330 PARK

Other books by Stanley Cohen

TAKING GARY FELDMAN

TELL US, JERRY SILVER

THE DIANE GAME

330 PARK

STANLEY COHEN

PRODUCED AND DEVELOPED
BY R. SMITH KILIPER

G.P. PUTNAM'S SONS
NEW YORK

SBN: 399–11901–9

Library of Congress Cataloging in Publication Data

Cohen, Stanley, 1928–
330 Park.

I. Title.
PZ4.C6783Th [PS3553.043]   813'.5'4   76-53027

To New York's FINEST,
but first and foremost,
to Lieutenant Frank Bolz

330 PARK

"How would you like to have a hundred thousand dollars?" Devereau asked.

"What kind of a question is that? Shit! Come on, man, I've never even seen that much money in one place."

"Well, I'm talking about having it." Devereau smiled. The young black's response to the first of the bait questions was right on target. Time for the second one. "Tell me something else. How would you like to live like some kind of Middle Eastern king? Fuck when and how you damn please. All kinds of beautiful women, white and black. Sound interesting?"

A broad smile. "I almost like that better'n the money."

The boy was just like the rest of them. Always interested in a little fancy meat for his dog. "Can you handle an M-14?"

"What's one got to do with the other?"

"That's not an answer. You're here to give answers. Can you handle an M-14?"

"Sure. I used a sixteen for two years. They're not all that different from fourteens. Played around with fourteens a coupla times."

"Perry tells me you just got out of prison," Devereau said. "What did you get caught trying to do?"

"Armed robbery."

"Here in the city?"

"Yeah."

"I'm surprised you drew any time just for armed robbery."

"It was because I cut this creep a little. I got zip to three and was in about a year."

"Armed robbery with a knife. How about that?" Devereau's tone was mocking. "When you made this unsuccessful attempt, how much planning did you put into it?"

"Planning?"

"Yes, planning. Or did you just walk in off the street?"

"I stood and watched the place for two nights before I went in. I was sure it couldn't miss."

"But it did. And if you'd made it, what would have been your take?"

"About four hundred dollars."

"Is that how much you expected?" Devereau asked. "Did you have good information when you picked your target?"

"Based on the traffic I saw going in and out, I thought I was gonna get fat on the place."

"Did you consider the four hundred high or low?"

The boy shrugged. "I guess I thought it was pretty good."

"Doesn't that seem rather stupid now? Putting your neck on the block for a dumb-ass little stickup where you didn't even know how much you could expect to get?"

"I guess it does."

"Then let me ask you again. How would you like to be handed a hundred thousand tax-free dollars?"

A slight smile and a change of expression. A knowing look. "What kind of shit are you looking to do, anyway?"

Devereau paused. Time to make him beg. "Listen, let's just forget the whole thing. Let's just say you were invited to a half-empty warehouse in Hunt's Point for nothing by some nut who asked you a bunch of dumb questions."

"Just a minute. I ain't ready to leave yet."

"What makes you think you've got a choice? As far as I'm concerned, you came looking for a job, and I didn't have anything for you."

"I want to know how to get in on this deal. Perry's in on it, and I want to be, too."

"What did Perry say it was?"

"He didn't. Said you'd tell me."

Devereau smiled. "Here you go again. You just finished a year in the slammer for a half-baked attempt that would have netted you exactly four hundred dollars if it had succeeded. And now you're gung-ho to get in on something new without knowing anything about it."

"I know I want in. You asked me if I'd like a hundred grand. The answer is a big fucking yes. And I'll do whatever I have to do to get it. For that kinda bread, I'm ready to take a few chances."

Devereau stared at him for several seconds. "Are you ready to answer some more questions?"

"Are we gonna get to the serious ones?"

"Don't you think they've all been serious?"

The boy wiped his palms on the knees of his pants. "Whatever, I'm ready."

Devereau opened the notebook on his desk and turned several pages, coming to an empty typed questionnaire. He took a pen and carefully printed the young man's name in the appropriate space at the top of the page. Archie Stoner. He scanned the page and then looked up. "What does the word 'subordinate' mean to you?"

"What kind of a question is that?" Stoner asked. "We playin' school or somethin'?"

"See you around." Devereau started to close the book.

"Hold it a minute, man. I told you I wanted in on this

thing, and I do, even if I have to put up with a bunch o' bull-shit."

"If you think this is bullshit, close the door when you leave."

"No, wait. I'm sorry. Let's start over. Gimme another shot. What was the question again?"

"The word 'subordinate.' What does it mean?"

"It means, like, you know, the one who reports to some-body further up. Like in the army, the noncom reports to an officer. The noncom is a subordinate. That what you mean?"

"Do you think the army system is a good one?"

"Sure. Somebody's got to give the orders."

"Are the right guys giving the orders?"

"You mean the officers? Sure. They're the ones with the training. I had a helluva good lieutenant when I was in Nam. Good captain, too."

"How would you expect an army to function if the officer system fell apart?"

"It couldn't."

"Do you have any problems seeing yourself in the role of subordinate?"

"Not for a hundred thousand dollars."

"What if the officer over you got a lot more?"

"Come on, man, I know where it's at." He thought a mo-ment. "Matter of fact, I might mention that I got a Good Conduct Medal when I was in the service."

Devereau nodded approvingly. "That gets you a few points." He made a couple of notations on the typed form. Then he looked up again. "What does the phrase 'doing your homework' mean to you?"

"You bringing up the liquor store again?"

Devereau smiled. "Obviously you get the message." He guided Stoner through the rest of the questions, including "total commitment," "patience," "secrecy," and "teamwork." He jotted notations as he went, satisfied that after he finished he'd know the man's behavioral strengths and weaknesses, his deep-rooted feelings about subordination to a white man, his dependability under stress.

Once he established a rhythm to the questioning, he jumped from subject to subject, carefully testing the young black's priorities, making sure Stoner wasn't contriving answers to give the desired impression.

As the time dragged on, Devereau sharpened the questions and used them to needle and irritate, to frustrate and enrage. "How would you feel if a white man called you a black son-of-a-bitch?"

"I wouldn't like it."

"What about stupid black son-of-a-bitch?"

"I'd like that less."

"What would you do about it?"

"Depends on the circumstances."

"Suppose I called you that a half-dozen times in the course of an hour? In front of a bunch of others?"

Stoner rubbed his palms again on the knees of his pants. "You take me on and I'll know it's because you think I can do you some good." He hesitated. "You're too damn smart to call me that, anyway. Unless you're testing me."

"What if somebody else did it?"

"I wouldn't lose my head. Not after this."

"Can you think of anything that would make you lose your head?"

He thought a moment. "Not now."

"You think you're that good?"

"The more I think about it, the better I get."

"I could make you blow without half-trying."

"You're a pro. The others won't be."

Devereau had started the questioning at nine o'clock, and over two hours had gone by. Stoner had stood up well. He was a prime candidate. "I understand you're not married," Devereau said. "That correct?"

"Yes."

"Thinking about getting married?"

"No."

"Have you any strong attachments to this country?"

"Meaning what?"

"Could you live somewhere else?"

"If I got a choice between livin' somewhere else with money and livin' here the way things are, it's no choice."

"Where are you living now?"

"Stayin' with a friend. She's got a coupla rooms in town."

"Where?"

"A Hundred and Eighteenth Street."

"Harlem?" Devereau asked.

"Yes."

"Niggertown?"

Stoner smiled. "You bet."

"What about family? You have any?"

"I'm out of touch. Have been for years."

"You sure?"

"I'm sure."

"Where are they?"

"I guess they're still in Detroit. Like I told you, I'm out of touch."

"What'd your father do?"

"He worked in a Ford plant."

"Have you got a job?"

"Like I said, I just got out. Not too much demand for me right now."

"Can you find a job?"

"I can look for one."

"Think you'll have any problems resisting the urge to go into another liquor store with a blade in your hand?"

"Don't worry about that."

Devereau made a summarizing notation on the page. "Plan to start coming here every Thursday night at seven-thirty."

Stoner took a deep breath. "Right. Now that we got that settled, what the fuck are you planning?"

"I thought we'd established that I was asking the questions here. Just get a job, and don't attract attention. Is that clear? Don't look for any new friends. You don't need them, and you'll only have problems explaining what you're going to be doing with your spare time. And just in case, work out a story now for Thursday nights. Come up with something that's believable. But above all, don't discuss anything I tell you with anyone. You get the picture?"

"I just wish you'd give me some idea what this is, and how long this Thursday-night business's gonna go on."

"You'll be briefed. The program of preparation will last a couple of months. But when you look for a job, you're looking for something permanent." Devereau got up from his desk.

The new recruit stood. "A hundred thousand dollars, no shit?"

Deverau smiled. "Minimum. But remember, no talk and no trouble. Because we won't tolerate a fuck-up."

"See you Thursday night." Stoner was weary but obviously pleased.

Devereau pulled a small black folder from the breast pocket of his fatigues and extracted a blank card. He jotted a phone number on it. "Call me tomorrow night at seven and tell me how you plan to explain your whereabouts on Thursday nights. I want to hear it before you use it."

After Stoner left, Devereau sat back down at the desk to study his notes. Stoner was a good find. Even if his friend Perry had briefed him on the right answers, it didn't matter. The important part was his character profile. He had the necessary level of talent, and he had integrity. And of course, a record.

Devereau turned to another page in the notebook and added Stoner's name to a list. Number thirty-three. Eight more to go for the required platoon of forty-one men. And the recruitment process was getting easier. At the outset it had been tough, and a few of the early recruits, like Floyd and Sally, might be problems. He'd have to keep an eye on them. He'd had to take what he could at the start, except for Lonnie Stroud, who'd served as a sergeant under him in Vietnam. And Benjy Sanchez, a twisted little gun-crazed Puerto Rican who'd been his company executioner over there. But as the number grew, Devereau had perfected his interview techniques. He had found that every recruit knew of another with just the right credentials, and the process had gained momentum. There were probably thousands of suitable misfits out there in that jungle of eight million animals who'd love the chance to take a flyer on this little operation. A hundred grand is a fat carrot. But forty-one men was all he needed.

Getting Luis a job at 330 Park had been the major coup. Almost a year in advance. A monumental example of long-range planning. Then finding Smokey, his "communications expert." In another couple of weeks he could start talking countdown. And a good thing. He couldn't keep the men's attention much longer without some promise of action.

Devereau glanced around the warehouse. He hated the place for its grime and its stench. But it was serving its purpose. The important thing was that it was nicely located and cheap. He looked at the rows of cots. He didn't anticipate two nights on one of them with much pleasure. But forty-eight hours after the landing, he could fill his life with sunshine and never think of Hunt's Point again.

He thumbed through the notebook to a section near the back. The financial-summary pages from the annual reports of all the tenants in 330 Park. The names were becoming familiar. Shenandoah. Stanco. Runyan. Goldwasser. Goodman. And of course, Root. All members of a new club. They just didn't know it yet.

The Root Corporation. His final bitter confrontation with the corporate director of personnel passed through his mind, and he felt a searing flush of heat. "I don't think you've been paying attention," he'd told the unctuous bastard. "I should be one of the operating officers of this outfit today. I've been here a long time. Before I left to return to the service in Vietnam, I practically ran the real-estate division of this company. During the two years I've been back, I've been jerked around like I don't count for much anymore."

"I'm afraid we instituted some new policies while you were away, Mr. Devereau, which create problems for us in your case. Big-business practices have undergone major changes in recent years. You really don't have the educational requisites for the kind of growth you seem to expect."

"Educational requisites? Whatever happened to 'college degree or equivalent'?"

"That kind of thing might help you at one of our plants. But not here at 330 Park. Would you like me to check the plants?"

"Would I what?"

"You needn't shout, Mr. Devereau."

"Listen to me. I was away those years because I was a POW. And before I left, Winfield Root himself told me what kind of promotion to expect from this company."

"Mr. Root is a nice old man. He's traveling in Europe at the moment and won't be back for quite some time."

"Then fuck you, you greasy son-of-a-bitch!" The words still echoed in Devereau's head as he thought about how he'd barely resisted the urge to hit the man before stomping out of his office and the building. He had been fired the next day.

After two months of unemployment, an agency got him the interview for the commercial claims adjuster's position and a glowing reference from Root, who'd returned from his trip abroad, got him the job. He declined the old man's offer to rehire him, because there was obviously nothing worth returning to at Root. Things had changed. Instead, he threw himself into the new job and thrived on "crushing the opposition" at every opportunity. But he constantly brooded about the Root Corporation, owner and principal tenant of the Root

Tower at 330 Park, occupant of four of the twenty-two floors in an office building he knew as if he'd designed it himself. And as he did, *the plan* began to form in his mind.

He closed the thick notebook and dropped it into his briefcase. No point in hanging around the rat's paradise any longer. Tomorrow was going to be a busy one at the office. A big case was about to come to a head. "Turn it over to Larry Devereau. Best in the business. He can spot a phony estimate quicker than anybody else around." Fuck it. Being the best claims adjuster in the business didn't pay. Two more months and they would never see him again.

He carefully locked the warehouse door and drove to his apartment in Yonkers. He didn't like the smell of the stairwell there much better than the warehouse. But five rooms for a hundred and thirty-five dollars made it worthwhile. And he only had to walk up to the third floor. Some of the slobs in the building had to walk up to six. The cheap rent left him most of his salary to pump into the preparations: the lease on the warehouse, the guns, the special equipment. The radios alone cost a couple hundred each, even with Smokey doing all the modifications. Two years' investment of time and money. Every nickel and every waking hour. But it would be worth it.

He entered the apartment and found a brushed-denim jacket on the floor just inside the door. Then, a navy sleeveless top. Slacks that matched the jacket. Pantyhose and bikinis, all balled up together. A trail leading toward his bedroom.

He stowed his briefcase inside the locked cabinet in the living room and began stripping off his own clothes. He turned on the glaring light in the bathroom and glanced at his face in the mirror. Then he ran a hand over his lean chest and abdomen. Not bad at all. Forty years old, and he could still pass for thirty. And perform like it, too.

He glanced downward at his genitals. An imperial cock emerging from an underbrush of sandy hair. He thought about Barbara curled up in his bed and decided to wash off the smell of the warehouse before going in.

He was glad she'd come over. She was much too important to the success of his operation to be ignored, even though she didn't know it. What a bonanza she'd been. He'd picked her up at a singles bar. "You come here to Rumm's often? You work nearby? Executive secretary at the Root Corporation? Over at 330 Park? Yeah, I know where that is. Me? I'm a claims adjuster for a big commercial underwriter. Why don't we go out and have a bite somewhere?" And maybe someday I'll tell you that I'd seen you around just before I left Root, and that I've been trailing you for the past week, waiting for you to go into someplace where I could approach you.

Devereau turned on the water in the big four-legged tub and cursed the ancient apartment house because the bathrooms had no showers. He sat down in the tub and jammed the rubber shower hose over the nozzle and began playing the anemic spray of water over his shoulders and back.

After toweling off, he went into the bedroom. She was sleeping peacefully, lying on her side, and when he yanked back the covers, she woke up, rolled over, and smiled at him, squinting from the overhead light. "Oh, hello, sweetheart," she said.

"What are you doing here?"

"I decided I couldn't wait until the weekend to see you. When you weren't here, I decided to surprise you. I must have dozed off."

"I don't like surprises," he said flatly.

"What time is it?"

"Past midnight. Almost one."

"Really? I *have* been asleep. But it doesn't matter. I planned to stay and go into the city with you tomorrow. Why are you so late? Weren't you at your reserve meeting?"

"I also don't like questions."

She looked pained. "Please, Larry. I'm not questioning

you. You didn't know I was coming." She forced a smile. "Aren't you a little glad to see me?"

He looked at her naked body. Then he reached out and began caressing one of her breasts, which was still warm from sleep. "No more surprises?"

She frowned slightly. "Do you have to take the fun out of everything?"

2

Devereau stood before the forty-one men sitting in the three curved rows of chairs. The men, about half of them black, sat quietly on the hard seats, some slouched, a few on the edges of their chairs. All listened attentively, even though they'd heard the speech several times before.

"Let's review a few things again," Devereau said. "As you move in, fire a few rounds. Aim at a piece of overstuffed furniture and rip it up with a shot or two. Pick any kind of target where you won't get ricochet. The idea is to scare the living shit out of them. After they've heard those fourteens and automatics a few times, they're going to do as they're told. I keep going over and over this point, because the whole plan depends on everybody in that building being scared out of their goddamn heads.

"But whatever you do, *don't hit anybody.* One dead body and all the rules change. There will be no killing unless I say so." Devereau picked one man in the group and fixed him with an unsmiling gaze. "That perfectly clear, Pedro, you trigger-happy son-of-a-bitch?"

A fat-faced man with greasy black hair answered. "You give the word, Dee. I do the work."

"That doesn't mean they shouldn't think you'd kill them without giving it a thought," Devereau continued. "Kick 'em around a little. It's for their own fucking good. We want absolute obedience from everyone in that building. Roll call is exactly five minutes after we land. Encourage them to assemble promptly and get quiet. Know what I mean by 'encourage'? After they've heard the rules, there should be no problems. Any questions?"

A large black man in the middle row raised his hand. "What are the chances somebody's got some kind of a gun in a desk drawer?"

"I'd say slim, Charlie," Devereau said. "You've got shock and surprise going for you. Take advantage. I want to hear teeth chattering all over that building. And if you don't have a few broads passing out with fright, you're no fucking good."

"You didn't answer my question, Dee."

"I don't think you'll be dealing with any face-offs in the opening minutes, and after they find out what's going on, it won't make sense for anybody to try anything."

"Listen, Dee, if some son-of-a-bitch come at me with a gun, I don't plan to let him shoot first."

Devereau hated even having to consider this possibility. "Keep your wits about you during those first minutes," he said finally. "Don't let some half-assed hero trick you into shooting him for nothing. I really can't imagine somebody with a little popgun coming at any of you, with the kind of firepower you'll be carrying. Jesus, everyone in that building is going to be too scared to know which way to walk." Devereau paused. "Any more questions?"

There was silence.

"You mean no one needs to know anything more? I must have done a better job training you guys than I thought. Come on. Anything else?"

"You still expect us to go back and nose around again tomorrow, like you said?" asked a skinny black named Floyd.

"Absolutely. Same routine as last time. Luis'll take you around in pairs. Every man is to know his floor like his own goddamn room. Tomorrow's the last chance. Monday's no good, because Palko will be back. And Tuesday's the day."

"But we been in and out of that fucking place three times," Floyd said.

"Once more will make four. What else?"

"We got it, Dee," said a hollow-chested youth sitting in the front row. "We been over it enough times."

"You can't know it too well, Pickett," Devereau snapped. "A guaranteed way to get knocked on your ass is to start thinking you're so smart you can't get smarter." Devereau actually liked Pickett, who was cold, unemotional, detached, good with guns, and quick to move decisively.

"Over the weekend, set up the story for your disappearance," Devereau said. "Get rid of your wheels and show up here Sunday evening by nine. Make sure no one suspects anything. If you're worried about your cover, go over it again with me."

"You mean we really got to sleep in this fucking hole for two nights?" Carlos, a flashy young Puerto Rican with two arrests for car theft.

"You sleep in this fucking hole for two nights," Devereau said.

"Christ, man, there's not even showers in this place. By Tuesday they'll smell us all over Park Avenue." He crossed his legs and dropped his hand on the ankle of his gleaming patent-leather boot.

"What's wrong with that?" Devereau said. "You be here Sunday night at nine."

"What's wrong with Monday night?" Little Benjy. A small wiry Puerto Rican with a perpetual grin.

"It's twenty-four hours after Sunday night," Devereau snapped.

"What'll we do here all day Monday?" Benjy asked.

23

"Think about Tuesday." Devereau had given considerable thought to his timetable. He wanted them waiting it out like troops huddled close on a landing craft, looking to the moment when the boat runs aground and they dash ashore. Let them spend the day talking, reading, watching TV, playing cards. But together, getting psyched up for the next day.

"Remember that we go by code numbers at all times after we land Tuesday," Devereau said. "Don't use any names. And one more time, if by some crazy chance some stupid broad gets turned on to one of you as the thing drags on into Tuesday night and Wednesday, forget it! Understand? There's plenty of time for that after we get out. Now, let's get on with tonight's business. We'll review the floor diagrams, starting with the second floor. Weapons check and reloading will begin with the top-floor team and work down. Run through the checkout on your radio after you leave the range. If any other questions come up, we can talk about them."

The men got up and began separating into groups. The old warehouse had a high ceiling supported on wooden posts. The windows were boarded up, and most of the area was poorly lit. At one end was the firing range, a remarkably soundproofed chamber set up for drill by two men at a time. Overhead pulleys and ropes allowed them to set targets at distances of up to a hundred feet. Targets were normal-size human outlines traced on pasteboard, with bull's-eyes in the middle of each chest.

Stroud unlocked several large cabinets with swinging doors just outside the range. Neatly arranged inside them, on numbered pegs, were matching automatic rifles and heavy army-style webbed belts with pistol holsters and carrying cases for several other pieces of gear. Each of the men at the range buckled on one of the belts and took a rifle.

At the other end of the warehouse was the barracks, forty-two cots arranged in five rows, each with a shoddy mattress, an army blanket, and a pillow. Near the cots were several card tables with chairs and a picnic table some twenty or twenty-five feet long with an oilcloth cover and low benches on each side of it. Against the wall was a stove and several old refrigerators.

Devereau walked through a door behind the kitchen leading to an ancient latrine. He urinated, then rinsed and dried his hands and went back to the conference area. A large easel stacked with placards roughly two feet by three feet stood by Devereau's desk. The front placard was blank.

Devereau lifted it off and leaned it against the side of the easel. The second sheet showed a flooring diagram, the word LOBBY printed across the top. "Okay," Devereau said, "Two-A and Two-B. Tell me what you're going to be doing next Tuesday morning."

3

Sunday night. Devereau checked off names as the troops wandered in. At nine-thirty, sixteen were still missing. Those present were occupied but restless. Some watched the old television. A group of five played blackjack around one of the card tables, the floor near them cluttered with beer cans. A few were already stretched out on the cots. Smokey Hampton was in the radio shop, leaning against the workbench, peering at a small electronics part through a curl of cigarette smoke.

Another walked in, and Devereau checked his watch again. Nine-forty-five. Everyone was to have shown up by nine. The lack of discipline was irritating. He had worked for weeks to establish military regimentation, but had never really achieved the degree he had wanted. They listened when he talked about the one-hundred big ones, the clean escape to the promised land, the life of a king. But they never really understood how his disciplinary bullshit was essential to the ultimate payoff.

Sally Panucci arrived just before ten. He was one member

27

of the team that made Devereau uneasy. Was he a little too soft, a little too sensitive? Were his roots in Brooklyn too deep? One of the other guys had brought him in, and he had been wildly enthusiastic, almost too much so. But he had withstood the hours of probing interrogation without a slip. He wasn't smart enough to do that if he was hiding something.

Sally was the only paisan in the group. And the only one without a record of any kind, a bad sign. Blacks and PR's who had a grudge against the system were preferred. Or drifters, like Pickett, who had no ties with anything. A paisan like Sally seemed much too human. Could he be a plant? Had the cops picked up a tip? For that matter, could *any* of the troops be a fink? Could any of them have outwitted him during the painstaking questioning? What if Sally had a tie with some syndicate, some "family"? All this work and investment, only to have a heist attempted on his heist. Or was Sally just what he'd suspected all along—an acceptable troop who was just a little too emotional?

As Sally passed, Devereau suddenly kicked him in the rump with all his strength. Taken totally by surprise, Sally almost left the ground, the suitcase dropping from his hand. He turned quickly to confront Devereau, his face enraged. "What the fuck do you call that?"

"A kick in the ass," Devereau answered coolly.

"What was it for?"

"I wanted to find out if you had balls."·

"You ever do that again and you'll find out what kinda balls I got!"

"Go have a beer." Devereau felt better. Sally's reactions had been clean, guileless. If Sally had been up to something, he'd have given himself away.

Between ten and eleven, more of the men turned up, and by eleven-fifteen they were all in the warehouse except one, Wayne Austin, Big Wayne, a rowdy but a good soldier. If

Devereau had wanted to guess in advance who'd be the last to show up, he'd have guessed Austin.

By midnight Austin still hadn't appeared. Devereau went over to Pickett, who was playing cards, and said, "Where's your buddy?"

"Bet I could guess. You didn't think he could go two nights without humping something, did you?"

"Go get him and bring him in."

"Got no wheels anymore. Remember?"

"The pickup's behind the building. Hampton's got the key in the drawer in there. Go find Austin and drag his ass in here."

Pickett slid his money off the table into his hand and stuffed it in his pocket. He picked up the key, went outside, and eased the truck out of the dark roofed alcove and into the street.

Two of Austin's favorite bars provided no leads, and the pool hall was closed. Sunday night, pushing one o'clock. The Bronx was getting quiet. Pickett finally found a guy they both knew in a little joint on 10th near 207th Street.

"Yeah, I saw him, tonight," the man said. "Judging from the way he was talking, I'd guess he's over terrorizing that little skinny turd and his child bride that you two are always joking about."

"You mean the Earl of Louisville?" Pickett asked.

"That's the one."

"Shit, I hope I can find that place tonight." Pickett borrowed the Bronx phone directory from the bartender and began studying it. His finger ran down a column of names and stopped, and his lips moved, repeating the address several times. "See you around," he said, and left.

It took him about ten minutes to find the building. When he did, he parked and walked up the filthy staircase to the third floor.

The door opened seconds after his knock, and a pitiful young man reached out with both hands and pulled Pickett into the dreary, littered apartment. "Oh, Lord, Jesus Christ, am I glad to see you," he said, almost in tears. He had a narrow face, large round glasses, a pointed nose that looked wet, a thin mustache, and buck teeth. He was consumptively frail. "Your animal friend is here again. He's in there." He paused. "Again," he said painfully, looking at the closed door. "Am I never to be free of this monstrous curse?" With his red-rimmed eyes and protruding front teeth, he looked like an unhappy rodent. They stood for a moment and listened to the heaving bed springs on the other side of the door.

"I warned him tonight," the little man said, suddenly pulling himself up to his full height, "that if he persists in coming here, and shows up again after tonight, I'll be forced to call the proper authorities. This can no longer be tolerated."

"Why, shit, Rodney, Wayne'd twist you right in half." Pickett walked over to the door, opened it, and stuck his head inside. "Hey, Wayne, how you doing?"

"Hey, Billy Pickett," came a voice back. "Be with you in a minute." The pounding springs paused and then resumed.

"This can't go on," Rodney repeated. "I'm going to put a stop to these visits, one way or another."

"Hell, Rodney, you oughta be glad you gotta friend like Wayne. Quit talking like you don't appreciate him. He takes care o' you, man, down at the job, right?"

The rhythmic noise on the other side of the door stopped. Seconds later, Wayne appeared at the door, naked, his clothes in his hand. He was a big boy with long reddish-brown hair and a broad, smiling face. His hulking white body was covered with freckles and a haze of curly orange hair. "It's gonna be a long dry spell coming up," he said with a grin. "I figgered I'd better stick me a little more muffin while I can. You want some, Billy? She's ready."

"Yeah?" Pickett said.

"No!" Rodney moaned.

Wayne fumbled in the pocket of the pants he was carrying

and brought out a tiny package. "You better put one of these on. God knows what she's liable to be carrying."

Pickett started to reach for the package and then drew his hand back and wiped it unconsciously on the side of his pants. "Naw, I'm not up for it tonight. Let's go. Dee sent me after you."

"I figured that much as soon as I saw you." Wayne went into the bathroom.

Rodney lit a cigarette and seemed to recover his composure. He smoked with a long holder, the cigarette drooping limply almost six inches from his face. He went over and put his head through the door to the bedroom. "Are you okay, my precious?"

"I'm just fine," was the very positive reply.

Wayne came out of the bathroom, buttoning his shirt. "Sure you won't have you a little while we're here, Billy?"

"We better get on back," Pickett said.

A short dumpy girl, still in her teens, came out of the bedroom, her faded print wraparound almost falling open. She walked over to Wayne and snuggled up under his arm, a stupid smile on her face.

Wayne gave her a quick squeeze and then slapped her firmly on her bottom. "We'll see you, Annie," he said. "Take care. See you, too, Rodney."

"I am going to kill you someday, Wayne," Rodney said.

"Shit, now, Rodney, what would you ever want to do a thing like that for?" Wayne's grin was broad and good-natured. "Is that what you learned in junior college?"

"He ain't ever going to do that, or anythin' else," the girl said. "He ain't ever going to do nothin' that amounts to anythin'."

"See you at work tomorrow, Wayne?" Rodney asked.

"Told you Friday. I'm gone. Me and Pickett's leavin' for California tomorrow."

They left the apartment and got back in the truck. When

they entered the warehouse, Devereau made no comment but merely bolted the door and went back to checking the food supplies. Pickett joined the one card game that was still going. A few men continued to watch the television. Wayne dropped on one of the cots and went to sleep. Back in the galley area, Devereau continued checking the cans and boxes that would feed forty-two men for the next day and a half.

4

"Joe Palko here."

"Joe, it's Bessie Gittelson."

"Hello, Bessie. You're the first to welcome me back from bein' away." The old receptionist on five was his favorite in the building, his private weather bureau and early warning system.

"Joe, I must talk to you."

"You're roasting, I'll bet. Or is it freezing this time?" He laughed. "I knew I couldn't trust Luis to take care of you."

"Joe, please. I must talk to you. It could be very important."

The absence of her usual easy banter finally registered. "Sure, Bessie. What's up?"

"Can you come up here?"

"You can't tell me over the phone?"

She didn't answer.

"Okay, Bessie, I'll be up in a little while. It's my first day back, and I got a few odds and ends. Maybe right after lunch."

She still didn't speak.

"Okay, Bessie, I'll be up in a few minutes." Something was really bugging her.

After listening to her account of how Luis, his assistant, had visited with the two strangers, he had to agree that she had reason to be concerned. As chief engineer at 330, he would have been told if the air-conditioning engineers had really been conducting a survey. She mentioned that Luis had previously brought around two other men as "painting estimators." Even when tenants chose to handle their own redecorating, the rental agreement clearly stated that he was to be kept advised so he could arrange use of the freight elevator and other details. That was part of his job.

The most suspicious aspect of Bessie's story was her certainty that both the supposed painters and the supposed engineers were one and the same. She even thought that Luis had brought the two men around a week or two earlier. And Luis always brought them on a day when he wasn't in the building. The rotten stench of some kind of setup was beginning to form.

He tried to keep Bessie from picking up his sense of alarm. No point in having her worry, at least until he'd tried to get a handle on it. "It's probably nothing," he said to her. "I'll talk to Luis and try to figure out what he's up to. If anything."

"Has he ever given you any reason to doubt him before?"

"He had a minor record, but you've got to give guys a chance. He was recommended by a guy named Devereau who used to work for Root, and so far, he's been all right."

Joe returned to his office, which was a desk in the middle of a large, basement room surrounded by two-hundred-horse-power pumps. He looked at the uniform rows of valves with handles like steering wheels, the maze of huge pipes and ducts, all insulated and painted different colors, and the wall arrays of instruments and lighted piping diagrams. Some office. But he had gotten used to working there in spite of the

34

heat and the loud hum from the machinery. It was the best location available below the lobby. He knew the room and its contents like his own bedroom. He knew the whole building that way.

Something had to be done about the need for improved security at 330. At the moment, the whole force consisted of the chief engineer, which was himself, his assistant, Luis, two porters, and the elevator starter. "We need an armed guard in this building," he'd once told Pederson, the rental agent. "We've got fourteen tenants and nearly six hundred people in this building."

"Who's going to pay for it? You know somebody who wants to work for nothing?"

"You're the landlords. Your company should pay for it."

"What are you, a wise guy? We'd have to add it to the rent. Do you happen to know how much around-the-clock security service goes for in this town? If we wanted to lay a few grand a year on everybody's rent, how many of your tenants would buy it?"

"Then don't ask 'em. Just do it."

But Pederson had just walked away.

Palko remembered the third-floor typewriter heist a year ago. A clean, simple job. They'd come in through a third-floor window from the building directly behind and taken all the typewriters on the third floor, the expensive IBM automatic recorders. Afterward the windows on the back of the building had been barred, but Palko was sure there were other weak spots.

He thought about the purse-snatcher he had confronted in the rear fire tower. He had been walking up one flight when the kid bolted through the door above and started down, his face a picture of guilt as he froze in his tracks, the pocketbook swinging from his fist. The kid had planned to race down to the next floor and walk calmly out to the elevators, having cleaned the purse in the stairwell and left it there. He'd grabbed the boy and handed him over to the police. It had been easy enough. But on many other occasions the petty thieves in the building had been armed with knives and guns and had pulled midday muggings in the elevators or fire towers without being challenged. He wasn't looking to get cut or shot.

At fifty he could still take care of himself. He'd always had to. Survival was a way of life in his neighborhood when he was growing up, and he never forgot the things he learned. He saw two years of combat action in the infantry in World War II. More good training. And he stayed in shape. He didn't weigh a pound more than he had in the Army. But he was unarmed, and paid to be the building engineer of the Root Tower, not to risk his neck tangling with every creep that wandered in off the street looking for a quick buck. Most of the time they were in and out without his ever seeing them. A security force was was needed to scare them away or deal with them when they came.

Whatever Luis was up to sounded too organized to be petty. But why would he pick the fifth floor? Berkowitz and Belz had the least fancy layout in the building. Nothing much worth stealing, at least compared to some of the other floors. What about all the very fancy drafting stuff and calculators and the computer and the new IBM machines with Dorfer, West on the third and fourth floors, for instance? Or the photography equipment with the outfit on the eighteenth? Or the computer setup the accounting firm used on ten?

Lots of the tenants even had furniture worth stealing. And expensive carpets. Stuff like that. The executive offices of the major tenants, the Root Corp., on twenty-one and twenty-two, the penthouse, for instance. But there was nothing special on five. No fancy furniture and no fancy equipment. Strictly a plain-pipe-rack spread. So what the hell could Luis be up to?

He heard Luis' chattering laugh and then the sound of footsteps in the tiled corridor.

"Hey, Joè, the water is all cleaned up." Luis was grinning. "I told the kid," he continued, "I said, 'Kid, the floors are not supposed to be covered with water down there. Next time you see water, don't just say to yourself, "Hey, there's water on the floor." Call me or Joe.' Jeez, what a stupido!"

Palko looked up at Luis. "Sit down, Lou," he said, nodding at the extra chair. He had tried not to tip his hand, but he saw Luis' expression change. "I got a call from Bessie Gittelson on the fifth floor." Luis' smile faded. "She said you brought in a coupla turkeys and took them on a tour of her shop Friday. What was that all about?" He watched Luis frown, then smile again.

"Oh, that was nothing," Luis said. "Couple my buddies wanted to see some of the building. No big deal. I show 'em around a little. That's all." Devereau had discussed this possible confrontation and told him how to deal with it.

"Bessie said you told her the guys were with the air-conditioner company. What kinda shit was that?"

"A little joke, Joe. No big deal." Luis was calm. "I figured I should have a little story if I'm gonna be taking 'em around. I made that up."

"She told me they were the same two turkeys you brought through once before. That time, you said they were painting contractors."

"No, she mistaken. That was two other friends of mine." Devereau hadn't coached him on how to handle that question.

Palko could easily see from Luis' eyes that something wasn't kosher. "She thinks you might have brought the same two around even before that with some other story."

"She's crazy. She's a crazy old broad."

"Luis, what the fuck are you up to?"

"Me? I'm not up to nothing. I just bring a couple friends around to see the place. No big deal."

"Why always when I'm not here?"

Luis forced a grin. "That's the reason. You're not here."

"What'd they want to see the place for?"

"They my friends. They want to see where I work. I tell them you're a good boss but you don't want no fooling around. That's why I want them to come when you not here."

"Why always the fifth floor? There's nothing interesting there."

"I take them on other floors, too."

"The same guys?"

"Sure."

"Luis, I think you're a lying son-of-a-bitch. I think you're up to no fucking good, and if you've got a brain in your head, you'll keep your friends outta here and forget whatever you got planned before it's too late. It won't be worth it!"

"Joe, you all wrong. Luis not up to nothing. He know better."

"I hope I'm wrong, Luis." The son-of-a-bitch was lying all over the place, and not about to back down on it, whatever it was. He had to get Luis out of there so he could use the phone. "Well, anyway, we may as well get back to work. Did you finish repairing the level indicator on the water tank last week?"

"No. You told me to stay below and keep my eye on things. You said wait till you get back. Right?"

"Well, I'm back."

"Sure, Joe." Luis grinned, but this time he could tell that Palko knew it was phony.

Palko allowed Luis plenty of time to get tools together and head for the roof. Then he called Terry, the receptionist on the ninth floor.

"Oh, hi, Joe."

"Terry, did Luis bring a couple of guys up to your place Friday and show them around?"

"Yes, as a matter of fact he did. Why?"

Could Luis have been on the level? "Who'd he say they were?"

38

"He said they were from the firm that installed the air-conditioning equipment."

"What'd they look like?"

"Like a couple of guys. Nothing special."

"Were they white? Black?"

"One was Puerto Rican and the other white. Why? What's happening?"

"Nothing, Terry. Thanks. I just wanted to see where he had taken them."

Bessie had told him one of the men had been white and one had been black. Could she have confused a Puerto Rican for a black? Bessie was sharper than that. He called the receptionist on eighteen. Yes, Luis had brought two men around on Friday to do an air-conditioning survey.

"One black guy and one white one?"

"No, they were both white."

"Are you sure?"

"Positive, Mr. Palko. I remember them well. One was a big red-headed fellow, and the other was smaller, and slim."

Joe's pulse began to race. He called the receptionist on the second floor. Luis had brought around a black guy and another who looked "Latin or something." The third floor reported a white man, definitely white, and one who was "distinctly Hispanic." The sixth floor reported two blacks.

"You're sure it was two black guys?"

"Yes, I am, Mr. Palko. Anything wrong?"

"Nothing wrong. Just checking. Thanks." Luis had taken a different pair of guys to every floor! Palko thought for a minute, then dialed the landlord's number and asked for Pederson.

"I'm sorry, Mr. Palko. Mr. Pederson's away from the office today."

"Where I can reach him?"

"If he calls in, I can ask him to call you. Can it wait?"

"I don't know."

"He plans to stop at 330 tomorrow afternoon. He wants to see you about something."

"Tomorrow afternoon? Are you sure?"

"That's what he told me. It's written on his desk calendar."

Palko exhaled. "If he calls in, ask him to give me a call, will you? Tell him it's very important. He can call me at home. Better still, give me his home phone. I'll call him if I don't hear from him."

"I'll give him the message, Mr. Palko. Mr. Pederson doesn't give out his home phone. To anyone."

"Shirley, this could be very important."

"I'm sorry, Mr. Palko. . . . You'll see him tomorrow."

Tomorrow. "Thanks, Shirley." He could alert Larsen, the foreman on the night crew, but he'd have to do it carefully to keep from scaring the pants off the old guy. There wasn't much else he could do. The cops would want some facts before they'd check the building. He'd just have to wait for Pederson. Maybe nothing would happen before tomorrow.

A few miles away, in the boarded-up warehouse Devereau dialed a number. "Barbara. How's my girl?"

"Oh, Larry, hi." She sounded relieved to hear his voice.

"How are things at the great Root Corporation?"

"You remember I told you we were having a board-of-directors meeting tomorrow. Winfield Root himself is coming, and you'd think they were getting ready for a coronation." She laughed. "Incidentally, is next weekend all set?"

"You got it."

"You won't have to cancel again?"

"Everything's all squared away."

"When will I hear from you?"

"Soon."

Barbara Meyner hung up the phone and just sat for a moment studying her hands. Larry always told her that they were lovely. Small, neat, and soft, he always said. The hands of a lady.

She thought about *his* hands. Sure and masculine, always well-groomed. She thought of the light-colored hair on the backs of them and shivered.

She thought about their first meeting, almost a year back, and wondered what prompted him to come into Rumm's on that particular night. "Fate," he always said when she felt giddy enough to ask. He'd always been attentive when they were together. And so sure of himself. But there were so many nagging questions. . . .

How old are you, Larry Devereau? Don't you ever plan to tell me? Must you always be so evasive when I ask? And moody? Where are you when I'm talking to you and I look up and see that your mind is elsewhere? And not just drifting. But racing. Computing. Can't you tell me? Why don't you want me to know?

Which is the real Larry Devereau? Is it the one who constantly makes and breaks dates and then comes back strong enough to charm me out of my clothes? Or the man whose eyes occasionally glaze over, letting me know I mustn't intrude? The man who one night said, "Shut up, I'm thinking something through." "But, Larry—" "I said shut up a few minutes." Larry, there's an element in you that frightens me. I only see glimpses of it. But it scares me. Larry, say something funny. Anything. Do you know that you've never made me laugh?

Why couldn't you have been someone a little less complex? Why you, with the smooth body and the incredible confidence and those frightening mood swings? Why not someone that's simple to deal with? And maybe someone with money? That wouldn't be bad. A man with real bread. Would be nice to get out of this office and away from this typewriter someday. Think you'll ever have money, Larry? . . .

I don't mean that. I really don't care. I just wish that you could be a little more constant. Sometimes I think that you can leave and come back in the middle of anything. I said "anything," Larry. What does it take to hold your attention?

. . . But when you come back, you sure can be worth waiting for. . . . Christ, I sound like I'm as big a sexist as you. I think you've made me that way. . . . Larry, I don't know how I feel about you. Because sometimes I don't think I know you at all. Maybe if you could just make me laugh one time. . . .

She looked down at the empty sheet in her typewriter and forced herself to go back to work.

5

Little Benjy opens fire with his M-14 and squeals hysterically as he pumps round after round into defenseless, crawling bodies in business suits, faceless men with arms outstretched, mouths open, eyes glazed. The bodies are thrown several feet by the impact of the shots. The bullets make tiny black holes in custom shirts as they enter and explode huge chunks of bloody flesh from the backs of the bodies as they pass on through. Blood splatters in all directions. Pedro's leathery face twitches slightly with each shot, but his expression remains impassive as he picks targets and drops them efficiently, men and women alike, some already on their knees, pleading, screaming, weeping. He spots one young miniskirted woman on the floor, struggling to get to her knees, her bottom exposed to the waist in pantyhose. He fires another bullet into her, causing her legs to straighten abruptly, dropping her body flat, where it remains still. . . . Attica! . . . Jesus, no! This is not the plan! Stop! Oh, God! Stop! You dumb shits! What the fuck did you do this for? . . . Yes, we're all going to be rich like Rockefeller. But all this blowing people up. . . . Executions are for conversation. Understand? Of course I trained you to handle those weapons like profession-als. Who knows what to expect? But I gave you no kill signal, no wave of the hand to just wade in and blast away. Boss, if it moves, I shoot. . . . What kind of movement did you see? . . . Boss, I saw it move. . . . You saw no guns. No one was coming at you. . . . Boss, I do not take chances. . . . No, damn you! Do you understand me? No! . . . Not no, Boss. Yes. What difference do it make, anyway? Like you say, we take and we go. Right? You told us everything will work. And we be far away soon after. Right, Boss? And then, what difference will it make? . . .

Devereau forced himself awake and rolled from his side onto his back. He stared into the shadowy darkness of the warehouse ceiling and listened to the varied breathing of the men around him. He couldn't clear his head of the grisly im-age of Pedro's facial tics as he pumped round after round into the same crawling female rump. What difference will it make? he asks. Jesus, what rank stupidity! The bus ride into town. The last chance to lecture on . . . on what? The intelligence of not killing? Simple everyday common sense. Nothing more. But it has to be done carefully. Can't take the edge off. They're keyed. Bristling. I outdid myself getting them up for it. They were perfect tonight. Just like a true military briefing. They knew every answer. Every detail. They couldn't be stumped. . . Why am I awake now? Fucking canned stew probably made with bad meat. Need this sleep. Could be up straight through for the next two nights. Got to get to sleep. . . . Sleep, you snoring bastards! You've got a job to do tomorrow. Be sharp like you were tonight. . . . We'll show the boys from Boston Latin. . . . But it's got to be done with finesse. Clean. No killing. Then we're the envy of the world. World! Wonder how the Manchester *Guardian* will write it up? Reuters? But it's got to be no killing. Better make the point again on the ride into town. No killing, and even the cops'll be jealous. The fucking cops'll wish they were us! We're going to be rich as kings. The boys from Boston Latin'll admire us for that. And we'll take the chest of gold and get back on the bus and go fly away. The envy of the world. . . . Put me down! It's not necessary to carry me off the field on your shoulders. Then again, the boys from Latin would probably be impressed. Not bad for a nothing kid from Dorchester. They can keep their fucking school. I'll be able to match fortunes with any of them. . . . Keep a hand on your hostage, you dumb bastard! No hostage and you're dead. Remember? . . . So much money. I'll buy a plantation down there. A villa with a spectacular view. . . . The guys in the office Friday. Jesus, was that a scene. . . . This is your last day, Larry. How does it feel after so long? You really taking that job in South America? Maybe I'd have the nerve to do it, too, if I was still single like you, Larry. We all wish you well. We'll miss you. No fooling. And this company's going to miss you. Yes, sir. Factory Underwriters is going to miss you. You've made this company a bundle, Larry. You're the toughest claims adjuster we ever had. Must have been your years in the service that made you so cool. Captain, wasn't it? . . . Yeah. . . . Vietnam? . . . And you were a POW, weren't you? . . . Yeah. And thanks, guys, for the kiss-off lunch. And for the watch. . . A watch! Let *them* watch. And let the boys from Latin watch. The kid from over in Dorchester is going to be doing all right. Wouldn't you say so, Rudy? Remember what you said during my one year at B.U.? . . . Devereau, you'll never be a millionaire. You haven't got what it takes. It's not that you're not a bright guy. You are. And quite articulate. Even surprisingly well read. And you're ambitious. But that's still not enough. The only way you'd ever acquire a million would be to steal it. Sure, I agree you still hear the Great American Success Stories, Larry. But they're stories about guys with exceptional brains and

exceptional talents. . . . Thank you, Rudy, for giving me
that little bit of information. I'm glad I joined you for a beer
that night. You placed me on the yellow-brick road and gave
me a shove. I'll write to you someday, in your raised ranch in
Nyack, and tell you all about it. A year of dreaming, Rudy.
Dreaming and speculating. Psyching myself up. Convincing
myself that I could do it if I was smart enough. And that I *was*
smart enough. Know when I started planning, Rudy? I'll tell
you when. It was right after I got out of the vegetable bin.
Can you see me a vegetable? Lining up for Valium pills three
times a day? Drawing pictures for the nice nurse? Working in
the flowerbeds? Me? . . . That company shrink saw through
me like I was a window. . . . If you'll sign this commitment
form, Mr. Devereau . . . Two weeks in the bin, Rudy. Me.
And I needed it. I was there, sweetheart. And it was great. Because I started putting things together. You know what was
wrong in my head, Rudy? I was getting derailed because I
wasn't going anywhere. Didn't have a goal. Well, I've got one
now. And I'm in it up to my hairline. Everything I've got. My
heart and soul. My head. My balls. Everything. Every penny
I own. Have you any idea what kind of bread I've got in this
thing, Rudy? The lease on the warehouse? All of that firepower and all of that ammunition? The radio equipment? And all
the rest? Why, just the room at the Waldorf is sixty a
day. . . .

Got to piss. That's the problem. Got to get up and piss.
Then I'll be able to sleep. This is stupid, lying here like an asshole, listening to all this snoring, not being able to sleep.
Must have been the canned stew. Must have been made with
bad meat. . . . Mr. Root, meet Mr. Devereau. Mr. Devereau, Mr. Root. . . . My pleasure, Mr. Devereau. I believe
we've met before. . . . That's correct, Mr. Root. You were
one hell of a man. You filled my head with dreams once. Do
you know I fantasized about occupying that big-ass office of
yours? And I will. But not under the same circumstances. Do

you know the meaning of "dream come true," Mr. Root? It's a carefully executed plan. Of course you know that, because you've been there and done it yourself. Right, Mr. Root? But you got old. While I was rotting in that fucking compound, you turned into an old man. They've squeezed all the piss out of you. Piss! Jesus, I'm going to float out of here in a minute. Got to get up and piss. In a minute. . . . Seven hundred rounds a minute. Beautiful. What exquisite weapons! Designed for jungle fighting. So? The whole fucking world's a jungle. Right? Incredible weapon. What firepower! Should have held out for the M-16's at any price. . . . Too much delay, he said. And too much risk. They're still in use by the army. Okay, then, you greasy little wet-nose gun merchant, get fourteens. . . . Quote: "The M-14 may be fired automatically or semiautomatically, it uses 7.62 NATO cartridges with 180 grain projectiles which have a velocity of 2,700 feet per second leaving the muzzle." And those army forty-fives. Jesus, just looking at those makes people die. Just looking. Been looking forward to seeing you again, Mr. Root. Now you can tell me all about how you got old and gave up running your company to become a fucking philanthropist. All you do now is give money away. Well, that's fine. And now's your chance to outdo yourself. That's right, Mr. Root, a new cause called Larry Devereau and company. These are my men, Mr. Root. And this is my friend Barbara. Do you know Barbara? Of course you do. She works here. Tell me, Mr. Root, did you go to Boston Latin? Bullshit, you did, Mr. Root. I've got the book on you. You're from Chillicothe, Ohio. But that's okay. Because you had what it took when you had to have it. All the brains and talent and drive you needed. You're my kind of man, Mr. Root. I'm going to enjoy working with you again. But if you'll excuse me a moment, I've got to piss. . . . No, Pedro, don't shoot Mr. Root! He's part of our plan, but only if he's alive. Do you know the definition of "nothing," Pedro? It's a dead hostage, you stupid Mexican wetback. Pedro, don't point that rifle at me, you dumb fuck! Don't you know you're dead without me? I'm your God Almighty. And don't you forget it. No, Pedro, put that gun down. Everything's going to work perfectly tomorrow. Isn't it, Luis? Are you telling me everything, Luis? Is that all that Palko said to you? It had better be. The decision is still go. There's no waiting God only knows how many months for the next board meeting. The troops have cut their cables. No turning back now. Decision is still go. What can anyone do to blunt our attack at this stage? Nothing. Wait'll they see our landing. Don't fuck around with us, Palko. Don't mess with us, and nobody gets hurt. All we want is a chest full of money. You screw around, somebody gets chopped up, and you can hold yourself directly responsible. Incidentally, I rather liked you, Palko. And thanks for hiring Luis. You know, I get the feeling you've got real talent. I get the feeling I'd like having you in this platoon. Interested? I'll make you one rich hunkie. I'll even offer you a commission. How'd you like to be one of my lieutenants, Palko? Why, I might just give you the honor of handling the old man. With respect, mind you. He may be old, but he still recognizes class. Mr. Root, will you pardon me a moment while I go relieve myself? How much longer am I going to lie here on this fucking cot with Pedro blowing up some upside-down broad and my fucking bladder about to rupture?

Devereau forced himself fully awake and sat up. The concrete floor was cold through his socks. His face stung from need for sleep, and he rubbed it with both hands. He felt around for his shoes.

He heard voices as he entered the glare and damp stench of the latrine and found big Charlie and Floyd having a smoke. "How much do you think. . . ?" Floyd was saying, but he stopped speaking abruptly as Devereau entered. Devereau studied their faces as they stared blankly at him, obviously taken by surprise by his unexpected presence.

Finally Charlie said, "Hello, Dee."

"What are you guys doing up?" Devereau asked. "You need all the sleep you can get."

"Just grabbing a smoke," Charlie said.

Floyd nodded without speaking.

Devereau went over to the urinal. His need was so severe that he had to concentrate on relaxing for several seconds to get his water to begin flowing. He thought fleetingly of a villa overlooking the sea and of a bathroom with a sun-flooded skylight over a marble step-down bath, all draped in luxurious fabrics, as he stared at the long, horizontal trough.

He finished and washed his hands. As he started out through the doorway, he hesitated and looked at the two men. "You guys get back to sleep."

"Yeah. We will, Dee," Charlie said.

Floyd waited until Devereau's footsteps receded. "How much do you think he's gonna get out of this job? A million?"

" I don't know," Charlie answered.

"You notice he never talks about how much he's taking from everybody in that building? You notice he never tells us what he's got in that notebook he keeps locked up in his briefcase?"

"We got a deal with him and I believe he's good for it. He promised us each a hundred grand if we get in and get out clean. And I can't see how his plan can miss. He's one smart son-of-a-bitch, Floyd. The smartest I think I ever met."

"Our ass is gonna be on the line tomorrow, too. I wanta know what he's gonna get out of it."

"Shit, he put the whole thing together. It's his show. Besides, do you know how much a hundred thousand bills is? Hell, did you ever see even *one* thousand bills?"

"When it come time to start counting that money out, he's gonna have to answer a few questions."

"Just don't fuck around with his plan. Okay? Just do your thing tomorrow like he trained you. Or maybe there won't be no counting party."

Floyd took two or three thoughtful drags on his cigarette. "I been discussing this with a couple the other guys. Don't you want to know the total take?"

Charlie hesitated a moment and then shrugged. "Maybe. Let's get to payday, and then maybe I will."

Floyd grinned. "Maybe we just won't wait." He flipped his cigarette butt through the air into the urinal.

"Hey," Charlie said, "don't you know that makes 'em soggy and hard to light?"

"Shit," Floyd said. They walked out, and as they approached the sleeping area, they began to tiptoe. Floyd hesitated next to Devereau and watched him sleep. Then he crouched and looked at the dim outline of the briefcase under the cot.

"Lose something, Five-B?"

Floyd hadn't even seen Devereau open his eyes. "No." He walked on toward his bunk, with Charlie following him.

6

Winfield Root was a grumpy little man of seventy-four, paunchy, with pink skin and thin, whitish hair. Nearly deaf, he always spoke in a loud and unexpectedly deep voice and was forever fiddling with the very latest in elaborate hearing aids.

Although many years past retirement age, Root retained his office in the tower. Located on the southeast corner of the penthouse floor, it was the nicest in the building, elegantly decorated, with richly colored Oriental rugs, antique paneling, and a splendid view of Park Avenue. The walls were hung with original paintings, including a small Rembrandt. Connected to the office was a full bath and dressing area, appointed in marble, the only private lavatory in 330.

The old man used his office for several hours a day, two or three days a week, when he wasn't traveling. He arrived early, usually before nine, in a chauffeur-driven Cadillac from his shore home on the Island. He spent the time in the city perched like a toy-sized puppy in his cavernous chair, constantly adjusting his hearing aid, consulting with his advisers on the many philanthropic and cultural interests that kept him occupied. Having drifted away from company business to become a patron of the arts, he had little to say about the day-to-day operation of the corporation. He left that to Donald Ronam, the president and chief executive officer. But he insisted on keeping his seat on the board of directors, and he attended all the board meetings, which he constantly interrupted with long advisory speeches. The other members of the board always listened attentively and discussed his recommendations at some length. But they seldom brought one of his proposals to a vote, much to his annoyance.

In the last two or three years, his sharpness had begun to fade more noticeably, and his total involvement with inconsequential detail seemed a clear sign of approaching senility. Prune Danish was an example. The nine-thirty board meeting was minutes away. The principal item of business was the company's divestment of a small West Virginia machine plant he had acquired years back, an operation which had initially yielded a nice profit but had become a loser among the more unified interests of the corporation. As the other board members milled around the conference room, the old man continued to berate his secretary of many years for the Danish she had bought to serve with coffee at the meeting.

Agnes Arrington, every inch a lady who carried her sixty-odd years with elegance, tried to calm him down. She explained that it had not been convenient to send someone up to the obscure little pastry shop on Third Avenue to get the finger-sized goodies she usually provided. Instead she had called the deli on Lexington, which would deliver. The old man insisted that delicatessen Danish were heavy and sticky, hardly suitable for a meeting of his board. She assured him that most of the board members adored the Danish from the deli, and she closed her ears as he grumbled on, thinking to herself that after so many years of loyalty, the thing she liked doing most for him was arranging his travel, particularly his cruises. She loved the idea of having him leave on slow boats.

A few miles away, an olive-drab bus entered Bruckner Boulevard in the Hunt's Point area. The windows of the bus were strongly tinted so that the passengers, men wearing army fatigue suits, were barely discernible from outside. Devereau stood near the front, holding on to an overhead luggage rack with his left hand and using his right to emphasize certain of his comments. He wore a pair of captain's bars on each shoulder.

The bus moved along Bruckner Boulevard to the Third Avenue Bridge, avoiding the Triborough toll booths. Devereau continued talking until finally Floyd said, "Jesus, Dee, if you don't quit telling us not to shoot anybody, we're going to start thinking you're chickenshit."

"The important thing is for you to understand why I keep telling you."

"We get the message."

Agnes Arrington poured coffee into fine white china cups from the walnut-paneled pantry in the boardroom. She made little jokes about the pastries, commenting that perhaps they were not as dainty as she usually served at board meetings, certainly not as dainty as the board members themselves, but she hoped they'd make do. Most of the men had already taken some and were eating with obvious delight. These were good, rich, sticky, New York-style Danish.

Winfield Root sipped his special tea and watched the others eat. After a few minutes, he asked that the pastry tray be passed to him, and upon studying them at length, pulled a prune Danish onto his plate with his fork. He took a bite and chewed in silence with the frown still on his face. He swallowed and took a larger bite but continued to frown.

Ronam suggested that they get started with the business at

hand. The other board members were largely corporate line or staff vice-presidents. There were a few outsiders: a banker, a clothing manufacturer, a member of the New York Stock Exchange, long-time associates of the Root family. Bruce Williston, young, with a cherubic face and a nearly bald head, managed the corporation's extensive Canadian activities.

Billy Marshall (William Maxwell Marshall III), a financial wunderkind and the corporation's youngest executive vice-president, handed out copies of the financial statement of a Sturdy Tool Foundry in West Virginia. The other board members began scanning it, except for Winfield Root who completely ignored his copy as he methodically ate his way through his own Danish.

Outside the closed door of the boardroom, everything was quiet. Since the twenty-second floor, or penthouse, was used exclusively for executive offices, and most of these executives were in the meeting, their secretaries tended to ease up on their work. Barbara Meyner, secretary to the corporate vice-president for manufacturing, browed through the Travel section of the previous Sunday's *Times* as she lingered over her coffee.

On the twenty-first floor of the tower, also occupied by the Root Corporation, it was business as usual, the employees totally unimpressed that the company's top dogs were having one of their big-deal, high-finance, pie-in-the-sky board meetings upstairs.

On the twentieth floor, Kennan, Schink, McGlothlin, and Perl, an advertising agency, entertained principals from a possible new client, a major California winery. The visitors stated they planned to appropriate an ad budget of two and a half million dollars to go after a substantially increased share of the market. Mike Kennan and his partner John McGlothlin discussed their proposed campaign in Kennan's office. Two of the agency's copywriters sat anxiously waiting for the signal to fold back the cover of their giant sketchpad and show their layouts, along with outlines of proposed copy, tables of media schedules, and budget figures, adding up to exactly two and a half million dollars.

The tenants on the nineteenth floor were Herder, Friedlund, Margolis, and Gump, Management Consultants. Bigtime headhunters. The foyer for the elevators was enlarged and lined with chairs and end tables displaying rows of magazines. A half-dozen neatly dressed young men sat waiting, sneaking looks from time to time at the blond that handled the switchboard. Periodically, another striking young woman appeared in a doorway and called one of the young men to his interview.

The eighteenth floor crackled with excitement. Rhodes, Guidera, Bunbury and Shaer, Industrial Designs. It was a day they'd all been waiting for, the day they were going to shoot the art for the sexy throw-rug ad for their staid carpet-mill client. Saxon Shaer was directing the photographic session himself, stating over and over, "Nothing must show, nothing must show," as he suggested pose after pose to the naked model, who struggled to hide all vital parts of herself from the eye of Jack Rhodes's camera. Stu Guidera, not one to miss so choice an occasion, stood with the model's agent behind Rhodes and made wisecracks. Horace Bunbury, having no interest in such matters, sat in his office, absorbed in paperwork.

On the seventeenth floor it was just another Tuesday morning for Widden, Sutzman, and Co., auditors, men not given to excitement.

The sixteenth floor was vacant. Fifteen and fourteen were filled with more of the offices of the Root Corporation. The tower had no thirteenth floor, and number twelve contained the corporate headquarters of Stanco Industries, a manufacturer of chemicals used in textile processing, with several plants in the Southeast. Eleven was vacant, and the tenth floor housed Kraft, Lutz, McMullen, and Perez, Account-

ants, a honeycomb of small offices where men sat at calculators and punched out numbers which they jotted into data
sheets to go to their computer room.

On the ninth floor, Terry sat before her switchboard, her
smile primed and ready. The next man off the elevator could
be Mr. Right. The offices behind her, Market Systems and
Surveys, Business Consultants, were active as usual. A panel
of housewives sat around a conference table with Dr. Gene
Schain, discussing a new concept in aerosol cleaners. Behind
a one-way mirror, Schain's staff members watched, taped,
and took notes.

The eighth floor was rented to Goodman and High, Ar-
chitects. The furnishings were sleek and contemporary, and
the walls were covered with renderings of shopping centers,
condominiums, and office buildings. In a large corner office
Mike Goodman sat with a client discussing plans for a new
luxury hotel in Fort Lauderdale.

In Goldwasser and Co., Securities Analysts, on the seventh
floor, old man Goldwasser sat at his desk, his swollen feet in
slippers, his belly rolling over his belt, reading *The Wall Street
Journal.* From time to time he took out his handkerchief and
wiped his florid face. In the other rooms on the floor, other
members of the firm were calling special clients to discuss actions that might be taken as soon as the market opened at ten.

In the corporate headquarters of Shenandoah Textile
Mills, on the sixth floor, the major topic of interest was the
end of a strike in one of their southern plants. On five, Bessie
Gittelson was on the phone, screening calls with great di-
plomacy to the various Berkowitzes and Belzes and other employees of Berkowitz and Belz, Importers.

On the third and fourth floors, both occupied by Dorfer,
West, and Associates, Architectural Engineers, the draftsmen
were still dawdling over their coffee, while the brass were in
conference in Dick Dorfer's office.

In Runyan Tool and Die Works, on the second floor, business was a little more relaxed than usual. Walter Scatliff, the executive V.P. and boss, was away on business. Frank Bertolini and the other executives were more easygoing.

In the lobby, Guillermo Rios, the elevator starter, fat and pompous in his red-gray-and-gilt uniform, briskly directed traffic into the four elevators, ruling his modest domain with authority. On the level below the lobby, Joe Palko sat at his desk, staring blankly at his phone. He kept playing back the brief conversation he'd had earlier with Luis. Something was brewing. He'd called Pederson again, and had again been told that Pete would be around to see him sometime in the afternoon.

It seemed to Devereau that his pulse accelerated with every green light that allowed the bus to move farther down Second Avenue in the sluggish morning traffic. He could actually hear his heartbeat, and as it grew faster, he found it hard to breathe. There could be no turning back.

He tried to distract himself by thinking about screwing Barbara, and he forcefully pushed all sorts of erotic images onto the screen of his mind. But the reality that he was wasting his time playing games with himself kept coming through, and his pulse rate continued to climb. He suddenly began to feel nauseated, and his armpits and palms and the soles of his feet felt wet. He couldn't allow the troops to sense his fear. He checked his watch. A few more minutes. They had passed Eighty-sixth, with traffic so far about as expected. At least, things were almost exactly on schedule. He had to hold himself together. He'd be all right as soon as they made their landing and the action got under way, like a quarterback who feels cold, stiff, and uncoordinated until the first time he gets hit.

Some of the men signaled their own nervousness with chatter and wisecracks. Others were quiet and brooding. Their weapons were in canvas bags at their feet. They joked in whispers about what Devereau would tell the fuzz if the fuzz stopped the bus and boarded. "We're on our way to an exercise at the Forty-second Infantry Division Armory down in the Village." Oh, of course, the fuzz would say, "Sure. With live ammunition?"

Luis stood on the roof, outside the elevator engine room, surveying Park Avenue. He wondered what banana-head on the night crew had brought a broad up to the engine room the night before. That had to be what had happened. What else? His guns were gone. And his mask. . . . Christ! Wet and sticky and stinking from fuck, lying there all wadded up in the middle of the floor. Of all nights to leave the engine-room door unlocked! What would Devereau say? But what the hell difference did it make? They had guns enough for a whole army. At least the banana-head didn't take the radio. That would have been trouble.

And what did he need with the mask? Palko already knew he was up to something. And in a day or two they'd be gone. The plan would work. Any minute now the call would come from the bus.

Luis pulled his radio out of the pouch on his webbed belt and turned it on. "Hey, Alfredo. You over there?"

Across the street, in room 11-S of the Waldorf-Astoria, a wiry little man, fifty-odd years old, sat in front of a window that overlooked Park Avenue. He wore earphones which were connected to a radio receiver-transmitter. As he looked past the gauzy curtain through the open window, he could see Luis on the roof. When he heard Luis' voice, he flipped a switch, grabbed a microphone, and said, "Hey, Luis, you forget to say the password."

"Hey, Alfredo. Boston," Luis answered, and giggled.

"That's better, Luis."

Devereau's furious voice exploded in their ears. "What are you two doing fooling around? Somebody could pick it up."

"Hey, Dee. We test the radios. That's all."

"We're at checkpoint A," Devereau said, still angry. "Estimate checkpoint B in three minutes and checkpoint C in six. Landing on schedule in ten minutes at oh-two after. Start cutting the elevators in exactly five minutes. Now, stop transmission until you hear from me."

Luis suddenly realized that it was all about to begin. He looked at his watch, which read 9:52. Checkpoint A was Seventy-second Street, B was Fifty-seventh, and C was Fifty-first and Third. He went back into the engine room and began watching the cabinets that contained the elevator switching relays. The indicators moved slowly up and down, telling him the exact location of each car. He looked at his watch. Four more minutes.

Barbara Meyner drew a circle around an ad for a dude ranch in Peekskill. She put the paper down and dialed the number listed. When a voice answered, she inquired about weekend rates, reservations, and directions, and jotted careful notes into her steno pad.

The bus reached Fifty-first street and turned toward Third. The men were quiet. The wisecracking had ended. Sally Panucci watched his hands, which were trembling, and wondered if he'd settle down once they were in the building. Devereau held himself in rigid physical control, but he felt certain his heartbeat was audible all over the bus. He turned and scanned the faces of the troops. Most of the men appeared as paralyzed by the significance of the moment as he. At that instant Big Charlie, who was driving the bus, drawled, "Okay, you fuckers, draw your assholes up tight, 'cause we're almost there." An explosion of laughter rippled the length of the bus, relieving the tension.

Car number two was the first to reach the lobby after 9:57, and as soon as the little red neon bulb glowed, indicating the elevator door was open, Luis threw the breaker, freezing the car in that position.

The bus crossed Third Avenue and moved into the block between Third and Lexington, following a yellow taxi. The traffic was tedious but consistent with Devereau's observations during the dry run. His watch read 9:59. They would arrive almost exactly on the ETA he had just given Luis.

At that moment the bus stopped abruptly, because a small panel truck in front of the taxi had suddenly parked. The truck driver climbed out, came around to the rear, and took out several cases of liquor. The hack began blowing his horn and waving his arms. The truck driver ignored him and took out a small two-wheeled carrier and wheeled the cases into a liquor store. Devereau glanced to his right and froze. The bus was stopped directly in front of the Seventeenth Precinct.

The cabbie waited until traffic in the left lane had let up and then whipped around the truck, shaking his fist in the direction of the liquor store as he did. There was no room for the bus to pull around, but it inched forward so that at least Devereau was not in direct line with precinct headquarters. The truck driver returned and pulled ahead to Lexington Avenue. Devereau checked his watched again. Ten straight up.

Guillermo Rios repeatedly pushed the "Close Door" button on car number two and wondered why nothing happened. The elevators—his whole world and only reason to exist—always worked perfectly. What could be wrong? A woman who had boarded car number four came over to tell him that it, too, seemed to have stopped running. Rios stepped out of the car and opened a metal cabinet on the lobby wall to call Palko. As Palko answered, a man from car number three approached him to complain.

In the board room on the penthouse level, Billy Marshall outlined the many arguments in favor of divesting the Corporation of Sturdy Tool. Winfield Root, still toying with his empty cup, hardly listened.

By the time Joe Palko appeared in the lobby, all four elevators had stopped on the ground floor, their doors open. The problem had to originate in the engine room. He went to the house phone and dialed, hoping that Luis, presumably out on the roof working on the water tank, might hear and answer. But Luis, leaning against a concrete column with his arms folded, just giggled. Would Palko eventually walk up twenty-two flights if nobody answered? Luis thought about how much fun it would be to draw his gun and shoot the phone. If he still had his gun. His smile faded, and he checked his watch. 10:02. He walked toward the passageway that led out onto the roof, kicking at his mask, which was still on the floor. When he reached the roof, he looked across Park and saw the bus pulling up to the red light. He went back inside, where the phone was still ringing. He picked the receiver off the hook and then hung it back up.

In the lobby, Palko heard the ringing stop and then the line go dead. He jiggled the hook. "Luis? Luis? Are you up there?" He pressed down the hook and dialed the engine-room extension again. The monotonous, unanswered ringing began once more. He looked at the increasing number of people waiting to get to upper floors, some of them beginning to get hostile because they were already late for appointments. Pederson's afternoon visit was going to be a couple of hours too late.

7

A sunny morning in mid-May on Park Avenue. Air quality, acceptable. The bus moved forward with the light and swung in a wide arc into the southbound lane of Park, stopping in front of the corner building, the Root Tower, 330 Park Avenue, next to the ITT Building and directly across from St. Bartholemew's.

As the bus made the turn, the troops pulled white cotton masks over their heads and stuffed their automatics into their holsters. Their movements took on a military precision as the doors opened and they poured from the bus in two neat columns. Pedestrians blinked with surprise and then watched coolly as the two rows of men stormed the double glass doors. Some publicity stunt, without question. Anything can happen in New York.

The first two soldiers held the doors open, and the rest funneled through, a couple at the rear carrying two large olive-drab crates, suggestive of caskets by their dimensions. As the troops entered the marble-and-terrazzo lobby, Guillermo

Rios strode gallantly forward in his gilt-trimmed coat, waving his arms. "Hey, what is this? You can't come in here like that."

A large black troop was the first to reach Rios. He brought the butt of his rifle down in a sweeping arc against the backs of Rios's knees, dropping Rios to the floor. Pushing Rios over with his foot, he pointed the muzzle of his rifle at Rios' eye. "You shut your fucking mouth and do as you're told, and maybe you get to keep your head." Rios blanched and then lost consciousness. A woman standing nearby screamed and crumpled to the floor.

Palko backed against a wall and remained quiet. Another of the soldiers thumped a young stockbroker in the chest with a rifle butt. The man dropped his briefcase and slid to the floor, begging not to be hurt. The other men and women who had been trying to get on elevators quickly backed against walls and on command from the troops also sank to the floor. Benjy looked for something to shoot in the bare lobby and finally found a small palm tree growing in a large wooden tub. His face lit up, and he pumped several rounds into the tub. At the sight of the bullets splintering wood, several women began crying hysterically.

Devereau found the scene reassuring. It was exactly as he had described it in his briefing lectures. The landing had been made and the beachhead secured. Their total control of the building could not be challenged. They had more than five hundred hostages. He looked at Palko and saw him as a soldier, lean and tough in suntans with no tie. Palko's face reflected a quiet acceptance of the fact that one does as he's told when facing a gun.

One of the troops pulled a heavy chain from his pocket, and looped it around the push handles on the glass doors leading to the street. He joined the ends with a padlock. Another soldier produced a spray can and began covering the glass with white paint. Two more soldiers started up to the second floor. Two others approached Palko and jabbed him with rifle barrels, pushing him toward the stairwell and down into the basement.

Big Charlie looked around and said, "Now, everybody do as you're told, and nobody gets hurt. Otherwise, gonna get messy." He put one foot on the still-unconscious Rios. "What we want you to do is go up to the floor you was planning to visit or go back to the floor you was coming from. We've been instructed to shoot anyone who gives us trouble. Floors two through seven take car number one"—he pointed at one of the elevators—"eight through twelve in number two, fourteen through eighteen in three, and the rest in four."

Devereau allowed himself a smile. The first sixty seconds had gone according to plan. The two packing crates were already stacked on elevator four, and the citizens were being hustled into their respective cars. Devereau followed the packing crates, carrying his briefcase.

The two soldiers who escorted Palko to the basement stood him against the wall while they searched him and went through his desk. "I got no gun," Palko said. "I don't like them." Satisfied, they made him sit on the floor against the wall. One of the soldiers sat in the desk chair to guard him. The other walked down the hall in the direction of the telephone terminal room. Palko studied his guard, obviously just a kid with a gun. He couldn't quite read the kid's eyes because of the mask, but the kid seemed a little nervous.

Two men, 2-A and 2-B according to Devereau's code, went up the back stairwell, pulled open the door to the second floor. They were Perry and Roberto—Perry, the handsome coffee-skinned black with a hard-on for the whole world, and Roberto, the smirking young Puerto Rican with the orange hair. They rushed into the second-floor foyer, startling the plain-faced receptionist at the desk. Perry jostled her breast with the muzzle of his rifle. "Let's go. Get up and get inside. Quick." Just as she appeared ready to scream in terror, he added, "And don't make a sound."

She stood up cautiously and raised her hands. "Let's go,"

he said. He slapped at her backside with the rifle barrel. "Come on, move it." She opened the door, and Perry pushed her through.

Roberto followed them, fired two rounds into a sofa, and then shouted, "Everybody do as we tell you and nobody will get hurt. You hear?" He fired two more rounds to a chorus of shouts and screams. Heads appeared in some of the doorways and then pulled quickly back. He fired one more time. "No funny stuff, you hear? You try anything, we shoot to kill. Now, everybody go into the conference room." He and Perry separated, each taking a corridor. They moved down the halls and entered each office, finding occupants in total confusion. Some crouched at windows in outside offices, looking down. Some had crawled into the kneeholes of desks or slipped into storage closets, where they cowered helplessly when the closet doors opened. The women, mostly secretaries at desks in areas outside of the individual offices, skittered nervously around and screamed whenever one of the troops came near to herd them along.

"Let's go, git your ass in gear," Perry repeated as he entered each office. "Do as you're told, and stay alive." He struck and shoved mercilessly with his rifle butt, deliberately inflicting pain.

In one of the larger offices Roberto found four men moving chaotically around, one of them about to put a chair through a window. Roberto fired into a chair, and the four threw their hands up. "Don't fuck around," Roberto said. "Just go in the conference room like nice boys. Okay?"

The roundup proceeded smoothly. When everyone was assembled, Roberto held them at gunpoint and Perry went back to survey the offices and check out the rest rooms.

On other floors the action followed similar patterns. The elevators, their power circuits reactivated by Luis, stopped at each floor, and two soldiers emerged, pointing their rifles at the receptionist. They carried out their assignment relentlessly, firing shots that echoed like minor explosions within the confined spaces of the office areas, provoking clumsy, fumbling panic and screaming hysteria. Men and women fell over one another, straining to avoid the punishing jabs from rifle butts.

On the fifth floor the two soldiers stormed across the empty foyer through the door where Bessie Gittelson sat to greet visitors. Despite their masks and weapons, she was almost certain they were the same two men who had visited the Friday before. She wondered where Luis was at the moment. And Joe Palko. Joe couldn't possibly be involved.

On the seventh floor, old Ben Goldwasser, hearing the shots and commotion, made no move but sat in his chair until one of the masked troops appeared at the door to his office. "Let's go quick," the man said. Goldwasser began struggling to his slippered feet, incapable of quicker movement because of his obesity and his age. "Come on, goddammit," the soldier shouted. He walked over to Goldwasser and shoved him in the back with his rifle butt. The old man lurched forward and crumpled slowly to the floor like some large animal settling to the ground to rest. The soldier kicked the collapsed body sharply. "Get up and get into the next office. Come on. Let's go."

Goldwasser said quietly, "I cannot move faster," His eyes were teary from physical pain, but he spoke in a restrained voice, maintaining his calm dignity.

The troop, suddenly realizing that the old man could not possibly go faster, said in a subdued tone, "Come on. We gotta get you into the next office." Holding his rifle aside in his left hand, he extended his right hand to the old man, and together the two strained and heaved until Goldwasser was finally back upright on his feet. They walked slowly into the bigger corner office, occupied by his son, the recently appointed president of the firm.

On the ninth floor Terry put on her best smile as she saw

the elevator stop but it quickly faded when the two troops came at her.

On the twelfth floor Avery Wissel, director of marketing for Stanco Industries, heard the shots and reached into the back of his lower-right-hand drawer and took out a twenty-five-caliber automatic. He had imagined this moment many times since buying the gun. He faced the door, holding the gun at his hip, cowboy-style. Seeing that his hand was trembling, he brought the gun up and steadied it with his left, the way cops did in television cop shows.

As soon as one of the masked men appeared in the doorway, he fired and missed. The recoil pushed the gun upward. He fired once more, hardly bothering to aim, and then held his hands in the air in surrender, the pistol still in his right fist.

The soldier, taken totally by surprise, stared at the pudgy little man who had surrendered before he even had a chance to shoot back. Frightened himself, the soldier said, "Why, you little shit, throw that thing over here before I blow you right out that window. Do you know how close you came to being dead meat?"

Wissel, a mass of tremors by this time, tossed the gun over. The soldier picked it up and dropped it into a large pocket on the front of his pants. "Let's go," he said. As Wissel moved by him into the corridor, he planted his boot in the small of Wissel's back and shoved. Wissel stumbled forward and fell down. The troop slapped him in the seat with his rifle butt, and Wissel quickly got up and moved on.

On the eighteenth floor troops 18-A and 18-B, Wayne Austin and Billy Pickett, stormed into the offices of Rhodes, Guidera, Bunbury, and Shaer, pushing the receptionist ahead of them. Pickett fired two rounds and began shouting instructions. A large man charged out of one of the offices to see what was creating the disturbance. He ran into Pickett, who thumped him brutally in the chest and face with his rifle butt. Hearing screams, someone opened the door to the usually sacrosant photographic studio, and Austin glimpsed the naked model under the lights. "Well, son-of-a-bitch," he said, walking past the various prop and makeup men "What've we got here, a little high-class coffee-break gang-bang? Cameras and everything."

"Who the hell are you?" Saxon Shaer asked.

"You keep your ass in line and I'm the man who may just let you live."

"Is this some kind of a gag?" Shaer said.

Austin fired a shot at a chair in the corner of the studio and the wood splintered from the impact of the bullet. "That look like some kind of a gag? Now, come on, let's go. Everybody into the big corner office."

"May I take my clothes?" the model asked. She defiantly made no attempt to cover herself.

"What for?" he answered. "You look just about perfect the way you are." His eyes traced her flawless, skinny body.

She took her light raincoat off a coatrack and slipped it on. Then she started for a door that led to a dressing room.

"Hey, where are you going?" Austin asked.

"My clothes?"

"You got on enough. Come on. Let's go."

On the twenty-second floor Little Benjy was the first off the elevator, followed by Stroud. The receptionist, an older woman, was on her feet screaming the moment she saw the guns. They had no trouble maneuvering the employees toward the boardroom where the Root directors were still meeting. Barbara gave a soft frightened gasp when she recognized Devereau. But she didn't speak and just watched silently as Benjy kicked the door to the conference room open. "All of you. Please sit very quiet, with your hands on the table." He walked to the far end of the room and aimed his M-14 at the seated board members.

Ronam, the president, watched Stroud jostle the rest of the floor's ten employees into the room. "Can somebody please explain all this?"

Benjy laughed. "You like to see me shoot something?" He

rapid-fired two rounds at an upholstered chair in the corner of the room, then quickly redirected his gun at Ronam.

"What do you want?" Ronam asked in a subdued tone.

Devereau entered and sat down at the end of the table near the windows. He placed his briefcase on the table and studied the board members at some length. Stroud shoved the ten other employees, all but two of them secretaries, into the end of the room behind Ronam. Then Stroud walked out.

"In answer to your question, Mr. Ronam," Devereau said, looking at his watch, "what we want is money. I will discuss the details with you later." He pulled out his radio and yanked up the antenna, carefully avoiding Barbara's frightened eyes. "Boston." He spoke at a voice level just louder than conversational. "Boston. Do you read me?"

"Good, Penthouse, clear and strong," came the answer. Alfredo sat at his window, nervously pulling aside the curtains and looking at 330's penthouse windows.

"Switch to transmit."

Alfredo flipped a couple of controls. "You're transmitting, Penthouse."

"Basement," Devereau said, a little louder. "Basement. Do you read me, Basement?"

Sally Panucci was seated at Palko's desk, his automatic in his right hand aimed at Palko and his radio pressed to his ear with his other. "Penthouse," Sally shouted. "We read, but just barely. Lotsa machine noise down here, like we figured. And lotsa concrete. But we read. Position is secure."

"Keep your volume on maximum. . . . Lobby. Do you read me?"

"Good shape, Penthouse. Position secure."

"Two-A. Do you read me?"

"No problems, Penthouse. Everything secure and working."

The board members watched in tight-lipped silence as Devereau carried out his roll call, moving up the tower, floor by floor, while a small, tenacious man wearing a similar mask stood next to him and kept an army rifle trained on them. Barbara Meyner, standing among the secretaries, watched and listened with special attention.

Devereau called to the sixth floor and received the "position-secure" report, the voice reaching him with remarkable clarity. Smokey Hampton's custom-engineered radio system was all he could have hoped for. Specially doctored three-watt portable units with extrafidelity speakers. Better than police units. And Smokey's answer to the question of vertical transmission through twenty-two floors of concrete was the portable receiver-transmitter on the eleventh floor of "the hotel across the street." The Waldorf-Astoria. "What it does," Smokey had explained, "is pick up the signals coming from any floor and reradiate them so that all signals travel nearly horizontal and don't have to go through so much concrete, just windows and outside walls."

The radio system had been just one more part of a plan so carefully detailed that it could not fail. Planning. Testing. Training. And then executing with crisp efficiency. A life's work telescoped into just a couple of years. And just a few days of real action. The latest in programs for early retirement. Fuck the boys from Boston Latin.

Execution had indeed been crisp. A high-rise on Park Avenue brought under total control in less than five minutes. And their position was impregnable. Unapproachable. Over five hundred high-priced hostages. And only one way in or out.

In Winfield Root's office, Stroud was working on the phone. He removed the square cover plate from the wall. He took from his pocket a device resembling a portable voltmeter, with a handle and two wires with alligator clips. He attached the clips to the two screws in the connecting box and set the controls on the instrument. Moving quickly into the next office, he attached an identical instrument to the phone connection there.

In the subbasement Hampton stood in the telephone terminal room studying the brightly colored wires that entered through a master conduit on one side of the room. The wires were separated into bunches, then into smaller clusters as they flowed up to the multibanked terminal board, where they were attached in pairs. On the opposite side of the terminal board the wires were pulled together in small ganglia as they left the board, and finally into one massive cable that went into a single conduit in a manner identical with the wiring pattern on the opposite side. Internal and external.

A cigarette hanging from his mouth, Hampton put on a set of earphones and carefully attached it to a small electronic monitoring device. Holding the palm-sized gadget in his right hand, he began touching the pairs of terminal screws, moving deftly down the rows of connectors, seeking the signals from the two tone oscillators Stroud was to have installed in the penthouse.

He stopped suddenly, checked two screws again, and nodded. Then he pulled a small dispenser of red tape from a pocket and marked the wires to those screws. He began testing again, and quickly found the other two. With these two sets of wires marked, he drew a pair of heavy nips from his pocket and began cutting wires, thinking about the poor slobs from the phone company who would be coming in a few days to reconnect that mass of spaghetti. Cutting around the two marked connections, he quickly isolated 330 Park's inhabitants from communication with the rest of the world. Only two lines remained, and Devereau controlled them both.

"Stereo," Devereau said. "All stations. Let's give them their orders."

On each floor of the building the two men in army fatigues and masks huddled the employees of that floor into a small group in an outside room with windows overlooking Park Avenue. The two men stood apart from each other, and each turned the volume control of his radio to maximum, directing the tiny but efficient speaker at the cluster of frightened people.

"This building is under a state of total siege," Devereau said. He read from a prepared speech in a notebook taken from his briefcase. "You are all prisoners. There is no possible means of escape. The only exit is through the main lobby, which is locked and heavily guarded. The police will not be able to approach this building for fear we will shoot you. This fear is well-founded. The men guarding you are fully trained and have been instructed to execute, if necessary, anyone who attempts to escape.

"You will be held until the terms of your release have been met. In a few minutes I will begin meeting with the senior executive of each firm to state the exact amount of money we will demand from that company. After the terms have been met, you will be released. This applies to everyone, with the exception of a few selected hostages who will remain with us until we have secured our escape route.

"When I am finished talking, you may go to your desks and resume your normal activities. Two soldiers will remain on each floor to guard you. You will not be able to communicate with anyone outside, as the phone lines have been cut. Your families will learn of your situation through the news media.

"If any of you have weapons of any kind, turn them over to my men. Do not attempt to overpower these guards. Any injury suffered by any of my troops will be answered immediately by the execution of innocent prisoners, and the person causing such injury may consider himself directly responsible for those lives. Executions will be at a rate of ten prisoners for each guard attacked.

"I urge your total cooperation. You will be allowed to leave immediately upon compliance with the terms of release."

Devereau closed his notebook and put it back in his briefcase. He continued to avoid Barbara's eyes, but a glimpse of her face revealed an inscrutable expression.

"You may all return to your desks," he said as he stood up, "except Mr. Root and Mr. Ronam. I need your two offices."

"I think I know you from somewhere," Root said suddenly.

The other board members looked at him incredulously.

"You're mistaken," Devereau snapped.

"Your voice is familiar," the old man persisted. "I'll probably remember in a while."

"That will be all," Devereau said, ignoring the old man, who looked much older than he had two years before.

"Of course I know you," Root said.

Devereau looked quickly back at him.

"We probably all know you," Root said. "Since you seem to know our names and where our offices are located." He looked around at the other board members. "It stands to reason, doesn't it? If he chose this building, it must be because of his familiarity with it."

"If you don't shut up, I'll close your mouth for you," Benjy said. He raised the butt of his rifle, but Devereau stopped him.

"Forget it." He picked up his briefcase and left the room.

"I am sure I know that man," Root said. "He is most familiar."

Barbara Meyner remained silent.

Devereau seated himself at Root's spacious desk and switched on his radio. He took out his notebook, read a phone number, and dialed. As soon as someone answered, he said, "Let me speak to the commissioner."

8

"Who's calling, please?"

"Let me speak to him at once. He'll be interested in what I want to tell him."

Doubtless one of the commissioner's buddies, playing wise guy. How else would he have had the private hot-line phone number? "The commissioner's out, sir. If you'll leave your name and number, I'll see that he gets it as soon as he gets back."

"Can he be reached quickly?"

"We can get a message to him if it's important. He's out of town. Be back in a couple days. Could you tell me who's calling, please?"

An impatient exhalation. "Let me speak to the second in command. Quickly."

This obviously wasn't one of the old man's cronies. "Who's calling, and how'd you get this number?"

"Just connect me with the next in command."

"The first deputy commissioner is out of town, too. There

are six other deputies. Tell me who's calling, and why, and maybe I can connect you to one."

Another brief pause. "Who the hell are you?"

"I'm Lieutenant Heinrich, one of the commissioner's aides. Who are you and how'd you get this number?"

"Okay, Lieutenant, you'll be the first to know. Let's see how well you and your SPRINT system handle it. I'm holding 330 Park Avenue for ransom. The entire building. Do you understand what I'm saying? I have an army of well-trained, heavily armed men at my command, and I am in absolute control. We have over five hundred hostages, and we expect complete cooperation from the police or we will begin to execute them."

"Hey! Who the hell is this?"

"You have all the information you need, Lieutenant. That's 330 Park, corner of Fifty-first. You'll call your dispatcher and have him tell the Seventeenth Precinct to send a car by. When they arrive, they'll see a bus in front of the building. Tell them to leave it alone, and as soon as they get here, we'll give them a little signal to let them know we mean business."

"Hey, how do I know this isn't some kinda crank call?"

"You don't know shit, Lieutenant. Now get moving."

"Who the hell is this?" Heinrich shouted again into the phone before he realized the line was dead.

After a minute he dialed the dispatcher in the communications center. "This crazy-ass call just came in over the P.C.'s phone. . . ." He hesitated. "But you'd better send a car to check it out. Possible hostage situation at 330 Park. Perpetrators could be heavily armed. . . ."

Devereau smiled at Stroud. "Tell Benjy to go up on the roof and get ready to do his thing." He glanced at his watch. "I figure they'll be here in two to three minutes. Certainly inside of five. Then we can start watching the scramble. You cover the foyer while he's on the roof."

76

The radio car stopped for the light at Fifty-first, and one of the cops pointed at the bus parked in front of the Root Tower. Traffic moved normally in all directions, and aside from the illegally parked bus, there was no sign of anything wrong.

Then someone appeared in a window halfway up the tower and waved something white, possibly a jacket. On another floor someone signaled SOS with a flashlight in a slightly darkened room. Several more people appeared in windows, waving their arms.

As the light changed and the radio car moved forward, the two cops saw that the wide glass entry doors had been sprayed white. They pulled past the bus and parked in front of the ITT Building, surveying the street before slowly opening the doors, their hands on their service revolvers. The driver stood in the door of the car, watching his partner, who walked toward the building. The few pedestrians in the vicinity looked at the cop curiously, and when he motioned to them to duck into the entrance of the ITT Building, they complied indifferently.

The cop approaching the glass building front tried to see through the paint into the interior. He got a glimpse of the lobby. All seemed quiet, but when he tried the door, he found it was chained.

Suddenly the light on top of the radio car exploded, and at almost the same instant, a rifle shot popped from somewhere high on the building. The cop by the car, jumped back, unhurt but confused. He drew his revolver, looking to see where the shot came from. He shouted to his partner, who was already moving away from the Root Tower toward the ITT Building.

The driver got back in the car and moved up the street as his partner herded spectators back from the street. "Stay in here out of sight," he said hurriedly. "Don't take no kinda chance. We don't know what we got out here yet." He hurried to the end of the ITT Building and slid back into the waiting radio car.

"This is car seventeen-Charlie," he called into the microphone. "Reporting a ten-thirteen. Repeat. Reporting a ten-thirteen. 330 Park. That's Fifty-first and Park. We were shot at from somewhere high up on the building."

The call went into the communications center, where it was recorded and monitored in various offices, including the commissioner's. Lieutenant Heinrich heard it and immediately called the chief of operations and the borough C.O. for Manhattan South, who was there at headquarters for a conference. Heinrich briefly related the details of his earlier phone call, and the borough C.O., an assistant chief inspector named O'Reilly, told him to make sure Harry Ziller was informed. Then O'Reilly ordered Emergency Service to set up a containment operation.

Radio cars were already moving to the vicinity. A 10-13—a threat on the life of a member of the force—always prompts quick action from other cops in the sector. As they moved in, their approximate locations known to the center, traffic was halted on Park Avenue from Forty-seventh to Fifty-fifth and on those crosstown streets from Lexington Avenue to Madison.

The mobilization moved efficiently. A fully equipped communications van was brought to Fiftieth and stationed between Park and Madison, just around the corner from 330, and a temporary headquarters was established. Two Emergency Service trucks were parked next to it, providing special weapons and other equipment if needed. Wooden police barricades were quickly set up to keep pedestrians out of the area. As soon as this was done, uniformed patrolmen and detectives swarmed into the buildings surrounding 330 Park, evacuating all offices with even a partial view of the Root Tower. Office personnel reacted calmly. Nothing is much of a surprise to New Yorkers.

But attempts to empty the northern and western rooms in the Waldorf-Astoria proved more difficult, as some occupants flatly refused to even unlock their doors, making it clear that they'd rather pull their blinds and take their chances. In room 11-S Alfredo almost dropped his transmitter when the cop at the door politely asked that he leave. Devereau had not prepared him for such a possibility, and he saw himself already on the way to jail. He meekly refused to go, and the voice on the other side of the door just told him to close his drapes and leave the room as soon as possible. Alfredo marveled that the cops left. It was further evidence of Devereau's magic.

Reporters in the press section on the second floor of police headquarters had been sitting around drinking coffee when they heard the dispatcher send the car to 330 Park. An unconfirmed hostage situation on Park Avenue. Perpetrators could be heavily armed. The call stood out from the usual gravelly static and routine business that came endlessly over the pressroom monitors. A few minutes later the 10-13 came in, and this grabbed their attention. Then, as they listened to the dispatcher in his controlled monotone lay out the details for the containment operation, they knew a potentially large story was unfolding, possibly even a whopper.

They began clamoring for an official comment and as much background as possible. A call was made to the Office of Public Information, only to learn that the deputy commissioner was away for the day, attending a function with the mayor. A lieutenant from that office called O'Reilly, and after they conferred for several minutes, O'Reilly agreed to go down to the pressroom. In view of the scope of the containment procedure taking place, the basic factual details as far as known had to be made public.

"Here's what we have so far, gentlemen," O'Reilly said. "I can tell you that we received a call that 330 Park Avenue is under siege, and the call came from a party claiming to be in charge of the operation. As you heard on your monitor, the radio car sent to investigate was fired upon by someone in or on the roof of the building. No injuries reported so far, and we have taken all necessary steps to cut off the area. Oh, yeah, one other thing, we received a call from the telephone company that all phones in the building have been disconnected. Apparently that doesn't include the one on which the call we received was made. That's about it for now, guys."

Within minutes the story was transmitted to all metropolitan and national newswires.

After Stroud returned from the foyer, Devereau told him to watch the hostages in the penthouse and then went into Winfield Root's private bathroom, carrying his briefcase. He quickly removed his mask, fatigues, and boots. He peeled off his underwear and socks and threw them into a wastebasket. After examining a large, clean, fluffy towel, he adjusted the shower and stepped under it. He picked up the fresh new bar of soap and smelled it. Real English lavender. He lathered and then stood under the heavy spray, watching it cascade down his body, cleansing away forever the last traces of the Hunt's Point warehouse.

He dried off, opened his briefcase, and took out a plastic bag containing clean socks and underwear. He opened the cabinet beneath the large mirror and found a barely used shaving brush and mug, also lavender, and an array of lotions and other toiletries. Instead of using the aerosol shit he'd brought in his briefcase, he savored the steaming-hot shave and the chilling sting of one of Root's expensive lotions.

"Would you like a shower?" he asked Stroud when he came out of the bathroom.

Stroud hesitated and then shrugged. He wasn't sure if it was an offer or an order. "Sure," he said finally.

"Go ahead," Devereau said. "Just keep the place neat."

"Right," Stroud said.

Devereau stood at the window of Root's office and watched

the world of Park Avenue gradually die before him. There was
no sign of life anywhere within his line of vision. Park Avenue
at eleven-thirty on a busy sunlit Tuesday—a ghost town. He
was impressed by the efficiency with which the force was
moving to get set up. It had taken only thirty minutes. Not
bad. A little ahead of schedule. And he had not seen one cop
during the whole process.

He opened his notebook to the page containing phone
numbers. The list included the numbers for the various news
services. He dialed API and asked for the city editor. As soon
as he was connected he asked, "Do you control what goes
onto the wire?"

"Metropolitan news is handled at this desk."

"What's your name?"

"Rick Barone. Look, would you tell me what you want?"

"Mr. Barone, I called to report that all occupants of 330
Park Avenue are being held hostage."

"Our reporter down at headquarters already called in the
story. If you know some additional details, we'd like to have
them."

"I can give you any information you want."

"Where are you calling from?"

"330 Park Avenue."

"I thought all the phone lines in the building had been
cut."

"All except those I've kept for my own use."

"How did you manage to keep yours when all the others got
cut?"

"I'm in command of this operation."

"You're what? Wait a minute. Are you telling me that
you're the one controlling that operation?" Barone signaled to
a rewrite man to pick up a phone and listen in.

"That's right, Mr. Barone."

"Jesus! I can't believe this. . . . Then again, if you were a
crank, you couldn't know about the story yet."

"We have over five hundred hostages in this building, Mr. Barone. We'll release them as our demands are met. If they are not met, we'll begin executions. We hope this will not prove necessary. I'm calling you to make sure the city is well informed of the situation, because I believe it will help expedite our demands."

"What are your demands?"

"Money, Mr. Barone."

"Would you care to tell me the amount?"

"Each company in the building will be expected to pay an amount commensurate with its financial standing. I have an army of men in here ready to shoot, and I'm sure you can see how publicity will help alert the people and make them realize that we are deadly serious. Your responsibility, Mr. Barone, will be to see that the city and the banking community in particular get that message."

Barone almost laughed. "Are you trying to tell me that if things don't go well, you're going to blame me?"

"Don't you agree you're in a position to help in the release of the hostages? Don't you think that you'd better do as I tell you?"

"Jesus. Now I've heard everything. Tell me. Any other details you'd like me to have? Anybody killed or injured?"

"There have been no casualties yet. Just state that we are in absolute control of the building and that we expect our demands to be met promptly, or we start killing hostages."

"That's it?"

"That's it."

"I'll bet you'd like this story on the national wire, too."

"What the hell's the matter with you? This is the biggest story you ever had!"

"I'll see what I can do for you"—Barone paused—"you miserable son-of-a-bitch!" He hung up abruptly and dialed the police.

*   *   *

The stunned captives of 330 Park moved about their floors of the building, nursing bruises and sharing the sense of shock over what had happened. The troops on each floor had left them to themselves and had set up guard posts by the elevators and stairwells. By guarding the only avenue of escape, they could control the whole floor from one spot. People in the offices kept picking up the dead phones, hoping for dial tones, struggling to accept the incredible fact that they were totally isolated, prisoners of the pair of coldly indifferent, brutal men in the foyer.

Many of the office workers had watched the police car appear and tried to signal. A few had seen the car fired on before it pulled away. As they saw all the traffic disappear, they knew the police were taking action. But what action? What could the police possibly do? One older woman flatly predicted mass murder. Others insisted the ransoms would be paid without question. But when would they be allowed to leave? And who would be the "few selected hostages" who would be taken along to ensure escape? One from each floor, maybe? And if so, how was that one chosen?

The Root Corporation directors remained in the boardroom, where they speculated on just how much would be asked. Root continued to insist that he knew the man in charge and would ultimately recall who he was. Outside, a group of secretaries gathered to discuss the situation, but Barbara Meyner remained alone at her desk, listening from a distance.

In Root's office Devereau had finished his calls. Nearly twelve noon. The other two wire services had been more respectful than the punk Barone. Before Barone was finished with the story of 330 Park, he'd be just like everyone else. Envious.

Time for one more call to police headquarters to Lieutenant Heinrich, minding the store for the commissioner.

Just as he reached for the phone, it rang. He glanced at Stroud and picked it up. "Yes?"

"Winfield?"

"Who?"

"Winfield Root? Is this his office? Do I have the right number?"

"You have the right number."

"Then may I speak with Mr. Root?"

"Are you aware of what's in progress here at 330 Park?"

"What are you talking about? Who is this? Let me speak to Mr. Root."

"The fucking media," Devereau muttered. "They're not getting the story out fast enough."

"What the hell's going on around there? Let me speak to Mr. Root."

"May I ask who's calling?" Devereau winked slyly at Stroud.

"This is Arnold Zeldes."

"No shit! Well, I'm sorry, Mr. Zeldes, but Mr. Root can't come to the phone just now. If you're a friend of his, surely you know that he's in a board meeting this morning."

"Oh, that's right."

"You peckerhead," Devereau said, grinning at Stroud.

"I'm sorry, I . . . Are you sure this is Mr. Winfield Root's line?"

"Mr. Root has been dispossessed of his office."

"He's what?"

"Go find a radio and you'll hear what's going on!" Devereau shouted. "But don't call back here. I want to keep this line clear so I can talk with the police. Understand?" Devereau slammed the phone down with a grin. Then he checked his notebook for the commissioner's number and dialed.

"The commissioner's office."

"That you, Lieutenant Heinrich?"

"Are you calling from 330 Park?"

"You're not Heinrich."

"My name is Ziller."

"Oh! Lieutenant Harry Ziller of the hostage squad. I figured it was about time for you to get into the act."

"I'm afraid you've got me at a disadvantage. I don't know your name."

"I'll see that you have all the information you need. Do as I tell you and everything'll be fine, Lieutenant Ziller." He gave "Lieutenant" sarcastic emphasis.

"We intend to cooperate fully with you. Our primary concern is the safety of the people in the building."

"Spoken like a trained negotiator, Lieutenant. Now, for openers, don't try gassing this building. My men all have masks and extra canisters of air. The tenants have nothing. Besides, if you start that kind of shit, we're liable to start throwing people off the roof. Do I make myself clear?"

"I told you we intend to cooperate fully. What else do you want?"

"Don't bother our bus. If you do, you'll only have to get us another. When we leave, we leave with hostages."

"When do you plan to leave?"

"As soon as we get what we came for."

"Which is what?"

"A great deal of money."

"Where do you plan to go?"

"Come, Lieutenant. I'm sure when we are ready to go, you'll see that we have an uninterrupted trip. Because, as I said, we'll have some rather high-class hostages."

"All right. What's your game plan?"

"I'll have a word with the chief honcho in each company in the building and then allow him to call his bank. When the money arrives and is counted, we let his people go. When all the money is in, we take our hostages and leave. And I'm counting on you to see that everything goes smoothly. If we are forced to kill anyone, you can hold yourself directly responsible."

"You'll have our cooperation. Let me give you another phone number to use."

"A temporary headquarters van around the corner?"

"You seem to know a lot about the way we operate."

"I used to be a cop," Devereau lied. They'd kill themselves trying to chase that one down. "Now, let me repeat, Lieutenant. We don't want to reduce the population. I'm basically a humanitarian. I just happen to like nice things. So don't force us to do something neither of us would want. See to it that things go smoothly. Okay?"

"I get the message," Ziller said. "What else?"

A pause. "Oh, yeah. One more thing. We'll be needing lunch. That's sandwiches and coffee for about six hundred people. I'd suggest the Waldorf. Okay, what's the new phone number?"

9

Lunch for six hundred people? Something new in hostage negotiations.

Ziller hung up the commissioner's phone and grabbed his hat. He was a stocky man in his forties, with dark hair and rumpled, poorly matched clothes. He rode the elevator down to the third floor and went into the central core of the Current Situation section, an oversized room with several large elevated TV screens around the walls. On one of them was a live telecast of 330 Park. A transmitter had already been set up in one of the observation points across the street from 330, and a portable aerial out a side window sent the signal back to a receiver in One Police Plaza.

Ziller joined a large group composed mostly of departmental upper echelon that stood and looked at the screen.

"Hey, Harry! You planning to try and nee-go-shee-ate that bunch outta there?"

Ziller looked around and spotted Dan Redmond, one of the deputy inspectors in charge of the Tactical Patrol Force. "It's the only way it can be done," Ziller answered.

"Shit! We'll have every man in the TPF going in there before this thing's cleaned up."

"The first thing we have to do is find out who's in charge and how he's set up. I just talked to him, and he sounds like he owns the place. It's gonna take a lot of time."

"My way's better," Redmond said.

"We've gotta go strictly by hostage guidelines, Dan. If we don't, we could have a disaster on our hands. I'm on my way to the van now to see if I can get some dialogue started."

"I'm gonna be looking over your shoulder, Harry. And I'm gonna have my guys moving the first time it looks like you're fucking up."

Ziller left without commenting further. Redmond was always trouble. And 330 Park fell in the TPF area under his jurisdiction. Which didn't improve the outlook for negotiation. Redmond was like a Pentagon general who believed that only wars provided opportunities for advancement. A tall and lean man who walked with a swagger, thumping his hard leather heels, he had earned himself the nickname "Cowboy," and as if to live up to it, he wore his special in a gun holster low on his right hip.

Ziller took the elevator to the parking garage in the basement. He should reach the van in twenty minutes. The man in charge of the operation was making noises like a tycoon entering a big financial negotiation holding all the cards. How would this perpetrator be classified? A whole new category. Super-grand larceny, using a building full of civilians for leverage. The case, no matter how finally resolved, could add a whole goddamn day to the hostage training program.

"Gentlemen, the last time I gave my talk here, I explained that hostage takers fell into three distinct categories. One, the professional criminal who has his escape unexpectedly blocked in the middle of a crime; two, a psychotic, someone with a twisted, depraved mind; and three, a terrorist or frantic group with some kind of cause. Now, gentlemen, I'm tellin' you of a fourth. We have the perpetrator of a carefully pre-planned and detailed hostage crime, who carries it out as a caper with crispness and precision.

"As I explained in the past, we've developed what we call a methodology of crisis intervention for dealing with hostage takers. It's designed to relax our felon's tensions and anxieties. The idea is to get our man to assess his situation rationally. And it works. We've got a track record to prove it. But in this fourth category, it's a whole new dance. Our man is *too* goddamn rational."

Or is he? Where's the chink? Where's his oversight? Or his weakness? He knows us well enough that he's predicting our moves. We've got to get a book on him so we can begin to anticipate him a little. . . .

With his siren shrieking, Ziller blazed his way up Lafayette, then Park Avenue and onto the ramp around Grand Central. He cut his siren and eased up to the barricade at Forty-seventh street. Surveying the wide street with its flowered esplanade, he said to the cops at the barricade, "When's the last time you ever saw Park Avenue look like that?"

Not waiting for an answer, he got out of his car and started to move the wooden barrier.

The patrolman frowned. "Chief O'Reilly says nobody crosses the line."

"It's okay. I'll take full responsibility. I'm Harry Ziller, chief of the hostage negotiating team. I just wanted to get a quick look at Park on the way over to the van."

"Oh." The cop acknowledged Ziller's role and lifted aside the barricade. "You're sure you want to drive in there?"

"Don't worry. Our man's got better sense than to start playing long-range artillery games." Then he grinned. "But I don't think I'll drive right up to Fiftieth. No use *trying* to stir 'em up."

He got back in his car and drove the two short blocks to Forty-ninth, staying to the left of the esplanade to be less of a target. He wondered as he drove, the only moving vehicle around, if he was being watched by the new supreme ruler of 330 Park, if he might, in fact, even be at the junction of the cross hairs of one of the king's riflemen. It was a low-percentage shot. He wasn't close. He was two, three blocks away. And it would make no sense. What would be accomplished? Still, he'd made a bonehead move. What if? He suddenly felt the dampness of a moment of terror. Self-imposed jeopardy. Stupidity! He should have gone around the other way. He could start weaving to keep some sharpshooter from drawing a bead on him . . . but that would be a sign of fear. . . . What the hell! They wouldn't try it. . . . A few more yards. . . .

He turned left into Forty-ninth, out of any possible line of fire, and came to another police barrier, set a few yards back from Park. He waved at the patrolman, who acknowledged him curiously and pulled the giant sawhorse to one side. The street was full of spectators, sensation-seekers, harassing the cops with questions, trying to learn the reason why all traffic on Park Avenue had been stopped.

Ziller drove the block to Madison, past another barrier, and then north on Madison in normal traffic. He turned right onto an empty Fiftieth and pulled behind the headquarters van. He was greeted by the silver-haired O'Reilly, Sergeant Murphy, and other members of the hostage team.

"You've got the bag, Harry," O'Reilly said. "You call the shots, and I'll see that you get what you ask for."

"I got a lulu for openers, chief. Would you believe sandwiches and drinks for six hundred people?" Then Ziller went down a checklist he had formulated while driving uptown. He fed the items to O'Reilly, who briskly reassigned each item to other men in the van. Getting information was the key.

First, the landlord of 330 Park was to be hustled over with a list of tenants and a layout of all the floors. Once the tenants were known, all major banks in town were to be contacted to determine which ones handled the funds for each. These banks would be briefed and advised to call the van for instructions if contacted by anyone in 330 Park.

The telephone company's assistance would be needed to establish which phones in the building were still operable, where each was located, and what the numbers were. This effort could probably be aided by reports from the cops at the various observation points. Only a few phones at most were still working, and it might be possible to determine where these were visually.

All radio and TV stations would be contacted and instructed to invite calls from anyone who had actually seen armed men entering 330 Park. One such call could provide an assessment of the size of the group involved. As luck would have it, no one in the ITT Building reported seeing the perpetrators enter 330.

A routine of regularly scheduled reports from all police observation points would be established. These reports would be made once an hour, and of course any unexpected observations would be called in at once. O'Reilly had a sketched layout of the area around 330 Park showing where the observers were stationed.

The FBI would be briefed and the FAA offices at the three airports would be contacted for information on all flight arrangements that might be related to an escape.

With these key preparatory steps under way, Ziller flopped into a chair and lit a cigarette. He would have liked a beer but beer was out for the duration. Twelve noon. The whole affair was less than two hours old. He glanced around the van and wondered how long he would be there. He was the chief contact for as long as a contact was needed. He would get to know the man, and the man would get to know him. He would not leave that phone.

He pushed his hat back on his head, his "Moe Penn" fedora, the Ziller trademark. "I'm an obvious cop," he'd once said at a cocktail party shortly after a successfully handled hostage situation. He'd shown up straight from work in his usual rumpled suit, dark-colored shirt, and poorly matched tie, and of course his hat.

"I just look like a cop," he'd said. "You can spot me coming a block away. If I'm gonna get ahead on the force, it'll never be in undercover work. It'll be because I'm a great salesman. What've you got you'd like me to talk you out of? Because I can do it. And just as important, I'm a pretty fair judge of people and what they're up to."

He had been a detective sergeant at the time the NYPD hostage negotiating team was formed, which was just after the incident involving the Israeli athletes at Munich. College-educated, and a comer on the force, he was regarded highly, a cop's cop, a perceptive, thorough, patient, analytical investigator, with more than twenty-five years in the department. He'd gotten his gold shield after only three years. He was assigned to the first group trained for the squad because he was an acknowledged persuasive talker, confident and quick-witted.

He had been promoted to lieutenant almost immediately after securing the release of three hostages and with the promotion came the title, chief negotiator. In this capacity he became known throughout the country, as police departments in other major cities sent men for training in New York's trend-setting program.

The phone in the van suddenly rang. Detective Paul Brauer, located in one of the police observation points, had some information.

"This guy I been watching, he's got to be the leader of the operation."

"What does he look like?" Ziller asked.

"He's got a white mask over his head. And he's wearing a set of G.I. fatigues. But he keeps parading around this fancy corner office like he's in charge of something. Big guy. I'd say

he's at least six feet, athletic, looks like he's got an army automatic in a holster. He's got another guy with him, a little
smaller, but dressed the same, mask and all, and this one's
carrying a G.I. rifle. A fourteen."

"What else?"

"The tall guy paces around and then sits at the desk and
uses the phone. There's a walkie-talkie on the desk, too. And
dig this. He's got army brass on his shoulders. Captain's bars.
We got a dead sure shot on him. He can't be as much as fifty
yards away."

"You outta your head?" Ziller shouted. "What we need
right now is more information. We've got to know everything
going on in that building. Exactly where's this turkey sitting,
and where are you?"

"He's in the southeast corner office of the top floor. Big
office. Very fancy. I'm watching from the twenty-third floor
of the ITT Building."

"Sounds like you're in the number-one spot. We'll want to
relieve you with a couple of the hostage team. Till they get
there, keep us posted on everything going on. If he so much
as scratches his ass, I wanta know about it."

Ziller hung up the phone. . . . A captain. What kind of a
man pulls a job like this wearing captain's bars? He'd said he
had an army in there. And they're in uniform. And he's the
officer in charge. The captain, whoever he is, is good. The
building's a fortress.

And his men are good. The job on the phones. Very professional. He has some pair of balls, our captain. Strutting
around that office, knowing we must be watching him from
fifty yards away, knowing we could take him out but
can't. . . . An ex-cop, he says. Could it be a dodge to keep us
chasing our tails? All that military stuff. Fourteens. Fatigues.
Captain's bars. O'Reilly can put somebody on it. A former
cop, a big boy, six-footer, with a military record, an officer
maybe. A captain. Or somebody who wanted to be a cap-

tain. . . . . Ex-cop or not, he has a pretty good handle on procedures.

How many men has he got? He's probably using the walkie-talkie for internal communication. But he can't get a signal up and down twenty floors through all those layers of concrete. He's got to have a substation somewhere outside the building. A repeater. Maybe the Waldorf. Easy place to rent a little well-suited space on a short-term basis and not be questioned. . . .

"Harry," Sergeant Murphy said. "We think we got us a number for the corner office where our man is sitting. We called the landlord's agent for the building, a guy named Pederson. He's on the way over with layouts of all floors. We gave him the location of the working phone, and he said it's the office of Winfield Root, chairman of the board of the prinicpal tenant. Ma Bell gave us the unlisted number."

"Why don't we try it?" Ziller said. He picked up the phone, studied the number for a second or two, and then dialed.

The phone rang one time. "Who is this?" a voice said impatiently.

"This is Lieutenant Ziller of the—"

"I figured it was you, Ziller."

"Well, it might not have been. It might have been someone calling the man whose phone it really is."

"Ziller, let me tell you something. We're going to have a rule about all future conversations between you and me. And it's very simple. Don't you call me. If I want to talk to you, I'll call you."

"Wouldn't it be better to consider this an open hot line? For the sake of the safety of the people in that building, which, I think, concerns both of us?"

"As long as you do exactly as I tell you, the people in this building have a good chance of walking away. Most of them, anyway."

"What's most of them?"

"Christ, Ziller, don't start that shit again. You know goddamn well we're going to take a few with us. Anyway, for now
everyone is safe as long as you do as you're told."

"What if I have a reason for calling?"

"If it's an emergency, okay. Otherwise, you just sit by your
phone and wait. But as long as you're on the line, let's discuss
lunch. What arrangements have you made? I'm getting hungry."

"The food is being prepared by the catering department at
the Waldorf. That much food on short notice takes a while."

"I want all sandwiches wrapped and labeled for easy iden-
tification. And send soda as well as coffee."

"If you'll guarantee their safety, I'll see if I can get the hotel
to have some of their staff deliver and serve the food."

"Jesus, Ziller, what do you take me for? I don't need any of
your bulls stumbling around this building in costume. Just deliver the food to the door. Just do as you're told and your precious hostages have the best chance."

"As I've said before, we'll cooperate in every way. The safety of the people in that building is our major concern. Oh,
one more question. I presume that since you're the one ordering the food, you're planning to pay for it."

No answer.

"My impression," Ziller said after a few seconds of silence,
"is that that's the way you'd want it."

Still no answer.

"I've really got to hand it to you," Ziller continued, "you're
pretty good. You really seem to be running a class operation.
That's why I figure you'll wanta pay for the food. You know
what I mean?"

"I know exactly what you mean, Ziller. And also the game
you're playing."

"Still, do you want to pay it?"

Another silence. Ziller chose to wait rather than say anything more.

Finally: "Okay, Ziller, tell the hotel to include a bill with the food."

"I didn't think I read you wrong," Ziller said. "How do you want to pay? You going to sign for it? Use a credit card?"

"Listen, you son-of-a-bitch! You're in no position to play games with me. You can tell the hotel I'll send cash as soon as I receive the first payoff."

"Would you like the chefs at the Waldorf to fix anything special for you and your men?"

"I think the percentages are with having me and my men pick from the lot. And I think this conversation has outlived its usefulness." He hung up.

Ziller quietly hung up his own phone and lit a cigarette. A case like no other, for sure. But he had to smile as he thought about the conversation. If nothing else, he had established one of the most important principles in any hostage negotiation. Always try to get something from the perpetrator in return for any request granted. Something in return for something. In this case it would be, of all things, money.

10

"The amount, Mr. Bertolini, is one and a half million dollars."

Frank Bertolini began to perspire heavily as he stared at the man in the strange white mask sitting behind the oversized desk. Bertolini was a mechanical engineer and the chief technical expert in Runyan Tool. He wore plain gabardine suits, which fitted tightly on his stocky body, and solid-color neckties. He had short-cropped auburn hair and thick, rimless glasses. The pocket of his white shirt bulged with an assortment of pens, pencils, and metal rules. He knew everything about machine tools but not very much about the ins and outs of top-level financial manipulations.

"Well?" Devereau paused and then asked, in an irritated tone, "Did you hear what I said?"

"I just don't know what you expect me to do." Bertolini looked at Stroud, who was lounging in an armchair, fondling his M-14.

"I expect you to call your firm's bank and tell them to bring the money over. As soon as it's delivered, we will release you and your co-workers."

"But I don't know how to handle such things. I've never been asked to . . . well, obviously, I've never had to do anything quite like this before."

"Are you the person in charge? Or should I be talking to someone else? Don't waste my time. According to my notes, you're generally in command when Walter Scatliff is away."

"Well, Scatliff leaves me in charge of operations while he's away. As is the case this week. But he runs the business. I don't even know how to start to do what you want."

"Why don't we execute one of your employees? Perhaps that will help you learn quickly."

"Please. I'm not trying to be difficult." Bertolini was conscious that his suit was clinging to him like a wet skin. "You've got to understand. I don't know much about the financial end of the business. I wouldn't know what bank to call, or who to ask for. I don't even know if we've got that kind of cash immediately available in the company's account."

"Would you like to see your firm's balance sheet, Mr. Bertolini? I have it here. Of course you've got the funds to meet my request. And much more. The amount I've specified is only about twenty-five percent of your company's present cash position. I'm not being greedy. You're not the only tenant in the building."

Bertolini stared helplessly at the floor.

"I'm losing my patience with you, Bertolini. Your bank is the Chase Manhattan, and I'll give you the number. I'm sure they're expecting your call. Now, get your ass in the next office and tell them to get the money over here."

"Look, could you get Karl Fenton up here to help me? He's our controller. Maybe between the two of us we can figure out how to handle this. I think we may need to try to reach Scatliff."

Devereau picked up his walkie-talkie. "I'll give the two of you ten minutes. Is that clear? Ten minutes to arrange to get that money over here. Otherwise, I'm going to show you a couple of tricks we've worked out to be persuasive." He switched the radio on and held it to his mouth. "Boston."

Ziller dialed the number.

After one ring: "What is it now?"

"The food is ready."

"Good. Bring it over."

"That's what I called about. Let's make sure all details are understood so that no problems develop."

"Such as?"

"We're not going to ask the hotel personnel to make the delivery. We're going to use uniformed cops. They'll be instructed not to touch their guns unless threatened. I presume you'll see to it that nothing happens. The food will be on large rolling hand trucks. Two men to a truck. They'll bring it to the door and move back. You are not to open the door until they signal you to do so. For the safety of the people in the building, we will not make any move toward the men who come out for the food. Is this agreed?"

"Sounds okay."

Ziller hung up. He did it abruptly, before the other party on the line could do so. Then he walked to the door of the van and looked outside, surveying the uniformed patrolmen for one who was roughly his own size.

Devereau stood at the window and stared at the deserted front of the Waldorf. He wished to hell they'd bring the food on over. He was suddenly starved. Fifteen minutes had passed since Ziller called, and he wanted to eat before the next interview. He picked up the phone and dialed the van, where the phone rang several times before it was picked up. "Ziller?"

Sergeant Murphy was taken by surprise. "Uh, this, uh . . . are you calling from 330 Park?"

"Where the hell is Ziller?"

"He can't come to the phone right now. This is one of his men. Can I help in any way?"

"Where'd he go?"

"He stepped away for a minute. I think he ducked into the restaurant to use the men's room."

"Sure he did," Devereau snapped.

"He'll be back in a few minutes. He'll call you."

"Sure he will," Devereau said, slamming down the phone. "That stupid son-of-a-bitch." He glanced down at Park Avenue and caught a glimpse of some movement. On Fiftieth, toward Lexington, three carts emerged from one of the cavernous parking-garage openings in the side of the Waldorf. Each was being pushed by two uniformed policemen who struggled with the cumbersome, four-wheeled carriers as they made their way up the slight incline to Park. The carts were designed for hotel corridors, and the rough uphill pavement was new to the small wheels.

The carts crossed Park, past the esplanade resplendent with red poppies and assorted greenery and onto the sidewalk, moving north toward the front of 330. The policemen appeared heavy and vaguely misshapen because of their bullet-proof vests. Devereau watched their slow progress until they moved out of his line of vision. "The stupid son-of-a-bitch," he repeated to himself. Then he walked out of his office to the elevators, where Benjy stood guard.

When he reached the lobby, he found Big Charlie squinting through a small peephole scratched in the paint. "They right in front?" Devereau asked.

"Yeah."

"Open the doors."

"I thought you said wait till they signaled."

"Open them."

Charlie took out a key and opened the padlock. He slid the chain away and pushed the doors apart. The six policemen turned around, startled. A couple of them reached toward their pistols and then pulled their hands back. One of them dropped to the pavement and reached toward his revolver, but seeing that the three masked men in the door were not aiming their weapons, he relaxed his arm.

Devereau looked at the six cops, who were no more than thirty feet away, and yelled, "Which of you is Harry Ziller?"

Ziller looked up momentarily, just enough to give himself away.

"Hi ya, Harry," Devereau said.

Ziller, trying to recover his composure, said, "Why don't you come on out and we'll talk this thing over?"

"We'll talk when I feel like talking. Get your ass back to that phone where you belong and take your boys with you. We'll bring the food in after you get the hell out of here. Now, move!" He nudged Charlie, who closed the door.

Ziller shouted, "You'll find the check on the first wagon." Then he nodded at the other cops. The six of them backed down Park toward Fiftieth. When they reached Fiftieth, Ziller stood behind the corner of the ITT Building and watched. After a few minutes six masked troops came out to the carts. Thus, there were at least six of them. Ziller walked back to the van and began removing the uniform and the vest. Murphy said, "He called while you were gone."

"No fooling," Ziller said.

"And we got a call from the Chase Manhattan Bank. He's asking a million and a half dollars for the release of the tenants of the second floor."

"For one floor?"

"That's what they said."

"What do you think he's got in mind for the whole building?"

Murphy didn't answer.

"What'd you tell the bank?" Ziller asked.

"I discussed it with Chief O'Reilly and we decided to tell them to make positive noises but stall for time. A little time, anyway. I said we'd be back to them. And to call us if he called again."

"That's fine," Ziller said. He handed the blue pants to the cop in Jockey shorts and began putting on his own. "Jesus, a million and a half for one floor. I wonder if there's enough cash in this whole city to get all those people outta there."

Devereau signaled Alfredo and then called for another broadcast. The employees on the various floors gathered without incident and listened to the man.

"As you know, you are all my prisoners, but there is no reason not to make things as pleasant as possible for the duration of the siege. In fact, I'd like to think of you as my guests." The tenants looked at one another and then at the armed guards holding the radios. "I know you must be getting hungry," Devereau continued, "and so I've arranged for lunch. It's been prepared by the Waldorf-Astoria, and it's here now, in the lobby. My men will be bringing it up to you in a few minutes."

"Jesus," said a clerk on eighteen, "I've always wanted to eat something from over there. I hope it's not my last meal."

The police van on Fiftieth was parked in front of a restaurant specializing in crêpes, which had reluctantly complied when Ziller sent in a cop for a ham sandwich. Ziller held it in his hand and watched as Pederson, the landlord's man, taped the diagrams of the Root Tower's various floors to the walls of the van.

Pederson was a large, athletic man. His eyes were clear blue and his thinning hair gray-blond. He knew the building well, and he pointed out the features of each floor with total familiarity. Ziller was intrigued by the penthouse and by the two levels of the basement. The other floors were routine and totally controlled by the elevator foyers. Seeing the diagram of the penthouse, its huge corner office and private bath, he began to get a picture of his man's personality. The throne room. The bridge. The captain's quarters.

And the labyrinthine basement layout fascinated Ziller. The tiny room with all the telephone wires that had been hit with such total efficiency. The equipment room with Palko's desk in the middle of it. The small room that contained nothing but circuit breakers and heavy solid-copper bus bars. Pederson said a man could touch a pair of the bus bars and damn near be vaporized by the magnitude of the current that would hit him. And at the end of a long, angled corridor was the service entrance onto Fifty-first Street.

Ziller asked Pederson about the staff in the building. Pederson felt reasonably certain Palko was straight. He'd known him for a long time. But Palko's helper was another story. A shifty man with a record. Palko had said to give the guy a break, that he'd never be rehabilitated if no one ever gave him a chance. As for the others, there were a couple of day porters he knew little about, but who were possible bad actors. The elevator starter hardly seemed bright enough to be implicated. The old foreman on the night cleanup crew was harmless, but he didn't know much about his crew. And there were all the employees of the various tenants who could be implicated.

"At least that narrows it down to a few hundred," Ziller said with a grin.

Dick Dorfer was escorted from the third floor to the penthouse by an overweight Cuban named Mario, code number 3-B, whose toes turned out when he walked. At one point, while entering the elevator, 3-B prodded Dorfer with his rifle butt and Dorfer quietly commented that it wasn't necessary, that he intended to go where he was told.

When they reached the penthouse, 3-B motioned to Dorfer to get off. As Dorfer stepped out, he was confronted by another of the troops, a small, wiry man, who pushed the muzzle of his rifle into Dorfer's stomach. As Dorfer was ushered to the corner office, the secretaries and the few other employees who sat around watched in a kind of fascinated horror.

Dorfer entered the big corner office and approached the large desk. Another masked man sat behind it. The desk was cleared except for a neat loose-leaf notebook in front of the man, and a walkie-talkie to one side. Another of the troops sat on the arm of a sofa, his M-14 held loosely across his lap. The monkey with a gun retreated from the room.

"Sit down, Mr. Dorfer." The man behind the desk spoke in a very businesslike manner and pointed at the chair.

"Thank you." Dorfer said it almost as a business reflex, something he did automatically when offered a chair. As he sat down, two gleaming pairs of captain's bars caught his eye. What kind of a sick joke . . .?

Dorfer pushed his fingers through his straight gray hair and settled into the chair. A tall, lean, middle-aged man with a prominent nose and large teeth, he always wore shirts that looked richly disheveled and small self-tied bow ties that drooped casually. He was soft-spoken, and when he smiled, the skin at the corners of his eyes wrinkled. He ran the large architectural engineering firm with competence and decisiveness, and he was respected, almost revered, by employees and clients alike.

"Mr. Dorfer, we want five hundred thousand dollars for the release of you and your people."

"Will we be released immediately upon delivery of the money?"

"Yes."

"This includes all personnel on both the third and fourth floors? We occupy both floors."

"I'm fully aware of who is on what floor, Mr. Dorfer."

"Then my next question is, how can I arrange to have the money brought to you? If all the phone lines in the building have been cut, how can I contact my bank?"

"They haven't all been cut. You can use the phone in that next office. I think you'll find it works perfectly."

"Have you a phone book? I don't know the number of our bank from memory."

"I'll give you the number. Incidentally, aren't you curious to know how I arrived at the amount?"

"Does it matter?" Dorfer asked with quiet resignation.

"I'm not a greedy man, Mr. Dorfer. I chose half a million after a study of your firm's financial statement. It is the exact amount of cash you can spare without getting into any real trouble."

"Your explanation really isn't important. I'm only interested in the safety of my—"

"Listen when I talk to you, you son-of-a-bitch!" Devereau snapped. Stroud, startled, jumped to his feet.

"I'm sorry," Dorfer said.

Devereau remained silent for a moment. Then he tore a scrap of paper from a blank sheet in his notebook and copied a phone number on it. "Here's your bank," he said. "Manufacturers Hanover. Correct?"

"Yes. That's correct."

"Then go into the next office and use the phone." Before Dorfer had time to get to his feet, Devereau said to Stroud, "Tell the boys on the second floor to go in and knock some heads. Good and hard. Then drag Bertolini back here. His bank is being a little too slow about delivering the money."

Dorfer stood up. "That type of thing won't be necessary in our case."

"Very good, Mr. Dorfer. It's much easier that way for all concerned."

The headquarters van was like a portable precinct station. Servicemen from Con Ed and Ma Bell had hooked up power and phones almost immediately. In addition to the six phone lines that had been activated, two radiophones were on hand for contact with the various observation teams.

The C.O.'s desk was at one end of the van, and Ziller had the "dedicated" phone, the phone used exclusively for calls to and from 330 Park, in a conference area at the other end. The walls in the conference area were covered with flooring diagrams and maps. In the middle of the van, six cops, two of them sergeants, manned the other phones, handling incoming and assignment calls, maintaining logs, receiving reports from the observation teams, and relaying the accumulating intelligence to Ziller and Murphy.

The street map of the area was marked with colored pins to show the deployment of police personnel. The van served as the control point for the inner perimeter of the containment operation. The outer perimeter was controlled by a second van on Fifty-second, between Park and Madison. One Emergency Service vehicle and an ambulance stood immediately behind the van on Fiftieth. Another was placed on Fifty-second, but east of Park, toward Lexington.

Ziller counted the cops deployed in the operation. Outer-perimeter police-line barriers located along Madison and Lexington from Forty-eighth to Fifty-fourth and across Park at both ends totaled eighteen barriers with two cops assigned to each. Thirty-six men. The inner perimeter consisted of barriers on both sides of Park at all the cross streets. This added up to twelve barriers, each manned by three cops—thirty-six more men. Then there were eight sharpshooter-observation teams in each of four buildings around 330 Park. Sixteen more cops. Counting the men in the vans and Emergency-Service trucks as well as the cops patrolling all nearby buildings, well over a hundred cops were involved. And more than sixty men had been used to evacuate the surrounding office buildings earlier that morning.

A sergeant came over and attracted Ziller's attention. "We got Manufacturers Hanover on the line. Our man's asking half a million dollars for the tenant on the third and fourth floors. Their chief executive wants it paid at once. Whadda you want to tell them?"

"Tell 'em to get the money ready," Ziller answered. "Let's see what he does with a payoff." Then to Murphy, "See that? See how easy I just let go of a half a million bucks? When you make lieutenant, you'll be able to do it, too."

The other sergeant appeared at the door. "We got Chase Manhattan on the phone again. The second-floor tenant is begging for the money. Says the man is having his apes rough people up. What shall I tell them?"

"A million and a half bucks." Ziller hesitated, but only for a moment. "Tell them to get it ready. If they've got that much." He turned to O'Reilly. "Might as well, chief. He can't spend it without leaving the building." Then, as an afterthought: "What in hell would you do with two million dollars? Tax-free, at that. And that's only three floors. He's got thirteen or fourteen more tenants."

When Manufacturers Hanover called back to say that the money was ready, Ziller ordered the van on Fifty-second to send a cop to pick it up and make the delivery. Since the bank was directly across Fifty-first from the Root Tower, the cop wouldn't have far to go with the money. Then Ziller dialed Winfield Root's unlisted number.

"What is it?"

"Your first payoff is ready."

"Which one?"

"Manufacturers Hanover. A half-million. Fifties and hundreds. In a briefcase. Just like you requested."

"Send it over."

"Then you'll release the people on the third and fourth floors?"

"After I count it. I hope you're telling those banks not to fuck around. It's a contribution you can make to the health of the people in this building."

"All the money'll be there," Ziller said. "We're sending it

over with a uniformed patrolman. He'll place it in front of the door and move back. You don't bother him and we won't bother the man you send out to pick it up."

"It's the only way to handle it, Harry baby. What's the percentage in anything else? All I want is the money. Besides, the man I send out, you don't want to hit."

"Oh?"

"Just get it over, Ziller." Devereau hung up in Ziller's ear and turned to Stroud. "Tell the guys in the basement we got a job for Joe Palko."

The first observation team to begin describing the payoff was located on the fourth floor of 345 Park, diagonally across the corner from 330. "He's coming out of the bank now, with the briefcase. Walking toward Fifty-first. Crossing. Very slowly. He's in front of 330. He's putting the case down in the street, maybe ten feet from the edge of the sidewalk. He's heading back. Jesus, look at him move now he ain't got the dough no more.

"No sign of any action by the door yet. . . . Wait. . . . Now. The door's open. Some tall slim guy in suntans. Christ, they must have shoved his ass out the door. I don't think he's one of them. No mask or weapons. Hey, they got a rope around his waist. They musta figured we might open fire on anybody they sent. They're covering him from the door. I see rifles. He's got the dough, and they're pulling him back in. That's it. All over."

None of the cops at the observation posts reported any further action for ten minutes. Then came the news that the doors were again open and some fifty people were pouring out. A cop at Fiftieth hailed them and hustled them into the computer showroom on the corner at Fiftieth for debriefing. A detective recorded each hostage's name and address because each one represented a separate charge of unlawful imprisonment, assault with a deadly weapon, extortion, grand larceny, and more. After the initial debriefing, principals were taken by the van to see Ziller. Others were simply released into Fiftieth Street. The exhilarated released hostages babbled and chattered during their debriefing about how things had been inside. Yes, there were two guards on each of their floors, and two more in the lobby. They had rifles and pistols. And radios. And the man running the thing kept having the guards crowd them into one room so he could give them speeches over the radios. He sure loved giving speeches. . . .

As the employees of Dorfer, West, and Associates were leaving the building, Devereau had all other employees gather in their stereo reception room. Looking out the windows, those on lower floors could see the departing people as they listened to his speech about how they would all be leaving as soon as their management took their safety into consideration and arranged the necessary "transfer of funds."

||

"Impressive operation," said one of the two men facing Devereau.

"A fine piece of workmanship," said the other. "I'd like to hang around and see how you handle the rest of it. But unfortunately, we have another appointment at three. So I guess we'll have to follow it through the newspapers."

Devereau studied them. How could they be so cool? The tone of their request to speak to "the man in charge" had completely intimidated his two soldiers on the twentieth floor. "These guys ain't fucking around," 20-B had said. "And they say they want to see you *now!*"

"Would you mind telling me who you are?" Devereau asked.

"We'd be glad to," said the taller of the two men. "I'm Louis Gianini. This is my brother, Pat." Louis wore a dark business suit, a white shirt and a conservative striped tie. Pat, though shorter, was similarly dressed, and the family resemblance was pronounced.

"I take it you're not with the firm on the twentieth floor," Devereau said. "You must be clients, then."

"Potential clients," Pat said.

"What sort of business are you in?"

"We have an interest in some wineries in northern California."

"Gianini Vineyards," Devereau said. "Of course. Good product. And you were talking advertising with the guys on twenty, I presume? What size campaign were you thinking about?"

"Why do you want to know?"

"It will help me decide what sort of demands I can place on your release."

"Let me ask you something," Louis Gianini said. His expression was one of irritation at having to waste time explaining the obvious. "I take it you spent a great deal of time laying out this operation."

"Yes." Devereau felt a vague sense of pressure. Gianini was the most totally confident person he had ever met.

"Did anyone like us figure in your plans?"

"I certainly expected to find quite a few people in the building who weren't tenants or employees."

"What did you plan to do about them?"

"I figured that I'd evaluate them as additional hostages. I looked upon them as possible windfalls."

"In our case," Louis said, "I think you should simply count us out. We have another appointment, and we'd like to leave. Our associates here in the city know where we are at the moment. We think that to detain us," he paused, "introduces an unnecessary element of risk into your proceedings. Why would you possibly want to do that?" Louis' voice was completely devoid of emotion.

Devereau began to sweat under his cotton mask. "Look. I think you'll agree that I hold all the cards at the moment."

"Don't you also think that your pot is already big enough

without us? We weren't really a part of your original plan. Why look for complications?" He looked at Devereau. "There is one other possibility, I suppose. Perhaps we could contact our associates here in town. They might be able to help you with certain phases of your operation."

Devereau was perspiring freely. "Thanks for the offer, but I just don't happen to think that I need your help, or anybody else's, for that matter."

"You fuck around with us and you're going to need a lot of help," Louis said abruptly.

Devereau glanced at Stroud, whose nervousness was apparent. "I'm really not terribly impressed by your threat," Devereau said at last. "Our withdrawal from this position is absolutely airtight. We'll have a police convoy to the airport tomorrow and then free passage out."

"But consider the element of risk I mentioned," said Louis. "Consider it very carefully. Are you sure it's worth it? Because I can assure you that it's real."

Devereau hesitated a moment and then said briskly, "There's no point in discussing this further, since you did not figure in our initial plans, and as I've said all along, we don't intend to be greedy. You're free to go."

"I think that's wise." Louis stood up. "It wouldn't have made much sense to threaten the operation unnecessarily." He held out his hand to Devereau. "Good luck, and our compliments. I'm quite impressed. Now, if you can have your men see us out. . . ."

Devereau nodded to Stroud and then picked up his radio.

The observation team in 345 Park called in that the doors were being opened again and that two men had come out. They were walking casually toward the Waldorf when one of the cops at the Fiftieth Street barricade motioned to them. He led them to the debriefing area and then, after a short period of questioning, to the door of the van where Ziller and Murphy stood waiting.

"How'd you two manage to get them to let you leave?" Ziller asked.

"We just told them we had another appointment," Louis Gianini said.

"Just like that?" Murphy asked.

"Just like that."

"I can't figure how he'd let the two of you just walk out of there."

"Well, I guess we managed to impress on him the urgency of our having to leave," Louis said quietly.

Ziller pushed back his hat and scratched his head. "Did we get your names and addresses for the record?"

"I'm Louis Gianini, from San Francisco. This is my brother, Pat. We were visiting the advertising agency on the twentieth floor."

Ziller smiled. "Oh. Nice meeting you two. Have a pleasant day."

Palko stared at the kid guarding him. The kid was out of his league. At the right moment, he'd be a cinch to take. A quick move, and he'd fold up like a kite with broken sticks. As for the other one, the smoker, Palko couldn't quite tell. He seemed so goddamn wrapped up in technical detail. Snooping around. Continuously. But it didn't matter. The opportunity was all that was needed.

Palko still seethed with the heat of resentment at being used as the dummy, the target, to walk outside and bring in the money. The kid had been scared shitless just ushering him up the steps to the lobby. He might have jumped him then. But the other details of timing weren't right. The two hoods in the lobby were a different story. The big black one who booted him out the door was probably capable of shooting if he'd gotten loose and made a break for it. The little one seemed pretty casual, too. Between the two of them, they had Rios lying on the floor, a whimpering idiot, by his precious goddamn elevators.

But the kid guarding him. All that was required was the right moment. And it was apparently going to be a long affair. Plenty of time. . . .

Ziller listened as Bertolini of *Runyan Tool,* the second company to be released, reviewed his story. He described his first interview, the raid that followed, his second trip to the penthouse, and finally, their release. The raid had been brutal. The two guards had come back in and hustled everyone on the floor into the conference room. One of the guards was black; the other was Puerto Rican.

Then, with blinds drawn, the guards began mercilessly beating on everyone. The employees huddled into one corner. The guards kicked and thumped with their rifle butts, hitting men and women indiscriminately. One of them fired his rifle as if to remind them that his ammunition was real. The other guard picked out Willie Leeper, a tiny, frail man, and yanked him from the group by his wrist. He threw Leeper to the floor and kicked him in the face.

As soon as the two masked guards had reduced the group to a state of complete shouting and screaming hysteria, they brought Bertolini and the controller, Fenton, back to the penthouse to call the bank again.

Ziller listened to the account of the beating and was sorry he had not rushed the money over faster. This was, of course, what the man wanted him to feel. His opponent fully understood the use of hostages in manipulating authorities. And his men were well-drilled in carrying out his instructions. They knew just how far to go to make the hostages beg for relief. Luckily, none of the injuries appeared to be serious, not even Leeper's, although the police insisted that everyone hurt be checked at a hospital.

Ziller thought about the man in charge in 330. So far he certainly did not seem homicidal. But what of his men? Would they kill against orders? And how many were there? The released hostages had reported two guards on their floor, two in the penthouse, and two in the lobby. Two on every floor then? The man said he had an army.

Ziller took another cup of coffee. Three o'clock was coming fast, when all the banks closed. And the vaults would close maybe an hour later, with time locks set to open at nine the next day.

Ziller guessed his man would probably work out the rest of the ransoms before the day was over and arrange delivery for the following day. Which meant he planned to stay there through the night.

One night. One night to devise a strategy to bust the thing up without losing hostages. But what kind of strategy? The place was impregnable. Who would the final hostages be? No one from the first three floors. One night. That can be a long goddamn period of time. A lot can happen. . . . It was time to get some dialogue going. Create a little anxiety. The guts of hostage negotiations. Jerry'll have some ideas when he arrives.

"I don't think you understand, Mr. Berkowitz," Devereau said. "You seem to feel you're in a position to bargain with me."

"But we haven't got the money. As I've tried to explain, if you'd asked me a few weeks ago, we could have managed." Melvin Berkowitz was the president of Berkowitz and Belz, Importers. He had been groomed for the role since childhood, when his father had built the business.

His father had long ago retired to condominium life in Miami Beach, as had his father's original partner, Harry Belz. Of the various sons and sons-in-law in the firm, Melvin had been heir apparent. A Wharton School graduate, he had been in the company for twenty years and had not only modernized business practices but had also made some rather gutsy decisions in recent years. The firm had done well under his control.

"A few weeks from now, we'd have the funds," he continued. "But today we have no cash position. We saw an opportunity to turn a fat . . ."—he hesitated—"to turn a good profit on all our available capital with virtually no risk, and so we took a flyer. But today . . ." Berkowitz sounded as if he were refusing a friend a loan.

Devereau looked at Stroud and nodded. Stroud got quickly to his feet and slapped Berkowitz with extreme force.

"What was that for?" The side of Berkowitz' already pinkish face began to redden, and drops of water formed in the corners of his eyes.

"Now, listen closely," Devereau said. "I'm going to give you a couple of minutes either to call your bank and get two hundred and fifty thousand dollars delivered over here, or we'll start executing the people on the fifth floor. I've analyzed your financial situation, and you can afford it."

"A month ago, yes. Two months from now, yes. But not today," whined Berkowitz.

"Let your bank finance you. I don't give a shit how you do it."

"My banker didn't like this deal we just made. Even though I told him it was a lead-pipe cinch. He won't budge. I know him."

"Mr. Berkowitz, you're playing with the lives of your employees."

"You've got to let me off the hook. We're small. You've got everybody else in the building. We could go maybe ten percent of that amount. Maybe twenty."

Stroud drew back his arm, this time with his fist clenched. Berkowitz cowered and Devereau waved Stroud off. "Don't bother bruising your knuckles," Devereau said. "I'm going to teach this fat son-of-a-bitch a lesson." He picked up his radio and called Alfredo. He then addressed 5-B. "Mr. Berkowitz says he doesn't have any money. Go in and find me a nice lady and take her up to the roof. Let me know who you get."

"What are you going to do?" Berkowitz asked.

"We're going to throw her off the roof."

"You can't be serious."

"Me? You're the one who'll be responsible for her death. We'll make that perfectly clear to the press."

Berkowitz squirmed in his chair. "This is some kind of trick. You couldn't possibly be serious."

"You'll be able to watch her drop by this window," Devereau said very calmly.

"An old lady named Gittelson," said a voice from the radio.

"Bessie Gittelson? Are you serious?" Berkowitz started to stand, and Stroud knocked him back into the chair.

"This is your last chance, Mr. Berkowitz, to call your bank and not have that woman's death on your head."

Berkowitz gripped the arms of his chair. "This is some kind of trick. I can tell. It's some kind of trick. You wouldn't dare."

"Just watch the window, Mr. Berkowitz. And remember. You could have prevented it."

"Let's go." Floyd prodded Bessie Gittelson with the muzzle of his M-14. He welcomed the chance to do something, because sitting around was making him edgy. Two soldiers would still be present on his floor, as the troops from the first three floors had been redistributed after their prisoners were released.

Floyd shoved Bessie off the elevator on twenty-two and pushed her past the masked guard to the rear stairwell leading up to the engine room. She yelled with pain after each jab, and finally began to sniffle and then cry. When they entered the engine room, she saw Luis' grinning face.

"Hello, Bessie."

"I knew you were mixed up in this. I knew it. I tried to warn Palko after you brought those men around. Luis, what are you going to do with me?"

"Take off your dress, Bessie."

"Luis?" She looked at his grinning face.

"Bessie, take off your dress."

"You need help?" Floyd grabbed the collar of her dress and yanked, ripping loose the fasteners at the back of the neck.

It happened so quickly the observation teams high enough to watch had no time to react. The distance from the door of the engine room to the brick railing around the edge of the roof was only a few feet. The door opened, and one of the masked men suddenly appeared. He ran to the edge of the roof carrying a female form in a brilliant red dress printed with large yellow flowers, heaved the body over the side, and disappeared back into the building. The body rolled end over end as it plummeted downward, then thudded near the edge of the wide sidewalk.

"Oh, God! Oh, Jesus!" moaned the cop near the top of 345 Park. "One of them just threw a broad off the roof."

"You monsters!" Berkowitz screamed. "How in the name of God? How?"

Stroud slammed his open hand across Berkowitz' face again.

"Why do you blame us?" Devereau said calmly. "You did it. We begged you to prevent it."

"My God! My God!" Berkowitz doubled over, his face against his knees. "That lovely old woman. She was like a second mother to me."

Stroud grabbed him by his hair and snapped his head back.

"Would you like to use the phone now, Mr. Berkowitz?" Devereau asked. "I have your bank's number right here. Or would you like to be responsible for another death?"

On the fifth floor, Mabel Pennington, another of the firm's older employees, who had worked with Bessie for years, spotted the vividly colored dress tumbling through the air and fainted. She had been the only one to see it. On several other floors of the building a few people had caught a glimpse of something falling but weren't certain what they'd seen. And the body had landed so close to the building that no one on any of the upper floors could see it.

On Fiftieth Street three members of the Emergency Service detail, equipped with bulletproof vests, climbed into the police ambulance and drove in front of the ITT Building. They held their weapons in readiness and watched the front door of the Root Tower. They were covered by the cops at the various rooftop observation posts. One of the policemen in the ambulance climbed out and approached the body. He knelt beside the lifelike form and then looked up in surprise. "Jesus, this is no broad!" he shouted. "It's a fucking dummy!" He slapped the mannequin's busted head back and forth as if to reassure himself it was not real, and then dragged the mannequin to the rear of the ambulance and climbed in. The driver backed away.

Bessie Gittelson was returned to her office in her slip with her eyes red and her makeup smeared and streaked. A few minutes later, a grief-stricken Melvin Berkowitz was brought back to the fifth floor. He cried out when he saw Bessie and dropped to his knees. She looked at him and began to cry again as she went over to comfort him.

Harry Ziller looked at the smashed mannequin in the ill-fitting red dress and smiled. Another bit of insight into his man. Then he said, "What the hell! Give it to Forensic."

The phone rang and Ziller picked it up quickly.

"Harry? Your men pick up the corpse off the sidewalk yet?"

"As a matter of fact, yes."

"This one was a warning. Next time, it will be the real

thing. If you're as smart a cop as I think you are, you won't get any wild ideas about testing me. Because you can't afford to take a chance on being wrong. Am I right?"

"You're right," Ziller answered.

12

"Sergeant Murphy speaking. May I help you?" Murphy's voice was deep and gruff, suited to his presence. One needed to work with him to discover his innate gentleness.

"Is this the special police number?" It was a young woman with a southern accent.

"Yes, it is."

"I just heard your announcement on my car radio. The one requesting eyewitness reports? You know, on those men going into 330 Park?"

"You mean you saw them?"

"I thought it was a publicity stunt. I would have called earlier, but I just now heard the announcement."

"How many men were there?"

"There was a whole busload of them. Thirty, at least. Maybe more."

"Were they armed?"

"Armed? Every single one had a rifle. Looked like some kind of army rifle. A pistol, too. They were wearing army worksuits, and these funny white masks over their faces. Kinda scary. I'm from Birmingham, and I grew up hearing stories about the Klan. Except, of course, these couldn't have been the Klan, because half of them were black. You could see their hands."

"Do you remember any other details?"

"That's really about it. They just came running out of both doors of the bus and into the building. Oh, yes. They were carrying these two big wooden boxes. I guess it wasn't a publicity stunt after all."

"What time do you think you saw them?"

"It was right about ten. I came into the city today with my husband. He works in the ITT Building. And I remember I left his office right about ten, and the bus pulled up just as I reached the sidewalk. I did some shopping, had lunch and caught the two-oh-two. As I was driving home from the Scarsdale station, I heard your announcement."

Murphy got her name and address and then gave Ziller the report. The man definitely had his full platoon.

An assault on 330 was clearly out of the question. Ziller reviewed the hostage-negotiation notebook in his mind. "Phase One is to enclose the quarry for whatever length of time is judged practical. Waiting time generally works in your favor. You need to think of Phase One in terms of four distinct operations: confine, contain, control, and consolidate. When it becomes obvious that the quarry's setup is too invulnerable and Phase One has outlived its usefulness, you try to push the situation into Phase Two, a mobile operation involving a selected and controlled route, with good communications every step of the way, until you can get your quarry into a new and more vulnerable situation. This gives you a look at the perpetrator, his firepower, and the condition of hostages. Then comes Phase Three, which is nothing more than a repeat of the four steps in Phase One, but in the new location. And at any point in the procedure, of course, you try to negotiate."

It was nice having a textbook procedure to refer to, but the trick was in applying the principles. So far, there was very little with which to negotiate. And no basis for forcing things into Phase Two. Not until after the man got all the money delivered. Nothing to do but wait and keep gathering intelligence.

An I.D. on the son-of-a-bitch would have been helpful. The checkout on the bus was no help. It had been arranged by phone, they said, by a Mr. Herman Krueger, who rented it without a driver. Sent a licensed operator over with the money to pick it up. At least that provided a book on one member of the platoon—the bus driver. Charlie Patterson, six-four, black, with a minor record. The puzzling thing was why the big bastard used his own license. But it's got to be him. The description checks out to the letter. But the man himself. Herman Krueger? That name has got to be as phony as the vacant lot in the Bronx he used for a business address. And there he sits. In his big corner office, filling a casket with hundred-dollar bills. . . .

"Hey, Harry."

Ziller looked up. Jerry Weissberger, the department's psychologist, had arrived.

"Looks like we finally got ourselves the big, big one we've been waiting for," Weissberger said.

"Penthouse-A. Lobby-A calling."

"Excuse me," Devereau said to Howard Goldwasser as if he were interrupting an ordinary business conversation. He picked up his walkie-talkie. "What is it, Lobby-A?"

"Chief, what do we need this fat-ass elevator boy for? We keep on tripping over the son-of-a-bitch, and he ain't worth no money, is he? Why don't we get rid of him?"

Devereau thought a few seconds. "Do it."

Guillermo Rios, who had just listened to Big Charlie's question, looked up at Charlie towering above him. He began inching away, sliding on the seat of his pants, propelling himself with his feet and the palms of his hands. "What you going to do now?" His voice was choked with terror.

"We decided you ain't worth keeping around, so we gonna get rid o' you. That's all."

Rios flung his arms around Charlie's knees.

"Hey! We ain't gonna hurt you, if that's what you worried about. We just gonna throw your ass outa here. Now, get up off the goddamn floor." Charlie walked over to the door and unfastened the padlocked chain. "Good-bye, man."

Rios burst into tears as he scrambled to his feet. He lurched out the door onto the sidewalk and looked around at the unfamiliar desolation of Park Avenue.

"Penthouse-A. Basement-B calling."

Devereau was considerably more annoyed by this second interruption. "What is it?" he shouted at Panucci.

"I just heard you release the elevator boy. Wouldn't the same be true for Joe Palko?"

"Absolutely not. Any number of things in this building could get screwed up, and we could need him."

"Okay, but why don't we hold him upstairs? What's the sense in having two of us holed up down here just watching one man?"

"Your orders are to maintain your post and control your prisoner. If that's more than you can handle, tell me, and I'll make the necessary adjustments."

"No, no." Panucci looked nervously at Palko, who was smiling. "I just called because it seemed a good idea to me. Besides, it's getting hot down here with all these fucking steam pipes." He hesitated. "It's okay. Forget it."

Devereau set the radio aside. "The amount of five hundred thousand, Mr. Goldwasser, is based on an analysis of your firm's financial position. As you can see, it only represents a minor percentage of your liquid assets. . . ."

Throughout the building the tedious waiting continued.

Employees were called together each time a tenant paid up and hostages were released. Devereau's harangues gave them hope, but also increased their impatience. The lower four floors had been evacuated. After the employees had left, some of the soldiers scrounged through the empty offices, looking for anything worth stealing that would fit in their pockets, before reporting to their secondary assignments on other floors.

The employees on six, Shenandoah Textile Mills, were waiting for the unimaginable quantity of two and one-half million dollars to secure their release. Their president, a J. Clark Akins III, who at forty-eight still had a full, thick head of brown hair, and who had just recently moved from the South, where the mills were located, had called a meeting in his office. "There didn't seem much choice, really. They are letting those go who pay up. And there is, of course, the reasonable chance they'll get caught and the money returned." He stroked his shock of bushy hair and smiled. "We use the biggest commercial bank in New York, and they don't have anywhere near that kind of cash on hand. They're going to have to get it from the Federal Reserve. So it may take a little while. But it's on the way."

On seven, the employees of Goldwasser and Company were waiting for Howard Goldwasser to return from the penthouse. On eight, Abe Feinberg, a gentle little wisp of a man in Adler Elevators, continued to contemplate requesting a private audience to explain that he was an outsider and not a member of the firm of Goodman and High. Perhaps on that basis he might be released at once.

On twelve, Ted Quirke, the credit manager for Stanco Chemicals, felt less philosophical about paying up. He decided to make another trip to the men's room and get another look at the guards. Maybe he could take them. He wasn't out of his league with a gun in his hand the way that idiot Wissel was. Wissel could have gotten himself killed, pulling that twenty-five on those creeps. Maybe the next trip to the men's room was the time to make his move. If he waited too much longer, the boss would be heading for the penthouse interview, and it would be too late to save all that dough.

On fifteen, Candy Dupree, an office temp, was becoming fascinated, almost obsessed, by the huge black soldier on her floor. The swelling in his pants had to be special. She was getting vibes that he could be a record-breaker, and as the evening approached, she was fast getting high on the fantasy of a little action.

On eighteen, Jessie Watts, everybody's favorite big old red-headed gal, the divorcee from West Virginia, was beginning to respond just slightly to the good-natured teasing of one of the troops out by the elevators. He was getting to her. She couldn't see much of him because of the mask and fatigue suit. But she could see he was a big old boy. And she could see his hands, which were freckled, and she figured if his hands were freckled, he was freckled all over, and probably red-headed, and when you put all that together with the way he talked, he was getting more than a little interesting.

The employees on the penthouse floor were kept in the most continuous state of tension. They spent the afternoon in grim fascination watching executives from the other floors being prodded at gunpoint by the vicious little guard who brought them in from the elevator. They occasionally heard the interviews with the "captain" develop into shouting matches. And they discussed among themselves the fact that since the building's occupants were being released, starting with the lower floors and working upward, and no apparent hostages were being held, perhaps all final hostages would be taken from the Root Corporation.

Most of the board members had remained in the conference room. Several were from outside the company and didn't have offices anyway. Since there wasn't much else to do, they tried to discuss their day's original agenda, among other things. But their discussion was little more than a list-less charade. Winfield Root, not to be intimidated by the day's developments, chose to leave the meeting. He had not thought of the principal intruder's name, but was sure he eventually would. He took over Billy Marshall's office, since his own was in use, and with Agnes Arrington he worked away at his philanthropic interests as if it were just another business day.

Barbara Meyner watched the traffic in and out of the corner office as she sat at her desk and typed mechanically at some work that had piled up. But she kept an eye on things, and as she did, she noted in particular the briefcases that were delivered to the corner office, wondering just how much they contained and where it would ultimately be spent.

The thought which perplexed her most was how she could have been so intimate with him for so long without picking up even a hint of what he was planning. She wrestled with the question of how she felt about him. She had cared about him, possibly even loved him in their better moments. Without ever being certain how he felt about her.

She had rationalized the subtle changes taking place in herself as a result of his influence. She had once been just another New York secretary, looking for "that ideal lasting relationship." She certainly wasn't that anymore. She'd given up on the split-level full of kids long ago. She knew it wasn't in the cards if she accepted him on his terms. And she had. And this was before he came bursting in with his mask and his goons.

In view of what was happening, she wondered which Barbara Meyner she really wanted to be, the old or the new. Perhaps it was the new, and she had been unknowingly preparing herself for it all along. If it was the new, how would he react?

Ziller and Weissberger talked to Bessie Gittelson at length. Of all the witnesses released from the fifth floor, she was clearly the most helpful. Her observations about the visitors

Luis had been bringing around the office over the last two months provided further insight into the depth of preparation that had gone into the coup. It was a masterpiece of planning, and the use of the mannequin was a show-boater to end them all.

"You got any ideas?" Ziller asked Weissberger after Bessie left.

Weissberger grinned. "I'll have to talk with this guy and find out where his head is. Then we can discuss the various psychological approaches."

"Smart-ass," Ziller said. "The next time the captain and I have a little chat, you can listen in and make your hotshot diagnosis."

Although a long-time shield-carrying member of the force, Jerry Weissberger had gotten a Ph.D. at night and had developed a limited practice as a clinical psychologist. He served on the force days and saw private patients after six P.M. Since a hostage negotiation was probably the most purely psychological act a cop could be called on to perform, he had been a key figure in the hostage program since its inception. He had helped develop the manual and train all personnel, both in the four-week intensive course for those assigned to the hostage squad and the one-day seminars attended by all superior officers.

He and Ziller were close friends; they worked together in the program and often traveled together to give seminars around the country. Ziller occasionally joked about how he had taught Weissberger to drink, moving him up from Dubonnet to straight scotch.

Weissberger and Ziller replayed the taped calls and discussed in detail the contacts and conversations Ziller had had with the captain. Weissberger agreed that the man probably wouldn't commit homicide unless really cornered. If then. But to what degree could he control the thirty or more misfits he had recruited? Most hostage situations involve a single perpetrator or a small, closely knit group. It was inconceivable that so large a group could be anything but unpredictable under prolonged conditions of stress.

"Hey, Harry." It was Chief O'Reilly, approaching with a tall, well-groomed stranger. The perfect gray suit and striped tie and slightly patronizing smile immediately suggested Ivy League to Ziller, who had had to claw his way through night school at City College to get his degree.

O'Reilly said, "Think you can get one guy out of that building with nothing but conversation?"

"One guy?" Ziller asked. "One of my favorite fantasies about now is getting them all out of there."

"This is a special situation. Very delicate. Meet Mr. Jarvis, from the State Department."

"Delighted to meet you, Lieutenant Ziller." Jarvis extended his hand. "And Lieutenant Weissberger. We have been contacted by the office of the minister of external affairs in Canada. As I'm sure you must know, this situation has been getting considerable publicity, and apparently a Canadian of some importance was attending a Root Corporation board meeting this morning. As soon as the news of this affair reached Toronto, his offices immediately began calling the minister of external affairs, who also happens to be his close personal friend."

"Look around," Ziller said. "Wouldn't you say we were doing everything we can to get him out?"

Jarvis stiffened. "Lieutenant, are you aware that the minister of external affairs is the Canadian equivalent of our secretary of state?"

Ziller looked at Weissberger, then back at Jarvis. "Mr. Jarvis, we're as anxious as you to get him out, but there are hundreds of lives in jeopardy in that building."

"Lieutenant, I am here in behalf of the State Department to ask that you treat this as a special matter and make every possible effort to get him out of that building immediately."

"They're in touch with the commissioner," O'Reilly said quietly.

Ziller picked up on the phone and began dialing. "Jarvis, how much money are you prepared to lay out?" Then he added in a more resigned voice, "What's the man's name?"

"Bruce Williston."

Ziller jotted the name on a pad and flipped a switch, putting the phone on a small speaker so the others could hear.

"What is it now? I'm busy and don't wish to be disturbed."

"I've called to ask . . . a favor," Ziller said.

"A favor!" He laughed. "Well, that's something new. One of New York's finest asking me for favors. Let's hear it. But don't expect much."

"Then let's say I've called to negotiate a deal."

"Ziller, don't take my time with a bunch of shit."

"This is important. I've called to ask you to release one particular hostage, and I'm prepared to offer you something in return."

"Who do you want?"

"His name is Williston, Bruce Williston. He's on the twenty-second floor and he's a Canadian. His government is involved, and with all the hostages you got, you'll never miss him."

"Why do you sound funny? Have you got this call on a speaker?"

"Yes. A man from the State Department is here now."

"Well! Not bad. An affair of State. Would the man from the State Department be willing to come over and take Mr. Williston's place? That seems fair. And I assume he's dedicated."

"We don't trade hostages. You know that."

"What if there's no choice?"

"You don't need him. You can afford to let one go."

"Then what's your deal? You said you wanted to negotiate his release."

"I'll personally see that you get good press for doing it."

"Ziller, you're wasting my time. I've got my own pipeline to the media, and it's just as good as yours."

"You know you'll get better press if it comes from us."

"Ziller, I've got your ass over a barrel, and you know it. If you want him out of here, you're going to have to come up with something real."

"I told you I was willing to negotiate. . . . Got any ideas?"

A pause. "Yeah, you son-of-a-bitch! You buy dinner."

"You got a deal. We'll send over a repeat of lunch."

"No deal. Have the hotel send over a menu. And call me back when you've had the press release written. I want to hear what goes on the wire before I let your man go. Now, get busy." He hung up.

Ziller carefully hung up the phone and took a deep breath. "Did you hear that egotistical son-of-a-bitch? Send over a menu, he says." He looked at Jarvis. "I assume you'll pick up that dinner tab. The department's got no budget to cover it." Then he said to Weissberger, "Now that you've had a firsthand look, what do you think of my man?"

"Seems to me that you and he have a strange kind of rapport," Jarvis said sarcastically.

"It's a start," Ziller answered quickly.

Suddenly the special phone rang. Ziller signaled for silence and picked it up.

"Ziller, get an ambulance over to the door of the building, and quick." The captain sounded rattled.

"What's happened?"

"Some creep bought himself a couple of M-14 slugs in the gut. Now, will you hurry?"

"Only one person hit?"

A pause. "Yeah, only one. But he's a mess, so move, goddammit!"

13

To the customers of Stanco, Ted Quirke was the world's toughest credit man. They had all learned to act when his quiet voice said, "If you don't plan to mail your check on time, do us both a favor and don't deduct the discount. Who needs the aggravation of all that extra paperwork? A day late is a day late." To the company's salesmen he was just as tough. "You think you got a hot new customer? A big hitter, you say? I'm the one that tells you when you got a new customer. A D&B is a start. Now, go back and get me a list of references."

To the executives of the company he was an absolutist. He made credit decisions on the basis of indisputable fact. "Hunches are for dummies. Whoever heard of a good emotional credit man?" When Quirke okayed one, it was safe. To his fellow employees, those not involved in his credit decisions, he was a warm, quick-witted, perceptive observer of the greater metropolitan scene and a sports fan. Everybody's favorite guy for lunch. Although he'd moved to Connecticut, he still revered Queens as his origin. "Don't identify me with

Brooklyn," he'd say. "I'm strictly Queens. I'm lace-curtain Irish, not shanty Irish."

He was of medium build and average height, but his appearance belied a key element of Ted Quirke's character. He was tough. He had an acute sense of justice and a little strain of vigilante blood. He had been among the first marines overseas in the Korean war, and although he hadn't liked combat, he'd been good at it. A sharpshooter, quick, smart, much-decorated, he'd been promoted to lieutenant in the field.

Quirke had already made two trips to the men's room to check out the guards. He was sure he could take them, and he knew he'd have to act soon, before his bosses arranged to ransom the company. A million or two bucks was a lot of dough to be giving to a bunch of trash for the privilege of walking out of the building. He'd trade the two guards for his company's release.

He sat at his desk with the door shut. Other employees didn't usually bother him when he closed his door. But he held the weapon below the level of the desk anyway. He didn't want some asshole to see it and blow his cover. He had two of the old G.I. automatics. He kept one at home in a night-table drawer and one in the office, stashed behind the hanging folders in his file drawer. He pressed the release and let the clip slide into his hand.

Then he took a half-dozen wide rubber bands out of his desk and slipped them over his left shoe, just above his ankle. He tried to position the weapon in them, but they didn't hold it tightly enough. He'd never be able to walk naturally. He tried doubling the rubber bands. Too tight. He stood up and stuffed the gun into the waist of his pants in the middle of his back. It would ride there long enough to get him to the men's room. Would the guards notice that he was wearing his jacket, when he hadn't worn it on his other trips? Not likely.

When he reached the foyer, he was stunned to find the

number of guards had increased from two to three. Still, he'd made up his mind.

He went into the men's room and into a stall. He slipped off his jacket and hung it up. He removed his tie. No need having that in his way. He tried rolling up his sleeves, and finally decided they were less cumbersome down. He listened to someone urinating. Nothing left to do but wait until he was sure the men's room was deserted. With the gun resting on the toilet-paper dispenser, he peeled off yards of the paper and swabbed his face and neck.

As he came through the door leading back into the foyer, he held the gun behind his hip. One of the guards was facing away, lighting a cigarette, his M-14 leaning against the wall. A break. At least the odds were somewhat closer to the original two-to-one. The other two guards were in a relaxed stance, holding their rifles.

Quirke raised his automatic and shouted, "Okay, you guys, freeze!" Both of the guards holding rifles whirled to face him. Quirke picked the one who seemed to be coming on first and fired, knocking him out of the fight, but before he could get off a shot at the other one, he felt two explosions of pain somewhere in the middle of his body. . . . And then he felt as if he floated into the air and slowly back to the floor, where he landed in a heap, facedown. He sensed that one of his legs was twitching as he struggled to get his breath. . . .

After a moment of immobility, the troop who'd shot Quirke walked over to where he lay. He was a rangy young black named Roosevelt Hinton who'd almost made it in semipro baseball the year before. Holding his rifle at arm's length and his finger on the trigger, he put the muzzle to Quirke's ear. "No!" yelled the other troop, a Puerto Rican named Miguel Sosa, who'd been lighting a cigarette.

"He woulda killed me," Hinton said.

"Don't do it. It a big mistake, man."

"Why not? Look what he did to Roberto. This creep's finished anyway. I'll be doing him a favor." Hinton kicked at the twitching leg.

"Just don't do it." Sosa had recovered enough from the shock to walk over and kneel by the wounded troop, Roberto Molina. He peeled the mask off the orange-haired Roberto and removed his belt. As he did, Roberto's radio fell out of its holder. "Not too bad," he said. "But a lotta blood. You better call Dee."

Roberto winced as Miguel examined him. "This is a bunch of shit, man," he said in pain. "Nobody tell me they'd have guns. He groaned. "Gimme back my radio. I want to keep up with what's going on. Stick it in my pocket. Okay, man?"

Sosa slid the compact radio into one of the large pockets on the leg of Roberto's fatigues.

The other employees of Stanco had heard the shots but decided it was wiser not to investigate. They'd wait, instead, for word on what had happened.

Devereau was just finishing up with Goodman from the eighth floor when the frantic call came from Hinton. He hustled Goodman out of the office and picked up his two-way radio.

"This is Twelve-A. We just had us a gunfight and I'm afraid we blew some little turd all over the place down here."

"No!" Devereau shuddered.

"I'm afraid, man, it's yes."

Devereau began to pull at the bottom of his mask. "Why, goddammit?"

"He came out of the men's room with a forty-five. He shot Roberto."

"How bad are they?"

"Roberto's messy, but he don't look that bad. This other one, Jesus, I think he's fucked."

"I'll be right down." Devereau hurried out of the room. After the elevator door closed behind him, he screamed a raging "No! No! No!" and slammed the metal wall several times with his fist. The car vibrated perceptibly in its descent.

When the elevator reached the twelfth floor, he was back in control, and he surveyed the bloody results of the gunplay in an unemotional, businesslike manner. He felt Quirke's pulse and briefly commented that it would be the police's responsibility to save him and that the idiot had brought it on himself. He told Hinton to get four of the extra troops from the evacuated floors to carry him to the door to be picked up by the police ambulance.

He looked at Roberto more carefully. Convinced his wound was minor, he instructed Hinton to have Roberto carried to the corner office on the fourth floor, where there was a couch. They were to stay with him. When Hinton questioned this, Devereau said, "It's a million-dollar wound, the kind that gets you sent home early. I've seen hundreds like it. Take it from an old field commander."

As he was about to go back in the elevator, the doors opened and Floyd walked into the foyer. "What the hell are you doing here?" Devereau asked. "Why did you leave your post?"

"I came to see what happen to Roberto."

"You're to stay at your post. I'll tell you anything you need to know."

"Now *you* listen," Floyd said. "Roberto's a good friend of mine. And when he gets hurt, don't you start giving me no fucking orders not to come check up on him. I wanta know how bad he got hit."

"You let me worry about it."

Floyd looked at Hinton. "How bad did he get it?"

Hinton shook his head.

Floyd looked back at Devereau. "Maybe you better send him with the other one. He might be better off out there than going down the fucking drain in here."

"I'll make that decision."

"You better make it right."

Devereau returned to the elevator. "If you're so goddamn anxious to help, you can help carry him down to the fourth floor. Then get back to your assigned post. That clear?" The door closed.

Floyd turned to the others. "We'll get the son-of-a-bitch."

"Roberto okay?" Benjy asked Devereau as he stepped from the car on the penthouse floor.

"Under control," he answered without pausing to talk further. He carefully avoided Barbara Meyner's eyes as he returned to Winfield Root's office.

He hurried to his desk and called Ziller. Then he went into the adjoining bathroom and closed and locked the door. He leaned against the wall and began to gag. He peeled off his mask and dropped to a sitting position on the closed toilet seat, where he slumped for several minutes, taking an occasional deep breath. He stood up, sponged water on his face, and dried it with meticulous care. He pulled the mask back on and returned to his desk.

Twenty-one stories below, the police ambulance was again on the sidewalk, in front of the open glass doors of 330 Park. Four masked men in fatigues carried the limp body of Ted Quirke. One of them grumbled in Spanish about the blood all over his sleeve. Two of the ambulance cops rolled the wheeled stretcher through the open doors into the lobby while two more cops with shotguns covered them. The troops lowered Quirke onto it.

The cops climbed in, and the ambulance pulled away, using a siren and pulsating lights.

As the ambulance headed South toward Bellevue Hospital, it passed a red Wells Fargo armored truck, heading north. The truck eased to a stop in front of 277 Park, the Chemical Bank Building. Two Fargo guards climbed from it and went into the bank, one of them carrying a large briefcase that contained a half-million dollars. The money was from Chemical Bank's Coin and Currency Department, located in their headquarters on Pine Street in the downtown financial district. It contained a hundred thousand dollars in recorded, or "marked," bills, which the bank always held in reserve for just such purposes. The money was the ransom for the employees of Goldwasser and Co., Securities Analysts.

Ziller took the call on his second phone to keep the designated phone clear at all times.

"Harry, this is Renzolo. Calling from Bellevue."

"Alphonse. You got there quick. How bad is he?"

"He was DOA, Harry. He didn't have a chance."

"Listen, Al, this is important. We got to keep a lid on this. As long as our captain believes the man to be alive, we got more to deal with. Talk to the medical examiner. Name's Polayes. Tell him to talk to the hospital director and have the victim listed as critical. And see that they tell the information desk right away. We can't afford to let the facts get out. Incidentally, what was the victim's name?"

"Ted Quirke."

"What floor of the building?"

"Stanco Industries, a chemicals outfit, whatever floor that is."

"Twelve. Get whatever else you can and get on back."

A line from a song trailed through Ziller's mind as he hung up the phone. "Billy, don't be a hero . . ." Heroes always seem to end up DOA. "Gentlemen, when you are dealing with a hostage situation, try to get word to the hostages to take it easy. Tell them not to try to be heroes. They need to know that even if it looks as if the police are doing nothing, what looks like nothing can be a great deal. It just isn't in the best interests of one's health to act impulsively around armed hostage takers. The waiting game usually works in favor of the hostage. . . ."

One of the detectives brought Ziller a report from a sharp-shooter-observation team. They had seen two of the troops helping a third one, who had obviously been shot, into the larger corner office on the fourth floor. The wounded man had apparently suffered a serious injury, but he was still fully conscious. He had his mask removed and had orange hair.

Ziller picked up the private phone and dialed.

"What is it?" Devereau said. "I don't wish to have you constantly calling."

"I thought you said only one person was shot over there."

"That's right. And I've turned him over to you. Hopefully, he'll survive. The asshole had no business attacking my men. He was shot in self-defense."

"One of your boys got hit, too. He's on the fourth floor."

"We'll take care of him ourselves."

"He's bleeding pretty heavy. You'd better get him to a hospital. I'll send an ambulance."

"I said we'd take care of him ourselves."

"Why don't you let him decide? Let me talk with him. When he knows his options, maybe he'll like my ideas better than lying there bleeding to death."

"You'll only talk to me, and only when I say so." Devereau hung up.

A minute later, the same observation team reported that the blinds had been drawn on the corner office on the fourth floor. And a minute after that, another team radioed that the drapes had been closed in the corner office of the penthouse. Ziller smiled at Weissberger. "He's taking himself off display. Think he's losing some of his cool?"

"How would you react?"

"Hey, Harry," Murphy called from his desk, "I think we finally found them. You guys come look at the scanner."

Ziller and Weissberger followed Murphy to where a detective sat before a boxlike radio device. The officer had been there much of the afternoon, fiddling with knobs and controls, scanning probable frequency ranges, looking for the band being used in 330 Park. Finally he had picked up a voice that matched the caller on Ziller's phone. The detective sat back with a satisfied smile as the captain's voice echoed in the van. Devereau was giving another lecture to his hostages.

". . . incident was of course unfortunate, but the man was a fool. My men will not hesitate to shoot anyone who challenges their authority, as demonstrated by the idiot who left in the police ambulance. I hope that no more of you will decide to leave in that manner. He's still alive. You may not be so lucky. On the other hand, all the occupants of floors two, three, four, and five have left. They walked out on their own power. It's much simpler that way. Floors six and seven should be leaving shortly. In complete safety.

"The rest of you will not be leaving until tomorrow. This is because bank vaults have time locks that cannot be opened. But the terms of your release will be established during the next few hours, and you will be allowed to leave in the morning as soon as the money is delivered. Until that time, think of yourselves as my guests and make yourselves as comfortable as possible. I am arranging to have dinner sent over from the hotel."

When it was obvious the man had finished, the detective operating the scanner said, "I thought we had him at the end of his last broadcast. After he closed his drapes, I decided to take a chance and leave it set there. He's using a spot in the business radio band. Not a bad choice, since the range is congested with dull office conversations, of little interest to hams who might be monitoring the airwaves for diversion."

With the frequency established, they discussed what other use might be made of this find. A car from the electronics unit of the intelligence division was sent out carrying a radio-direction-finding set, or RDF unit. A second unit was set up in the van. With these units set for the captain's frequency, the men operating them would wait for his next broadcast and triangulate on the signal in an effort to pinpoint the location of the repeater they were certain the perpetrators had to be using.

Ziller discussed the status of things briefly with Weissberger and then went back to the designated phone and dialed. It was important to maintain dialogue, look for openings to create anxiety.

"I want to read you the press release," Ziller said. "We want to get Williston out of there."

"Let's hear it," Devereau said. Ziller detected a distracted tone to his voice.

"'A spokesman for the New York Police Department has announced that the leader of the group of men holding the tenants of 330 Park Avenue for ransom has cooperated with the police in releasing one hostage before his ransom was paid. The freed man was a Canadian businessman. The police negotiated his release to ease government concern that his confinement would strain relations with Canada.' Okay?"

"It's fine," Devereau said. "How's the idiot at the hospital?"

"He's listed as critical."

"He brought it on himself. No one asked him to pull a gun."

"You know that if he doesn't make it, you've got homicide added to the charges and that ups the ante. If you'd like to negotiate an end to this whole affair, now'd be the time to do it. I can probably get you a better deal while he's still alive."

"Are you out of your head, Ziller? Do you think I give a shit about that creep? I told you, my men acted in self-defense."

"You can have your counsel tell that to the judge."

"Listen, you son-of-a-bitch, one thing I can do without is your smart mouth. I just changed my mind about Williston. I want one million dollars for him."

"I wasn't trying to be smart. But that's beside the point. You and I made a deal. Aren't you good for your word?"

"I don't make deals with you."

"If that's the way you want it. But keep in mind that it's a

144

two-way street. If I can't expect anything from you, don't expect anything from me."

"What could I possibly want from you?"

"You can never tell."

"Get a million dollars over here and we'll let your man go. And get that menu over here from the hotel. I want a decent meal tonight."

"No deal. We'll just send over sandwiches like at lunch."

"Listen, you son-of-a-bitch! Don't play games. I'll go back to our original deal, but get that menu over here. The meal I'm planning to serve tonight is going to be a news story in itself. And it could take some time to prepare."

"We'll have a cop bring the menu right over. And we'll put out the news release as soon as Williston is free. Incidentally, how's your wounded man over there?"

Devereau hung up, but not before he had heard Ziller's question.

14

"Boston."

"Boston."

The detectives in the radio car jumped. Their man had started transmitting. On the seat between them was a metal box roughly a foot square and about four inches high. On its top was a compass with a plastic pointer containing a metallic element.

"Penthouse-A calling Lobby-A."

The detectives quickly began moving the pointer around, looking for the man's repeater, the source of the signal.

"Penthouse-A to Lobby-A." A pause. "Penthouse-A to Penthouse-B. Stroud. You pick me up all right?" A pause. "You do? Then transmit back and let's see if I'm receiving."

"Penthouse-B to Penthouse-A."

"Son-of-a-bitch! This little motherfucker transmits, but it's stopped receiving. We'll have to get Smokey on it. Let me use yours." An extended pause. "Penthouse-A to Lobby-A."

"Right here, baby. What's going on up there, anyway?"

"My unit went out. I was sending but not receiving. Two things. A cop'll be bringing over a menu from the hotel. After it arrives, I'll be releasing one hostage from the penthouse floor. Also, we're expecting the payoffs for the sixth and seventh floors. The seventh will arrive first. Could show up anytime. You read me?"

"Has a nigger got black balls?"

All troops in the building followed this exchange. Devereau had repeatedly lectured the men on the importance of monitoring their radios at all times. They were to know everything that was happening and be prepared for any emergency. Each soldier carried enough batteries to see him through at least forty-eight hours of continuous operation.

The radio car parked on Fifty-third between Lexington and Park completed its scan and called in to report two nodes, one considerably stronger than the other. Within minutes the other RDF operator in the van had located the nodes and fixed bearings on them. The two sets of bearings were plotted on a scale map. The weaker signal came from the vicinity of 330 Park, as expected. The stronger one appeared to be coming from the Waldorf-Astoria, specifically the northwest corner of the hotel.

In the Greenpoint section of Brooklyn two detectives from the Thirteenth District robbery squad walked into the dispatcher's office of a trucking terminal. The man was just winding up his work for the day.

The cops presented their shields and began asking for information about a Charlie Patterson.

"You're too late," the dispatcher answered. "He moved to Detroit this past weekend."

"Have you got anything that established that? You know, the fact that he's actually there?" one of the detectives asked.

"That's what he told me he was doing. He quit last Thursday. Asked for a letter of recommendation."

The detective described Charlie Patterson, and when the dispatcher said it certainly sounded like the same man, the cop said that they had reason to believe Patterson was involved in the business at 330 Park Avenue.

"Christ!" the dispatcher said. "I heard about that on the radio."

The detective explained how the bus had been leased using Charlie's special operator's license, and all descriptions had matched up. His license address had led to his place in Bedford-Stuyvesant, and working with the Housing Authority police, they had checked housing records to come up with his place of employment.

"Then I think I got you another one of the boys you're looking for," the dispatcher said. "A buddy of Charlie's named Floyd Washington. Said he was going to Detroit with Charlie. Floyd worked here in the terminal. Nasty little guy, Floyd. I'm not surprised he's into something like that. But Charlie, Jesus, he was a good man! I hated to lose him."

In the financial district of lower Manhattan, Richard Quinnell left the Federal Reserve Building and started back for his own office at Citibank. Although he worked for the biggest commercial bank in New York, its coin and currency department couldn't handle the ransom for Shenandoah Textile. Quinnell had gone to the Federal Reserve to sign the necessary papers to arrange a transfer.

He'd be late getting home, and though his wife had planned a small dinner party that night, he wasn't concerned. How often does a banker have the opportunity to arrange a two-and-one-half-million-dollar ransom payment? And what better material could one have to keep a midweek dinner party alive than to have played such a role in what had to be the biggest ongoing news story in the world? Just another ho-hum day in the life of your average everyday banker. Not bad conversational fare to go with martinis and hot cheese puffs.

He thought about the stuffed-shirt Federal Reserve executives who had handled the paperwork. Sitting there on more than seventeen billion dollars in bullion, over a quarter of all the monetary gold in the free world, they had been considerably less impressed by the significance of the 330 Park situation. It was interesting, perhaps, but their main concern with it was that it had kept them from leaving for home on time. In discussing it, they'd speculated with a certain amount of annoyance on the number of similar transactions they'd probably have to make for other banks with accounts in 330 Park. Bureaucrats. No imagination.

On the backside of the Federal Reserve Building, the flexible steel curtain in front of the loading area rumbled upward. An armed guard stepped out to halt traffic on Maiden Lane. Then a silver Brinks truck backed out, turned, and headed uptown in the rush-hour traffic. It carried two large canvas bags of money to Citibank's Park Avenue Headquarters at 399 Park. At the same time, the Chemical Bank, eight blocks away, was arranging payment for Goldwasser & Co., and to the surprise of its manager, the cop in charge placed the large Waldorf menu on top of the packets of hundred-dollar bills.

Stroud entered the boardroom and said, "One of you men Bruce Williston?"

Of the ten board members who had been present when the meeting started that morning, five still sat listlessly around the table. Williston stared nervously at the slim masked troop with his rifle. "Why do you want him?"

"We're cuttin' him loose."

A flush of pink traveled up Williston's face to his prematurely bald scalp. "What does that mean?" He touched his forefinger to the bridge of his nose to adjust his metal-rimmed glasses.

"We're lettin' him go. Sendin' him on his way."

"You mean you're releasing him," Ronam said.

"That's what I said."

Williston smiled. "In that case, I'm Bruce Williston."

Ronam said, "May I ask why only Williston?"

"We're honorin' a request by the State Department. We're trying to be patriotic."

"Sorry about that, guys," Williston said, hesitating a moment, embarrassed by his good fortune. "Too bad we can't all be Canadian, eh?"

"You ready to go?" Stroud asked.

Williston grabbed the yellow pad on which he had been writing, dropped it into his briefcase, and stood up. "I'm quite ready."

Stroud escorted Williston out to the elevators, where Benjy stood guard alone. "Take him to the lobby," Stroud said. "I'll cover for you here till you get back."

The elevator door opened, and as Williston started to walk on, Benjy hit him viciously in the stomach. Williston dropped his briefcase and doubled over. "Why did you do that?" he gasped.

"You're too happy to leave your friends behind," Benjy answered. He prodded Williston and followed him into the elevator. Stroud pushed Williston's briefcase into the car with his foot. Williston's face reflected extreme terror as the door closed with only the two of them in the car.

"You understand, of course, Dr. Schain," Devereau said, "that you will not be leaving until tomorrow. You and your employees will have to do the best you can tonight. You won't be alone, though. Everyone from the ninth floor up will still be here. But I can promise you an excellent meal tonight. The Waldorf has promised to serve their finest. And tomorrow morning, right after the banks open and your money is delivered, you and your people will be released."

"I do have one request to make," Schain said. "I'd like to call my wife and assure her that I'm okay."

"We've decided that since we have only two working

phones and there are so many people in the building, personal calls are out of the question. I'm sure you can understand. Besides, I'm sure she's been listening to the radio or television and knows the hostages are being well treated."

Schain looked earnestly at Devereau. "My wife had open heart surgery a few weeks ago. I'd rather not have her feel anxious. It upsets her not to hear from me when anything happens that . . ."

"Well, I think we can make an exception. But don't tell anyone that I allowed you this privilege. I don't wish to have to deal with a barrage of similar requests. And keep the call brief and to the point. My associate"—he nodded at Stroud—"will show you to the phone and then back to the elevator."

Schain walked ahead of Stroud into the next office. He picked up the phone and dialed.

"Hello!" A very loud child's voice.

"Barry, let me speak to Mom."

"Jeez, are you going to be late again? I thought we were going to the ball game."

"Let me speak to your . . ." Schain stopped as if he'd just remembered something. After hesitating he said softly, "Barry, is she there?"

"Did you forget? She had her quarterfinal singles match this afternoon, and then she was staying at the club because we were going to the game. . . ." The child's voice filled the room.

Stroud glanced at the guilty look on Schain's face and then ripped the phone out of his hand. He slapped Schain's face, knocking his glasses to the floor. "You crawly son-of-a-bitch! Get the fuck out of here!"

In the corner office Devereau sat at his desk, studying the Waldorf's catering menu.

Ziller studied his pencil notes: "Charlie Patterson, 29, black, 6'4", 230 pounds, truck driver, minor record, burglary, one arrest; Floyd Washington, 32, black, about 5'9", 150 pounds, equipment operator in trucking terminal, minor record, car theft and burglary, two arrests, one conviction, considered to be a troublemaker; Luis Rodriguez, 34, 5'8", 130 pounds, assistant to the chief engineer of 330 Park, two arrests, armed robbery, dealing in stolen goods, one conviction." And another man named Stroud and another named Smokey, who's a radio expert, and a third with orange hair who has a bullet in him and could be bleeding to death. . . . Not a lot of information, but a start. . . .

"Harry!" Murphy was calling from the other end of the van. "I got a call from the team using the field strength meter over at the hotel. They can't find the man's repeater. He must be keeping it turned off between transmissions."

Ziller thought about the word "Boston." Obviously the signal to tell his operator on the repeater to turn it on. "Let's get every one of those meters we've got in the department into the hotel so that the next time they broadcast, we can find their boy."

"Hey, Harry!" It was O'Reilly. "The commissioner and the mayor are here."

Ziller jumped up as several men crowded into the small area before his desk. The mayor. The commissioner. The first deputy commissioner. The deputy commissioner for public affairs. The chief of operations. And lurking behind them, naturally, was Dan Redmond. The mayor extended his hand and said, "How's it going, Lieutenant?"

Ziller took the mayor's hand and hesitated before speaking. He glanced at the commissioner, whose eyes seemed to be asking: How long's it going to take to clean this thing up? The overtime is costing a fucking fortune.

One question at a time. He looked back at the mayor, wondering how to tell him what he wanted to hear.

15

"This is the CBS evening news, with Walter Cronkite."

"Good evening. One of the most spectacular heists ever attempted is taking place at this moment here in New York City. At ten o'clock this morning a platoon of men estimated at between thirty and forty arrived in a chartered bus and entered 330 Park Avenue, a twenty-two-story office building at Fifty-first and Park, in the heart of one of New York's most fashionable areas of high-rise office buildings. . . ."

Devereau listened to the rest of Cronkite's report on 330 Park and snapped off the television set. He closed the wood-paneled doors in front of it. Not bad. Cronkite had been . . . yes, respectful. Cronkite, the dean. Later, maybe, the other networks, to see how they'd treated it, but for the moment, the dean was respectful. Which meant the nation would be respectful. And much of the world. Not bad at all.

He picked up the phone and dialed.

"Ziller."

"Hello there, Lieutenant. By any chance did you happen to catch Cronkite's opening remarks?"

"I'm afraid I've been a little too busy to watch TV."

"Too bad. He did a nice number. I thought he was very discerning as to the quality of my workmanship."

"I'll try to catch a look at tomorrow's *Times*. Maybe you'll even make the front page."

"You can count on it," Devereau snapped. Then, in a more controlled tone: "Ziller, what I called you about, I'm anxious to get on with dinner. And I'd like to cover the details directly with the hotel. I want you to call them and tell them to expect a call from me. And tell them I'll expect their absolute cooperation. That should satisfy the terms of our deal."

"Whatever you say."

"Do you need their number? I have it right here. Incidentally, how's the creep at Bellevue?"

"No change."

"His idiocy was inexcusable. He had no business putting my men in that position. . . . Sounds as if you're using your phone speaker. Who's around there in the van? Anybody interesting?"

"Just some of my co-workers."

After Ziller got the phone number and ended the conversation, he wheeled in his chair to face the group of men who had been standing behind him: the mayor, the P.C. and all his side men—O'Reilly, Murphy, Weissberger, Redmond.

A deputy commissioner asked with a mock smile, "Is this the same negotiating technique you've used on other cases, Lieutenant?" His smile widened slightly. "Is this the sort of thing for which we created the hostage team?" His tone was short.

Ziller felt heat rise up his neck and face. He glanced at Redmond's smirking expression.

"It wasn't the moment for any kind of negotiating ploy,"

Weissberger interjected. "Our subject is on a high at the moment. He's very high, in fact. Any attempt to negotiate anything at this point would have been counterproductive. Some of our earlier exchanges were quite effective, I thought. He was responding to the needle pretty well. I'm confident we can get to him. But it's going to take lots of time. And infinite patience. It's going to be a long night."

"And keep in mind we did talk the Canadian out of there," Ziller said. "In exchange for a meal for the people in the building."

"Out of whose budget?" the deputy commissioner asked.

"I can't say that I have the answer to that as yet, sir. Unless the State Department takes it. Which reminds me. I told him I'd call the hotel and call him right back."

Ziller explained that he expected the more serious aspects of the negotiations to begin late that night, and breathed a sigh of relief when the delegation from City Hall finally left. He was just about to grab another cup of coffee when the banquet manager at the Waldorf called to complain about Devereau's demands. It appeared he was planning to serve a banquet. To complicate things further, food would have to be delivered to twelve different floors. In addition to the elaborate food, he had also demanded vintage wine, crystal stemware, good china, and the Waldorf's famous gold service for the penthouse.

"It all fits," Weissberger said.

"He knows what he's paying for it," Ziller said. "Look at the dough he gave up when he made the deal."

"I think he's more interested in the review he'll get from *Time* magazine. He's really flying right now. He figures Quirke to pull through and the whole operation to go as planned."

"It's gonna be a nice dinner party. Wonder if we can wangle an invitation?"

"Why don't you give him a call?"

Ziller grinned. "Let's get us some sandwiches, anyway. And while we eat, maybe we can figure out how to really start needling the son-of-a-bitch. It's time we got this case moving."

Devereau lined the three briefcases up on his desk. The money was, as usual, packed exactly as specified in his demands. The cases were locked. The keys were in sealed envelopes, taped to the tops of the cases.

He had trained himself to assess the contents of a case quickly and accurately. A standard packet contained one hundred hundred-dollar bills. If the bills were new, the packet measured three-eighths of an inch in thickness. Older bills measured around one-half inch. Not that the contents of a packet, as indicated by the banding strip, would ever be wrong. Bankers were to be trusted. Money was sacred to them.

Knowing the thickness of a packet, he had a good idea of the number of packets in any given stack. A four-inch stack usually contained nine packets, or nine hundred bills. And if these were all hundreds, the stack contained ninety thousand dollars. The average briefcase held ten stacks. Thus, if all bills were hundreds and the case had an interior height of around four inches, the case would carry up to nine hundred thousand dollars without crowding. With a little crowding, it just might accommodate a million. By riffling a packet or two and counting the packets in one stack, he knew the count in the case.

Devereau checked the contents of the cases before him. The money was all there. Two and a half million dollars. Had anyone other than an employee at the mint ever seen so much cash? He relocked the cases, labeled them, and dropped the keys into one of the large pockets in his fatigues.

The money itself was stored with the rest in the casketlike packing crate along the wall behind the desk.

On the eighteenth floor Jessie Watts strolled out to the reception area once again. She eyed the taller of the two guards and smiled.

"You were about to say . . ." he said to her.

She grinned. "Me? You must be mistaken."

"Aw, come on, I know you was about to say something to me."

"Shoot. When I'm ready to say something to you, I'll say it. I'm not bashful." She opened the door to the ladies' room and disappeared inside.

"You see that?" Wayne Austin said to Billy Pickett. "That red-headed gal's got X-ray eyes. She can see right through these pants I'm wearing just like I don't even have 'em on. And she's got her eye on something she likes inside there. And she's done made up her mind she's gonna have herself a little taste of it 'fore this night is over."

"Did you forget what Dee said about not screwing around?"

"You don't 'spect me to pass that up, do you, Billy? Man, she's table grade. Besides, we'll have extra troops on this floor just as soon as the next group of hostages is released."

"Christ, is tail all you ever think about?"

"Me? What about her? Look how many times she's been out here to check up on me."

"You must be right. Nobody needs to piss that often."

"Boston."

"Boston here."

"Penthouse-A calling Six-A and Six-B."

"This is Six-A. Come in, Penthouse-A."

"Think your prisoners would like to leave?"

"Want me to ask 'em?"

"Don't ask 'em, tell 'em. They're not invited for dinner."

"Penthouse-A to Lobby-A. You listening?"

"Sixth floor getting ready to walk."

"Just checking. Okay. Penthouse-A to all stations. I want a stereo in five minutes. I repeat. All stations. Stereo in five minutes. That's it till then, but stay tuned."

"Good evening." Devereau sat with his elbows on the desk. Stroud's walkie-talkie stood directly in front of him on top of his briefcase. He spoke into the mouthpiece of the unit as if he were a commentator speaking into a microphone, addressing a radio audience. In Ronam's adjacent office, Smokey Hampton sat at the walnut table, Devereau's dismantled radio spread in front of him.

In the boardroom the employees of Root stood silently between Stroud, who held Hampton's radio, and Benjy. Winfield Root sat at the conference table, his brow deeply creased. He still hadn't placed the voice.

"I have two important announcements to make. First, the employees of Shenandoah Textile, on the sixth floor, are being released. This means that all floors through seven have been allowed to leave. I had planned to have more of you out by now, but delays by the police have put things a little behind schedule. As a result, the rest of you will have to wait through the night. . . ."

A flurry of whispers greeted this announcement. No more speculation was necessary. Most employees on the upper floors had already decided that this was their likely fate, but what would happen during the long hours of the night? What were the cops doing besides diverting traffic?

"I hope you will make yourselves as comfortable as possible," Devereau continued. "I certainly want your stay to be as pleasant as circumstances will allow. Which brings me to my second announcement. I have ordered dinner for all of you from the Waldorf-Astoria. It will be over very shortly. I selected the dishes and wines myself, and I feel sure that you will enjoy your meal."

On the twentieth floor John McGlothlin thought about the night as an unexpected opportunity to return to the little upright piano in his office and work on his secret project, a musical about the advertising business. On eighteen, Saxon Shaer said to his partner Rhodes, "Did I hear him say wines?" as the two of them thoughtfully watched the lean-hipped model who had earlier been posing for the carpet ad.

On the fifteenth floor Candy Dupree continued to study the bulge in the pants of the husky black troop holding the radio. On twelve, the employees of Stanco stared with intense hatred and fantasies of vengeance at the two guards holding the radios. One of them had shot Ted Quirke. On the ninth floor, Terry Alvarez, the receptionist, began to reconsider all the men of Market Systems. Even the married ones. Tension could make people behave in strange ways, even a Jewish prince like Dr. Schain himself.

Devereau was finishing up his broadcast. "During the evening, I will continue to discuss terms of release with the principals of the remaining firms. And tomorrow morning, as soon as the banks reopen and the money is delivered, I'll allow you to leave. I would like to emphasize again the importance of your continued cooperation. There will be at least three troops on every floor throughout the night. I think you've already seen evidence of the stupidity of challenging them. I hope you'll choose to walk out of here healthy rather than be carried. I trust I'm making myself clear. . . . Thank you."

Around the corner, in the headquarters van, Ziller pushed back his hat and took a deep breath. "What do you think of that little speech?"

"Did you notice how his tone of voice changed near the end?" Weissberger said. "He started out like Santa Claus, but ended up mean. And did you notice how many times he said 'I' during his last minute or two? Let's play it back. The son-of-a-bitch is really high right now. We'll have to talk about how far we want to bring him down. And how to go about doing it. . . ."

"Hey, Lieutenant Ziller." It was one of the detectives who manned the phones. "The boys over the hotel have located the repeater. Corner room. Eleventh floor."

"Good job." Ziller said.

"They want to know if you want them to move in and take him."

"No!" Ziller said quickly. "Tell 'em to take it easy. Tell 'em just to sit on 'im till I give 'em the word." He looked at Weissberger. "There's another small step along the way. We'll get the son-of-a-bitch."

16

Jordan Kraft, the president of Kraft, Lutz, McMullen, and Perez, Accountants, was ushered into the corner office of the penthouse floor. The chair behind the desk was empty. The guard who had escorted him dropped into the big armchair, where he sat fondling his M-14.

Kraft looked around, wondering when the man in charge would appear. The guard who'd brought him in and who talked like a redneck southerner did not have the voice that had made the stereo speeches. Kraft noticed the briefcase on the desk, and of course the walkie-talkie, and the packing crate behind the desk, its lid pushed slightly to one side to allow a glimpse of a row of other briefcases, standing upright.

Kraft looked at the masked guard in the armchair.

"Jus' take it easy," the guard said. "He'll be here in a minute."

"I've got all night," Kraft answered. "At least, that's what I've been led to understand."

"You understand right." The guard scrutinized Kraft. "You just do nothing but figures all day?"

"The computer does the figuring. All we do is feed the numbers in."

"Don't that get old in a hurry?"

"Sometimes."

"You ever in the service?"

"Yes."

"Like it?"

"Not too much."

"Ever kill anybody?"

"I was a navigator in the Air Force."

"That a real silk suit you're wearing?"

"No."

"It's a nice suit. I like the way it looks."

"Thank you."

"That hair of yours. Do you comb it or just bend it where you want it to go?"

Kraft smiled and ran his hand back across his shapeless bush of wire hair. "I don't do much of anything to it. Looks about the same before and after."

"Can you cut it with a scissors or do you need nips?"

Kraft laughed. "Is it your job to warm up the audience before the star comes on?"

The guard stiffened in the big chair. "Don't get fancy. We got a license to hurt people."

Kraft's smile faded. "We're all well aware of that."

"I'd take that suit offa you, only it wouldn't fit. I might take it anyways, and give it to somebody."

While Kraft was trying to think of a safe response, a door opened and another man in fatigues appeared. He was taller and carried himself in an assured manner. Kraft immediately noticed the captain's bars.

"How do you do, Mr. Kraft," the man said. "I'm expecting dinner to be served very shortly. But I thought we might as

well get our little business discussion out of the way before-
hand. Then you'll be able to go back and relax and enjoy your
meal."

At street level Park Avenue was assuming its evening character. The sun was gone, as was most of the daylight, and the
sodium-vapor streetlamps compensated with their yellow-
white illumination. The street was strangely quiet, and many
of the windows looking directly onto it were dark, but the city
surrounding Park Avenue was very much alive. The Pan Am
Building towered regally over it at Forty-fifth. As the sky darkened, lighted windows in the skyline grew more brilliant.

An NYPD building-and-maintenance truck followed a radio car slowly out of one of the large open bays on the side of
the Waldorf, "The Well," as this entrance was often called by
the cops in the Seventeenth Precinct. The big van, with blue-
and-white markings like radio cars, moved up to Park and
turned north in the southbound lane, unmindful of the one-
way signs. It went the short block to Fifty-first, then maneu-
vered backward to bring its tailgate to the edge of the wide
sidewalk just behind the parked bus.

Four cops wearing heavy ceramic vests and carrying carbines emerged from the radio car to provide cover. Two uniformed officers climbed down from the passenger side of the
cab and went around to the rear of the van. The corrugated
rear door rolled into the ceiling, and two more officers inside
pushed a cart completely covered by a white tablecloth onto
the motorized tailgate. One officer rode down with the cart,
holding it with both hands to prevent any mishaps.

The doors to 330 were opened by three masked soldiers
holding rifles. "Jus' push it on in through the door," the tall
black one said. "We'll take it from there." He nodded to one
of the others, who slung his rifle over his back and then pulled
the cart into the lobby.

The officers struggled with cart after cart, transporting

them to the pavement on the narrow steel tailgate, managing somehow to avoid the complete disaster of having one go over the edge. As they sweated over them, the tall guard in the doorway maintained a taunting supervisory running commentary, "Easy does it . . . careful now, boy . . . not too fast . . . a little more to the left . . . steady . . . steady . . . watch it . . ." After the last cart was inside the door, he said to the cops, "Nice job, boys. I'll personally see to it you're well taken care of when we sign the check."

The guards began pulling tablecloths off the carts. In the middle of each cart stood a placard numbered between eight and twenty-two. Pedro was fascinated by the solid gold dishes on number twenty-two. Charlie reached into a bowl of iced shrimp and grabbed a handful. He began dipping them into the red sauce and stuffing them into his mouth. The third guard, Perry walked from cart to cart lifting the covers on the heated serving pieces and studying trays of canapés. "Jesus, what classy shit!" he said. "Old Dee's really done things right this time." He took a couple of iced shrimp and dunked them. "We gotta check these plates so we'll know what floor to eat on," Perry said with his mouth full.

"Take a plate now," Charlie said, "and then let's get this shit on upstairs."

Perry looked at the undershelf of one of the carts. "Christ, dig this wine."

"Forget the wine," Charlie said.

Pedro began lifting the bright silver covers on the hot serving trays. He stuck his finger in a tray of chicken curry and then licked it. Satisfied it was the spiciest thing he'd find, he filled one of the gold plates. He found a pepper shaker and sprinkled it heavily. He grabbed a napkin off the cart where he'd found the plate and unrolled it. His face lit up when he came to the solid gold service inside. Perry and Charlie went from cart to cart, picking things that appealed to them. Then they filled cups with black coffee from one of the gleaming urns that stood at the corner of each cart. Charlie took a separate plate and piled it with a selection of pastries for dessert. Pedro was already sitting on the floor, his back against a wall, eating out of gold.

"Okay, let's get this stuff loaded," Charlie said. He picked up his radio. "Boston."

"Boston."

"Lobby-A to the engine room."

"Engine room here. Hey, baby."

"We gettin' ready to load the food and bring it up. Usin' all cars."

"Save me somethin' good, now, man."

Both Charlie, in the lobby, and Luis, in the engine room above the penthouse, could watch the movements of all the elevators. Both men had been instructed to monitor elevator travel at all times, being sure all movements were accountable. Every trip was to be preceded by radio communication. Another of Devereau's controls.

Charlie and Perry loaded the cars, one cart to a car, and began delivering them. Within ten minutes they were all on their respective floors, being sampled by the guards. Charlie called Devereau, and Devereau called for another quick stereo to announce in a most gracious manner that dinner was being served. He even suggested taking dinner and wine first and coming back for desert and coffee.

Any reluctance or indifference the employees had about eating dissolved away when they saw the spectacle of the food. They quickly organized into lines and moved around the carts, piling their plates, ignoring the guards, who stood back to allow them free movement. Lunch had been light and they were hungry. The thoughts of the long day and the pain many had suffered seemed remote. A party-like atmosphere developed as they returned to their desks with dishes laden and dripping, linen napkins, and crystal glasses of estate-bottled French wines.

The twelfth floor was an exception. The employees were silent as they dutifully took food and ate as if at a funeral, even though the guards had brought the cart into the office area, away from the heavily bloodstained carpet in the foyer.

The hotel had equaled its reputation in preparing the meal. Although each cart held a different selection, all offered impressive arrays of exquisite food. Appetizers included shrimp, trays of mixed canapés, sturgeon, caviar, salmon, ham, assorted cheeses, Dungeness crab fingers, hot appetizers such as fried shrimp, chicken livers in bacon, and oysters Rockefeller. There were massive carvings of roast beef, ham, and turkey, all sliced and then carefully placed back on the frame or bone and glazed, hot serving dishes of beef Stroganoff and curries and delicately prepared vegetable casseroles, several kinds of salads, baskets of crisp rolls, and a variety of desserts, including Viennese pastries, cakes, sliced cheesecakes, and the Waldorf's famous macaroons.

The cart on the penthouse floor featured an ice sculpture of a leaping fish that held a dish of black caviar. Winfield Root moved around the cart with his gold plate, making his selections as if he were at one of his own parties. The others also ate heartily in spite of the menacing presence of the small, fierce guard with the M-14.

The strange festiveness continued on all floors until most employees had eaten themselves into a distressed state. Although most had been working across the street from the Waldorf for years, many had never eaten in any of its restaurants or dining room. The spectacular food was all they'd imagined it to be. The guards waited until employees had completed their first round and then took a plate of food and coffee. They sat on the floor and ate, their backs to the wall between the elevators, their M-14's across their laps. .

Devereau selected sparingly, caviar, crab fingers, a slice of rare roast beef. After hesitating a moment, he finally poured a small amount of the vintage red Bordeaux into one of the gold-trimmed wine glasses. As he was about to walk back to his office, Barbara appeared and began putting a little more meat on her plate. She followed him around the table, standing quite near him at times, but she did not speak to him.

In the headquarters van around the corner on Fiftieth, Ziller and Weissberger and the other cops took the logical opportunity of the dinner lull to eat dinner themselves, and they had plates of food brought in from the crepe restaurant. The dinner hour had to be working in their favor. Hostages and captors were in very close contact, sharing a memorable feast.

Devereau savored the rich coffee a minute or two longer and then put the gold cup and saucer with the gold teaspoon aside. Stroud and Smokey were in Ronam's office. He picked up his radio. "Boston."

"Boston here."

"Penthouse-A to Four-A."

"Four-A here."

"Proceed to the eighth floor and get dinner for yourself, Four-B and Two-B. Suggest you look around for something to use as a tray so you can manage in one trip—"

"Dee, we gotta talk to you. We gotta get some help for Roberto. I think this hit he got is a little worse than—"

"You dumb bastard! Stick to code names."

"I don't give a shit about code names. Roberto's losing a lot of blood. I think we gotta get him some help."

"I'll be down to see him shortly. Meanwhile, you see to it that all three of you get fed."

"Dee, this is Roberto." The voice was weak, the words separated by gasps. "Listen, man, you get me some help, you hear? Money ain't gonna do me no fucking good if I'm dead."

"I'm aware of your condition, and I promise you I'll get you a doctor in plenty of time."

"I hear you, man, only it's my fucking blood. Dee . . . get me some help."

"Take it easy. I'll see you in a few minutes. Penthouse-A to Basement-B and engine room. Basement-B, I'll be sending engine room down to take over. You bring Palko up here to the penthouse so you and he can eat. And I want to meet Mr. Palko. Both of you got that?"

"Engine room to Penthouse-A. When do *I* eat?"

"Walk down and pick up a plate on the way. Either of you have any further questions?" No response. "Then ten-four," Devereau said.

Within minutes Luis showed up, a silly grin on his face.

"Where's your mask?" Devereau shouted. "And where the hell are your weapons?"

"The mask got lost. The cleanup crew, I think. Somebody use it for a jizz-rag. I couldn't put it on. And the guns, I guess they take them, too."

"Didn't you even look for the goddamn things?" Devereau said, staring at Luis.

"The mask don't make a shit," Luis said. "Everybody here know I'm mixed up in this thing. What is the difference, anyway? We'll be outta here tomorrow."

"You dumb shit! Didn't you leave that room locked up last night?"

Luis shrugged. "I thought I did."

Devereau shook his head. "You can't go down there unarmed," he said finally. He pulled out his own automatic and tossed it to Luis. "See if you can avoid losing this one."

"Everything gonna be okay, " Luis said.

"Jesus," Devereau said. "I wonder how many more fuck-ups this caper can survive?" He sat for a moment, after watching Luis' hurried retreat. Then he took his cup and saucer and went out for more coffee. Luis was shoveling food onto one of the gold plates, one thing on top of another.

"I going right now," Luis said. He stacked a fancy pastry on the pile in his plate and then pushed the elevator button.

"Got silverware?" Devereau asked.

"No. Where?"

Devereau handed him a rolled napkin. "You're going to like this when you open it."

The elevator door opened. Luis stepped in and was gone.

Devereau took his hot coffee back to the desk. Good coffee. Exceptional. Black. Astringent. Bracing. . . . His reverie was broken by the radio. "Boston."

"Engine room calling Penthouse-A from basement."

Devereau put down his coffee and picked up the radio. "What is it, engine room?"

"They gone." Luis shouted. "Nobody's down here. Sally. Palko. Nobody."

17

"How can they be gone?"

"I don't know. They just gone."

"Penthouse-A to Lobby-A. You listening to this?"

"Every word."

"Where can they be?"

"They ain't been through the lobby. And they ain't been on the number-four car, which is the only one that goes down there."

"Then how could they get out?"

"All I know is they didn't come this way."

"Go down and take a look around. Then call me."

Within minutes Big Charlie was back on the radio. "No trace o' nobody. Like Luis said, Dee, they gone."

Devereau wiped his damp palms on his thighs. He thought about how much he wanted another shower, how much he wanted to just stand under the healing warm water.

"Four-A calling Penthouse-A."

"What, goddammit?"

"When you coming down here to look at Roberto?"

"Haven't you been listenin' to what's going on?"

"Roberto's passed out, man. You gotta do something."

"One thing at a time!"

"Then this is the one thing, man. Turn him over to the cops. Doing a coupla years beats being dead."

"I'll be down there in a minute. As soon as I learn what happened to those two in the basement. Now, end transmission. Ten-four."

"Hey, Dee!" It was Luis.

"What?"

"The service entrance is open. The door to Fifty-first Street!"

"You sure?"

"'Course I'm sure. It's padlocked all the time. Me and Palko have the only keys."

A wave of nausea swept over Devereau. Less than ten minutes ago he had been giving a dinner party. The picture of a dam crept into his mind. A dam holding back a vast body of water. A small hole appeared near the bottom of it, and a rivulet of water began to flow. The hole spread as if the dam were composed of nothing but sand. Another hole appeared, near the first, and he had the feeling, as he watched both holes enlarge, that as soon as the two expanded to meet, the whole dam would wash away. . . .

He took a deep breath. "Lock the door again."

"You think they've gone?"

"It doesn't matter. Fuck them both. We don't need them. We're still in control here. Absolute control. They were both problems. Nothing's changed. Two less problems, that's all. Ten-four." He looked at Stroud and Smokey, who had come in from Ronam's office. "The radio fixed?" he asked Smokey.

"It's all right now." Smokey placed it on his desk.

"I need you back in the basement," Devereau said to

174

Smokey. "I'll send somebody down to cover it with you, but I want Luis back up on top."

After Smokey had left, Devereau said to Stroud, "I knew that son-of-a-bitch Panucci was no good."

"Palko must have jumped him," Stroud said.

"That weak son-of-a-bitch couldn't even hold one man captive with an M-14 and an automatic. Fuck 'em both! We don't need 'em!"

"Hey, Dee," Stroud said quietly. "Come on, now. Take it easy."

Devereau got up and started toward the elevators. "I've got to go to the fourth floor and see Roberto. Call and tell 'em I'm coming."

Ziller and Weissberger sat by the large brown radio unit that was monitoring the captain's private communications network in 330 Park. Ziller turned to one of the detectives handling the phones. "Get me the observation team across Fifty-first. The one in Manufacturers Hanover."

Within minutes the detective handed Ziller the receiver. "You guys still awake over there?" Ziller asked.

"Jesus Christ! That all you called for?"

"Well, if you're awake, why didn't you tell me two guys walked out of the back door of our fortress?"

"Nobody's come out o' there, Lieutenant. Christ, don't you know we'd have sent up a rocket if they had?"

"That's what I figured. Okay. Keep an eye on that door." Ziller turned to Weissberger. "Well, sport, what do you make of that?"

Weissberger shook his head. "The two of them are floating around in there somewhere. And obviously neither the captain nor any of the rest of his army knows it. It'll be interesting to see where they surface next."

"The plot thickens, eh, Watson?" Then, in a more subdued

tone: "You know, this makes me damn nervous. Because we got no idea who's doing what to whom. I've got to assume Palko took Sally—whoever-the-hell Sally is. The question now is, what did he do with him? And more important, what's he planning on doing next? One hero was quite enough for today."

Roberto Molina was unconscious but breathing. The three men struggled to get his fatigues unfastened enough so they could examine the wound in back as well as in front. They were unable to rip the coarse fabric of the fatigues, and finally one of the troops began looking around the offices, returning in a minute or two with a large pair of scissors. They hacked away at the cloth until the nature and extent of the wound was in view. One of the troops got up and ran toward the elevator foyer and the men's room.

Devereau reached in with his fingers. "You have to hold all this stuff inside," he said. "Like this. You have to keep it where it can stay wet. You can't let it get dried out."

"You talking to me?" He was the troop named Archie Stoner.

"Yes, you. Now, get your hand in here."

"I can't do it."

"We've got to get help. When I saw this thing before, it looked superficial. But Jesus, that slug really made a mess coming out. Now, get your hand down here and hold all this stuff in until I can get help."

"I can't, Dee. I can't."

"Goddammit, you can and you will. Now, do it. Right where I've got *my* hand. Think of it as something else. Meat you're about to cook. A chicken you're cleaning. Any damn thing. But get your hand down here."

"I ain't touching that, Dee."

"Goddammit, he'd do it for you. Now, you do as I say."

Devereau pulled his bloody hand back and wiped it off on the sofa.

"Dee, I like Roberto, and I wanta help him, but I can't touch that stuff."

"You'll do exactly as I say, or goddammit, I'll . . ." Devereau made a move for his automatic before he remembered that Luis had it.

Stoner was on his feet, his own handgun drawn and aimed at Devereau. "I ain't about to put my hand in that, Dee."

Devereau stared at Stoner's gun for several seconds. "Let me use your radio."

Stoner handed it to him.

Devereau held it in front of his mouth. "Boston."

People on all floors stood patiently in their familiar stereo positions and listened, through the haze of the memorable meal they'd just had, to the man's latest message. Some even wished they were doctors so they could do as the man asked. Give a little help to the one injured troop and and then be allowed to leave.

On the nineteenth floor Philip Gump of Herder, Friedlund, Morgolis, and Gump, Management Consultants, exchanged looks with his visitor, Dr. Ira Goldenbaum, as they listened. But he said nothing because he agreed with the message he read in the barely perceptible shake of Goldenbaum's head: anyone who admits to being a doctor will almost certainly become a permanent hostage to take care of all battle wounds suffered by the members of this little army.

Goldenbaum was an industrial doctor, an old-timer who had given up the pressures of private practice years back to run the dispensary and do the routine physicals for a big chemical company in New Jersey. One of Gump's clients needed such a man, and Goldenbaum had driven in to discuss changing companies.

Goldenbaum thought about the classic "Is there a doctor in the house?" coming from the man holding 330 Park, who was momentarily willing to bestow concessions and privileges on anyone with the necessary training. But Goldenbaum wanted to go home when the siege finally ended. He had been thinking all day that such a contingency might develop, and he didn't want to become physician to this regiment of criminals when it attempted its withdrawal. Besides, he had no instruments, no supplies. Let the man on the radio seek a different solution to the problem. The police had ambulances standing by.

Devereau listened to Roberto's erratic breathing as he waited another minute or two for a response. He finally signed off and told Stoner to just stay with Roberto until he could get help. When he reached the elevator foyer, he found Four-B, a car thief named Angel Gonzales, who had just come out of the men's room and reeked of puke. Gonzales refused to go back into the room where Roberto lay, because, as he put it, of the smell.

Devereau got back to the penthouse office and told Stroud to keep an eye on things a little longer because he had to take a shower. He looked at his hand, which still had traces of Roberto's blood on it.

"Ain't you gonna do something about Roberto first?"

Devereau avoided Stroud's eyes. "It'll have to wait a few more minutes." He paused. "I've got to decide what to do." He disappeared into the bathroom, and within minutes the shower was running.

Ziller studied the diagram of 330 Park. Wherever possible, he tried to identify the criminal on a particular floor. The list of names was growing. Luis Rodriguez had spent most of the day in the elevator engine room. Charlie Patterson was the big man in the lobby. Floyd Washington was in the building somewhere. Somebody named Stroud was in the penthouse,

along with the captain, who was sometimes refered to as D.
And Palko was in there. And somebody named Sally. Probably a paisan named Sal. These two could be anywhere. Even
the captain himself didn't know these two were in the building. But they were there. . . .

And Smokey Hampton. The electronics boys on the force
knew of him. Smokey Hampton, Mr. Bug. A real talent. Constantly being questioned on illegal wiretaps. Possessing and
selling the equipment. The whole list. But no convictions.
Mixed up with more than a couple of the less scrupulous private investigators in town, helping them bust up big-money
marriages. . . .

And Roberto. Poor son-of-a-bitch! A Puerto Rican named
Roberto with orange hair? An easy one for the M.O. section
guys. Roberto Molina, upper grand larceny, auto theft, disor-
derly conduct, youthful offender, assault with a dangerous
weapon. He had been indicted for the robbery of a supermar-
ket in Queens; no conviction. His alleged associate had been a
black named Perry Snodgrass. Could Snodgrass be in the
building too? Could he be one of the A's or B's? . . .

Every floor had an A and a B. Two guys to a floor? Some
operation. How the hell did the captain ever put together an
army of forty guys and keep them in line? But he's getting rattled. Too many little pieces falling out of place. Too much
room for screw-ups. Nobody could hold it all straight and
keep his cool. . . .

He doesn't want to kill. Could be his downfall. But how far
can he be pushed? We don't find this out by trial and error.
And what about the rest of those monkeys? Who knows what's
holding them together? One of them could freak out all over
the place. Long fucking night ahead. . . .

The phone. Well! Hello, D. I thought you'd never call. I'll
bet you want to talk about an orange-haired kid that's next to
dead. Right? Let's just see if'm right. . . . "Ziller."

"Ziller, I want you to get a surgeon over here right away.

Someone capable and equipped to button up a serious abdominal bullet wound. Everything's coming out his back. Whoever you send will be perfectly safe and will be released as soon as the job is done."

"You know that's impossible. It's against our rules to voluntarily add hostages under any conditions. We'll send an ambulance for your man."

"We'll give up a hostage in exchange. Five hostages. And we'll still let the doctor go."

"Not for a hundred trade-offs. You've studied our M.O. You know how we operate."

"Ziller, if this man dies, I'll hold you responsible."

"Feel free."

"Ziller, you get a fucking doctor over here or we kill a few hostages."

"Don't do it. You kill one person and it's a whole new ball game, and that's not what you want. What you want is money. Stick to your game plan. Anyway, I think your boy Roberto's hit too bad. He needs hospital equipment to have a chance."

"How do you know how bad . . . ? How did you know his name was Roberto?"

"Listen, the kid is better off in our hands than dead. Give him a break. He can't help you."

"Panucci! That little shit Sally Panucci told you."

"Look, instead of trying to get us to send in a doctor, you better start thinking about letting the rest of your hostages go. And coming out yourself. The longer you hole up, the greater the chance of more accidents happening. As for Roberto, he's already unconscious. You know he's got little hope without gettin' to a hospital. Let the kid live."

"How'd you know he's unconscious?"

"Why, you just told me how I knew everything."

"Bullshit! Palko and Panucci were out of here before I got word Roberto passed out. . . . Which I got by radio. . . .

Why, you son-of-a-bitch! You're plugged into our radio! You found our channel! Or have you got Panucci's unit?"

"What's important is to get Roberto some help."

"You just might have one of our radios," Devereau said thoughtfully. "I can't know for sure. If you do, you'll be able to follow everything that's going on. Even though you can't do anything about it. But its also possible you *don't* have one of our units. You may have located our frequency on your equipment. On the chance that that's the case, I think I'll try to tune you out."

"How? Your units have two channels?"

"You don't know? Then you couldn't have one of our radios. Thanks for tipping me off, Ziller, because now I can get rid of you again." He paused. "Get your fucking ambulance over here. That creep on twelve messed Roberto up pretty bad."

"It's on the way."

"I'll let you listen to my orders on this, Lieutenant Ziller, and hope that's the last thing you'll hear on our network."

Within seconds his voice was coming out of the radio monitor. "Boston." Ziller and the others gathered to listen.

"Boston."

"All stations. I've examined Two-B. His condition is out of control without hospital care. In view of this, I've sent for an ambulance. There was no choice."

"I want one man from floors eight through twelve to report to the fourth floor so Roberto can be carried out without being moved from his sofa. Now, one more announcement. All stations, switch your radios to channel B. I repeat, all stations, switch your radios to channel B. And with that, good night, Lieutenant Ziller."

Ziller looked around at the other policemen. "Well, what do you think, Jerry?"

"I think he's incredible," Weissberger answered. "And he's flying again, because he just won himself another battle."

"Dual-channel radios, no less," Ziller said. "Gotta say one thing. He's resourceful. And we haven't got the time to pick up his second channel." Ziller paused for a moment. "But he hasn't won this battle, because it ain't over." His tone became determined, almost desperate. "The time has come to move in and take the repeater. Murphy . . ."

The observation team on the fifth floor of the ITT Building spotted a glowing cigarette in the darkness of the fifth-floor corner office of the Root Tower. One of them quickly focused a portable night-viewing device, their "Owl-eye," a light-amplification unit capable of revealing the contents of a darkened room by the light from a single cigarette. They studied the man smoking for several minutes. He was sitting calmly at a desk in the darkness, enjoying his cigarette.

One of the detectives dialed a phone, using the carefully shielded beam of a tiny penlight to see the numbers on the dial. "Let me speak to Ziller," he said.

"Ziller."

"Lieutenant, this is Martinez."

"Julio. Whatcha got?"

"This is crazy."

"I don't doubt it. Lay it on me, anyway."

"One of the men in there is sitting in a dark office on the fifth floor, by himself, smoking a cigarette."

"One of the troops?"

"He's wearing fatigues. He's got an M-14 and a radio on the desk in front of him."

"What about the mask?"

"He ain't wearing it."

"What does he look like?"

"Thin face. He's sitting down, but I'd guess he's tall and fairly slim. Short light hair. Bad complexion. Noticeably pocked."

"Keep watching him. Let us know every move he makes."

Ziller turned to Weissberger and said, "Looks like Palko has surfaced."

"Where do you think Sally Panucci is?" Weissberger asked. "And in what condition?"

"God only knows," Ziller answered. "But what's worrying me is having a civilian in there, armed and in costume, thinking up ways to get into the action."

"It's going to be an interesting night," Weissberger said.

"Stick around," Ziller said.

18

The ambulance was waiting. The six men carrying the sofa hated their load. It was heavy, and Roberto was giving off a distinct and unpleasant odor. Just as Angel said. He refused to help carry it. He wouldn't come near. Getting the sofa onto the elevator was a problem, too. They finally managed to get it aboard by lifting one end above their heads and holding Roberto in place. They looked away and held their breath during the short ride down. Once on the terrazzo of the lobby, they were able to slide it at arm's length. And gulp air.

They pushed the sofa toward the door. Charlie unlocked the chain, and he and Pedro pulled the doors open. The sidewalk was alive with cops, some waiting by the wheeled stretcher, others with shotguns providing cover. Charlie and Pedro stood with their M-14's and exchanged looks with the Special Service cops while the other troops carried the couch to the sidewalk.

Archie Stoner suddenly remembered that Roberto's radio was still in one of his pockets. He started to go after it, but the others restrained him. The stretcher was already disappearing into the ambulance. They watched as it headed downtown, lights flashing. The blood-soaked sofa remained in the middle of the sidewalk.

Floyd hung back as the other men returned to their assigned floors. Charlie sensed that Floyd wanted to talk and followed him to a corner of the lobby. Floyd opened the door to the fire tower and stepped through. Charlie followed him.

"All right," Charlie said. "What?"

Floyd held up a small transistor radio. "I picked this up off a desk upstairs, and I been listening to it."

"Don't imagine anybody's gonna run after you to get it back."

"I been listening to the news."

"They talking about us?"

"You know how much bread he's already got up there?"

"No."

"Over five million bills."

Charlie remained silent.

"Do you know how much that is, man?" Floyd's eyes gleamed through the slits in his mask. "And that's just from a few companies. He ain't got to some of the big ones yet. Like the one that owns the whole building."

"So what?"

"So what? Shit, man! I been figuring. He's already got enough to give all of us our hundred and still have more'n a million left. You know what that means?"

Charlie didn't answer.

"That means we're getting a royal fucking," Floyd said. "That's what that means."

"This is his show. We work for him. He made us a deal and we took it. He's paying for everything and arranging everything."

"That's bullshit. You already saw what happened to Roberto. I say we go to him and do a little renegotiating."

"When's the last time you had a hundred grand? You know how much that is?"

"Charlie, get smart, man. You know what else they been sayin' on the radio? The cops been asking for information on anyone that quit their job last Thursday. That make you think of anybody in particular?"

"Listen. For now he's the onliest way we got of gettin' outa here. Let's get where we're goin' and then talk to him."

"My way's better. We got to talk to him now."

"Nobody likes money better'n me, Floyd. You know that. But if we don't get outta here, no amount of money's gonna make a difference."

"I don't like getting screwed. I'm gonna talk to some of the other boys 'n' see what they think."

The rooms near room 11-S in the Waldorf had been evacuated earlier, and the corridor was filled with cops and detectives who moved silently on the heavily padded carpeting, talking when necessary in guarded whispers. In rooms adjacent to 11-S, detectives sat with stethoscopes pressed to the walls.

Across the hall Murphy sat in one of the bedrooms talking to Ziller on the phone, planning strategy. They had to catch Boston when he was away from his radio so 330 Park wouldn't know what had happened. The problem was the hour. They might have gotten in earlier with room service when the man ordered dinner. But chances were he wouldn't order anything else, and any attempt to force the door might give him too much time to call the captain.

"Hold it," Murphy said suddenly. A detective was signaling from the corridor. He put down the phone and walked toward the door. The detective met him and whispered something. Murphy came back to the phone. "Harry. We got a shot right now. Looks good. I'll call you in a few minutes."

Murphy went into the corridor and glanced into one of the

adjacent rooms where the detective with the stethoscope made an affirmative gesture with his fist. A cluster of cops poised around the door to room 11-S. One of them turned a passkey in the lock as soundlessly as possible. As expected, the door didn't budge. On a signal from Murphy, a cop put a fire ax through the upper panel of the door. He reached quickly through with his hand and turned the dead latch and lifted off the chain.

The hapless little man in the bathroom had managed to stand up, but he had not had time to pull up his pants. And with his arms poking frantically at the ceiling as he looked at the guns aimed at him, his pants remained around his ankles. Murphy grinned broadly. One of the secrets in handling stake-outs is knowing the exact moment to move in. And in this particular case, well, there are certain noises in nature which are unmistakable.

One of the detectives in the van yelled to Ziller that Renzolo was calling from the ambulance.

"Alphonse. How bad is this one?"

"He's a mess, Harry. A few hours earlier and his chances woulda been a lot better. But the reason I called now, he's still got his radio on him."

"Jesus, lemme see if I can stop Murphy. Get back here with it as quick as you can." He hurriedly dialed the hotel, but he was sixty seconds too late.

Murphy explained how they'd broken in. The man handling the repeater radio was "a dried-up little Hispanic named Alfredo Medina."

Ziller told Murphy they'd just acquired a radio and to keep the repeater unit where it was. The unit was to be left "on" and Murphy was to pick a cop to sit by it and say "Boston" every time the call came in from 330. The cop had to sound as much like Medina as possible. Murphy asked what the cop should do if someone from 330 tried to make conversation.

"Tell him to make conversation back," Ziller answered. He then suggested they talk to the old guy and try to get a handle.

Murphy said Medina claimed that he didn't know who the captain was and added that someone had done a good job of convincing the old man that he could refuse to answer questions and get away with it, or maybe he just had more to fear from the captain than from the police.

As soon as Ziller finished talking to Murphy, a detective named Zocco phoned. Zocco had been handling incoming calls responding to the radio and TV requests for information on possible perpetrators. "This guy sounds good to me, Lieutenant. Claims he has a feeling he might know the guy in charge of the whole thing. And he sounds like a real straight type. A solid citizen. Lives out in Nyack. I asked him lots of questions and got good answers. He doesn't read like some turkey who's just trying to make the scene. Whadd'ya think?"

They reviewed the details of Zocco's interrogation of the caller. Ziller told him to have the Rockland County police run him down to the van. It was worth checking out.

"What time do your bankers get to their offices?" Devereau asked.

"I really don't know," Ronam answered. "I'd guess nine-thirty."

"We'll put you on the phone at nine tomorrow morning and give you exactly ninety minutes to get the money out of the Federal Reserve and over here. We want to pull out as early as possible, tomorrow."

"You can't be serious about the amount."

"What, seven million dollars? It's only roughly a quarter of your cash surplus. What are you complaining about?"

"That's a great deal of money."

"I've been thinking about increasing it. Why the hell not? This whole thing has lost its intellectual appeal, anyway. Two people have been shot as a result of the stupidity of that asshole on the twelfth floor. A couple of other things have screwed up. . . ." Devereau rattled on, as if talking to himself, as if Ronam weren't in the room. "All the kick's gone out of it. The goddamn cops keep interfering. . . . But the bastards know they're dealing with the biggest thing in their fucking lives. You can bet on that. The biggest thing in their whole fucking lives. Time to teach them a lesson. . . ."

"Couldn't you reconsider on the amount of money?"

Devereau looked up abruptly. "The amount is ten million dollars!"

"Ten!"

Stroud brought his hand down across Ronam's face. "Who the fuck do you think you are?" he snapped.

"Don't you know better than to yell at me?" Devereau asked. "Do you want me to increase the amount again? How does twelve sound?"

Completely subdued, Ronam said quietly, "I apologize for shouting."

"In that case, we'll leave the amount at ten."

"And you'll let everyone out of here then?"

"As soon as I count the money."

Ronam weighed that last statement a moment. "Are you planning to take some of our employees as hostages when you leave?"

"We'll let you know tomorrow."

"Can't you tell me now?"

"Your nagging questions are making it difficult for me to continue to treat you with the dignity called for by your position. Isn't it better not to know? If I told you now that I was taking you with me, think how poorly you'd rest through the night." He turned to Stroud. "I've had enough of him. Get his ass out of here."

Stroud gripped Ronam's arm and led him out.

Devereau opened his notebook. He had originally intended taking the floors in exact ascending order, but he was behind his timetable. And since the Root Corporation was to make the single largest contribution, he'd decided to lock it up and then proceed with the others.

Raising the ante had been easy. An extra three million dollars by merely saying the words. Most satisfying. He could have had more. Why limit the take to only a quarter of each firm's cash surplus? Why not half? Why not all? No. That lacked class. A half. Half the cash position. That had an elegance about it. The first eight firms had gotten off light. It pays to be on a lower floor. The rest? Increase to one-half. . . .

He began turning pages in his notebook, one for each individual company in the building. On each page he drew a single precise line through the number jotted there and wrote another one beneath it. It was obviously just as easy to ask for a half as to ask for a quarter. Particularly when the other party to the negotiation could only say, "Whatever you say, sir." Unilateral negotiations. A contradiction of terms? So? This was not an exercise in semantics. This was a demonstration of achievement through superior intellect. . . . Right, Rudy? Didn't I tell you, sweetheart? What do you think of this kid now? How about it, Boston Latin? Not bad for the kid from Dorchester. . . .

A slight noise made him look up. Barbara Meyner was standing in front of him. "What are you doing in here?"

"Nobody saw me come in. I was careful." She slid into Stroud's empty chair. "I understand a lot of things now," she said. "I've been thinking about it all day. It's no fun to realize you've been used, but I don't give a damn, and I'll tell you why. It doesn't matter why you started seeing me. No one can convince me that you didn't really get involved."

"It was great."

"Then let me get to the point. I'm not concerned with what the past means. Only what's ahead. . . . Take me with you."

He remained silent.

"We can just pretend I'm one of your hostages," she said. "Don't you see? It'll be easy. And if you think we've had something special up till now, can you imagine . . . ?"

"Did you know that I was fired by the Root Corporation?" He said it abruptly, changing the subject.

"You what?"

"I was fired by this company. Can you believe that I was once one of the old man's favorites? Then *he* went out of style. He got old and turned into a little old lady. And I became 'a problem' for the director of personnel." Devereau laughed. "I should send my guys to kick that son-of-a-bitch's ass all over the twenty-first floor. Except that, in the final analysis, he did me a favor."

"I don't remember ever seeing you here."

"I left shortly after you were hired."

"But you remembered *me*." She smiled. "There are others you could have picked. True?"

"True."

"Do you know what it felt like to recognize you this morning? And do you know what people are saying about you, and this whole business, and what you're doing?"

"Of course I do."

"Why, this is the most incredible . . . "

"It's my life's work." He leaned forward. "Can you possibly understand that?"

"How much money will you have when you leave?"

"Considerable."

"And where will you go?"

"Forget it, Barbara."

"I don't even care where. Larry, I want to go with you."

"You must be out of your goddamn head."

"Why? What do I have here that's so wonderful? A secretarial job? One and a half rooms in the East Seventies? Larry, I've been thinking about it all day. Look how easy it would be to take me as a hostage."

"I can't see where you fit into things any longer."

The excitement faded from her expression. "You mean you don't need me? Is that it? Do you know, you once told me the most hateful three words in our language are 'who needs you?'"

"Look, you can't stay here. As for going along tomorrow, if you feel what we've had till now was good, let it end that way. Keep what you've got."

"I don't believe that's what you want." Visibly shaken, she looked at him for a few seconds and then got up to leave.

Winfield Root appeared in the doorway. He saw Barbara and said, "Why are you in here? Do you know this man?"

"Yes," she answered quickly.

"How?"

"He's my lover." She said it without hesitation.

Root frowned and touched his hearing aid as if he wasn't certain it was working. "Devereau, I just remembered who you are."

"Congratulations," Devereau said.

"What you are doing is an outrage. It could end in tragedy."

"It won't be my fault if that happens. I've taken every possible precaution. What I can't control are acts of stupidity like the one that occurred on the twelfth floor."

"Larry, there are easier ways of making a great deal of money than this. Why didn't you come to me?"

"This seems to be working very well."

"The down-side risk is rather great if you fail, don't you think?"

"I don't intend to fail."

The old man's expression changed. His face became almost elfin. "What's your bottom line? What do you expect to net?"

"Enough to justify my investment and my commitment."

"And it's tax-free," the old man commented with his playful smile.

"And completely negotiable," Devereau added.

"I feel like I'm listening to a conversation between two dear old friends," Barbara observed.

"That once was true," Devereau said.

"You may as well remove your mask," the old man said. "We know who you are."

"You realize that that places you in a position of considerable jeopardy," Devereau said.

Root looked at him. "I'd be hard pressed to believe that."

"I'd still recommend that you treat the information with great discretion. The police don't yet know my identity." He looked up at Stroud, who had returned, and then back at Barbara and the old man. "Now, if you two will excuse me." He nodded at Stroud. "Please show them out."

After they had left the room, Devereau picked up the receiver and dialed Ziller. "How's Roberto?" he asked.

"His prospects would have been better if you hadn't kept him without help for six hours."

"Goddammit! Just give me a factual report."

"Why don't you break this thing up before we have more shooting? It's bound to come."

"Just give me the report on Roberto."

"They took him into the operating room. That's all we know."

"Why can't you talk to the point like that all the time?" He paused a moment. "Incidentally, just in case you *do* have Sally Panucci's radio, which I doubt, don't try to use it for transmitting. Or I won't be responsible for what may happen. Is that clear? *You'll* have to assume that responsibility. I think I'll call the media again and explain the situation so the public will know who's to blame if any other incidents occur."

"What's so bad if I tune in and chat with some of your boys?"

"You direct all communications to me."

"But what if I wanta talk to Charlie Patterson? Or Luis Rodriguez? Or Floyd Washington?"

"Listen, you son-of-a-bitch—"

"Or maybe Smokey Hampton? Or Stroud?"

A prolonged pause. "Ziller, if I hear your voice coming out of this radio, I'll kill a hostage. That clear?"

"But I don't understand. Can't you control your men well enough so that nothing I could say would get to them?"

"I told you how it's going to be. Feel like testing me?"

"But why? You've got it made. As long as you've got even one hostage, you know there's no way we can touch you. And what you want is to show the world a clean, successful caper with you making lots of money and no killing. Right?"

"Then let's keep it that way."

"So what can it hurt if I chat with a few o' your guys?"

"Don't push me, Ziller."

"Look, I'm not on the radio now. It's just you and me."

"So?"

"So we can be realistic. You made a mistake starting this whole thing. Walk away from it now, before it gets more complicated. You know that as the night wears on, things are gonna start happening in that building. And even if you're not willing, give your men a little freedom of choice. Maybe some of them'll feel like getting out now. That's all I wanna talk to them about. Just tell them if they leave now, they get the best deal."

"Ziller, I'm telling you again. If you go on our radio, I'll have one of the hostages executed. And now I'm sick of wasting time talking to you. I've got work to do." He hung up.

Ziller turned to Weissberger. "Whaddaya think?"

Weissberger rolled his eyes. "I don't think he's got the stomach for killing. Still, he keeps reiterating the threat. And by doing that, he's pushing himself into a corner. But you've got one thing going for you. He was on the phone, not the radio. He doesn't have to worry about losing face."

"You know," said Ziller, "I have a feeling he knows exactly what he's doing."

"You going to call his bluff?"

"When the time is right. I've gotta reach his soldiers. We have to start breaking this thing up."

Just then O 'Reilly came in leading a stranger. "Harry, this is the man from Nyack who thinks he knows our captain."

The stranger shook hands and said his name was Rudy Milzer. When he heard the radio announcement, he remembered a friend of his who'd left his company the previous Thursday. Milzer said that when he talked to Detective Zocco, every question Zocco asked seemed to fit his friend exactly.

"Let's get him on the phone," Ziller said. "You can listen on the speaker. But don't say anything, even if you recognize him." Ziller started to dial.

Before he finished dialing, a "Boston" issued from Roberto's radio, which stood on his desk.

"Boston," answered the cop on the repeater. His accent was close if not perfect. Ziller smiled. New York cops are versatile.

"Penthouse-A calling Twelve-A."

"Twelve-A here."

"Bring me Donald Gertziger right away. Time for his interview. . . ."

"That's him!" Milzer said. "Christ, yes, it's him."

"What's his name?" Ziller asked.

"Larry Devereau."

19

Midnight. Behind the barriers on Park Avenue, the level of activity was still unusually high. The night was clear, and curious onlookers continued watching the best free entertainment in town. This was the real thing. The biggest event in New York in a long time.

Many of the people in the crowd had friends or relatives in 330 Park, and their presence was a vigil. To others it was a circus. The operator of a frankfurter cart set himself up near the van on Fiftieth and was enjoying a brisk business.

Cops milled around in great numbers, some occasionally in bulky bulletproof vests, carrying shotguns and other heavy weapons. A PBA food-service truck moved in and out of the sealed-off areas, serving coffee and soda and sandwiches on hard rolls to cops on the inner barriers or wherever they found them. In addition, an unsolicited Salvation Army truck circulated beyond the outer perimeter, providing coffee and lemonade and the more spartan Salvation Army sandwiches for any of the traffic-control officers who wanted them. New

York cops had a special appreciation for the Salvation Army, because somehow their truck always seemed to be able to find hungry cops on special duty.

A few newsmen, some with cameras, and TV crews moved among the crowds, waiting for the next bit of action. The street was strewn with TV cables. Some of the other newsmen sat at the bar in the crepe restaurant discussing, among other things, where they'd set up if the restaurant decided to close.

A wholesome-looking young girl walked among the crowds, engaging men in conversation. As soon as she got a rap going, she revealed that she was a hooker and a good one. "Wanta go out?" she asked. "We could leave awhile and come back."

A flatbed truck carrying a huge object covered with canvas groaned up Forty-ninth and stopped alongside the Waldorf. Its lumbering journey had brought it from the police hangar at Floyd Bennett Field in South Brooklyn, across the Manhattan Bridge and up Third Avenue. Two cops climbed from the cab and mounted the deck of the trailer, where they removed the canvas, revealing the department's emergency-rescue vehicle, a monstrous device weighing twenty-one tons and resembling an oversized tank. Although not equipped with weapons of any kind, it was converted from an outdated G.I. armored personnel carrier and constructed of bulletproof armor. O'Reilly, following procedures, had had it brought to the scene.

In the police van Ziller and Weissberger interviewed Milzer at length about Devereau. Milzer recalled conversations from months and years back that meshed dramatically with their observations and conclusions about the man in the penthouse.

O'Reilly, refreshed after a short nap, was on the phone to the current-situation desk at headquarters. He instructed the desk to call a complete tactical think-tank session for two A.M. at Seventeenth Precinct headquarters. He approved overtime if necessary for the two busloads of cops from the Tactical Patrol unit being deployed in the area, and arranged for additional men if needed. Should a shooting war break out, a very large complement of men would be required to deal with the forty men in 330. The Mobile Security Force, the six best sharpshooters in the department, were already stationed with the observation units in surrounding buildings.

In the penthouse Devereau interviewed Donald Gertziger, the general manager of Stanco Industries. Devereau was terse and impatient. He still had four more interviews to go, and he wanted to get them out of the way quickly. He was hours behind his schedule and no longer bothered to be polite. He simply glanced at the new number jotted on the notebook page and told Gertziger that three million dollars delivered in the morning would get him and his employees released alive. Devereau mentioned Quirke, emphasizing that Quirke had obviously been an idiot. Stroud stood over Gertziger, poised to respond to any reaction Gertziger might make. Gertziger accepted the information and instructions without reaction, and Stroud led him away.

In the engine room above the penthouse, Luis sat on a metal folding chair, monitoring the movements of the cars by watching the link chains and pointers on the consoles. When he was just sitting with nothing to do, he kicked at his balled-up mask on the floor, pushing it back and forth between his feet, fantasizing about what had taken place the night before when the mask had been used for cleaning up.

On the other occupied floors, employees, still aglow from the food and wine, were beginning to show the fatiguing effects of what was surely the most memorable day of their lives. But a night lay ahead of them in which they would hope to get some rest. The trick was getting comfortable. Executives with posh offices were faced with decisions on whether to keep their luxury to themselves or share it with employees in less posh surroundings. Some offices with thick carpeting became dormitories. Employees were thrown together under

the most extenuating conditions, and a close, giddy camarad-
erie had developed.

In the penthouse Winfield Root stretched full-length on the
sofa in Billy Marshall's office. Marshall sat deep in his large
chair with his feet on the desk, fully awake, wondering where
and how he'd ever find a situation that would allow him a little
sleep. He finally got up and went out to find some of the other
board members to see how they were managing. Barbara
Meyner sat at her desk, her arms crossed, staring into space.
She was very much awake.

On the elevator foyers the number of troops on each floor
has been increased to three. Those from the evacuated floors
had been redistrubuted. They began to relax their images as
sources of terror as the late hours approached. Employees
who came out to use the rest rooms often smiled at them and
occasionally even spoke a few words of inconsequential small
talk. For some of the employees the troops had become faceless benevolent protectors, men who were simply there to
guard them.

On the twentieth floor John McGlothlin plinked away at his
little spinet. On the eighteenth floor, the photographer's
model turned down the offers of office hospitality from Shaer
and Rhodes. She chose instead the sofa in Horace Bunbury's
office. He was obviously the safest of the lot. On the ninth
floor Terry Alvarez sat and talked with two other secretaries,
who were getting drowsy. Terry was fully awake, and she fre-
quently glanced at the closed door to Gene Schain's big corner office.

On the fifth floor Joe Palko sat in the dark, estimating the
number of drags left in the Camel he was smoking. The observation team in the darkened room in the ITT Building
watched him through their Owl-eye. He took another drag
and then ground the cigarette out. With this source of illumination gone, the cops lost sight of him for a moment. Then
they saw a column of light as he opened the door to the office

and walked out. They called Ziller to tell him that Palko had left, and Ziller told them to keep an eye out for him to reappear, there or elsewhere. He had the other observation teams briefed as well. Palko could be making some kind of move.

Palko walked silently through the fifth-floor offices, past old Bessie's desk, and into the deserted foyer. He had put on the mask. He stood for a moment and looked back and forth, moving finally toward the rear, or west, stairwell. He opened the door and started upstairs, walking lightly on the rubber cleats of his work shoes. He was dressed in the full gear of one of the troops—fatigues, the webbed belt with the radio and military handgun, and the M-14 rifle.

He walked up three flights, then paused to rest. He had to pace himself. After a couple of minutes, he started upward again. Taking the kid they'd left him with in the basement had been just as easy as he'd expected. He had been sitting on the floor, his back to the wall, and the kid had been at the desk holding the M-14. He'd gotten up casually and walked toward the kid, who sat up and pointed the rifle. "Hey! Where d'ya think you're going?" the kid had said, obviously scared out of his mind. He wasn't about to shoot anybody. "Relax," Palko had said. "Take it easy. I just wanna get another pack o' cigarettes outta the drawer here."

Once he reached the desk, it was all over. He leaned over as if to open a drawer and then grabbed the rifle barrel and pushed it upward. He slapped the kid hard and wrenched the gun out of his hands. "Now, take off the mask," he'd said. One look, and he knew he'd been right all along. A baby. A baby with guns he wasn't about to use on anybody. They'd picked the wrong one to leave guarding Joe Palko.

He'd taken the boy down into the subbasement and into the small power room that contained the circuit breakers and bus bars for the electric-power input to the building. "Now, strip," he'd told the kid. "Down to your skivvies. And after I leave you here, if you're smart you'll just sit right over here against the wall and stay away from all this copper. Because if you touch any of it the wrong way, you'll light up like a torch. You know what I mean? Matter of a couple seconds, and you'll be completely cooked. And just so's you won't be tempted to fool around with nothing, I'd better put the light out." He'd reached up with the barrel of the rifle and poked through the protective metal grille around the bulb, cracking it. It sparkled and fizzled out in a couple of seconds.

"You gonna leave me here in the dark?" the kid had asked.

"Look at it this way. You could get in trouble out there, running around with all these guns."

"But in the dark?" The kid had sounded choked.

"Just sit down and stay cool. And don't let the rats get you." Palko had walked out and locked the door, leaving the cell in pitch blackness. The kid'd started screaming as he heard the key turn, screaming his lungs out, but Palko had just kept on walking. They'd never hear him in the upper basement when they came back because of all the concrete and the noise of the heavy equipment.

Palko stopped to rest again. A few more floors to go. Leaving the back door unlocked had seemed a pretty good bet to make the rest of them think he'd taken the kid and left. And it had worked. Luis had found it open right on schedule . . . Luis . . . "Give Rodriguez a break," he'd told Pederson. "He seems like a decent enough guy to me, and if we don't give these guys with these minor records some kind of a break, what chance have we got of ever rehabilitating any of them? Besides, what kinda trouble can he get into as my assistant?" Palko started climbing again.

Luis looked up when he heard Palko's footsteps entering the engine room. "Hey, man," he said. He could see it was one of the troops, but he couldn't recognize which. "Hey, I can't tell who you are with the mask. . . ." Palko continued to walk toward him. Luis glanced at his shoes. They looked familiar. But whose? "Hey, man, which of the guys are you?"

Palko drew back his fist and slammed the side of Luis' head with all his strength, knocking him to the floor. Dazed, Luis tried to get to his feet, and Palko, resisting the urge to hit him with the butt of his rifle, swung his fist again, knocking him flat on the floor. Luis tried to roll over and get to his knees again, and Palko kicked him in the jaw, dropping him back. Luis was still barely conscious but smart enough not to try to get up again. Through the haze he had finally recognized Palko's shoes, and he tried to reach his handgun.

Palko stomped his hand, pulling the gun from Luis' holster. "Hey, pal," he said, "I guess you were up to something, after all." He stuffed Luis' gun into his own belt and then hit Luis once more on the point of his chin. Luis' head snapped back. "I may not hit you too much more, pal, because it's getting to be too hard on my hand. So take it easy and . . ."

"Boston."

Palko froze.

"Boston."

"Penthouse-B to Lobby-A and engine room. Advising movement on car four. Floors twenty-two to seventeen to eighteen and back to twenty-two."

"Lobby-A to Penthouse-B. Read you."

"Penthouse-B to Seventeen-A. Am coming to return Sutzman."

"Seventeen-A to Penthouse-B. Read you."

"Penthouse-B to Eighteen-A. Coming to pick up Shaer."

"Eighteen-A to Penthouse-B. Read you."

"Ten-four."

Palko looked down at Luis, who was still moving, not quite unconscious, but clearly unable to get off the floor. He walked quickly over to a tall metal cabinet and took out a thick extension cord and a pair of heavy-duty pliers. He returned to Luis and rolled him over on his stomach, cut a section of wire, and lashed Luis's hands together behind his back. "When I hired you, Pederson asked me if I could trust you." He stood up and pulled Luis to his feet. "I said, 'Sure, Pete.'" He sat Luis on the chair, forcing his arms over the chair back. "That's what I said. 'Sure, Pete.'"

Palko cut another section of the wire and tied Luis' arms to the steel frame. He used another length around Luis' waist. "'I'll take full responsibility,'" he said to the semiconscious Luis. "'Leave it to me,' I said." He cut two more short sections of wire and used them to bind Luis' ankles to the legs of the chair. He checked and tested all his knots. "Yeah, looks good."

Palko glanced around again. "Y'know, Lou, I think you oughta stay very quiet for a while. Know what I mean?" He picked Luis' mask up and after looking at it for a moment, stuffed it into Luis' bloody mouth. Luis' eyes flew open, and he tried to spit the ball of fabric out. "Now, take it easy, pal," Palko said, holding his hand on Luis' face. "I told you I think you need to keep very quiet for a while." He took another piece of wire and pulled it tight around Luis' head to hold the wadding in place. The wire cut into the corners of Luis' open mouth. He still tried to shout, but the sound was almost completely muffled, a barely audible bleat.

"You know, I'm starving," Palko said. "I didn't get none of that feast the rest of you guys had. I'll bet it was good, huh? Pretty good? That's some hotel over there. And there don't seem to be any way I can get any real soon at this point. I gotta eat something. I guess the time has come for me to sample those old G.I. biscuits." He walked over to a stack of corrugated cartons imprinted with civil-defense markings and ripped one open. "You know how long this stuff's been here? How many years? Jeez! You guys get fed by the Waldorf, and look what I get." He opened a tin and began eating. "Christ, this stuff is awful! But what're you gonna do? Maybe somewhere later I'll get to pick over a few leftovers from you guys." He continued eating. "Like to try some of these? Guess you can get used to 'em if you have to." He dropped the tin back onto the opened carton.

"Listen, I gotta be running along. But you stay up here and keep an eye on things. And gimme your keys in case I might need some extra ones." He reached into Luis' pocket and pulled out his keyring. Luis continued to look at him with a wide-eyed, silent stare. "I'll leave you your radio so you can keep up with what's going on."

He pulled Luis and his chair across the room to the door, opened it, and hung the back of the chair on the doorknob. Luis' feet were suspended several inches off the floor. "I put it on the line for you, remember? I said I'd take the responsibility for giving you a chance!"

He walked out the door and pulled it closed, leaving Luis swinging on the knob. Then he took one of the master keys out of his pocket. He had three of them—his own, Luis', and the one he'd found in the kid's fatigue suit. Apparently Luis' key had been copied for every troop in the platoon. He put the kid's key in the lock and then smashed the side of the key with his heel, breaking it off. If he had to get back into the room, he knew of another route. He started down the stairs.

"Boston."

Palko hesitated for a moment and then continued walking.

"Boston."

"Penthouse-B to Lobby-A and engine room. Advising movement on car four. Floors twenty-two to eighteen to nineteen and back to twenty-two."

"Lobby-A to Penthouse-B. Read you."

"How about you, engine room?"

Palko took two or three more steps.

"Come in, engine room."

Palko was between the twentieth and nineteenth floors.

"I repeat. Engine room. Come in, engine room."

Palko was between the nineteenth and eighteenth floors.

"Penthouse-B to Penthouse-A. Engine room not maintaining radio contact. Gonna walk up and take a look before making the elevator run."

"Penthouse-A to Penthouse-B. Make it quick. And kick the son-of-a-bitch's ass for falling asleep."

Palko reached the landing of the sixteenth floor, which was vacant. He hesitated for a moment. Would they have anyone stationed on an empty floor? He pressed his ear to the door and then peered under it. There didn't appear to be any light. He stood up and put his master key in the lock. He felt sweat running down his back.

The door opened onto a dark foyer. Wiping his face with his sleeve, he used the key again to enter the dark office area. Then he reached inside his fatigue suit to his shirt pocket and drew out his penlight. The offices were totally bare, the floors tiled. He went into the southeast corner office and again lit a cigarette.

The upper observation team in the ITT Building spotted the glow and turned their Owl-eye on him. They called their observation in to the van.

"Penthouse-B to Penthouse-A. Something up here looks queer. The door to the engine room's locked. And there's a key broken off in the lock. I tried banging on the lock, even with my rifle butt, and I ain't getting no answer. I don't like the looks of this."

"Penthouse-A to Penthouse-B. You're armed, for Christ's sake. Shoot the fucking lock. Blast the goddamn door open."

20

Jessie McMurtry had had very little trouble getting Haskell
Watts to marry her. In fact, she had him convinced that they
had a marriage made in heaven. He'd come to Charleston,
West Virginia, from his home in South Carolina, sporting a
crisp new degree in chemical engineering, all set to go to work
for Union Carbide. Jessie was a local girl, good-looking, full of
fun, very easy to get along with, and most of all, unbelievable
in the rack. After they got married, their first year or so was an
extended honeymoon.

But as time passed, there were moments when Haskell
questioned the divine origin of his marriage. Jessie could be a
little *too* outgoing at times. And sometimes her sexual insatia-
bility was too much of a good thing. Still, life in Charleston
was generally not too bad.

When Carbide promoted Haskell to a job in corporate
headquarters at 270 Park Avenue, they moved to the Big Ap-
ple. He was a sharp engineer, and after a year or so it became
obvious that he was doing extremely well. And he was on a

fast track. The first time he took Jessie to a social function where they were exposed to some corporate brass, it also became obvious that Jessie had not been growing along with him. As he met other women, Jessie seemed to get coarser. Before long, the marriage just didn't work anymore.

But Jessie Watts liked the big city. She was a skilled secretary, and she wasn't moving back to the hills of West Virginia when the demand for capable secretaries was so great in a swinging town like New York. Since she was making good money, she got herself a studio unit on the East Side and joined the singles race. Her pretty face and appealing drawl won her numerous dates, but she soon realized they were no more than one-night stands. And the tougher it got, the stronger she came on. She sensed that she was scaring the good ones away before they had a chance to put the make on her, but she couldn't seem to behave any other way. Restraint was not one of her attributes. Her needs called for lots of strong sex, and she telegraphed it.

She had been feeling particularly raunchy from playing back a near-miss the night before when the two masked guards came crashing into the office during the morning. The big one with freckled hands gave off that special electricity she sometimes felt when a one-nighter turned out to be like a week in the woods. She knew it was stupid to even think twice about him, but still. . . . She kept making trips out to the ladies' room, and as the evening progressed, it became clear that he shared her interest.

She glanced around the office. It was past twelve-thirty and things were getting pretty quiet. Nobody'd noticed that she'd been running to the ladies' room every little while. At least, nobody'd said anything. Maybe she'd just wander back out there and see what he was up to. . . .

"Here she comes again," Wayne Austin said to the other two troops as she walked through the door. "When did you boys ever see anything look that sweet?" He said it to them for her benefit. Then to her, "Hey, there, cutie."

"Hey, yourself," she answered. "Horses eat hay."

"You sure must be nervous about something, you come out to the head so often. What you so nervous about?"

"What makes you think I'm nervous? Maybe I just come out to wash my hands."

"They must be gettin' pretty clean by now."

"I'm just a clean girl."

"I think you been coming out here to see me. Bet you think this whole business is pretty excitin', don'chu?"

"I'm scared of all those guns, I don't mind telling you."

"No need to be. No need to be atall. I wouldn't hurt a pretty thing like you. Matter of fact, I'd like to do somethin' with you that would just feel pure good."

"With you?"

"Well, lookie there. Judgin' from that smile, you think it's a pretty good idea."

"Shoot. I don't even know what you look like."

"What difference does that make?"

"What difference? What kinda girl do you think I am?" She looked at Pickett and the other troop.

"I hope you're the kind I like," Austin said.

"What kind is that?"

"The kind that likes to do the same things I like to do." He rotated his hips just slightly as he said it.

"You're crazy. You know that?"

"Then why're you smilin'?"

She looked at Pickett again.

Austin said, "Why don't you and me sneak off for a smoke? These two boys'll stay here and mind the store for us."

"For a smoke?"

"Yeah. When's the last time you did anything as exciting as goin' off for a smoke with me?"

"What if one of your guns went off?"

"They ain't gonna go off no way unless I pull the trigger. And that ain't what I have in mind to pull. Going for that smoke could turn out to be the best part about this whole deal."

"You're just crazy out of your head."

"Come on, now. We ain't gonna have us a chance after tomorrow."

She looked at the other two for a moment. "Let's just say that suppose the idea did appeal to me. Not that it does. But just for the sake of talking about it. There's still no way we could."

"Are you kiddin'? Let's go. You leave the details to me."

"Go where?"

"We'll go down to the sixteenth floor. Sixteen's empty." He leaned his rifle against the wall and grabbed two cushions off a sofa facing the elevators. "These are to sit on while we smoke." He grabbed her hand. "Come on. Let's go." He pulled her over to the rear stairwell.

Pickett said, "Hey, you silly shit, you been listening to what's been coming over the radio. Don't you think you oughta wait and see what's going on upstairs?"

Austin released her hand and turned off his radio. "We won't be all that long. We're just going for a little smoke. Right, honey? You boys cover for me." He pulled the girl after him and disappeared through the door.

"That dumb bastard," Pickett said. to the other troop. "When his pecker gets hard, a fucking earthquake wouldn't stop him."

Palko stood in the dark, listening to the conversation on the radio. Penthouse-B sounded badly shaken.

"What is it, Penthouse-B?"

"Dee, you better come up here."

"Stick to code. What the hell's the matter with you? You

sound like you just saw a fucking ghost. And why do I need to come up there?"

"Just come up here, Dee. You hear me? And remember, I just did what you told me."

"Tell me what this is all about. I've got lots to do."

"Goddammit, just come up here!"

A pause. "I'm on my way. Ten-four."

Palko heard voices, live ones, and footsteps, coming toward him in the darkness. He turned squarely toward the sounds and held the M-14 in a firing position. He released the safety on the rifle. He remembered the radio and reached down and fumbled until he found the switch to turn it off. He could not remember having ever felt his blood pounding so furiously. In a moment they would be face-to-face in the darkness.

Then he heard the silly cackle of a female. Someone had brought a broad! Most likely one of the troops. Had to be. Nobody else had the freedom to move around. But what broad would take up with one of those creeps? . . . Still they were coming toward him. How the hell did he handle it?

"Let's take the big corner office."

Palko tensed up.

"Wait." The girl. "Let's go in here instead. I like the way the moon comes in through the window."

Palko exhaled slowly as he heard them walk into the office next to the one in which he stood. Their voices reverberated in the absolute bareness of the empty office area.

"You gonna close the door?" The female.

"Don't know what for. Nobody else around."

Palko relaxed slightly. Nothing to do but stay very cool for the moment.

"Boston."

"Boston."

"Larry?"

"Who the hell is this?"

"Larry, this is Lieutenant Ziller. Look, I wouldn't a called you on the radio, but I tried calling you on the phone and nobody answered. I got an idea for you. . . ."

"Goddammit, Ziller, get off my radio." Devereau turned his back to the sight of Luis' corpse suspended in the chair.

"Now, wait a minute. Take it easy. Lemme tell you why I'm calling, and—"

"I said get off this radio!"

"But it was the only way I could reach you. And I'm not asking to talk to Charlie Patterson or Floyd Washington or Stroud or Smokey or Luis Rodriguez or—"

"Attention, all stations! Ignore this son-of-a-bitch! There's no way he can stop us. Do you understand? There is absolutely no way he can stop us as long as we stick to our plan. I don't care how many names he's learned. Don't get taken in. We've got the hostages, and he can't touch us. Understand? Now, Ziller, you stay off our goddamn radio or we start killing hostages, and you can take the rap."

"But that wouldn't help you. At least listen to my idea. Ask some of your men if you shouldn't listen. Ask Patterson, or Hampton, or Rodriguez . . ."

"You can forget Rodriguez."

"Why?"

"He's dead."

"What happened to him?"

"That's what we're trying to figure out. Now, get off the goddamn radio."

"Was he shot?"

"Yes."

"By whom?"

"That's not the question."

"Whaddaya mean that's not the question?"

"Just what I said."

"Maybe he's still alive. We'll send an ambulance."

"He's dead."

"You can never be too sure. Why don't you leave that to the doctors and the medical examiner?"

"He's dead, you mother-fucker! Don't you think I can tell a dead man when I see one?" Devereau was shouting.

"Jesus. We got to stop all this shooting, Larry. Listen. Maybe some of your men would like to talk about coming out. Now's the time to get the best deal. Before anything else happens. To them or the hostages."

"They're not interested in your goddamn deals, Ziller! So get off the fucking radio!"

"How do you know, Larry? Let'em talk for themselves."

"Goddammit, Ziller, you're pushing me and you're gonna pay!"

"Then listen to what I'm calling you about. I promise you it's worth hearing. Just listen for a minute."

A pause. "Make it quick."

"Look, Larry. You know how we operate. We're interested in one thing, and one thing only—the safety of the hostages. And one hostage is as good as a thousand. If you had no more than one hostage per floor, you'd be just as secure as you are right now. And think how much easier your work would be. You could consolidate. Have everything under much better control. Less chance of any more accidents."

"You'd like that, wouldn't you, you son-of-a-bitch? You'd like getting a bunch of my prisoners out of here with just talk. Well, you can forget it, Ziller. I've heard nothing of interest."

"Then you do like the idea a little. Only you want something for the hostages. Wanta talk a deal? What kinda deal have you got in mind?"

"Hear that, men? Hear that, all stations? Does it remove any doubt from your mind as to who's in charge? Just get off the radio, Ziller. I'll call you when and if I feel like talking."

"For example, you could let just the women go. Look at all the potential problems you could avoid by doing that."

"If I want to talk, I'll call you."

"For all you know, some of your guys could be off somewhere with a broad right now."

"No chance of that. I know exactly where every man is at all times."

"Maybe so. But anything's possible. And you sure could avoid a lot of grief by getting all the women out of there."

"I'll make that decision."

"What about your men? Any of you guys want to talk to me? Charlie? Floyd? Smokey? . . ."

"Nobody speaks to him," Devereau shouted. "That's an order. . . . Ziller, I'm warning you."

"I just want to give them a chance. Let them know I'm as close as their radios. Listen, Larry, I'm ready to talk anytime."

"Fuck you, Ziller," Devereau said. "And ten-four." He looked at Stroud and had to control the sense of futility that was flooding him. Ziller had complete access to all their communications. Ziller practically walked among them. Calling him Larry. And Luis, who knew the most about the building, was dead. How had it happened? Who hung him there? A fucking phantom was loose in the building. Devereau kicked lightly at the edge of the suspended chair and watched Luis' corpse swing back and forth.

"Whadda ya wanta do with him?" Stroud asked. Devereau seemed to be in a trance. "Dee? Whadda ya wanta do with him?"

Devereau stared at Stroud for a moment. Then he said in a very restrained voice, "You bagged him. I guess you get to take him home."

"Come on, Dee. Whadda ya wanta . . ."

"Boston."

"Boston."

"Basement-A calling Penthouse-A."

Devereau looked at Stroud. After hesitating a moment longer, he held the radio to his mouth. "What is it, Basement-A?"

"We just found Sally."

"You what?"

"We just found Sally. Joe Palko locked him up in the sub-basement. Left him in the dark in the power room. Took his clothes, guns, radio, everything."

Devereau looked at Stroud. Palko was loose in the building! In full uniform, armed, masked, with a radio. . . .

"Sally was off the wall," Smokey continued. "Sitting there in the dark screaming about rats. It's gonna take a while to settle him down. Is there someplace we can get some booze or something? Dee?"

Palko was the phantom. He'd have to think a little about how to deal with this new development.

"Dee? You still there?"

"What is it?"

"You hear what I said?"

"We got booze in the penthouse office," Stroud said. "There's a whole bar in there."

"What about Sally? Where ya wanta take him?"

"Put him on one of the lower floors, say five," Stroud said. "I'll send you a bottle o' somethin' down there. Ten-four." Stroud looked at Devereau. "Whadda ya say, Dee? You all right?"

"Of course I'm all right. Let's go back to the office."

"Where'd you learn to do that so good?" Austin asked. "In West Virginia?"

"Nng."

"They must know something in West Virginia that they don't know in Kentucky where I come from."

"Nng."

"Any other time I'd say we could just go right on with you doin' exactly what you're doin' till about late Thursday afternoon. Of next week. But under the circumstances, much as I hate to stop you, I guess we'd better get on down to it."

A brief pause. "Okay."

"Man, that was good."

"We're just gettin' started, love. That was just the beginnin'. I'm gonna make you remember me."

Palko stood absolutely motionless, because the slightest sound carried so well. He considered tiptoeing by them. The chances were good he'd make it. They were over by the windows and pretty well occupied. But he decided not to risk it just yet. The biggest problem was that he couldn't turn his radio back on and follow whatever was happening. . . .

"Here. Lemme help you get that thing off. Anybody ever tell you that you had some kinda boobs? Your nipples are just like a coupla little hickory nuts. I never felt such hard nipples. . . . Where's the catch on these fuckin' pants?"

"I'll get it. I don't know what you're thinking about me right now. Considerin' I don't know your name and I've never even seen your face. But I do know that I just don't care."

"Here, now, lemme just peel these little ol' things off and give you a kiss on that pretty little belly of yours."

"Ohhh, God. . . . Hey, that mask kinda tickles."

"Come on down here. Guess maybe now you know why I brought these two cushions."

"You said it was so we could get on 'em and smoke."

"Wouldn't you say we were startin' to smoke a little?"

"Oh, honey, I'm not just smokin'. I'm gonna burn this place down. Is this big ol' thing all covered with freckles, too? I can't quite see in the dark."

"Honey, I'm just one big ol' freckled country boy from scalp to asshole."

"I really like doing it with your mask on. Makes it kinda special. Now I know how girls felt with Zorro."

"Zorro? Hell, he was prob'ly a country boy, too. . . . Man, you must be just about the softest, squeeziest lady that ever left West Virginia. . . . You about ready to start sawin' a few logs?"

"Honey, I've been ready since early this afternoon."

Their conversation gave way to soft thrashing sounds. Palko, his hand clutched about his silent radio, continued his vigil.

Devereau was back in the penthouse, seated at his desk. He picked up his radio. "Boston."

"Boston."

"Penthouse-A to Joe Palko. I repeat. Penthouse-A to Joe Palko. Attention, Joe. We are fully aware of your presence in this building. So are the police, because they are somehow tuned into our radios.

"Let me begin by complimenting you. Your handling of our man who was left to guard you was beautifully done. As you know, we have retrieved him, and he will be fine. But your planned execution of Luis was an absolute masterpiece.

"However I do not believe the police will excuse you of all responsibility for his execution. Even though you didn't actually fire the shots. But if you look at things my way, I can't see that it matters how the police take it.

"Joe, you have demonstrated to my satisfaction that you are both gutsy and resourceful. As a result, I have a most interesting offer to make to you. It may be a little unexpected. But then, I do the unexpected. Joe, come in with us. To begin with, I'll make you wealthy beyond your wildest dreams. Besides, in view of the circumstances, I can't see that your other options are anywhere near as attractive. So, do as follows. Proceed from wherever you are to the penthouse. I'm in the southeast corner office. My men are all listening and are aware of this proposal. I presume you know how to operate your radio unit. Use it now to establish communication." Devereau stared at his watch.

After fifteen or twenty seconds: "Joe Palko. Do you hear me? Joe, you're perfectly safe. You cannot be located by a radio signal." He waited a few more seconds. "Joe Palko. Do you hear me? If you're not familiar with the radio, here's what you do. Press the control switch on the side and talk into the speaker. We'll hear you. . . . Joe Palko. Do you read me?"

"He ain't gonna answer," Stroud said.

"Sure he will. If he heard me."

"No way."

"Do you think he's stupid? There are forty of us and one of him."

"You serious about wanting him with us?"

"With Luis gone, we need him. Besides, he's good."

"He's straight. How can you trust him?"

"Weren't you listening? Look at the stakes. And he's on the hook for Luis. What choice has he got? Besides, once we get to him, we own him. The trick is getting to him."

"Dee. This is Floyd."

Devereau grabbed the radio. "Stick to code."

"Code, shit! You heard the cop."

"What do you want?"

"We ain't with you on this Palko deal. If he set Luis up and almost killed Sally, we ain't about to get buddy-buddy."

"You let me handle it."

"Fuck him. He didn't answer you, no way."

"He may not have heard me."

"He got Sally's radio, ain't he? He heard you."

"How the hell can you be sure?"

"How much was you planning to give *him* on payday?"

"You cool it and let me run things. Your insubordination will do nothing but screw things up." Devereau was beginning to raise his voice.

"The other two guys on this floor are with *me*, they say fuck Palko."

"I said cool it!" Devereau shouted.

"And we say let's find the son-of-a-bitch!"

Devereau looked at Stroud. "We've got a problem," he said, away from the radio.

"Hear what I said?" Floyd snapped.

Devereau put his mouth to his radio. "Joe Palko. Do you read me? Please come in."

"He ain't gonna talk to you," Floyd said. "We gonna have to find the son-of-a-bitch. And we say let's start looking."

"He's wearing a mask. You won't know him when you see him. I don't want any shooting."

"Larry, this is Harry Ziller."

"Stay the hell out of this!" Devereau screamed.

"Listen a minute. You've got to do something to prevent a lot of unnecessary shooting."

Devereau looked at Stroud, who nodded. Devereau pulled at his mask. "Joe Palko!" he said frantically into the radio. "Joe Palko, establish commVnciation!"

"I done told you," Floyd said. "We gotta go find him."

"Larry," Ziller said. "Your whole operation could get screwed up if you don't proceed carefully at this point. You've got to get your men to cool down before they do anything. You can't afford to let them go storming around that building looking for somebody to shoot at. You know the kind of things that are gonna happen. . . ."

Devereau snapped his fingers. "Son-of-a-bitch, I just thought of how to do it! Attention, all stations!" He paused to study his diagram of the building. "All relocated men except those in the basement or on five proceed to the foyer of seventeen and reassemble to form a search party. Wait there for Penthouse-B, who will arrive shortly with detailed orders for carrying out the search.

"And one more detail. *All* stations. *All* personnel. I repeat. *All* personnel! Remove your masks! This will prevent any accidents due to mistaken identification. Remove your masks but hold them for possible future use. Ten-four." Devereau leaned back and peeled off his own mask. Then he went into the bathroom and splashed his face with water.

"Wanta get it one more time?" Wayne Austin asked softly.

"Think you can, I mean, without restin' or anything?"

"Are you kiddin'? For the likes o' you, this little ol' freckled rooster o' mine would stay up all night."

"All I can say is, you boys gotta start comin' and takin' over this building a coupla times a week."

In the next office, Palko waited patiently, wishing they would get through with it and leave.

Finally, the sounds of their movements stopped, and an absolute quiet settled over them. Then he began to snore. After several minutes, she woke him. They made small talk about getting dressed and going back upstairs. She talked about how hot and sweaty they both were and how her hair must be a sight. But she didn't care. She figured people would guess. They'd been gone quite a while. But she didn't care about that either.

Palko listened to them get up and begin fumbling with their clothes. He exhaled with relief as he heard them walk out of the room and toward the stairs.

"Ain't you gonna take back the sofa cushions?" she asked.

"You kiddin'? Let the night crew figure out what they're doing here."

Palko heard the door to the foyer open and close, and for a moment everything was quiet.

Wayne and Jessie walked across the elevator foyer which was lit only by a tiny red bulb. They walked with their arms around each other. As they approached the door to the rear firetower, she looked at him and kissed his mouth through the hole in his mask. He reached down and gave one of the cheeks of her rump a firm squeeze. He pulled the door open and they stepped through.

"There's the son-of-a-bitch!" Floyd Washington shouted.

He was the lead man of four unmasked troops coming to search the sixteenth floor. Jessie screamed as Floyd opened fire. Wayne's body jerked around crazily as the slugs hit him. One of the bullets passed through his body and shattered her wrist. She fell back, and as she watched Wayne slide to the floor, her continuous, prolonged, repeated screams echoed up and down the concrete stairwell.

21

The men were all dressed informally and their faces reflected the fact that they'd been aroused from sleep. They began gathering in the squad room on the second floor of Seventeenth Precinct headquarters across the hall from the inspector's office.

A lanky lieutenant named Bob Selcker called the meeting to order. He was one of the department's College Joe career cops, a comer, college-trained in administration with a minor in criminology. He was in the department's Planning Bureau and had made these meetings one of his specialties. One of the bureau's stenographers sat with his fingers poised over his Stenotype.

A representative was present from New York Steam because 330 Park used city steam. Con Ed was represented at the meeting, as were Ma Bell, the Department of Buildings, and the Health and Hospitals Corp. A man from the Sanitation Department was there because some of their heavy equipment, such as a payloader, might be needed to crash a door. He made it clear he would provide the equipment but not the operator; he would have his men train Emergency Service cops on the spot.

Also at the meeting were men from the FBI, the FAA, and the Port Authority. A delegate from the Triborough Bridge and Tunnel Authority was present because a Phase 2 might call for a caravan involving one of those exit routes. Airport management reps had arrived from all three airports, and two USAF officers were there to discuss air pursuit if necessary. A State Department man, accompanied by one of his flunkies, was invited to discuss possible places for such a flight to land where the U.S. had no reciprocal agreements. Algeria seemed one likely spot. A couple of South American countries were other possibilities.

The representative from the Federal Reserve was most vociferous about the lack of necessity for his presence, but Selcker insisted that his quick cooperation at some point could be vital to hostage safety. The fire department was represented to cover many possibilities including fires started by tear gas or use of rescue equipment such as high ladders. A total of eight or nine cops of various ranks, including the precinct inspector, completed the group.

Selcker, having been briefed at length by Ziller and O'Reilly in the van, conducted the meeting, reviewing all aspects of hostage safety and possible capture of the perpetrators. Constant watch would have to be kept to prevent any independent action, such as an attack by friends of a hostage, or just some nut looking for headlines.

Selcker also reviewed all elements in a possible assault on 330. This would be done from the top down, by TIE, Team Insertion and Extraction, depositing Emergency Service Unit personnel on the roof by helicopter and pushing the action toward lower floors. A simultaneous assault might be made at the street level, where the building was presently ringed by "concertina wire," or expandable coils of barbed wire.

This case was destined to be a classic, Selcker told the group. One of the biggest deployments of department personnel for a crime situation in the city's history was in effect. The case could ultimately have its own chapter in procedural manuals, not just in New York, but across the country and even around the world.

Palko drew quietly on his cigarette. He'd have to start taking it easy on the pack, which was going fast. He didn't want to run out, and he wasn't going to be able to just stroll back down to his desk and pull another pack out of the drawer. Not when he was the object of an armed manhunt. At least he was in one of the safest spots in the building for the moment. He'd turned on his radio just after he heard the shots. Two or three minutes had passed before anybody spoke, but once they started talking, he was able to put the pieces together. The poor kid with the broad. At least he'd left this world with his cock still damp. How many guys ever get to go like that?

The sixteenth floor would be safe for a while. The lead man in the penthouse, Larry, the cop called him, had announced that if the kid with the broad had been on sixteen, Palko wouldn't very likely be there.

Larry had sounded like he might be falling apart. Things weren't going exactly according to his plan. When he started screaming about how he'd told them no shooting, men all over the building began standing up for the troop that'd shot the kid. They figured since the kid was wearing the mask, it had to be Palko. Sounded like the line of command was getting stretched pretty tight.

And the cop, Ziller, was right in the middle of every conversation. Offering deals to the troops. Sending an ambulance for the girl. And for the kid. Maybe he wasn't dead yet, the lieutenant said. He was dead, Larry told him. The guy that shot him thought he had Joe Palko, and he really blasted away.

* * *

Saxon Shaer continued to sit quietly in the chair facing the twenty-second-floor elevators. He occupied himself by observing the behavior of the vicious little guard who paced back and forth across the foyer. Shaer had been stranded for well over an hour, ever since the first guard who had been taking him back to the eighteenth floor had gone to check the engine room.

Since that time, he had been left to figure out as best he could what was going on, listening to most of the action on the little guard's radio. What an evening it had been! Following the memorable dinner, for entertainment he'd been treated to a live-action show, one destined to go down in history for sure, with two real-life homicides. Both of them their own men. Killed by their own men. And one of the dead was that creep Luis.

And while he sat there, he began to feel new respect for the NYPD as he listened to the police lieutenant's constant presence in the affair, pulling all sorts of psychological strings. The cop knew what the hell he was doing. How had they gotten access to the radio frequency so easily? And learned the names of so many of the troops? The police were with it. He was impressed.

And the moment when the guards all took off the masks. Most interesting. The faceless monsters became people. Of sorts. The madman running the show didn't look like a madman at all. A good-looking guy. Looked a little familiar. Handsome, tall, he'd make a great leading man. And obviously a bright guy. Able to select very good wines. And to swing back and forth from being reasonably articulate to being the kind of street-fighting savage necessary to control his nasty little army of animals. Except that control seemed to be slipping.

He thought about the chick who got messed up with the troop. They'd said she was from the eighteenth floor. Would have to be Jessie. Those steaming pants of hers finally got her into trouble. Too bad. Basically a decent kid. Hopefully she wasn't hurt too bad. The others on the floor probably haven't even missed her yet. They're probably asleep after all that wine.

"I need an idea," Devereau said to Stroud. "Something to turn things around. Like in a football game when you need a big play to change the momentum of the game."

Stroud sat in the big chair studying his M-14.

"Do you know how badly things are fucked up?" Devereau said. "And I can't even figure out how it happened. Three men wasted! Over what? And those morons down there sound mutinous! Don't those dumb son-of-a-bitches know that if they deviate from the plan, they'll get buried? Every cop in this city is sitting outside, with some kind of heavy weapon trained on this building. The only way we'll ever walk out of here is according to plan. How many months have I been lecturing to these assholes on the importance of sticking to the plan? There's no way we could ever win a shooting war."

"You gotta get Joe Palko." Stroud didn't look up from his thoughtful examination of his gun. "Gettin' him would put you back in control."

"You got any hot ideas on how we get him? He knows holes and corners in this building we'd never find. Not without Luis."

"Pick very patient boys for your search party. Not Floyd, not Benjy, not Pedro. Let Smokey lead it."

"We need Smokey in the basement."

"For what?"

Devereau reflected on Stroud's comment for a moment. Then he began to study his diagram of the building, jotting the names of several troops on a page of his notebook. When he finished, he picked up his radio. "Boston."

"Boston."

"The following men will report to the penthouse at once: Basement-A, Twelve-B . . . ."

After he had signed off, his phone rang. He let it ring ten times before picking it up. "What the fuck do you want?"

"You organizing another search party for Palko?"

"What's it to you?"

"I just hope you're a little more careful than you were last time, Larry. You know how we operate. If there's any more gunplay, we may be forced into moving on the building."

"You wouldn't dare. We've still got hundreds of hostages. If we have to, we'll start executing them."

"What'll that get you? Just remember what helps your cause and what doesn't."

"You get the girl okay?"

"She's at Bellevue, being treated. Your men were a little rough with her."

"Some cunts pick the damnedest times to let their crotches take over their heads."

"Some men, too."

"You through?"

"You sure you wouldn't like to talk about a deal?"

"You're right on schedule, Ziller. I just wanted to hear you dribble your shit one more time before hanging up in your face." He slammed down the receiver.

Ziller flipped off the phone speaker.

"You call that progress?" said Dan Redmond. "I'm ordering the assault force into place, ready to move in." He had been prominent among the profusion of high-level department personnel in and out of the van during the late hours, and he had been slowly building his case for positive action.

"Things are going pretty good," Ziller said quietly.

"Good? Sounded to me like he's jerking you around any way he likes."

"That's the way this game is played. Ask Jerry how he thinks

we're doing. Besides, you gotta remember that 330 is still full
of civilians. Even if we win a shoot-out, we lose."

"Look, we just had a couple of out-and-out homicides. Any
more shooting, and we mount an assault."

"Where were you during the last three inspector's funer-
als?" The most recent was for a young cop shot in the Bronx.

"Serving as a pallbearer," Redmond snapped.

Ziller looked at O'Reilly, whose quiet nod reminded him
that Redmond had a direct wire to one of the deputy commis-
sioners. And procedures could be interpreted to call for mobilization at that point. There was really nothing wrong with
having the assault force in place. The trick would be keeping
Redmond from ordering an attack before it made sense. Poli-
tics. Life-and-death decisions could swing on who's got the
best lines to the top.

Redmond had started giving orders. The big chopper would
be brought in from Floyd Bennett Field to deposit the TIE
team on the roof. The Matilda would be taken to Fifty-first
Street and held in readiness to batter the rear entrance. In
that event the ERV would be used to create a diversion on
Park Avenue, or possibly go in through the front doors.

One of Redmond's deputies left the van and walked a few
yards up Fiftieth Street to a police bus, a converted city bus,
painted to conform to NYPD code. It was filled with TPF
cops, many of them dozing, others quietly talking and smoking. The floor of the bus was littered with empty plastic cups
and waxed paper from sandwiches. "Okay, guys," Redmond's
man said, "it looks like some of you may be flying, tonight.
You're off to the park to get set up."

Devereau nervously faced the assemblage. He had tapped
Smokey to lead the search party, as Stroud had suggested,
and picked Big Charlie, Miguel Sosa, and four others to help.
This still left two men on all the occupied floors, two in the

lobby, two in the basement and two with Sally Panucci on the fifth floor. Devereau abandoned the engine room, deciding that he couldn't spare a man for it and Pedro's surveillance of elevator travel from the lobby should be adequate. Besides, no one wanted to stay near Luis' body.

Devereau began the briefing by emphasizing caution. Any more gunplay could bring an assault on the building, which would probably blow the whole operation. Palko had to be taken peaceably. This shouldn't be so tough. There were seven of them and only one of him.

The seven members of the group nodded their approval of his plan, and he found huge relief in this expression of confidence. One of his major fears was that the platoon would split into factions. He had watched Big Charlie's face during the brief meeting. He saw no indication that Charlie would turn sour, regardless of what kind of pitch Floyd might lay on him. Charlie was solid. Or perhaps he was simply smart enough to know his only hope was to stay with the plan.

Candy Dupree's deification of the black penis had begun in her fantasy world during her teen years. It had started with an offhand remark made by one of the white boys she ran with, one of the number she had screwed in back seats and stairwells and wooded areas and, a couple of times, even porch swings. She and her schoolmates had floated many a used condom on the town pond.

The boy had quipped that one of the black athletes in their high school had a cock that when hard was like a vibrating loaf of rye bread. The comment triggered a parade of vivid pictures in Candy's mind, and she became obsessed with the image of that huge, glistening black thing forcibly penetrating her soft white flesh. But it was only food for her imagination; she never seriously considered the possibility for herself. No such thing could ever happen where she lived.

A couple of years out of school, she moved to New York

City from her hometown in western Pennsylvania, and although she discovered that black studs with white chicks wouldn't draw so much as a glance in New York, she still couldn't seriously imagine acting out her fantasy. She had lived a lifetime with that as an unquestioned taboo.

When the two masked troops crashed into the office that morning, hitting and shoving, inflicting pain and blazing away with live ammunition, she had been absolutely electrified by the huge black. Her dream had materialized at last. And the circumstances surrounding it—guns, masks, brutality . . . .

As the afternoon progressed, Puddin' Thompson realized that the broad in the tight striped sweater was one of those kinky chicks that had a thing for black men. She never said anything. She just came out from time to time for one excuse or another and stared at his joint. After a while, whenever he saw her coming, he slouched his pelvis forward to tease the little bitch.

By late evening he was sure. She had sniffed him out, and she was hot as a stove. He liked the idea. No white broad had ever looked twice at him before. He had hated taking off his mask. It had been one of the things he'd liked most about the whole idea of joining the caper. As for the broad, he figured that as soon as she laid eyes on the right side of his face, which was a mottle of pink-and-white burn-scar tissue, she'd cool off in a hurry.

But when she showed up at three in the morning, she just stood for a moment, transfixed. She glanced at Floyd and then brought her eyes back to Puddin's face.

"Never saw nothin' like that?" Puddin' said bitterly.

"Never saw nothing like you."

"Meanin' what?"

"What do you think I mean?"

She was still hot. He looked at Floyd, who was absolutely bug-eyed. "Don't start nothin' you can't finish," he said.

She smiled. "If I was to start something, I'd finish it."

"Well, let's go." He motioned to her to follow him through the door to the front stairwell. He wanted to avoid the rear stairs—Wayne Austin was still on the landing, one flight up.

"What the fuck's the matter with you?" Floyd said. "You outta your fuckin' tree? With all that's goin' on right now? Look what happen to Austin."

Puddin' smiled. "No chance of somebody not recognizin' me. Not with the mask off. Won't be no rough stuff this time."

"Who's Austin?" the girl asked.

"One of our boys who took a broad on the sixteenth floor and got hisself killed," Floyd said.

"He what?"

"You wanta see him? Go out that door right there. He's one flight up."

Her face paled. "I don't know what kind of sick joke this is . . ."

"Joke, shit!" Floyd walked over to the rear stairwell and pushed the door open. "Step out there and see what kinda joke it is."

She looked at Puddin'. "I was just making talk. I'm not really interested. . . ."

"You started somethin'," Puddin' said, "and you gonna finish it." He moved toward her and grabbed her hand. "Now, le's go."

"Man," Floyd said, "this is dumb."

"I won't be but a few minutes. Jus' stay here till I get back."

Floyd suddenly grinned. "Long as you made up your mind, why don't you stay right here and we can both jump her?"

"I'm going back into the office," the girl said. "This isn't quite what I had in mind. Please let me go."

"What make you think you got a choice?" Puddin' said. He wrenched her hand as he dragged her into the front stairwell and up one flight to sixteen. Without releasing her hand, he unlocked the door to the foyer and stopped just inside the office area.

"Where are we going?" she asked.

"We's arrived."

"But it's dark. And there's nothing but a bare floor."

"You don't need to see nothin'. Jus' get down on your knees," he said, forcing her down by one hand and unzipping his fly with his other. "Now, reach in and take it out."

"Goddamn you, you black son-of-a-bitch! The way I had it pictured, it was going to be something really special. I don't want this. Let's just go back and forget the whole thing."

He slid his fingers into her hair and then tightened them into a fist. "This is the way it's gonna be, so quit talking and open your mouth."

A few feet away, Joe Palko, uncomfortably cramped inside the door of an air-return duct, listened patiently. He had been leaving the sixteenth floor when he heard the search party coming, and he'd managed to slip into the duct and pull the sheet-metal door shut only seconds before the searchers reached him. They had decided to take a quick look on sixteen before going to lower, more likely floors. If Luis had been with them, the air duct would have been one of the first places to look.

Palko stood on narrow metal braces that jutted into the duct. If he slipped, he would slide down toward the plenum on fifteen. The air circulating system was designed around units of two floors to a circulating fan. His footing was shaky, but he froze himself into a rigid stance to wait out the scene just beyond his door. He began to wonder if every troop in the platoon was going to have to hump a broad right under his nose before he'd be able to leave the sixteenth floor.

One of his legs began to cramp and he moved it slightly for relief. As he did, his foot tapped against the wall of the duct.

"What was that?" the girl asked.

"Jus' a noise," Puddin' said.

22

The busload of cops drove up to Grand Army Plaza, in front of the Plaza Hotel where it was met by a NYPD jeep, a special vehicle mounted with overhead banks of floodlights. The jeep, driven by Park Precinct police, led the bus into the park to the Sheep Meadow. It stopped there and switched on its floods, illuminating the open field. Several cops piled off the bus and trotted to the middle of the floodlit area, where they paced off a square roughly a hundred feet on a side, which they lit with flares.

Within minutes a large helicopter thundered overhead, hovered a moment, and then lowered itself to the ground. The big Sikorsky chopper, capable of carrying up to sixteen men, was on one of its rare flights from Floyd Bennett Field. It was seldom used because it took more than one hundred gallons of fuel an hour to keep it aloft, but Dan Redmond was not about to let the night pass without getting it into the air.

* * *

Inside 330 Park the occupied office areas were quiet. Most employees were sleeping soundly; others were groping around trying to find positions that were comfortable enough to allow them to sleep. They were remote from the activity in the foyers and stairwells, insulated by floors and walls of thick concrete, and were not aware of all the action that had taken place in the last couple of hours. In the lobby Pedro and Perry Snodgrass were on guard. On five two troops sat with Sally Panucci, who was stretched out on a sofa, thrashing around in restless sleep, having swallowed half a quart of whiskey. The search party was working its way downward, checking with the troops on each floor. They split into two groups as they left each floor, to cover both stairwells, regrouping in the next foyer. If this first run-through failed to uncover Palko, they planned to start back up and check the occupied floors. He had to be somewhere in the building.

Floyd Washington was going from floor to floor, pitching, threatening, cajoling, like a candidate behind the scenes at a convention, lining up his votes. He carefully avoided the search party. Big Charlie was the only man on it he wanted or hoped to get, and he wasn't sure he could count on Charlie.

In the penthouse Devereau was pulling himself together. Things were still in control; that was the beauty of using hostages. The secret was in maintaining cool and moving according to the plan. The mishaps so far had been minor. Three men lost. He still had many more than he needed.

He sent Stroud to return Shaer to eighteen and pick up Herder on nineteen, the same mission he had sent him on two hours earlier when Stroud decided to stop and see why Luis didn't respond to radio contact.

Stroud had to wake several people on nineteen before finding Herder. He roused the stocky gray-haired man out of a heavy sleep and led him toward the penthouse, where he was told that he and his employees would be allowed to leave the building for a half-million dollars. He would be brought back to the penthouse to call his bank when it opened. For the moment, he could return to his office and go back to sleep.

Elsewhere on the penthouse floor, nearly everyone was asleep. Winfield Root, on the couch in Billy Marshall's office, had dozed off slightly after ten. Marshall and Ronam had lain down soon after, fashioning beds of sorts out of overstuffed chairs. But Barbara Meyner still sat at her desk, her arms folded, staring into the shadows.

On the fifteenth floor Dave Goldmann, a Root Corporation attorney, woke up with a strong need to urinate. Too much wine with dinner. He went out to the foyer and was shaken to find the floor unguarded. They had left! A lone M-14 rifle stood leaning against the wall.

He walked quickly over to the door of one stairwell, stuck his head through, and listened. Nothing. He checked the other stairwell. No sound of any kind. He rushed back into the office area and began frantically waking people up, saying that the siege had obviously ended and the troops had taken their leave. As evidenced by the gun they'd left behind. Since the phones were dead, there was no way they could call anyone for an explanation. The important thing was that the floor was unguarded, and he saw no reason why they shouldn't try to get the hell out. Everyone agreed and began moving toward the elevators.

Just as they started through the door to the foyer, the front stairwell door opened and Candy Dupree walked through, followed by the tall black troop with the shockingly disfigured face. Several women gasped. The troop pushed Candy out of his way and drew his automatic. "Well," he said, "everybody decide to go for a little walk?" Keeping the handgun pointed at the group, he went over to his M-14 and picked it up. "Now, everybody jus' go back inside, and there won't be no trouble."

The stunned employees kept staring at the two of them.

"He forced me to go with him," Candy finally said. "There was nothing I could do."

Goldmann observed that she didn't seem much worse off for the experience. He began to recall the rather strange vibrations he had been getting from her in recent weeks. "You don't have to explain," he said.

On the twelfth floor, the two troops who had been guarding it, Roosevelt Hinton and Archie Stoner, strode into the office area, snapping on the overhead lights. The people in the various rooms woke reluctantly, squinting at the sudden brightness.

Hinton finally stopped by a man stretched out on the carpeted floor with a small pillow under his head. He walked over and kicked the man's foot.

"Wha . . . ?" The man looked up into the blinding glare of the overhead fixture.

"Get up," Hinton said. "I want your clothes."

The man on the floor rubbed his eyes and looked around. "What's going on? What time is it?"

Hinton kicked the man in the side and then held the muzzle of his M-14 to the man's face. "It's time for you to stand up and take off your clothes. Now, move!"

The man looked at the gun barrel and tried to roll away from it. Hinton kicked him again. "I said get up!" He reached down and grabbed the man's hair, pulling him to his feet.

"What's this all about?"

"Just gimme your clothes and don't ask so many fucking questions and you'll be all right. You can keep your socks and underwear. I'll take the rest."

The man started unbuttoning his shirt, then stopped and reached into his pants pockets. "Let me just empty my pockets," he said.

"Leave it. You might have somethin' in there I want. Jus' get on with it." Hinton glanced around and spotted the man's jacket hanging on a rack behind the door. Collecting the rest of the man's clothes, he said, "Take it easy," and walked out. Just outside the office, he met Stoner, who was also carrying an armful of clothes. "Get yourself some nice threads?" he asked Stoner.

"I stripped the head man, Gertziger, himself," Stoner said. "Shit, man, I don't fuck around."

Outside the building the police observers noted the sudden random pattern of lights popping on and off on various floors. In several cases they were able to watch as an employee was forced to give his clothes to a troop. They reported their observations to Ziller, who discussed this new information with Weissberger. It was a most interesting development.

Devereau was almost pleased when the phone rang. Things were settling down, easing back onto plan. He had finished the last interview, which was with Mike Kennan of the ad agency on twenty. He had doubled his originally planned ransom, as he had done in all the interviews after Ronam's, and the total amount of "funds to be transferred" now exceeded twenty million dollars. A handsome amount, by any standards.

Twenty million dollars. Over five already in. Right there in the room. For real. He'd checked it himself. And things were going right again. On plan. . . . And now Ziller was calling to provide a few laughs, a few minutes of diversion. Time to relax and enjoy him a little. . . .

He picked up the phone after a dozen or so rings. "Hiya, Harry!" He said it like a Shriner meeting an old friend at an annual convention.

"Hiya, Dee," Ziller answered, picking up on Devereau's mood. "How's it going?"

"Real well, as a matter of fact." He looked at Stroud and nodded.

"Hope I didn't wake you up."

"I'm having too much fun to sleep."

"Any problems? Anything I can help you with?"

"Just don't do anything foolish, Harry. And there shouldn't be any problems."

"Y'know, Dee, this is quite a caper."

"I'm inclined to agree."

"I mean, no matter how it turns out, it's still some story."

"I'm depending on you, Lieutenant, to see that it turns out right. I'm just as opposed to violence as you are."

"That goes without saying. But that's not what I was leading up to. I was just thinking that this would make a terrific story."

"It's more than that, Harry. We're making history."

"Agreed. Which is exactly why I'm calling. Y'know, there's a hell of a book in this piece of business. The problem is, there's only one person that could write it. And that's you."

"Jesus, Ziller. Is that what you called about? All right. Who knows, maybe someday I'll write about it. Or more likely, pay somebody to ghost it for me."

"Now, wait a minute, Dee. I couldn't get into this discussion with just any perpetrator I run into on the job. Most of them are professional hoods or kids who grab a couple hostages trying to escape. You're an artist. You really planned this thing. Worked it out in great detail. Even invested a lotta your own money. You've got a real stake in this."

"And I intend to collect."

"But there could be more than one way of doing it."

"And you're gonna suggest that I give up and write a book. At least you're amusing, Harry."

"Hold it a minute. You know what a best-seller earns? You could make a million bucks."

"Thanks for the tip."

"Lemme finish. Let's say you escape tomorrow as planned. You're gonna have enormous expenses. The cost of getting to where you're going. The payoffs at the other end. Every-

body's gonna know what your take was. This'll all be in the
news. Do you think they'll settle for the original amount? And
the same is true for all your guys. You're gonna be on the
hook, Larry. Your take could evaporate a lot faster'n you
think. The more you get, the more everybody's gonna want.
Right? And I presume you're planning to leave the country.
Right? Do you really wanna do that? You won't be able to
come back so easy. Or go anywhere we've got reciprocal
agreements. That doesn't leave you many desirable places to
go. Right?"

"Jesus, Ziller, you just told me how smart I was. Don't you
think I've thought about all these things?"

"Dee, there's a million ways this thing could go wrong.
What if some of your guys cop out or turn on you and screw
up your whole plan?"

"Ziller, the world is full of 'what ifs.' I laid this thing out
carefully. I have all sorts of contingency plans. If there's any
more violence, it'll probably be your fault. And I'll see to it
that the world knows it."

"Now, let's look at another approach. Suppose you threw in
the towel—"

"Forget it."

"Lemme finish. With no record and a good attorney, what
would you get? Six months? A year? What have you got so far?
Unlawful imprisonment? Assault? And we can indicate that
you came out voluntarily. That's good for points. And you
could spend the year writing the book. You'd end up making a
bundle. And come out of it a big celebrity. A superstar. The
public loves a confessed ex-anything. You know that. You'd
probably make all the talk shows. And you wouldn't have to
leave the country. And you'd have no expenses. The state
would even supply the paper and the typewriter."

"How's Quirke?"

"No change."

"You finished now?"

"Listen, all I'm suggesting is that you play the percentages. I'm telling you, Larry, my way's better."

"Well done, Ziller. But I've got a counterproposal. You're a pretty good man yourself. How'd you like to join our side? I'll make you rich as a king."

"Larry, you'd be playing it smart if you'd consider ending this thing and coming on out. You could be a lot closer to a collapse of your whole setup than you think. And if that happens, well, just remember, I'm here to help if you'll let me."

"You never stop selling, do you, Ziller? Just keep doing your job, and nothing will go wrong." Devereau hung up.

Ziller turned to face the group standing around him. "Hear him asking about Quirke? He was checking to see if his bridges were burned."

Weissberger nodded. "I'd agree. We've got him thinking."

"Sounded like a bunch of bullshit to me," Redmond snapped. "We've got the assault force mobilized, and I've got a feeling we're going to need it very soon."

"An assault is out of the question right now," Ziller said quickly. "But I think something else is going to break, for which we'll need your men. All we can do for the moment is sit tight and keep an eye on things."

"We just may have to take that decision out of your hands," Redmond said.

"Based on our experience, I think it will be in the best interests of the hostages to wait," Ziller said.

O'Reilly's expression suggested that he'd do what he could to restrain Redmond but that ultimately the decision could come down to a political power struggle. And Redmond had some lines that led directly to the PC himself.

After hanging up the phone, Devereau looked at Stroud without speaking. He could sense that Stroud hardly-understood how it was possible to be so glib with the cop in charge, right in the middle of all that was going on. But he didn't see any sign that Stroud questioned his judgment. Good. Things were beginning to take shape.

With the call from Ziller out of the way, he felt the onset of a lull, a chance to rest and refresh himself for when things would pick up again. And with that thought came a totally overwhelming sense of fatigue. He had not slept well the preceding night. He told Stroud to keep an eye on things and let him stay asleep as long as it was safe to do so. If Ziller called back, he was not to be disturbed unless it was important. Then he stretched out on the puffy four-cushioned sofa, propping one of the cushions for a pillow. He turned on his side and was asleep in minutes.

23

A long table. Twenty, thirty, forty feet long. A white embroidered damask cloth. Gold candlebra, tall, slim tapers flickering. Crystal stemware, trimmed in gold, dark wine reflecting light from a vast chandelier. Dazzling sunlight, warmth, all-healing warmth, sand, clear green water, warm, mirror-calm, transparent to the sandy bottom. Crumbs in a gold plate, coffee from gold service into a gold cup and saucer and spoon, rich, black, aromatic coffee, exhilarating to the senses. . . . Why are you touching my shoulder? Servants are not supposed to touch. Stand back against the wall and wait to be summoned. A snap of my fingers and you walk forward from your station against the wall. . . . Yellowish stucco, gleaming dark brown wood, arches, arch after arch after arch. . . . Barbara, naked, on her back, smiling, silken flawless skin, childlike, fragile, pink-white, pubic floss nearly invisible. . . . Don't touch me! If I want you, I'll signal, but as long as you're here, more coffee, and more port, and the drapes, pull the drapes, the blinding glare, clear sky, the jet's

245

vapor trail, evaporating. . . . Why do you keep touching my shoulder? . . . "What is it?"

"You better wake up." It was Stroud.

"What the hell for? I need some rest."

"You just better wake up."

Devereau shifted onto his back and gazed at the ceiling for a moment. He held up his arm and checked his watch. Four o'clock. He'd been asleep for fifteen minutes. "Okay, now that I'm up, why'd you wake me?"

"Look around."

Devereau raised himself on an elbow and looked past Stroud. Then he sat bolt upright, fully awake. Floyd. In a suit and tie. Puddin'. Rosey Hinton. Archie Stoner. Angel Gonzales. . . . All dressed in ill-fitting business suits, shirts, ties. But all holding their M-14's aimed more or less in his direction. . . . Perry Snodgrass, Mario. . . . "What the fuck are you bastards up to?" Devereau said finally. He made a quick count. Eleven of them altogether. Contingency plans began to spin through his mind.

"We're leavin' now," Floyd said.

"Going where? What the fuck are you talking about?" Devereau asked. Floyd was obviously spokesman for the group.

"We're gettin' out now," Floyd said.

"Haven't you been listening to me these last few months? Are you smarter than I am? You stupid shits, every cop in New York is outside this building. There's just one way out of here, and that's in that bus, protected by hostages."

"We know a better way," Floyd said.

"Which is . . . ?"

"Jus' give us the fucking money and we'll go."

Devereau surveyed the group. Charlie wasn't there. Or Smokey. Or Benjy or Pedro or Miguel Sosa. Nothing but the troublemakers. "You dumb fucks ought to have your heads examined," he said. "You can't make it without me."

"We think we've got a better chance alone. We don't think you're ever gonna leave this building."

Devereau smiled. "You guys are fucking yourselves."

"Jus' give us the money."

"You're making a mistake," Devereau said. "But if this is what you want to do. Okay. We'll have to manage without you." He turned to the big crate behind him and pushed the cover aside. After examining the contents, he pulled out one of the briefcases. Reaching into his pocket, he drew out the labeled keys and selected the right one. Then he unlocked the case and flashed the tightly packed money at Floyd. "There's a million and a half dollars in here, thanks to the second-floor tenants. Since there's eleven of you, this is substantially more than your share. But take it and good luck."

"We ain't jus' takin' that one," Floyd said. "We're takin' 'em all."

Devereau's jaw dropped. "You're taking this one. And no more."

Floyd raised his M-14 and aimed it a little more directly at Devereau. The others followed his lead. "We taking all of that money," Floyd said quietly. "You got plenty more comin' in tomorrow. We never was happy with the way you was dividin' things up, anyway. This'll be more like the way we think the pie supposed to be cut."

Devereau looked at the eleven rifles and then glanced at Stroud, who was stunned. "Let's talk about this a minute," he said. "Put your rifles down and—"

Floyd fired past Devereau into the wall. Then he pointed the gun at the middle of Devereau's chest. "Ain't nothin' to talk about. We're takin' all this bread and leavin'. Everybody else can stay with the plan, and there'll be plenty more bread for you and them tomorrow. Now we prepared to leave you alone long as you don't fuck around with us. You wanta hand us the rest of those cases?"

"You guys are dead," Devereau said. "You're nothing without me. You never were." He turned as he talked and began pulling the briefcases out of the crate and lining them up on the desk. "Firing that shot was a stupid-ass trick. Don't you know that? Don't you think the police heard it?"

"Give us the keys, too," Floyd said.

Devereau took the handful of tiny keys with string tags from his pocket and dropped them on the desk. Then he smiled. He had just made a decision.

Floyd moved forward, keeping his eyes and gun on Devereau. He picked up the little tangle of tags and keys and slid it into his pocket. Then he grabbed one of the cases. Enough of the others followed him up to the desk to take the other seven. They began to retreat from the room, some of them backing out to cover Devereau and Stroud until the last minute.

"You guys look just like big businessmen," Devereau quipped. "Rifles and all." He paused. "And now you've got the money to prove it. Right?" He paused again as he watched the last of them file out. "Except that you're dead without me, you assholes!" he shouted after them.

Stroud started to protest, but Devereau just smiled.

"They took five million dollars," Stroud whispered.

Devereau didn't answer. He just waited until he was sure Floyd's group was out of earshot. Then he picked up the phone and dialed. "Hello, Lieutenant Ziller . . ."

The group of eleven reached the elevator, where Benjy, startled when they had first appeared in the street clothes, was even more confused on seeing them with the briefcases. Benjy was Devereau's trained animal. Floyd had never even considered asking him to join the counteraction. Benjy had heard the shot and saw that they had the money, but it was one against eleven, and he let them pass. As soon as they went into the stairwell, he hustled down the hall to Devereau's office. He found Devereau using the telephone while Stroud stood by.

Devereau's call touched off a flurry of activity in the police

van. All observation teams were alerted to watch for movement of any kind. Eleven men, business suits, briefcases, still
armed. Then Ziller and the others studied a map of the block
bounded by Park, Madison, Fiftieth, and Fifty-first. The ITT
Building and the Root Tower fronted on Park Avenue. The
crepe restaurant, a low, two-story affair, was on Fiftieth, adjacent to the rear of the ITT Building. All other structures were
vacant, scheduled to be razed for construction of a new high-
rise. These buildings included the archdiocese headquarters
facing Madison, the old stone structure with the circular
driveway. Just behind it on the Fifty-first Street side was a
small private parking lot. In the center of the block, surrounded by buildings and hidden from view, was a small formal garden, owned by the archdiocese.

An order went out on the police radio to alert the containment team, and cops on Fifty-first and Madison moved
around, focusing their attention on the vacant buildings
along Fifty-first. Some carried shotguns, others rifles with
scopes. Within minutes, although the area was still outwardly
deserted, cops were everywhere, concealed behind vehicles
or corners or in doorways, alerted for any sign of activity.

Floyd led his renegades down the rear fire tower, past sixteen, where the corpse of Wayne Austin still lay in a heap. He
avoided using the elevators for fear Devereau would cut the
power and trap them between floors. When they reached
eleven, Floyd unlocked the door into the office area, where
an eight-foot painter's ladder leaned against a wall. He and
Luis had left it there the preceding Friday, and he had
checked it again before making his rounds.

They carried the ladder out to the fire-tower landing and
eased it over the edge, where it came to rest on the roof of the
building immediately adjacent, 34 East Fifty-first, a nine-story
brick structure among those destined to be leveled. One after
another, the eleven men went over the railing and down the
ladder, onto the roof of the other building. As the men saw

that their movements were invisible to the street, they realized that Floyd's plans had been as carefully made as Devereau's.

But when they reached the roof, Floyd hesitated and gazed all around for a full minute. He held up his hand to keep the others quiet. "Somethin' ain't right," he said finally. "Oughta be some traffic on Madison or somewhere I can hear." He listened a little longer and then shook his head resolutely. "Somethin's wrong out here. And I don't like it."

"What are you talking about?" Hinton asked.

"It's too fuckin' quiet. I don't like the way it feels."

"Man, are you crazy? Course it's quiet. It's four in the fuckin' morning, and the cops got the traffic blocked off."

"I'm going back," Floyd said. He made the statement with the same total assurance that he had displayed earlier in getting them to mutiny.

"Are you nuts? This is your plan. And it's gonna work. One hour from now we're gonna be loose right here in this city with a half-million bills apiece. Jus' like you said."

"What are you gonna do if you get back in there?" Stoner asked.

"I don't know yet," Floyd said. "All I know is, I don't like the way this smells out here, and I'm goin' back. You can stay with me or keep goin'."

Floyd's unexpected action threw the other ten into total confusion. They chattered among themselves and finally elected to stay with Floyd's original plan. "You gonna take any of the bread?" Stoner asked.

"I'm taking this one," Floyd said, swinging the bag he was holding. "You can slice up the rest. You'll still get more'n three times what Dee had in mind for ya."

"What about the keys?" Perry shouted.

"Bust 'em open," Floyd yelled back.

The men watched Floyd climb the ladder and then they started down the steel fire escape on the back of the building.

Their footsteps reverberated in the stillness, echoing off the walls of the surrounding structures. They stopped and just stood for several seconds, waiting for quiet. They started downward again, slowly, tiptoeing, but the steel of the stair treads responded to even the most restrained steps, and the stairwell began to develop a soft harmonic that expanded gradually into a low hum. When they neared the bottom, they quit tiptoeing and rushed, landing finally on a concrete area enclosed by the buildings.

The noise from the stairs had been heard by one of the observation teams, who spotted the ten men threading along the ground across the tiny garden to the rear of a small building facing Fifty-first and adjacent to the archdiocese. He watched as one of them put a fire ax into the door of the empty building, and the group disappeared inside.

The cop radioed the van and within minutes a dozen or more TPF cops filed from the back door of the restaurant and took positions overlooking the rear entrance of the building the men had entered.

Ten or fifteen minutes passed. Then the front door of the empty building opened and two men stepped out casually onto the sidewalk. They were dressed in business suits and one of them carried a briefcase. They walked as if they were just leaving their office on any business day, and they started up the sidewalk toward Madison Avenue.

A cop waiting by the Lamston store across from them yelled, "Police! Don't move!" They stopped and turned back toward Park, where another yelled, "Police! Don't move! Get your hands up!" The man with the briefcase dashed back into the building, while the other pulled a handgun. A barrage of shots exploded around him, and he was knocked to the sidewalk. After a few seconds, a voice on a police bullhorn boomed, "Everybody stay under cover. Don't leave your cover."

Quiet enveloped the area once more. The man who had

been hit lay still on the pavement. The police held their positions.

Another ten minutes passed, and the back door to the little four-story building inched open. The men inside tiptoed out. After seven or eight men were outside the door, a cop on the roof of the restaurant yelled, "Police! Don't move!" and several of the policemen turned on Port-o-lites, small hand-held floods. Another cop shouted, "Freeze, you motherfuckers! Hands on your heads!" Several of the men plunged back through the door, while others hopped around, bumping into one another, undecided about which way to run. Two dashed toward the archdiocese building and dived through a glass window into a basement room. The police held their fire.

Those remaining rushed through the ornate steel gate that separated the garden from the small parking area. One of them quickly put the butt of a handgun through the side window of an old panel truck parked there. He opened the door and slid inside onto his back with his head under the dash. Another held a flashlight for him. The others, obscured by the steel gate from the police in back and protected from Fifty-first Street by the truck, watched nervously while the man worked under the dash.

In a matter of seconds he had the truck running and slipped behind the wheel as the rest climbed in. The engine rumbled uncertainly for a moment and then began to pick up, gradually smoothing out. He backed the truck onto Fifty-first and cut sharply, heading toward Park Avenue, where he turned north after steering to the left of the coiled barbed wire.

As he was getting underway, the cops on Madison began running around, shouting and waving to one another, signaling for a radio car. Within seconds, a car carrying four policemen was giving chase. It jumped a curb and traveled a few yards on the sidewalk to get around the barrier. A few seconds later another radio car pulled up Fifty-first from east of Park and headed north. And in less than a minute still another car had joined the pursuit.

The aging truck bore down on the police barrier at Fifty-fifth. The two cops stationed there ran to get out of the way. The driver, planning to crash the barrier, reached within a few yards of it and then suddenly began braking. He was on a collision path with a massive steel refuse truck chugging west on Fifty-fifth, just starting across the intersection beyond the barrier. He cut his wheels sharply, but his vehicle, going much too fast, went into a skid, rammed the wooden barrier broadsides, and slammed against the side of the refuse truck.

Seconds later, the first radio car arrived, followed by three others. They pulled up and turned at angles, encircling the truck. Cops leaped from the cars and draped themselves over the hoods, leveling shotguns and service revolvers at the doors of the truck, which had not yet opened. The chase had lasted five blocks. The driver of the refuse truck looked down curiously on the proceedings from his elevated window. Something had finally happened that made one night a little different from all others.

The police radio frequency was frenzied with activity, and groups of cops gathered in little conferences on Madison. Those holding stakeout positions from behind or facing the small building on Fifty-first stayed in place. Several minutes passed, and then the cops on Madison watched as a fire engine followed by a hook-and-ladder truck came up Madison. One of the cops directed them to the curb just below Fiftieth to stand by.

With the fire equipment at hand, a plainclothes cop wearing a police-blue windbreaker stood up behind a police truck and raised a bullhorn. Hustling over to him from a few yards away came a "gasman," a uniformed cop carrying a fat-barreled launcher and wearing a loose vest which had rows of pockets filled with tear-gas projectiles. *"Okay, you in there,"* the cop shouted into the bullhorn. *"We know you're in the building. You're covered from all sides. We know who you are and we know you've got no hostages. We'll give you exactly five minutes and then we're shooting in tear gas. Make it easy on yourselves and come out with your hands on your heads."*

He brought the horn down and checked his watch. The sky was beginning to turn gray. He raised the horn again. *"Two more minutes and we start lobbing in the tear gas. Drop all weapons and come out, hands on your heads."* He waited two more minutes and pointed at the building. The gasman raised his clumsy-looking weapon and put a thirty-seven-millimeter "flite-rite," through a fourth-floor window. The cop with the bullhorn lifted it again. *"We're gonna fill the building if we have to. Come on out and save yourself some pain."* The gasman waited another minute or so and pointed again. Another projectile sailed through a third-floor window.

The front door swung open, and a voice yelled, "Hold it, goddammit!" Three men came walking out, their hands on their heads.

"Where's the money?" asked the cop with the bullhorn.

"You want it, motherfucker? You just go in there and find it."

More little meetings on Madison Avenue. More frenzied radio activity. Raised voices. Shouting. Arguments. And then, more waiting. The sky gradually grew lighter. A police bus came through Fiftieth to Madison and stopped. Some fifteen uniformed cops climbed out of the bus, all wearing vests and carrying shotguns or carbines. After a hurried briefing on the layout of the archdiocese building, the cops entered the auxiliary office structure and made their way into the main building, where they began checking the rooms.

One group reached an upper-floor corridor and heard several hurried footsteps, followed by a closing door. They moved quickly to the door, flanked it, turned the knob carefully without standing directly in front of it, then kicked it open.

"Don't shoot! Don't shoot!" The man in the beam of the light held both arms rigidly above his head. One of the legs of his expensive beige suit was ripped just below the knee. He had an army automatic in his left hand, and a thin leather briefcase dangled from his right.

Another group of cops found a trail of blood spots in the basement corridor. They followed it until they came to the main foyer, where a young light-skinned black sat slumped against the wall. His left leg was crimson from the upper thigh down, and he gripped at it with both hands. A briefcase lay on the floor next to him, and he had an army automatic in his belt. "What kept ya?" he asked the cops in a weakened, breathy voice, looking up into their lights.

"Throw out the gun with your fingertips, very slowly," one of the cops said.

"Jesus, do you think I'm stupid?" He struggled to pull the weapon from his waist. "Don't worry. You ain't got enough on me to make me suicidal."

"Boston."

"Boston."

"Larry? This is Lieutenant Ziller. We—"

"What the fuck are you doing on the radio? Why didn't you call on the phone?"

"I tried but couldn't seem to get through."

"You're lying, you son-of-a-bitch!"

"I'm telling you. Anyway, we rounded up all your guys. I'm sorry to have to tell you that one of 'em pulled out a weapon, and I'm afraid he got blown away."

"I have no further interest in them. What I want is the money. Did you recover it all?"

"I think so. We haven't finished—"

"Ziller, I want all of that money returned within thirty minutes, or I'm gonna take the president of Root Corporation and blow his brains out. And I'll shoot another member of the board every thirty minutes until that money is back in here. Do I make myself understood?"

24

"We'll do it," Ziller said. "But for Crissakes, don't harm any of the hostages."

"That's better," Devereau said.

"Only, there's no way we can get it back to you in thirty minutes."

A slight pause. "Listen, you son-of-a-bitch, it's time you get the message."

"Now, take it easy, Larry. I told you we'd cooperate. But, it's gonna take a little time. You're not leaving till after the banks open and you get the rest of the money. Right? . . . Larry, you still there?"

Devereau was busy giving Stroud some detailed instructions.

"Larry, are you there?" Ziller repeated.

"I assume you've got observers in position to watch the windows of my office," Devereau said coolly.

"What do you mean?"

"Wake the son-of-a-bitches. Because I'm getting ready to open the drapes and give them something to look at."

"Larry, take it easy. Don't do anything to screw up your plan. Larry? . . ." Ziller covered the mouthpiece of the radio and told Murphy to alert the upper observation team in the ITT Building.

The message hardly reached them before the drapes to the big corner office were opened. The observers saw one of the troops prod a middle-aged man, rumpled and groggy, his hands tied behind him, into the room. The man was pushed into a chair in the corner of the office farthest from the windows, while the troop—his body protected by his hostage— kept the muzzle of his rifle to the man's ear. No one else was in view.

"Okay, Ziller," Devereau said into the radio. "That's Ronam in the chair, the president of Root. You've got exactly thirty minutes to get that money back over here, or we decorate the walls of this office with Mr. Ronam's brains."

"Listen to me, Larry. I said we'd return the money. But we've got to count it first." Ziller looked up at the men surrounding him. These included Mike Bayne from the district attorney's office, frowning his disapproval. "You know about police work, Larry. You know about maintaining the chain of evidence. I don't have the authority to return it until it's all been properly vouchered."

"Twenty-nine minutes, Ziller."

"Larry, we'll give you the dough as soon as we check it. Just stay cool."

"You've got twenty-eight minutes left."

Ziller began to perspire. He sensed a trace of something in Devereau's voice that he had not heard before. How far could the man be pushed at this point? Experience had taught that deadline threats can usually be shrugged off. There had not been a single one in his experience that had been kept. Still, a sixteenth-inch of movement on that troop's trigger finger

would blow Ronam away. And the troop was a totally unknown quantity.

"Larry, you're going to have to understand something.
Now, I'm only interested in hostage safety. I'd return the
money in a minute, but there's other groups involved, and
we're talking about five million bucks. I got the D.A.'s office
on my back. And the borough commander. Somebody could
have reached into one of those cases and taken himself a
handful."

"Ziller, your problems don't interest me. You've got
twenty-seven minutes."

"Look. We'll start checking it out right away, and we should
get the first case back to you within the thirty minutes. We'll
probably have all six cases back in a couple hours."

"Did you say six cases?"

"Yeah."

"There should be eight."

Ziller hesitated. "Hey, you're right."

"How many men did you pick up?"

Ziller paused to consult his notes. "We account for nine
guys, one of 'em dead."

"Nine? There were eleven. I told you eleven. Goddammit!
What's the matter with you stupid cops?"

"We're still looking for the other two," Ziller said.

"Stupid cops! I lay 'em right in your laps, and you blow it.
Jesus! What do I have to do? Do you at least have names?
Let's see who's missing."

They reviewed the list and also the tag notations on the
cases that had been recovered. Floyd Washington and Mario
Blanco were still at large, holding two briefcases containing
two million dollars.

"You find the son-of-a-bitches!" Devereau screamed. "Do
you hear me? Find them. I want them caught."

"What does Blanco look like?"

"He's a fat-ass Cuban. Check your files. He's got a record a mile long. But find him quick. He left here wearing a tan suit. And Ziller, you've got twenty-three minutes to get the other six cases back, or Ronam's a dead man."

Ziller looked at the men around him. Redmond was obviously looking for the least excuse to launch his assault. He, too, had picked up the change in Devereau's voice.

The six cases of money had been tagged as evidence and were still in the van. Three million dollars. They did not appear to have been opened. The cops who had brought in the money were still waiting for their memo books to be signed in receipt. The eight men captured had been taken to the Seventeenth, and Hinton's body had been picked up and hauled away.

"Twenty-two minutes, Ziller."

Ziller looked at Weissberger and said, away from the radio, "How does he sound to you?"

Weissberger hesitated. "Different."

"You got any ideas?"

"Let me think a minute," Weissberger answered. "Keep him talking. Get him to ventilate. Try to keep changing his thought patterns."

"We're going in," Redmond snapped.

"Wait!" Ziller said. He took a deep breath and turned back to the radio. "Larry, I got an idea." He spoke calmly. All the troops in the building were tuned in, as well. "As I told you, the chief in charge of the tactical forces is here listening, and he thinks it's time to charge the building. You know and I know that that won't serve our interests, but you're going to have to show some sign of cooperation or I won't be able to stop him."

"Twenty minutes, Ziller."

"Look, I got a possible deal for you. I'll send the money back, but—"

"No!" Bayne snarled in the background.

"But you've got to give me something in return," Ziller continued. "Something I can use to cool them down. In other words, let's do some trading. You want the money. Right? And I want some hostages outta there. So pick out the hostages you need for leverage when the banks open and let the rest go."

"Ziller, I told you I'm not interested in your problems. You've got about nineteen minutes."

"Larry! F'Crissakes, think about it. What have you got if we move in? Not the money. Nothing. It'll be over. Don't you understand? I'm trying to help you. Whether I like it or not. And I don't. But hostage safety is my job. You know goddamn well a shooting war will get you nowhere. So we've got to do some dealing. You help me, I'll help you."

A pause. "Okay, Ziller, return the money and maybe I'll release a couple of hostages."

"Come on, Larry. You know that's not good enough. Christ, what do you need with all those people, anyway? Think about it. They're in your way. Pick the ones you need, and chase the rest the hell out. You get to name the deal as long as you're reasonable."

A lengthy silence. Ziller waited. He didn't want to risk oversell.

"Okay," Devereau said finally. "Here's what I'll do."

Ziller sighed and sat back in his chair. Devereau's voice had returned to its earlier coolness.

After Devereau had finished, Bayne touched Ziller's shoulder. "I will not permit you to send that money back in there. At least, not until it's been properly processed."

Ziller stood up. "What's the matter with you? I got four hundred people I'm trying to get out of there alive. If any of them are hurt, the newspapers are gonna hear about the D.A.'s office's preoccupation with money." Ziller glanced at O'Reilly, and he could tell he had the chief's support. "We'll give the stuff a quick check right here and sign it out."

Bayne clenched his jaw but remained silent.

In the penthouse office Devereau sat at his desk, collecting his thoughts. He had closed the drapes, but Ronam still sat in the chair in the corner. Ronam had been an interesting study of a man in absolute terror. Poor son-of-a-bitch! Still, it had brought Ziller to his knees.

Ziller was playing right into his hands, begging him to take the money back in return for the hostages he'd wanted to unload anyway. The trick had been to use them for the best possible return, and Ziller had worked it out for him. Ziller was getting to be one of his best men.

And he was finished with the mutinous faction of his platoon. They'd been used when they were needed and then gotten what they deserved. That son-of-a-bitch Floyd Washington was out of his hair. And Hinton. Dead in the street.

Time for the next step. He pressed the talk button on his radio. "Boston."

"Boston."

"Attention all stations!" He began laying it out for his men. In brisk military fashion. Ziller had to be impressed. The hostage-cash exchange, conceived on the spot, was clean. Easily controlled. And foolproof.

The troops were to rouse all prisoners and assemble them for a final address. Three hostages had been selected to remain from each firm. They were key employees and would be brought to the twenty-first floor and held there. The operation was then to be consolidated on the top two floors of the building.

All other hostages would be conducted to the second floor by elevator. The search team would temporarily suspend its efforts and assist in the movements of the prisoners to ensure that the operation proceeded in an orderly fashion. From the second floor, the prisoners would be led single file down the front stairwell to the lobby. After each case of money was handed through the door and checked by Stroud, fifty hostages would be allowed to leave the building. When all six cases were inside, the remaining hostages would be dismissed. If at that point the police attempted to rush the building, the remaining hostages in the penthouse would be executed.

"Hey, Dee," said one of the troops. "What about Joe Palko?"

"He is no longer of any real value to us. So why worry about him?"

"But he set up Luis. And in a way, Austin."

"Austin set himself up."

"He still set up Luis."

"Then watch for him. If he shows, bring him up here—alive. Anything else before I talk to the hostages?"

Silence.

"Have you any questions, Ziller?" Devereau asked. His voice was calm and confident.

"The whole arrangement sounds reasonable to me, Larry. Except that you're keeping more hostages than you need. All you need is one from each firm. The more you trim, the better off you'll be."

"Leave that decision to me."

"And you guys be careful," Ziller said. "We've managed so far to keep the gunplay from getting outta hand. The one man who was wounded is still alive. So the charges are still minor."

"That's enough, Ziller," Devereau said impatiently.

"Larry, I'm just tryin' to answer questions for your guys. Unlawful imprisonment and assault is all they got so far. Pretty small stuff. Especially if they come out voluntarily."

"I said knock it off, Ziller. Pay no attention to the son-of-a-bitch."

"Lieutenant?" said one of the troops.

"Right here," Ziller said.

"Which one of you is that?" Devereau shouted.

"Lieutenant, what if one of us just wanted to walk out? What do you think we'd get?"

"What the fuck's the matter with you?" Devereau screamed. "We're on our way! Have you lost your senses?"

"Depends on your record," Ziller answered, ignoring Devereau. "With a few minor counts, maybe as much as a year. With no record, even less. Nothing's happened yet. Coming out voluntarily makes it still better, of course. But if anything goes wrong, the game changes. For everybody. Whether you had anything to do with it or not."

"Ziller, you're asking for it." Devereau's voice was tense.

"Lieutenant, what about the chances of getting picked off by a cop if one of us should decide to walk out?"

"Lemme just answer this one, Larry. We won't fire on you. Mix in with the hostages and lace your fingers together on top of your head. I'll guarantee your safety."

"The next one of you that talks to that motherfucker is out," Devereau shouted. "Is that clear? Out!"

Silence.

"Which of you was talking to him?" Devereau yelled.

Continued silence.

"Speak up!" Devereau screamed.

No one answered.

"Well, at least you've got the message. We're in control. Everything's working according to plan. Now, let's get on with it. You have your assignments. I will address the hostages in exactly ten minutes."

"And remember what I told you," Ziller said. "If you want to come out, we guarantee your safety." ·

"Ziller!" Devereau's voice was shrill. "Ronam's still in that chair. If your voice shows up on this radio once more, we pull the trigger. Understand?"

"If that happens," Ziller said, "every one of you in there will be held responsible."

"Ziller?" Devereau's voice was soft. "This building's a fortress. Do you know how many people we could shoot before you could get through the door? Don't test me."

The radio remained silent for a full minute.

"Ten-four," Devereau finally said.

Ziller sat back.

"How much more abuse are you going to take from him?" Redmond asked.

"What abuse?" Ziller looked at Weissberger. "Do you think he's for real?"

"You planning to test him?" Weissberger asked.

"You're supposed to tell me."

"What would you do if I told you I thought he was faking? Push him?"

"Not right away," Ziller answered. "Let's get the cash ready to return." He glanced at Bayne, who was livid, and added, "It's only money."

"It's also evidence," Bayne snapped.

"We have to get the people out," O'Reilly said quietly.

Murphy lifted the lid on one of the briefcases. He had forced the locks with a screwdriver.

"A million bucks," Ziller said. "Right here, in one neat little pile. Do you know how many years we'd have to be on the job to pay that back?"

Joe Palko slowly opened the latch on the sheet-metal door to the duct where he had been hiding. With Luis dead, it was probably the safest place in the building. But a chance was near at hand to make his break.

He had been in the same cramped position for hours, his feet on the narrow strips of metal inside the duct, his knees and forearms pressed out against the sides so he wouldn't slide down to the fifteenth floor. His body ached, particularly his legs. The rifle slung over his back had grown oppressively heavy. And the mask was stifling.

It was time to make his move. He pushed the door open, gripped the top of the frame with both hands, and swung his body out. After rubbing his forearms to bring the blood back, he leaned his rifle against the wall and lit a cigarette. A little light came in through the office windows. It was almost dawn.

He was waiting for the captain to start speaking on the radio, because that would mean that everyone, including the troops, would be inside office areas on every occupied floor. No one would be in the stairwells, and the basement would be empty. After the hostages were released, the captain was planning to guard the basement. He had to make his dash out the service entrance during the speech.

He walked out into the elevator foyer and stood pressing the radio to his ear, waiting for the lecture to start. Suddenly he heard a key in the door to the front stairwell. He turned off the radio and slid it into the holder on his belt. He lifted his rifle and released the safety. The door eased open, and a man came through pushing the door with his back. Despite the poor light, he could make out that the man was small and black and dressed in a business suit. He carried a briefcase in one hand and his shoes in the other.

The man turned and stopped abruptly when he saw Palko, his eyes going first to the rifle and then the mask. After a minute he began to smile. "You must be Joe Palko," he said. "No one else is still wearing a mask."

"Who are you?" Palko asked. "One of the troops?"

"You know what's in this case?" the man asked.

"Money?"

"You got any idea how much?"

"No."

"How about a million and a half?"

"If you say so."

"Wanta know somethin' else? Me and you's about to become partners."

"That a fact?" Palko kept his gun trained on the man.

"That's a fact. In business you don't need to be 'ssociated for a long time in order to cut a deal. All you need is for both sides to have somethin' the other one wants."

Palko declined to comment.

"How would you like to get . . . ?" He hesitated, studying Palko. "How would you like to have a half-million dollars?"

"I guess you figure that's what you got that I want," Palko said. "Now, what have I got that you want?"

"You know this building inside out. All you gotta do is hide me in here somewhere till all this shit is over with and everybody outta here. And we become business partners, jus' like that. Y'see? Nobody know I'm in this building. They all think I left."

"And you're proposin' to divide that money with me?"

"Listen, half a million, just for hidin' me is pretty good."

"I thought you said partners."

"Okay, then halfs. One and one."

"Just checking. But it doesn't matter, because I don't want any part of that money."

"Are you crazy? Shit, man, you'd never have to do another thing the rest of your life."

"Why don't you take that briefcase and turn yourself in before something happens?"

"Hey, man, I don' believe you. I'm offering you three-quarters of a million dollars just for hidin' me."

"I don't want any part of it. I think you need to turn yourself in to the police."

"I still don't believe you. Wait a minute. Lemme put on my shoes." He set the briefcase down, bent over, and slipped a foot into one of the shoes. "Man must be weird to turn down this much money."

Palko was silent.

The man pushed a foot into the other shoe and began tying it. "So I guess you are weird." He got to his feet, and as he did, he pulled the army automatic from his belt and fired.

The slug hit Palko in the fleshy part of his shoulder. The troop fired again and missed. Palko lifted his own rifle and fired a round. He rapid-fired several more times and watched the man go down.

Seeing no movement whatever, Palko walked over, his rifle

still cocked. "Jesus, what'd you make me do that for?" he said softly. "Those shots'll probably draw a crowd." He snapped his radio back on. The man upstairs was talking. "Well, maybe they didn't hear anything," he said to the silent form. "But I ain't got time to get outta here now. He's about to finish his speech. And what am I gonna do with you so you don't lead 'em to me?"

Palko listened to the voice on the radio for a moment. "You fucked me up," he said to the body. "You nearly killed me, too." He leaned the rifle against the wall and grabbed the body by the jacket collar, pulling it toward the rear stairwell. He opened the door and dumped it onto the body already lying on the landing. "Stay here with your buddy," Palko said.

Back in the foyer, he grabbed the rifle and the briefcase and reluctantly returned to his hiding place in the sheet-metal duct. He was suddenly conscious that his shoulder was starting to burn.

25

"Good morning," Devereau said to his radio audience. "I wouldn't have gotten you up quite so early were it not for the fact that I have some exciting news. With the exception of a few key hostages, I am going to order your release in a few minutes. And as soon as the banks open and the necessary transfer of funds is made, the rest of you will be free too."

His message was received with a wave of emotional and exhilarating relief. But those who listened carefully knew he would need some hostages to take along on his withdrawal. Whom would he select, and why?

"I have been assured by the police," he continued, "that they will cooperate. The hostages chosen to remain will be brought to the twenty-first floor. The rest of you will be taken to two, and from there led out. I urge your full cooperation. Lieutenant Ziller, do you have any comments you would like to make at this time?" Devereau's tone was that of a chairman, allowing a new committee member a few words.

Ziller was taken by surprise. "Uh, yes, please do exactly as you're told. If any of you had been thinking about trying to be a hero, forget it. At this stage we are just anxious to get you all out safely."

"Thank you, Lieutenant. And now—"

"And you men with the guns, remember what I told you. A lot can still go wrong, and you're—"

"Shut up, Ziller!"

"You're way ahead if you come out voluntarily."

"Ziller, what did I tell you?"

"Forgive me, Larry. I just wanted to repeat that one point. So think about it, all of you."

"Don't listen to that son-of-a-bitch! You hear me?"

"You asked me to comment," Ziller said.

"Only to the prisoners," Devereau snapped. He looked up at the people surrounding him. The directors of the Root Corporation and their staff had all recognized him by now. "Ziller," he said calmly, "if you cross me one more time, I am going to carry out my threat to execute Ronam. Is that perfectly clear?" He watched the effect this statement had on the group before him.

"I hope you won't," Ziller said. "Remember, up to now, no one is facing a homicide charge."

"If I do shoot, you will have been responsible."

"That may or may not be true in the eyes of a jury."

"There will be no jury. There will be no trial."

"Dee?"

"Who's that?"

"Dee, this is Sally. I think you better let me go."

"You're still drunk. Calm down and you'll be all right."

"I was, but not anymore. I know what I'm doing. I can't go with you over there. I've had it, and I want to go home. So lemme go out and take my chances."

Devereau glanced at the members of the board. "You sound like you're finished, Panucci. I can't use you anymore. Get the hell out."

"Hear that, Lieutenant? I'm coming out. This is Sal Panucci. Okay?"

"Got it, Sal. Anybody else?"

"Dee?" Another one of the troops.

"I won't tolerate any more defections!" Devereau shouted. "You hear me? I'm ordering the men in the lobby to shoot any other member of the platoon who tries to leave."

"Larry." It was Ziller. "I'd think that over. If a man doesn't want to stay with you, what do you need him for?"

Devereau caught Barbara Meyner's eye for an instant. She was watching him with intense interest, but he couldn't quite read her expression. "Let me repeat what I said earlier," he said. "We're in complete control. We're proceeding exactly according to plan, and we can't be challenged. What possible reason would any of you have for quitting at this point? To give yourself up and go to prison?"

"Larry, lemme just mention," Ziller said, "things can still go wrong, guys. The easy way out could still be walking out with your hands on your heads. Think about it."

"My order about additional defectors stands," Devereau said. He waited for several seconds, noting the silence. "Ziller, it's time we began the exchange. We expect the first briefcase in ten minutes."

"Lieutenant?"

"Who's that?" Devereau asked quickly.

"Lieutenant, this is Joe Palko, the chief engineer of the building."

"Hello, Joe."

"Lieutenant, I ain't a party to what's going on here today. I hope you know that."

"We do, Joe."

"All I wanna do is to get out of here. Only, I can't just walk out. These guys've been looking for me for hours, and I'm not gonna take any chances on what some of 'em's got in mind."

"We couldn't care less about him at this point, Ziller,"

Devereau said. "As far as I'm concerned, he can proceed to the lobby and leave with the other hostages."

"What do you think, Lieutenant? The others might feel differently."

"Joe, I don't think you have to worry as far as Larry is concerned. But as long as you're in a place where they can't find you, maybe you better stay there. Keep your radio on, but don't transmit anymore, unless you have to."

"He's perfectly safe," Devereau said. "He can leave."

"Why don't we proceed with the exchange?" Ziller said.

Daylight. A pair of radio cars and a special equipment truck drove into Park Avenue and stopped in front of 330, just outside of the coil of barbed wire. A dozen or so cops, all carrying rifles or shotguns, climbed from the three vehicles and lined up behind them, using them as cover. The bloody couch that had been used to carry Roberto Molina still sat on the wide sidewalk.

Several more cops came down the sidewalk from Fiftieth. One of them was carrying a briefcase, while another was holding a wooden pole some twelve feet in length. They stopped just short of the door to 330 Park and one of the cops suspended the briefcase by the handle on the end of the pole. He reached out and dropped it just in front of the door.

"Boston."

"Boston."

"Dee?"

"What is it?"

"Tell your lieutenant friend we're not gonna go ahead with this thing until he get that fucking firing squad away from the front door. What's he tryin' to pull?"

"You listening, Ziller?"

"They're not going to fire on your guys. Not unless your guys start firing first. They're there to cover the cops delivering the dough. One of my co-workers believes in heavy cover.

Christ, what're you worryin' about? You've still got a building full of hostages."

"They weren't there the first time the money got delivered. We ain't goin' out there till they leave."

"Ziller, get 'em the hell out of there. You know damn well we're not going to fire on the cops delivering the money."

"I'll see what I can do."

The cops behind the three vehicles climbed back into them, and the vehicles drove away. The front door of 330 Park opened, and one of the troops stepped quickly outside and grabbed the money.

Ten minutes later the doors to 330 Park opened again and a stream of people poured out. The first things they saw were the bloodstained sofa, the bus, and the coiled barbed wire. A policeman called to them from in front of the ITT Building. They ran toward him and were led into the computer show-room on the corner, where detectives took down their iden-tification. Each hostage represented a distinct and separate charge against all perpetrators.

After the employees had been interviewed, they were allowed to go out the side door of the showroom, where they were greeted by excited crowds and the press. They flung their arms upward, shouting their relief as they looked around the crowd for family and friends. Reunions were emotional: crushing embraces, screaming, laughter, body-shaking weep-ing, kissing, and frantic chatter about what it had been like and how it was to be out. Two of the men who had been re-leased were in underwear, and a few uninvolved spectators pointed at them and sniggered about what could possibly have led to that.

After the fifty hostages had been released, things inside 330 Park quieted down. The cop who had used the long pole to deposit the first case walked up to the sofa without the pole and dropped the second case. Before he was back into the sheltering entrance of the ITT Building, one of the troops was out for it and back into the lobby. Several minutes passed, and then more employees came rushing out of the building to disappear into the computer center.

Sally Panucci forced his way past the line of employees in the stairwell and came into the lobby. Big Charlie was running things there while Stroud sat off to one side, waiting for the next delivery. Pedro stood by, along with Miguel Sosa, Smokey, Rick Dominguez, Wally Cothron, Raymond Galloway, and Hector Collazo. Sally looked at Miguel, who had a very strange expression on his face as their eyes met. The line of hostages extended from the open stairwell toward the middle of the lobby.

"Charlie," Sally said. "Like I told Dee, I'm going out."

Big Charlie smiled. "Just means less people when it come time to divide the money. Why don'cha take off your belt and leave it?"

"Wait a minute." Miguel Sosa walked toward him.

"What?" Sally looked up apprehensively.

Sosa leaned his rifle against the wall. Then he began unbuckling his own belt. "I'm going too."

Charlie's jaw dropped.

"Miguel?" Hector Collazo looked up in surprise.

Stroud got to his feet. "You're crazy, Miguel. Anyway, Dee said nobody else can walk out except Sally."

"Would you shoot to stop me?" Miguel asked.

"What you wanna go out for, Miguel?" Charlie asked. "Man, I thought you was with us. I thought you was part of the hard core."

"I was on the twelfth floor yesterday when Roberto got it. There's a lotta cops out there. I don't think things are going as perfect as Dee says. I been thinkin' it over, and I'm going out." His tone was resolute.

Collazo appeared stunned. "If Miguel goes out, that must

mean . . . Shit!" He looked around at Charlie and Stroud and then at the door. "Miguel," he said softly. "Do you know somethin' you don't tell me yet?"

"I'm going out."

Collazo looked stricken. "You think I should go, too?"

"Do what you want to do."

Collazo looked at Charlie inquisitively.

"Ain't nobody *in here* gonna shoot ya, if that what you won-derin'," Charlie said. "Man, if you like going to jail, then, shit, go."

"If Miguel is goin'," Collazo said, "that good enough for me." He leaned his rifle against the wall and then unhooked his belt.

"Don't you think we better check this with Dee?" Stroud drew out his radio.

"Shit, no need stirrin' that up," Charlie said. "Let 'em go."

"Le's get on with it," Raymond Galloway said. "There's more bread out there." He opened the door and came back with another briefcase, which he handed to Stroud.

Within minutes the door opened again and another line of hostages scurried frantically along the sidewalk. Interspersed among them were three men in G.I. fatigues with their hands on their heads.

Galloway brought in still another case and Stroud opened it, checking to see that the bundles of money were solid. Stroud gave Charlie a nod and Charlie directed the line of employees to proceed. He counted them as they moved to-ward the door, counting aloud as he grasped each employee lightly by the arm. Charlie came to two of the troops in civil-ian clothes and almost missed noticing them. The other troops had immediately recognized them and were watching anxiously to see what Charlie would do.

Charlie stopped the line. "You got to be jokin'," he said.

"We're goin' out, Charlie," one of them said.

"Who you goin' to tell the bulls you are?" Charlie asked.

"The idea is to disappear into the crowd," the other one said.

"You ain't seen the setup out there," Charlie said. "You gotta go through a police lineup and and identify yourself."

The two men looked at each other. "We can fake that."

Charlie looked at the hostages behind them and then looked back at them. His expression suggested that they were among the stupidest people in the world. "You go through that door, you go to jail."

"We're goin' out," the younger one said. "We think we can make it."

Stroud was about to interrupt, but Charlie held up his hand. Then he waved the two men on out. When they reached the sidewalk, they saw the barbed wire for the first time. There were no crowds in sight. They stopped, looked in all directions, and saw they had no choice but to follow along with the hostages. As they entered the showroom, the copywriter from the twentieth floor, still in his Jockey shorts, pointed them out to the police. A few feet beyond was the side door to Fiftieth Street and the noisy, congested throngs of people.

After all six cases were back inside 330 and all floors except twenty-one and twenty-two had been completely evacuated, Charlie radioed Devereau and reported on the defectors. By the time all employees were out, a total of ten troops had quit, four in civilian clothes. Devereau, particularly surprised about Miguel Sosa, accepted the news with reasonable control. He opened his notebook and began writing.

On the twenty-first floor, Billy Pickett, having delivered Rhodes, Guidera, and Shaer from eighteen, went into the men's room to take a leak. After finishing, he lit a cigarette and leaned against the wall to collect his thoughts. It had been a long night, and he ached from exhaustion. He wondered who was smart, the bunch who gave up, or Dee, who said they had it made.

The caper had been a "why-the-hell-not-do-it?" thing at the beginning. He and Wayne had no roots anywhere. Dee said the thing couldn't fail. And he'd sounded like the smartest fucking genius in the world when he talked about it. And Wayne had sold him on the idea of being rich. Only, Wayne's ass was dead now, and he wasn't all that sure of his own chances. Pickett wanted to check Wayne's body, get his knife out of his pocket. And a few other things. His wallet. His book of names and numbers. All that other junk he carried around. To remember him by. Longtime buddies. In and out of a lotta shit together. . . .

Pickett left the men's room. He nodded at one of the other troops and ducked into the rear stairwell. Five floors down. He took his time. He really wasn't in a hurry to see Wayne's corpse again. When the sixteenth-floor landing came into view, he saw the other body heaped on top of Wayne's and rolled it over to get a look at his face.

Suddenly the door from the sixteenth-floor foyer opened, and Pickett looked up. A tall slim man with light hair and a pocked face. In fatigues. But not one of the troops. Palko!

The man saw him and quickly retreated. Pickett started after him, carrying his M-14 in readiness. When he reached the foyer, the door to the office area was already closing. Pickett stopped and pulled out his radio. "Boston."

"Boston."

"Dee, I found Palko. I'm on sixteen, by the elevator. I got the son-of-a-bitch trapped in the offices."

"Hold there. I'll send some men to help you. And remember, you've got to take him alive. That clear? Alive!"

"Dee. Another thing. Floyd's down here too."

"Doing what?"

"Not much. Somebody shot him full o' holes."

26

Devereau had been devising a new deployment of his forces when the call came in from Pickett. He had seventeen men left, eighteen including himself. With the mutiny over and the defectors gone, those still with him should be solid. And with the hostages consolidated on two floors, he had more than enough troops.

After receiving Pickett's call, he wondered why Floyd had come back. He carefully selected men from the earlier search party to send to the sixteenth floor. Smokey. Cothron. Galloway. Rick Dominguez. He wished he still had the steadying influence of Sosa in the group, but Sosa was gone. Who could account for the occasional vagaries of the Latin mind? The one person he did not want in the search group was Pedro. Galloway showed occasional impulsiveness but should be safe in a controlled situation. Pedro would stay in the lobby with Charlie.

Ziller and the others in the van were monitoring Devereau's instructions. Redmond wanted to plunge ahead with an assault on the building to counter the search for Palko. Ziller wouldn't agree. It was too late for that. The search party was already on the sixteenth floor. A rushed assault meant nothing less than an all-out shooting war. That made no sense. They could only hope that somehow Palko would survive the search.

But Ziller did detect a tactical chink in Devereau's setup. The men on the lower levels did not have hostages for protection. Without radio contact with the upper floors, they would be isolated. And this contact could be broken by simply turning off the repeater. The radios would not carry vertically through twenty-two floors of concrete, which was why Devereau had set up the repeater in the first place.

Ziller proposed one possible alternate use of some of Redmond's power. He suggested bringing up the ERV, the tank parked on Forty-ninth, and parading it in front of 330 for its psychological impact. In the famous John and Al's Williamsburg siege in Brooklyn some years before, the very presence of the monstrous contraption had contributed to the surrender of all four perpetrators.

When Pickett's call and Devereau's follow-up instructions were received by the troops in the lobby, the four men tapped for the search party moved quickly into one of the elevators and pressed the button for the sixteenth floor. Pedro, hearing that Palko was cornered, dashed into the elevator just before the door closed. Charlie shouted, "Hey, you Mexican son-of-a-bitch! You come back here." But the elevator was already moving.

The five troops reached the sixteenth floor, where Pickett stood waiting. They talked briefly. They were six hunters surrounding a trapped animal. They looked at the door and remembered that Palko was similarly armed. He could be waiting on the other side to blast anybody coming through. They would have to move defensively. Take no chances.

Pedro stood back and fired three shots through it at different angles. Then Pickett reached out, turned the knob, and kicked it open. After a few seconds, he stepped through, rifle first, and looked around.

Smokey followed and shouted, "Joe Palko! Come on out with your hands up and we'll hold our fire! Joe Palko! Do you hear me? Come on out! Hands up! And we won't shoot!"

After waiting a few seconds Smokey repeated the call, louder. Hearing nothing, they looked at one another. Raymond Galloway held up a clenched fist as he looked at the others. Pedro's deep-set eyes gleamed.

They moved forward cautiously, checking room after room, shooting through every closed door before kicking it open. Finally they reassembled back in the foyer, certain Palko was still somewhere on the floor. Suddenly Smokey pointed at a sheet-metal door with a swing latch. It apparently provided access to some kind of air duct inside the service closet. That had to be the hole through which Palko had disappeared.

The men turned to face the metal door. Smokey called to Joe Palko inside the duct, offering him safety if he came out. When Smokey received no answer, he told the men where to stand for cover and how to get the swing latch lifted.

"No need to let him get first shot," Pedro said, and he fired a round into the duct, chest-high.

"No!" Smokey shouted. "Jesus, what'd you do that for?"

"Come on, now Smoke," Galloway said. "You don't think we oughta take a chance on him blastin' away at us? Pedro, man, I think you shot too high. What if he was squattin' down?" Galloway put an M-14 slug lower down in the duct.

"Jesus, you bastards, no more!" Smokey shouted, but Pedro fired off another round.

"I want me a little of that before we open that door," Pickett said in his characteristic understated tone. He fired into the duct.

Pedro fired twice more.

"Well, shit, man, if that's the way it going to be, okay." Rick Dominguez fired two shots.

Pedro, Galloway, and Pickett each fired several more times into the duct, peppering it from head height to knee level and from one side to the other.

"That's enough!" Smokey was trembling. He had been involved in shady penny-ante stuff all his life, but this was an execution. The first he had ever witnessed. And from close range. And like it or not, he was a party to it. He'd joined the caper to be the electronics man.

"Now we'll see," Pedro said, and walked over to the sheet-metal door.

Galloway held his rifle up, ready to cover for Pedro if Palko just happened to have survived that fusillade and was about to emerge, blazing away with his own rifle.

Pedro lifted the swing latch and pulled the door open. The space was empty. Palko was truly the invisible man.

Pickett rushed over to the duct and looked up, then down. "The son-of-a-bitch is one floor down! Let's go git 'im."

Smokey was powerless to stop them. They were out the door and down the back stairwell. By the time he reached them, they were on the fifteenth floor emptying their rifles into the duct. Smokey shouted, but they heard nothing.

"*Now* we'll see," Pedro said. His black eyes glistened under his heavy brows as he walked over to the door and opened it. Even Palko's face had taken several slugs. They had finally nailed the invisible man.

Smokey stared at him. Why had he stayed there? He must have heard the commotion on sixteen. Although Smokey hated getting closer to the blood-splashed body, he went over and examined the latch. Both inside and outside arms were designed to operate as one, being attached through a single bolt with fasteners into the handles on both sides of the door. Unfortunately for the dead man, the inside fastener was deformed, and he had been trapped.

The hunt was over. The fox had been ripped into fur and blood by the hounds. The troops looked at one another. "Okay," Raymond Galloway said finally, "At least we kept him from gettin' us first. What now?"

"This was a stupid thing to do," Cothron said.

"I wasn't going to let him shoot me first," Pedro said.

Galloway looked at Smokey. "The point is, man, it's done. Now what?"

"I don't know," Smokey said.

"What's the problem?" Pickett said. "Nobody knows about this but us. Who says we have to ever tell anyone?" Pickett closed and latched the door. "We'll just tell Dee the Phantom got away again. Anybody see anything wrong with that? Shit, we'll be outta here'n a couple hours."

"I'm going out now," Cothron said. "I'm going out there and do everything I can to convince the cops I left before this happened."

"You going to tell them who shot him?" Pedro asked.

"I'll tell 'em anything I have to tell 'em to make sure they know I didn't do it."

"That not too good for us," Pedro said. He pulled his automatic from his holster.

"Jesus, Pedro, put that thing away!" Smokey shouted.

Before any of the others could move, Pedro fired three times, point-blank, at Cothron's chest.

The police observers in the ITT building had seen and reported the search team when it was running around some of the outside offices on the sixteenth floor, occasionally firing through a door. Little could be done, and Ziller hoped Palko would manage to elude them again. The observers did not see the M-14's being fired into the duct on either floor, because it was located at the core of the building. They might have heard the shots several hours earlier, during the still hours before daybreak. But it was eight o'clock, and the city's ambient hum prevailed once again, even though Park Avenue was without traffic.

Ziller was greatly relieved when Smokey radioed Devereau to report that Joe Palko had managed to escape again, this time through an air duct. Devereau told the troops to abandon the search and return to their stations. Palko was to be ignored as long as he stayed out of sight. If he surfaced, he was to be taken alive, if at all possible.

Ziller and the others listened as Devereau checked assignments with the remaining members of the platoon. Devereau continued to use his code numbers for his men, and as he quoted the numbers, Ziller looked at his notes. The code numbers had all been nailed down. Murphy and the rest of the backup team had been gathering this intelligence by debriefing the defecting troops. Devereau had three men including Smokey Hampton in the basement, four including Charlie Patterson in the lobby, four including one named Pickett on twenty-one. He, Stroud, Benjy Sanchez, and Raymond Galloway were on the penthouse floor, and three troops including a hot dog named Rick Dominguez were stationed by the elevator motors. Eighteen men.

Ziller continued rehashing the situation with Weissberger and the others. If the case was to be moved toward a conclusion, a face-to-face confrontation would probably be essential. And prior to that, the number of perpetrators had to be reduced further if possible. If those on the lower levels were to be made vulnerable by cutting off radio contact with the upper floors, Devereau would have to be distracted so that he'd have no reason to use his radio. This could be done by getting him on the phone and keeping him there for as long as necessary. It also provided an opportunity to keep him ventilating.

A detailed plan of action began to solidify in Ziller's mind. After noting that Redmond was out of earshot, Ziller proposed sending Emergency Service personnel to probe the lower floors. O'Reilly, who was tired of battling with Redmond, asked how they'd quiet Redmond down if they didn't hand that mission over to him and his TPF boys. Ziller explained that it could be done and still go by the book. The Tactical Patrol Force was to be used for outer-perimeter contacts. Inner-perimeter actions were to be handled by the ESD.

Ziller poured himself another glass of milk as he outlined his plan. It helped quiet the little animal that had begun scurrying around clawing at his stomach lining.

There were so many actions to coordinate. So many details to keep straight. The whole ponderous sequence of events had to be put into motion, and everything had to come off in the proper order. He looked around at the others. O'Reilly. Weissberger. Murphy. Bayne. Captain Daniels of the ESD. "We all set on everything?" he asked.

Redmond approached just as everyone was getting up from the table. A quick meeting had obviously just been completed and action decisions made. "Hey what's going on?" he asked.

"We're gonna need your help," Ziller answered. "The chief'll bring you up-to-date." He picked up his glass of milk and drained it. He sat back for a few seconds to collect his thoughts while he watched Redmond look around, trying to figure out what he'd missed by slipping out for a cup of coffee. Then he picked up the designated phone and dialed.

27

Devereau was pleased when the phone began to ring. Ziller was finally getting the message that he was to do as he was told and stay off the radio. He was beginning to have respect. Let the phone ring. A good opportunity to keep the son-of-a-bitch off balance.

Another hour or so, and the banks would open. Twenty million dollars! The entire world would take note. And the name of Larry Devereau would become a household word.

"Boston."

"Boston."

"Lieutenant Ziller calling the penthouse. Larry, are you there?"

"What do you want!"

"Why don't you pick up your phone? Christ, you tell me to call by phone, and you don't even pick the thing up."

"We're talking. What's on your mind?"

"Not on the radio."

"What's wrong with radio? Let my men listen. There's

nothing you could say at this point that would make a damn. They know we're on our way and you're going to cooperate."

Ziller hesitated. "Look. Larry, this is private."

"Such as?"

"If I tell you over the radio, it won't be private anymore. Christ, pick up the phone!"

Devereau paused. "Okay, Harry. Why not?" He picked up the receiver. "All right, I'm on the phone. And from the sound of things, you're on your speaker, so this conversation isn't all that private."

"Most of 'em got sleepy and went home."

"Yeah, Harry, sure they did. But get to the point. I haven't got all day."

Ziller exhaled silently and nodded at one of the backup detectives from the hostage squad. "Uh, coupla things, Larry." He watched as the detective promptly radioed the cop manning the repeater in room 11-S in the Waldorf.

"Come on, Ziller. Get on with it."

"Take it easy. For openers, why don't we talk about breakfast? It's past eight o'clock. Everybody over there must be gettin' hungry. And you know how people are till they get their coffee in the morning. And considerin' what your tastes were at dinner last night, maybe we can do a little wheelin' and dealin'. You know, maybe trade a few hostages for some eggs Benedict." He looked at Weisberger as he spoke, noting Weissberger's smile and nod of concurrence.

While he was talking, the other phases of his plan were being launched. Murphy was winding up his final briefing of the ESD squad. The twelve men watched as he traced once again the floor plans of the crucial levels of the building. They could expect three troops in the basement and four in the lobby. The ESD cops had been on duty throughout the night, alternating with another equivalent detail on two-hour shifts of full alert. One of them joked nervously that he was glad to get the overtime, that he'd finally have a week almost as good as his brother-in-law, the carpet mechanic.

Outside the van on Fiftieth, O'Reilly was rounding up reporters to brief them while the ESD detail headed for the service entrance of 330 carrying in their vehicle a six-inch diameter concrete-filled steel pipe called Matilda.

". . . so drop it, Ziller. I'm not interested in breakfast. I just want to get the rest of the money and get out of here."

"Then let's say you settle for a couple urns of coffee and some doughnuts. Okay?"

On Forty-ninth two cops in mechanic's garb climbed onto the ERV tank. A few seconds later, its engine thundered to life and labored unevenly as it warmed up. Then it advanced slowly toward Park, with bystanders cheering at its progress. The cops at the police barriers pulled them aside, and the menacing hulk moved past the flowered esplanade onto the sidewalk.

". . . but, Larry, I'm serious about the hostages. What's the point in keeping so many? Like I said earlier, all you need is one from each of the companies in the building. As long as you've got the honcho with the clout to call the bank, what do you want the others for?"

The observation team in 345 Park coordinated the ESD detail with the distraction provided by the ERV. They were to allow the tank three minutes directly in front of the building and then signal the ESD cops to proceed.

The ERV moved along the sidewalk in front of the Colgate Building. It reached Fiftieth, eased off the curb, and crossed the street. It moved in front of the Root Tower, too close to the building to be seen by occupants in upper floors.

". . . like I've been sayin', Larry, you can call the shots as long as you're reasonable."

"Ziller, what's that racket out there?"

"What racket?"

"What do you mean, what racket? It sounds like a tank coming down the middle of Park Avenue."

"I can barely hear it. Could it be one of those big garbage trucks, maybe over behind the hotel?"

"Come on, Ziller, you son-of-a-bitch! You're playing with fire. Don't forget, we've still got the gun to Ronam's head. And there's lots more where he came from."

"And that's another matter. You've had that man sitting there for over two hours. If he has a heart attack, you're as guilty of murder as if you put a bullet through his head."

"Hold it a minute." Devereau turned to Stroud. "Call Charlie and find out what's making all that racket." Then, back into the phone, "Ziller, I'm warning you. Don't fuck around with me. We intend to leave as planned, and I don't care who we have to put away to do it. . . . "

The tank bucked as it rolled over the couch in front of 330, crushing it almost flat. The three men in the lobby watched it rumble by. It passed within a few feet of them, and they wondered what the hell it was and if the cops intended at some point to crash through the glass wall. Pedro wanted to open the door and throw his grenade at it, but Charlie, noting the words "Police Rescue Ambulance" brightly painted on its side, chose to watch and wait. It occurred to him though that the tank could easily enter the lobby and that maybe they needed a few hostages for protection.

He decided to call Smokey in the basement to come up and see the thing and talk about having a few hostages on the lower levels. Rather than stir Devereau up by calling Smokey on the radio, he sent Pedro down for him. Pedro returned with Smokey and the other two troops from the basement. Everybody wanted to see the tank.

After the tank reached Fifty-first, it turned completely around in the middle of the street and started back the other way, climbing over the curb and passing once more in front of 330.

"Like I said, Larry," Ziller was saying, "As long as you keep all of your prisoners alive, we have no choice but to keep our distance and cooperate."

"Hold it a minute." Devereau covered the phone with his hand and looked up at Stroud, who had just rushed in, gesturing frantically. "Well? What is it?"

"I can't reach the lobby by radio."

"Maybe it's your unit. Try a different one."

"I tried three different ones. It ain't the radios. Alfredo ain't answerin'."

"What?" He looked out the window at the Waldorf and listened for a moment to the thundering drone coming from the street. "Send Galloway down to see what's going on. I want him back in three minutes." He watched Stroud hurry out of the room and then put the phone back to his mouth. "I hope you're not trying to pull something, Ziller, because I won't tolerate it. Do you understand?"

"Larry, what are you talking about?"

"First of all, I want to know what that goddamn noise is in the street. Second, I want to know why I can't reach my men on the lower floors by radio."

"Okay." Like the manual says, never get caught in a lie. Never risk losing credibility with the hostage taker. "I found out about the noise. It's our emergency-rescue vehicle. It's like a tank, only without any guns. You're probably familiar with it. It's actually used mainly as an ambulance, and we got one hot shot in the department, every time anything happens in the city, he insists on using it. He's trying to get a federal grant to buy a couple more."

"You planning to crash the lobby?"

"Are you kidding? All the hostages you've got in there?"

"Then what about our radios? Have you cut off our transmitter?"

"I'll look into it."

"Just don't play dumb cop with me. You must have known right off that if we were going to use portables throughout this building, we'd need an outside repeater transmitter. What I want to know is, did you find it and turn it off? Because if you did, I want it back on, and quick."

"Of course we knew you had to have a repeater. I told you I'd check into it."

When Galloway reached the lobby, he found all six troops with their noses pressed to the glass, looking out. The tank was making its third ear-splitting pass in front of the door, humping just slightly as it rolled over the remains of the couch.

On Fifty-first, outside the service entrance to the building, the twelve ESD cops watched a window in 345 Park. The group was led by Captain Daniels, a grandfather who barely looked forty, and Sergeant Gus Miller, raspy-voiced and wearing a turtleneck shirt. Daniels checked his watch and then pulled on his gas mask, adjusting it for a good seal. The others followed Daniels' every move. He was one of those rarities on the force, a cop revered by his subordinates.

A light flashed in the window in 345 Park. The six cops who had been carrying Matilda picked it up and began measuring the door for a shot. They moved back, stood poised for a moment, and then brought it forward with a rush. The door broke open.

Daniels and Miller scrambled into the service corridor, followed by those not carrying the ram. Those handling it quickly set it down and grabbed their weapons, falling in behind the others. The team filed into the basement, advancing cautiously toward the stairs to the lobby. When they reached the door, Daniels unlocked it and pushed it open a crack. All seven troops were lined up with their faces to the glass.

Daniels paused, concentrating on the sound of the ERV. When it reached its maximum intensity, he pushed the door open, and the cops hustled through, assuming positions offering the best possible cover in the the bare lobby. Several flattened themselves into the insets of the elevators, two crouched behind the one large potted tree, several others dropped themselves prone on the floor. All of them aimed their weapons at the backs of the seven men at the front of the lobby.

On a signal from Daniels three of the cops pulled out gas canisters, yanked the pins, and hurled them the length of the lobby. The canisters hissed and sputtered, and the choking fumes billowed upward, enveloping the troops.

As the gas hit them, they whirled to catch a glimpse of the dozen cops, who looked like men from another planet in their goggle-eyed masks and bulky bulletproof vests. A couple of the troops fumbled for their own gas masks, but it was too late. They dropped them and fell to the floor, gasping, trying to find a pocket of fresh air. Galloway started firing his M-14 wildly in the direction of the cops, and the crack of his rifle was answered by the boom, boom, boom of a pump-action shotgun. He crumpled to the floor, bleeding from multiple wounds. The troop nearest to him was hit in the arm by one of the pellets.

Pedro hurled himself against the glass, trying to break it with his shoulder. He bounced back and tried again with his rifle butt before dropping to the floor. Smokey immediately recognized the futility of the situation, throwing his hands up and running toward the cops. Charlie got out his keyring and tried to open the doors, but the fumes overpowered him. Unable to see, he dropped the keys and plunged after Smokey. Then the rest of them followed, running or crawling, screaming from the agony of the gas in their faces.

Galloway remained by the door, smearing the terrazzo with blood as he struggled to move away from the hissing canisters.

Finally, two of the cops ran to him and grabbed his shoulders, pulling him toward the rear of the lobby, painting an uneven red line on the gleaming floor. Two more cops knelt over Sergeant Miller, who had taken an M-14 slug in the thigh. The rest of them forced the troops face down and snapped handcuffs on their wrists behind their backs.

"Goddammit, Ziller, I don't know what you're trying to accomplish with this phone call. I only know that you're going to do exactly as I say."

"Larry, I told you we'd do that. Listen, you're well situated, and you're in control, and we're going to cooperate. Now, there's something I'd like to ask you to do for me, and that's to give Ronam a break. He's been in the chair over two hours, and he's no young man. Give him a rest and put somebody else there."

"Shut up a minute." Devereau covered the phone and looked up at Stroud. "Well?"

"Galloway ain't back. It's been over five minutes. He's had plenty o' time."

"Jesus Christ, go down there and see what's going on!"

"I ain't going down there."

Devereau's jaw dropped open. "What do you mean you're not going down there? Go see what's happening. That's an order."

"I said I ain't going down there." Stroud's tone was quiet but final.

Devereau paused. What was happening downstairs? "I really need you here anyway," he said to Stroud. "Send one of the other men. Wait. You better send two men. Pick one from upstairs and one from twenty-one. Tell them to be quick. Two minutes." He held up two fingers. Then he uncovered the phone. "Listen, Ziller, too many things are happening around here that smell like you. And I don't like it. There are things going on I can't explain. Like the man I sent to the lob-

by to report back in three minutes! That was nearly ten minutes ago!"

"How am I supposed to know what's happening over there?
You've got control of that building, and I'm a block away.
Matter of fact, I'm beginning to think maybe that's our problem. We need to get together and talk about the situation
face-to-face."

One of the cops in the lobby spotted the movement of an
elevator by the lights above the elevator doors. When the
doors slid open, the two troops found themselves staring into
the muzzles of seven or eight poised weapons held by cops in
gas masks. Then they saw their buddies facedown on the floor
and picked up the smell of the tear gas. Then they saw Galloway.

"How many times must I tell you, Ziller? I don't have to discuss anything with you. Look, I haven't yet figured out why
you made this call, but I want to get off the phone."

"Listen, Larry, you're interested in getting the rest of the
money, and I'm interested in getting everybody out of there
safely. We've got plenty to talk about. Let's arrange a meeting. If I'm willing to come and talk a deal, will you let your extra hostages go?"

"You want to come here?" Devereau's tone changed. "Are
you offering yourself as a hostage in exchange for the others?
I just might be willing to consider that."

"You know we never exchange hostages."

"How do you know I won't just take you prisoner?"

"We're gonna have to talk about the—"

"Shut up a minute." Devereau looked up at Stroud. "What
now?" He covered the mouthpiece of the phone.

"You tell me. They didn't come back."

"Then send two more."

"Dee, something's wrong."

"Tell one of the men upstairs to go out on the roof and take
a look around."

"Dee, he'd be a sittin' duck."

"There's no chance of them firing on one of my men. We've got hostages."

"If you wanna tell one o' those two boys to go out on the roof, you go ahead and do it. Only, you must be tired 'cause I think you've quit thinking. Somethin's happened downstairs."

Devereau's expression suddenly changed. He stared at the phone in his hand as if it were something he wanted to destroy. He looked at his watch. Ziller had kept him on the phone bullshitting about nothing for close to a half-hour. He'd been suckered! The call was a diversion. The tank. The dead radios. What *had* happened downstairs? He put the phone back to his mouth. "Ziller!" But Ziller wasn't even there. He heard a dial tone.

In his rage, he had difficulty dialing. As soon as Ziller picked up, he yelled, "Ziller, you cocksucker!"

"Take it easy. I hung up because I thought you'd put your phone down."

"Ziller, I want some answers, and I want them quick!"

"As a matter of fact, I do have some new information for you. Nine more of your men came out."

"What are you talking about? That's impossible."

"Listen, I know you must be surprised. But it's a fact. I don't have all their names yet. One of 'em's Charlie Patterson."

"Ziller, you're a lying son-of-a-bitch!"

"Larry, I'm telling you the truth. But it doesn't make any difference. You've still got plenty of men. You're still in control of the situation. And as long as you keep all of those people in there healthy, we're going to cooperate with you. So let's get together and try to come up with a hard deal."

"I want those men back."

"Larry, you know we can't do that."

"You send them back or I start executing, beginning with Ronam."

"But that makes no sense. You're still in good shape. And those hostages, live and healthy, are your ticket out. Look, I'm offering to get together and discuss the situation face-to-face. Do you realize we've been in constant contact for nearly twenty hours and we've never actually met? It's time we did."

"I recognize the speech, Ziller. It's word for word right out of the manual. But, then, what else would I expect from you? That's why you're going to be living on a cop's salary for the rest of your life." He paused. "Okay, Lieutenant, time for a face-to-face meeting. But on my terms." His tone had changed again. He sounded calmer. "I want you here in my office in exactly ten minutes."

28

"That's not the way it works, Larry. We set up a meeting on neutral turf. Then I come back to my people and see what they say. You gotta remember, I'm not the final authority here, so it pays for you to try to be reasonable."

"How about the area in front of the elevators on the twenty-second floor? I'll see that it's cleared of my men."

"Come on, Larry. I'd hardly call that neutral."

"All right, Ziller, what do you propose? I could use a laugh."

"I was thinking maybe the lobby of the building. It's empty now."

"Why are we wasting our time talking? The banks are going to be opening shortly. I've got work to do."

"Keep in mind, Larry, that wherever we meet, there's no way we can hold you, because of the hostages. We could meet in the street, for that matter. You see *Dog Day Afternoon?*"

"Look, Ziller, either you get serious or let's forget it. My final offer is the twentieth floor."

"What's wrong with the lobby? Don't you understand? We can't lay a finger on you because of the hostages."

"Ziller, how are my men up here going to know what's happening in the lobby?"

"We'll turn your repeater back on."

"And then turn it back off? I learn from my mistakes, Ziller. The twentieth floor."

"Okay, suppose we talk twentieth floor for a minute. You are to come alone, unarmed, and keep all of your men on twenty-one or above."

"How soon can you be here?" A trace of eagerness hurried his question.

"After you give me your personal guarantee that I will be able to leave safely."

"You've got it. When can I expect you?"

"Twenty minutes?"

"Why so long?"

"How's fifteen?"

"I'll be waiting for you. Incidentally, Ziller, how long have you controlled my repeater?"

"I don't remember exactly. Last night sometime."

"And you waited until this morning to use it?" Devereau's tone was faintly appreciative. Respect for an adversary.

Ziller remained silent.

"Not bad, Harry." A genuine compliment. "Now, play your cards right and maybe you'll get your precious hostages. A few today and the rest a little later."

"I want to make another condition for this meeting of ours. Take the gun away from Ronam's head and let him out of that chair."

"Now you're getting pushy, Ziller. If that's one of your objectives, bring it to the table. I'll see what you've got to offer in return. Didn't you say we were getting together to do a little business?"

"Listen, Larry, we're worried about what the pressure could

do to that man. If anything happens to him, we got a problem."

"Maybe I need to execute one hostage. Maybe then you'd cut out all the horseshit and get up here."

"We've been over that. The minute one citizen gets it, the caper's over."

"Now, let me tell you something, you son-of-a-bitch! You and your buddies listening there with you. You've been saying that over and over again. And it's bullshit. I could kill a half dozen if I wanted to. And if I still had thirty left, you'd still have to squat on command from me."

"Larry, as long as everybody stays healthy, we're going to give you plenty of room. You've got a chance to pull off a real class number here. So don't screw it up at this stage. Okay? Now, I'll see you in fifteen minutes."

Ziller turned off the phone.

"You call that a negotiation?" Weissberger asked quickly. He was being glib, but his eyes reflected fear for his friend.

"I've done better." Ziller looked away.

"You're not really planning to just go right up to the twentieth floor?" Weissberger stared at Ziller incredulously. "Why, shit, you know he's going to grab you. He must be laughing and thinking you're the dumbest cop in New York. After all you've done to him, you're planning to go in there and let him get even?"

"Just can the bullshit and help me get ready," Ziller said. "Besides, I'm not going alone. I'm planning to take along a lot of help."

"You're still going the last leg of the trip alone."

Ziller put his right foot on a chair and pulled up his pants leg. "Jerry, lemme borrow your ankle holster."

"He's going to take that off of you first thing," Weissberger said.

"That's what I'm counting on," Ziller answered. "Then maybe he won't look for the other one." He spent a minute or two adjusting the holster. Then he transferred his own thirty-eight into it. "Now for the one I don't plan for him to find." He sent a detective out to his car to get the crotch holster and twenty-five automatic from the gun box in his trunk.

O'Reilly said, "Harry, don't you think we oughta try holding awhile and see if we can wait him out? He's gotta come down sooner or later."

"Why has he gotta?" Ziller asked. "He's consolidated now. And he's down to eight men. He can sit there as long as he wants and make all kinds of demands. There's no way we're gonna make any progress without some face-to-face dialogue. I'm planning to have Daniels and a squad of his guys just one floor down backing me up. I'll be all right. Besides, I gotta couple of tricks up my sleeve if the situation looks like it's getting too close."

"If you're really going in there," O'Reilly said, "I want you to wear a kel-kit, or some kind of transmitter. The first sound we hear that we don't like, I'm sending in every man we got. Understood?"

Ziller unbuckled his belt and let down his pants. The detective handed him the crotch holster, which consisted of a double thickness strap of wide elastic. He stretched it tight around his hips over his shorts, having trouble getting the hooks to join. "I bought this thing fifteen years ago," he said to Weissberger. "When I was doin' undercover. It seems to have shrunk quite a bit."

He checked his twenty-five automatic, pressed the gun into the holster, and adjusted it directly over his pubic area. No one would search him there. He dropped his shirt over it and pulled up his pants. No impression of the gun was visible. But it was also rather inaccessible, one of the facts of life about well-concealed weapons.

"Do me a favor," Weissberger said. "When you get in there, do whatever's necessary to save me the trouble of breaking in a new chief negotiator and traveling companion."

"Just tell me everything you can think of that I might be able to use in there," Ziller said.

"The usual stuff applies," Weissberger said. "You already know it all."

Devereau stood in front of the elevators on the twentieth floor and occupied himself by scanning the block letters emblazoned on the wall. Kennan, Schink, McGlothlin, and Perl. Ziller should be getting there any minute. Unbelievable. He'd actually volunteered to come.

Everything was set. Only eight men left? Enough. Tactically deployed, eight men could be like a battalion. And Ziller was walking right in like it was a sold-out game and someone had given him a free pass. Just when things were getting a little uncertain, the son-of-a-bitch volunteered. The crazy bounce that turns the game around. They took all of my pawns, I'll take their knight.

Ziller could see all the way across the East River as he walked toward Park with Daniels and the ESD cops. Ziller was wearing a short-sleeved shirt and a baseball cap with a NYPD emblem. He wore one of the reinforced ceramic mini-vests under his shirt. And it chafed. On his belt, along with the empty holster, he wore two radios, one of which was Devereau's. The other was a police unit, tuned to the Special Operations Division frequency. The channel-selector switch had been removed so that the radio, if taken, could not be tuned to the situation frequency, Channel 2.

He had the "pack of Winstons" in his shirt pocket, with the pinhole microphone and the antenna coil inside the pack. No court order was needed for the bug because he was part of the scene being monitored.

"You already know it all," Jerry had said, always the psychologist.

"Course I do. But lay it on me, anyway. Everything you can think of."

"The main thing is to keep him ventilating. You want his head puffed up so big, it's lifting him off the ground. But don't be too obvious. And stay out of his space. Give him plenty of room. He won't take being crowded. And don't do any negotiating in a crowd. Try to keep him separated, if possible. Don't make him compete for your attention."

"What else?"

"Slow down the pace. Wait very patiently for him to make a mistake. If he feels pushed, he's going to stay alert."

"That's it? That's all you can think of?"

"That about covers the principles," Weissberger had answered. "The rest is in the application."

Ziller glanced at the crowds of onlookers behind the barrier as he and Daniels and the others turned the corner in front of the ITT Building. The gallery was growing. The story had kept the press and media hopping, and everybody wanted a look, because it wasn't over. The biggest show in town in a long time. A few people shouted comments at them as they walked by. Most were encouragement, but many were heckles. He was on his way to risk getting his ass blown off, and to some, he was still a clown.

Ziller could still smell tear gas as they entered the lobby. The three burned-out canisters were still on the floor, lying amidst areas of fresh blood. The pile of webbed-belts, guns, radios, and other equipment lay near one wall. A dozen uniformed cops occupied the area around the rear stairwell.

Redmond was involved in a heated argument with Inspector Milford, of Forensic, who wanted his guys to get to work processing the area, one of the key crime scenes. Three detectives with large suitcases and photographic equipment stood waiting. Redmond was explaining in a raised voice that it would have to wait, that the action was still taking place. He was in charge and was just sending in his men to occupy all lower floors. Milford, always the lawyer, concerned for evidence and its presentation in court, maintained that the action was on the three upper floors and that the lobby had to be protected.

Ziller took a radio from his belt and paused while Daniels asked for absolute quiet. Then Ziller held it to his mouth. "Boston." He waited a few seconds and repeated it. "Boston. . . . Larry?"

"Well! I take it my repeater is back in operation."

"Nothing to it. Larry, I'm in the lobby. If I guarantee to keep the repeater on and guarantee you absolute freedom to return, how about you coming down here?"

"Ziller, we already agreed to the terms for our meeting. I'm waiting as agreed on twenty. Come on up. You can use an elevator."

"We have to talk first."

"What about?"

"My brass put some conditions on my comin' up there."

"Such as?"

"They want some more people out of there. As a gesture of good faith on your part."

"Stick to your deal, Ziller."

"Now, wait a minute. It's against the manual for me to come up there. And you know it. So—"

"I guaranteed your safety. Remember?"

"Let me finish. They said it's not enough. They want you to show them something. Look. You're down to eight guys, and you've lots more hostages than you need. Keep one from each floor and send down the rest and I'll come up."

"Cut the shit, Ziller."

"Larry, I got orders. I'll have to go back to the van and renegotiate there. Think about it. It works in your favor."

"If I send a few hostages down, are you coming on up?"

"That's my deal. If you send enough."

"Here's my offer, Ziller. I'll send one per firm of the firms still here. That makes seven coming out."

"Larry. You can do a little better than that. Look. You've

got three per floor from six floors and a bunch from the top floor. If you wanta do business, make a reasonable offer."

"Ziller, I'll go to ten, and that's it. Ten people. You want to come up or shall we talk again in a week or so?"

"I'll have to call the van. Can you hold it a minute?"

"A minute. No more."

Ziller released the talk switch on the radio. "A windfall," he said to Daniels. "I didn't expect him to give up anything. We already had a deal. But I figured it was worth a try."

"He's anxious to get you up there," Daniels said quietly. "I hope you know what you're doing."

"Stay near," Ziller said. His smile was uneasy. "And pay close attention." He patted the pack of cigarettes in his pocket. Then he lifted the radio back to his mouth. "Larry?"

"Well?"

"You got a deal. Send out ten and I'm on the way."

"I'll have to go back to my office and look at my notes to know who to release. It'll take a few minutes, but they'll be coming down. And, Ziller, just so there's no misunderstanding, if you don't show, or if you don't come alone, we're going to pull some triggers. These radios will go two floors without the repeater. Do I make myself clear?"

"Looking forward to meeting you, Larry. A deal's a deal."

Several minutes passed before they heard anything else. Devereau's voice came over the radio, telling Twenty-one-A to bring six persons on twenty-one out to the foyer to await further instructions. He listed their names, and after several more minutes he told Twenty-one-A that Twenty-two-B would be bringing four people by elevator to twenty-one, and all ten would be sent to the lobby. Two or three more minutes went by and then the cops watched the tiny lights in the brass plate above the elevator doors tracing the journey down.

The elevator opened, and the ten exhilarated people scrambled out. Then one of the three women spotted the blood and turned pale: "Couldn't that have been cleaned up before we were brought through the lobby?" she asked.

"Just be careful and don't step in it," one of the cops answered.

After the ten employees had been led out of the building, Ziller pressed the talk button on the radio. "Larry?"

"Well?"

"The ten people are out. You kept your side of the deal, so I'm coming up. Same elevator. Starting now."

"Alone, of course."

"I said I'd be coming alone." Never get caught in a lie. "There are other cops around, Larry. You know that. But I'll be coming to twenty by myself."

"Then come ahead."

Ziller and Daniels and the squad of cops walked onto the elevator, and Daniels pressed the button for eighteen. The door closed, and the elevator started up. The air was close in the car, and the residual tear gas on Daniels' clothes became noticeable. A couple of the cops rubbed at their eyes. One of the cops tapped on another's vest. Every man on the car was wearing one.

They reached the eighteenth floor and hurried out of the car into the welcome fresh air of the foyer. Ziller held the radio to his mouth. "Larry?"

"Where are you?"

"I'm on eighteen."

"Eighteen? Why eighteen? You're supposed to come direct to twenty."

"I'm comin'. I'm gonna walk the rest of the way." When approaching a perpetrator, keep him advised. Avoid surprises. A startled man can react irrationally. "I'm coming up the rear stairwell, Larry. Starting now."

Ziller opened the door to the rear stairs, and then the sense of the situation engulfed him. His mind began darting about wildly. The African violets in his windowless office downtown. The lines of his wife's flanks. The clutter in his garage at home. His first fuck-up as a rookie. The morning of his wedding day. His knees wanted to lock, and he could hardly get his breath.

He turned and looked at Daniels, noting the gray in his friend's close-cropped hair. Daniels always looked for a little gray at other men's temples. A sign of stability, he said. Ziller adjusted his cap and started up the steps.

When he reached the landing on the next floor, he spoke into his radio. "Larry?"

"Where are you now?"

"I'm on nineteen and starting on up. When I get to twenty, you want me to open the door, or are you going to do it?"

"Either way. Call it."

"I'll open it. Okay?"

"Come ahead."

Ziller started up the last flight and his pulse continued to accelerate. A drink. A double scotch. Jesus fucking Christ, what was up those steps? When he reached the landing on the twentieth floor, he called, "Larry?"

"Where are you now?"

"I'm on twenty. Right outside the door. I'll knock before opening it. Then I'll open it and come on in. Okay?"

"Come on in."

Ziller tapped several times on the door. Then he gripped the knob. One of the most frightening moments of his life. He turned his hand, but the knob wouldn't move. He glanced at the printing on the door a few inches from his nose. "No reentry this floor." The door was locked! He wanted to laugh out loud.

He backed a step or two away from the door and raised the radio. "Larry. Hey! The door's locked and I don't have a key." He waited a few seconds, hearing nothing. "Larry. You gonna open it?" He heard footsteps, and then the knob turned and the door moved an inch or two toward him. He reached for the handle and pulled it slowly open.

They studied each other. Devereau stood in the middle of the foyer, his radio in his hand, the talk button depressed. Ziller stayed in the doorway with the door open.

"We finally meet," Devereau said.

"How is it going?"

"On plan."

"Any problems?"

"Not at the moment. Come in and have a seat."

"I'm comfortable where I am."

"As a matter of fact, let's go upstairs to my office."

"No. This is fine."

"At least come all the way in. That door opens outward, and no key's necessary, should you decide you want to dash out. I'm unarmed. And alone."

Ziller walked a few steps into the foyer. "Okay, Larry. I'll accept your hospitality."

"Since you've come this far, why don't we go up to my office? We'll be much more comfortable there."

"I'm quite satisfied with this. It's more neutral. We made a deal, remember?"

"Then let's sit down and talk." Devereau eased himself into a deep chair next to a low coffee table. He pointed to another chair with a straight back which he'd placed near the middle of the carpeted foyer before Ziller arrived. "Sit there, Harry. It's perfect for you. Easy to get out of, and it's nice and high, which, I know, is important to you. See? I'm trying to cooperate and play your game right down the line." He leaned back and stretched his legs.

Ziller sat down cautiously and looked around, noting the several closed doors.

"Well, where do we start, Harry? This is supposed to be a negotiation. Make me an offer."

"Larry, your best bet is to give this whole thing up and come on out."

"Come on, Harry. Don't waste my time with that kind of drivel. You're supposed to come up with something to start a reasonable negotiation. All I want is to be one of the richest men in the world. I'll protect your precious hostages as long as you see that I stay on schedule. State what you have in mind, not just for me, but for the rest of your audience."

"The rest of my audience?"

"Are you going to try and tell me you're not wired for sound?"

"I've got two radios, one of yours and a police unit. But they don't transmit unless I turn 'em on." He touched his hand to the two radios on his belt.

"The question, Harry, is what else have you got?"

"Isn't two enough? One of yours and one of ours?"

"Aren't you uncomfortable with that vest under your shirt?"

"Sure, but it's regulation. You know they'd never let me come in here without it."

Devereau continued studying Ziller. "Give me one of your cigarettes, Harry."

"Don't you have some of your own? I've only got a couple left, and I don't want to run out."

"I left mine upstairs. Let me have one of yours."

"All right." Ziller carefully took the package from his shirt pocket and shook a cigarette upward. He lifted it out with his fingers and then stood up, extending the single cigarette to Devereau.

"Let me see the package, Harry."

"What for? You object to my fingers or something?"

"I'd like to see the package. Because if it's got a bug in it, we're finished. I'm not interested in negotiating in front of your little gallery down there."

Ziller grinned.

"You son-of-a-bitch!" Devereau said. "What a cornball trick!"

"I wouldn't have been allowed to come without some kind of transmitter."

"If we're going to talk, you'll have to get rid of it."

"Let me tell them I'm turning it off. Otherwise, they might do something unexpected." He held the pack in front of him. "This is Harry Ziller. We're continuing our discussions without the transmitter. So I'm turning it off at this time. The situation is completely satisfactory. There's no cause for alarm. Ten-four." He opened the pack and slid the mechanism out. "See that little thing? That's the microphone." He twisted a wire loose, leaving the device obviously inoperative. "Now we're alone."

"How do I know that wasn't an obvious bug to keep me from spotting another one somewhere else?"

"It was the only one. Now we can talk."

Devereau looked at Ziller's smile. His expression had distinctly changed. "Okay. Go ahead. Talk."

"You're going to have a problem getting out of here on your own, even with hostages. I frankly don't think you can do it. Once you leave this building, there will be too many unknowns."

"Are you going to make some suggestions?"

"Only that you give the whole thing up without the right kind of help. I could get you out of here and on your way. If I were so inclined."

Devereau looked at Ziller with mild surprise. "I must admit, I didn't expect that. I guess you don't have another bug."

"I'm just making small talk, you understand. Look, we've got one helluva lotta men on the job out there. Your forces are cut way down. Even with hostages, you're gonna have problems pulling it off."

"Keep in mind, Lieutenant, that I might just have you. Maybe you just realized what a bonehead play you made by coming here, and you've suddenly started thinking about survival. But regardless, I'm interested. What do you have in mind?"

"What do *I* have in mind? I want to hear something from you."

"Why should I trust you?"

"What are your options? Think about it for a minute."

"I don't need you. Except maybe as a hostage."

"You got plenty of hostages. What you need is one who's on your side."

"Oh? What's that going to cost me?"

"What's it worth to you?"

"I'd be willing to make it worthwhile if I went for it. How would we arrange payment for services rendered?"

"I'm sure we could figure something out between the two of us as we move along. We're a coupla pretty smart boys. The important thing is, we would have to make it look right to make it work."

"Who ever heard of trusting a cop?" Devereau said reflectively.

"What's the matter with you? Is there some reason why we don't like nice things, too? Play the whole scene through, Larry."

"If you had this sort of thing in mind, why'd you wait till now to come up with it?"

Ziller hesitated. "How could I, before now? It's the first time we've been alone."

Devereau stared at Ziller for a full minute without speaking. "If you had to get that bug turned off before you could talk, why didn't you just do it when you got here? Why'd you wait for me to spot it?"

Ziller hesitated again. "You're not thinking. I was sure you'd spot it. And I had to be sure it would sound right for them. If you hadn't noticed it, I'd have given you a hint."

"If you had this in mind, why didn't you call for a face-to-face before I lost so many men?"

"I couldn't, Larry. It just wouldn't go down if too many got away. Besides, what do you need with 'em? They'd just be trouble at the other end. You know that."

"Those answers took you a little too long, Harry. Nice try. But I think I'd better stick to plan rather than start making last-minute deals with cops."

"You're going to blow it, Larry. Play it through, for Crissakes."

"I'll take my chances." He picked up the ashtray off the table.

"What are you getting ready to do?"

Without answering, Devereau tossed the ashtray across the foyer toward one of the elevator doors. It struck the door and fell to the carpet. The door slid open, and two of Devereau's troops walked out, their rifles pointed at Ziller. "Why don't we go upstairs to my office?" Devereau said.

"I figured you to be a man of your word. Can't believe I read you wrong."

"Harry, who says this game is played by the Marquis of Queensberry rules?"

29

A rope stretched from one of the front doors to the rear of the lobby. Two identical signs hung from the rope:

CRIME SCENE
KEEP OUT
NYPD

The roped-off area included roughly half of the lobby but did not block the path from the elevators to the doors. Two of the forensic detectives took photographs: the spray-painted glass front, the areas of blood, the bullet holes in the potted tree. . . .

Redmond sent his men to search and occupy the lower floors of the building. Two men would remain on each floor. As they entered the stairs, he cautioned them to walk silently and remove anything that made any kind of noise, because sounds would carry up the stairwell.

On the eighteenth floor Daniels and his men stood quietly

in the foyer and waited. One of the men had been designated the communicator for the squad, and he wore an earpiece in each ear. One was tuned to the silent "pack of Winstons" in Ziller's pocket, and the other brought in the situation frequency, Channel 2.

Pickett, Carlos, and a black troop named Felton Lampert stood guard in the foyer of the twenty-first floor. Pickett and Carlos had gone with Devereau to set the trap for the cop, and while they were gone, Lampert, standing alone, had become extremely anxious. If the hostages had made any kind of move, he wouldn't have known how to deal with it. He was relieved when the other two returned.

Inside the office area on twenty-one the twelve remaining hostages sat discussing the situation. The group consisted of two principals from each of six firms in the building, and although they'd worked there for years, most had never met. Saxon Shaer, having spent two hours witnessing some of the action during the night, talked about what he knew. Mike Kennan, a student of history, commented as he listened to Shaer that the man running things sounded like one of those rare egos, a Napoleon, who never used staff of any kind for planning or decision-making.

The hostages on twenty-two were closer to the action, and although concerned for Ronam, they'd become fascinated with Devereau. He was a prime example of the kind of shark they'd occasionally encountered in the business world. It was difficult not to admire his ability to keep recovering from one apparent setback after another. When they saw him return to the floor with the cop as prisoner, they decided the man's resourcefulness was endless.

Ziller had calmed down by the time he reached Devereau's office. The suspense of the confrontation was past. He'd studied the way things were laid out as he was led through the corridors of the twenty-second floor. One troop stood in the foyer. The one named Stroud had stayed in the office along with the one who had the gun to Ronam's head. As soon as they entered, Devereau sent the two men used in springing the trap back to the twenty-first floor.

"Search him," Devereau said to Stroud.

Ziller sensed that Stroud had an urge to be rough about it, to "give him a toss." He felt his pulse begin to quicken again as he wondered how thorough Stroud would be.

The glint in Stroud's eye softened. "Would you mind putting your hands flat on the wall?" His tone was almost polite. He couldn't overcome his innate restraint when around the men in blue.

"Don't miss anything," Devereau said.

Ziller took the several steps over to the wall, glancing at Ronam as he did. Ronam's complexion was ashen, and his eyes reflected terror. Ziller put his hands against the wall. After twenty-five years on the force, he was on the receiving end of a search.

Stroud checked Ziller's left leg to a point well above the knee. He then went to the right ankle and immediately felt the holster and the thirty-eight. He pulled up Ziller's pants leg and yanked out the revolver. "Well, lookie here," he drawled. He stuffed the gun into his own belt.

"You son-of-a-bitch!" Devereau said.

"It's a regulation," Ziller said. "There was no coming without it."

"You told me you were coming unarmed," Devereau snapped.

"I told you that I would come to the twentieth floor to meet you if you'd come unarmed."

Devereau said to Stroud, "That was too easy. Go over him good. He's probably got a twenty-five in one of his pockets."

Ziller felt the perspiration drenching his body as Stroud's hands finished working up his right leg and then squeezed the contents of his hip and back pockets. Did either of them know about crotch holsters? Would Stroud reach for another man's crotch? Especially a cop's? Stroud took the two radios off his belt and then began feeling around his waist just inside the belt. Finally, he moved to Ziller's chest. "Never saw one of these vests up close before," he said. "You're not countin' on this thing stoppin' an M-14 slug?"

"I hope I'm not going to find out," Ziller said. "But I had to wear it. Another regulation."

Stroud reached under Ziller's shirt and explored on both sides of the vest and around the straps. After satisfying his curiosity, he pulled off Ziller's cap and examined it. He put it back on Ziller's head and yanked the visor down over his eyes. He touched at Ziller's shirt pocket. Nothing but a pack of cigarettes.

"Are we about finished?" Ziller asked, looking at Devereau.

"Sit over here, Harry." He pointed at one of the armchairs in front of the desk.

Ziller walked over and sat down. "Now, maybe we can talk some more," he said.

"Go ahead."

"What are your plans?"

"To use you as my prime hostage."

"Then why don't you let the others go? How many have you got on the twenty-first floor? Twelve? And only three men to watch them?"

"How do you know I've got three men down there?"

"Well, you had eight all together. And you have four on this floor, one by the elevators and three in this room. And you sent the other two back to twenty-one. So I figure you either got four on twenty-one or three there and one upstairs."

"You give me the feeling you're trying to lay this all out for someone besides me. Are you wearing another bug, by any chance?"

"You know better than that. My interest is getting everyone safely out of here . . ."

"Boston."

Devereau picked up the radio. "What is it?"

"This is Pickett. We're sittin' with the doors to both stairs propped open like you said, and we're beginnin' to hear things like you said we might. Sounds like a lot going on somewhere down there."

Devereau looked at Ziller. "What kind of shit are you up to?"

"I'm not up to anything. They probably hear cops checking out the lower floors. I told you when I was in the lobby that there were cops around. But they won't come up here."

"I'm going to give you your police unit. Call your friends and tell them to pull back." Then he brought his own radio to his mouth. "Things should quiet down. I'm having our boy here tell them to withdraw. Let me know if they don't."

Stroud got up and handed Ziller his police radio. Ziller called O'Reilly and told him to have Redmond hold up any further advance. Then he placed the radio on the desk. "Why don't we get back to the subject of your plans?" he said to Devereau.

"My plans should be fairly obvious to you by now. And they're such that merely knowing them doesn't help you much in trying to stop them. That's the beautiful thing about having hostages. You don't have to run. And you can't be pushed. Right?"

"We're gonna do whatever's necessary to keep everybody safe."

"You're goddamn right you will. And you're sounding like a cop again."

"How much longer do you expect to be here?"

"Well, there are seven more money deliveries to be made."

"What about hostages? How many do you plan to take with you?"

"Whatever we need. Wait and see."

"Why don't you start calling the banks and getting the money in?"

"What's the hurry?"

"You want to take your time, go ahead. You planning to leave in your bus?"

"Yes."

"To the airport?"

"See? I told you you'd know."

"JFK?"

"I think so. The planes there are generally geared for longer flights."

"You all set on the amounts you want paid by each company?"

"Of course."

"Root's the biggest, I imagine."

"Certainly."

"It's past ten. Why don't you release Ronam and let him call his bank?"

"Boston!" It was Devereau's radio. "Larry?"

Devereau took the radio off his desk. "What is it?"

"We still hear the cops movin' up. We can't be sure, but that's the way it sounds."

"Ziller, I thought you told them to back off."

"I did. Your men are probably just feeling anxious."

Devereau hesitated, then spoke into his radio. "Our boy here told them to back off, and I think they did. But if you hear them again, call me."

"I think they're hearing footsteps," Ziller said. "Which is why, if I were you, I'd get on with it before something goes wrong."

Devereau looked at Stroud, then at the stony-faced Ronam with Benjy behind him. He glanced around at the windows, particularly in the direction of the ITT Building, which was very close. "Look, Ziller, if anybody's going to wage any psychological warfare around here, it's going to be me. Time to change things a little." He got up and closed the drapes. "Now, let your friends wonder what the hell's going on."

"That could be a mistake," Ziller said. "Don't you think it's safer if they can see that everything's okay?"

"Fuck 'em," Devereau said.

"Okay." Ziller shrugged. The gesture was for effect, but he was wondering just what action O'Reilly would take now that his last means of surveillance was lost. "You were saying before, you'd decided on the hostages you planned to take besides myself."

"Hold it a minute." Devereau looked at Stroud. "Go out there and bring Mattie down from upstairs and put him with Rick by the elevators. We don't need anybody up top, and I want them doubled up out here." He watched Stroud leave and then looked back at Ziller. "The first cop that comes near any of my advanced guard, we pull the trigger on Ronam. Understood? Now. Do you want to get back on your radio and tell your people?"

Ziller studied the wild light in Devereau's eyes. What was he capable of doing? Time to try to cool things back down. "I agree we should call as a precaution, but I don't think you have to worry. They're going to stay back. But if you wanta play it even safer, you oughta open the drapes."

"Just call."

Ziller told O'Reilly that there were three men on twenty-one and two in the foyer of twenty-two and they were not to be approached because any such action would result in Ronam's death.

"Whatever you say, Harry," O'Reilly's voice squawked from the radio. "You get that last transmission, Redmond?"

"Yeah, chief. I read direct."

Ziller looked at Devereau, who seemed momentarily absorbed by the police dialogue. "Larry?"

Devereau looked up.

"Larry, we were just startin' to talk about who you plan to take out with you when you leave."

Devereau looked at him. "You for one."

"You told me that already. Who else?"

"Why don't you wait and see?"

"Haven't you planned that all out?"

"What would you expect?"

"I would expect that you had."

Stroud walked back into the room and sat down in the chair facing Ziller. "All set," he said.

Devereau continued staring at Ziller. "My final hostages, in addition to you, will consist of the board of directors of Root Corporation. Plus one more."

"One more?"

"A little diversion for myself, you might say."

"Meaning?"

Devereau looked at Stroud. "Bring Barbara in here."

"A broad?" Ziller said. He watched Stroud leave.

"Barbara Meyner?" It was Ronam. A new look of shock added to the pain already on his face. "I can't believe she'd have anything to do with you."

"Shut up!" Benjy jabbed him sharply in the back of his head with the rifle barrel. Ronam winced in pain.

"That's enough, Benjy," Devereau said. Then, to Ronam: "She'd have everything to do with me."

Ronam said, "Why don't you let me call the bank and get on with it?"

Benjy jabbed him again. "What I tell you?"

"I said stop it, Benjy."

Ziller caught a glimpse of Benjy's right hand. His finger twitched on the trigger. "Larry, it might be a good idea to let him call. It's going to take a while to get the money."

"In time," Devereau said. "I want you to meet Barbara."

Stroud returned with a young woman.

Ziller looked her over. Barbara Miner? Good-looking biscuit. A little worn down from the long night, but still a nice dolly. A part of this whole business? Judging from the look on her face, she wasn't a willing participant.

"Sit down, Barb," Devereau said. "I was just telling Lieutenant Ziller that I planned to take you along."

She sat down but didn't speak.

"You did say you wanted to go with us," Devereau said to her.

She didn't respond.

"You remember," he said. "Last night?"

She looked down.

"And I've been thinking about it. Barb, that's the way I want it, too. I'd be disappointed if I couldn't take you with me."

"What do you want from me?" she said finally.

"Barbara, forget about our converstion last night. I want to take you with me to share my success." He seemed to wither under her gaze. "Think about it, Barbara. I really want you to go with me."

She looked at Ziller.

He studied her direct gaze. She was clean. And she wasn't apologizing for anything. She had simply been taken by a pro, but it was finished.

"I'd like to return to my desk now," she said to Devereau.

"I want you to stay." His tone was cooler. "Besides, I can't believe you don't want to be in here. A major event in history is taking place in this room."

She sat back and folded her arms.

Devereau's expression changed. He was becoming increasingly irritated.

"Larry," Ziller said, "let's get on with the business at hand."

30

"You should have notified our office before taking that step," Farrent said.

"Will you get off my back?" O'Reilly shouted.

"Look at the situation. Ziller is in there, a prisoner, and we have no line of communication whatsoever. You needed clearance before you let him go in." Farrent's gleaming bald head reddened slightly. He was an inspector attached to the office of the chief of operations. He had shown up after Ziller left with Daniels for 330 Park.

O'Reilly stood up. "You think I don't know what the situation is? I've been here the whole goddamn night. And I don't need you to come wandering in here at ten in the morning and decide you're gonna personally break my chops. You wanta take over this case on behalf of your office? Or do you want me to run it? If I'm gonna run it, don't stand around and tell me what I shoulda done. I don't need that for shit."

"I just think you should have covered your ass," Farrent said, backing down. "Why are you flying off at me?"

"Look," O'Reilly said. "We gave it a lot of thought and de-cided to go ahead. And if we'd called your office, you'd have said play it by ear, anyway. The fact of the matter is, he's in there, and let's hope to God it was the right thing to do." O'Reilly looked at Weissberger, but Weissberger stayed quiet-ly outside the conversation. He was upset about Ziller risking his neck, but he wanted no part of an interoffice dogfight.

One of the detectives came over to tell O'Reilly that Cap-tain Daniels was going to try to move his team closer to the top floor.

"Good," O'Reilly said, looking at Farrent.

The subdued Farrent nodded.

On the eighteenth floor Daniels slowly opened the door to the front stairwell. Although their shoes were all rubber-soled, the men filed through in their stocking feet. They made it to the landing on the nineteenth floor and stopped, listen-ing to the conversation drifting down from the open doorway on twenty-one.

They stood absolutely motionless for a minute and listened. Could they make one more floor? The dialogue on twenty-one had stopped. Maybe they'd already been heard.

Daniels pointed at the door into the nineteenth, and one of his men unlocked it as carefully as possible. The men padded through, and after the door was closed, turned radios back on and began lacing their shoes.

"Boston. . . . Larry? It's Pickett again."

"What is it?"

"Those fuckers are up to something."

"Did you hear anything?"

"I'm not sure."

"Why don't you go out in the stairwell and take a look around?"

"Fuck that."

"Then just keep your door open, and if you hear anything, let me know."

"How much longer do you figure we'll be here?"

"Let me worry about that. Ten-four." Devereau put down the radio and looked at Ziller. "I trust you believe there's live ammunition in that rifle." He nodded toward Benjy.

"Of course I believe it. Why?"

"You don't need him to fire off a round just to prove it to you?"

"I think you know what that will accomplish. The first shot that's fired. . . ."

"Then would you please tell me what your friends are doing downstairs? Any tricks and Ronam's a dead man."

"I don't know what they're up to," Ziller said. "I told you there were cops down there. That's all I know. You heard your guy. He wasn't sure he heard anything."

"He must have heard something."

Ziller studied Devereau's silent expression. The constant calls from twenty-one were upsetting him. Had they really heard anything? Maybe Daniels was trying to get closer. And the rejection by the girl had burned him. Easy to see why he wanted to take her along. Only, she wanted no part of it. Time to ease things a little. "I got an idea," Ziller said.

"About what?"

"The sounds your men heard. Maybe it was Joe Palko changing his location."

"Anything's possible."

"Why don't you start calling the banks?" Ziller asked. "I'm curious to see how much you're going to end up with."

"Shortly." Devereau seemed preoccupied.

"How much more do you plan to bring in?"

"More than your mind can grasp." He said it with strong emphasis, glancing over at Barbara, who sat on the couch avoiding his glance.

"How are you planning on carrying it all out?" Ziller asked. "You've got eight guys left, as well as the hostages."

"I have something in mind."

"Hey, cop!" It was Benjy. "We let you carry it."

"Shut up, Benjy," Devereau said. He seemed deep in thought, as if Ziller's questions had raised other problems he hadn't considered.

"Hey, cop. You carry it, and I keep a gun in your ribs." Benjy gave his annoying little giggle.

"I said shut up!" Devereau snapped.

Stroud stood up. "Knock it off, Benjy."

"Who the fuck tell you to tell me what to do?" Benjy said. He poked Ronam's head in a gesture of defiance. "I talking to the cop. Hey, cop. You carry the money. I escort you out."

"Ignore him," Devereau said.

Ziller thought about Benjy's finger on the trigger and suddenly felt a slight chill. Benjy was not to be ignored. "We'll have to make more than one trip, Benjy. I've only got two hands."

"See that, Stroud? The cop talk to me."

"Benjy, will you shut the hell up?" Devereau said.

Barbara raised her eyes, sensing an ominous change in the room.

"Can't you please get him away from me?" Ronam pleaded. "Why don't you let me call our bank and request your money?"

"You shut your mouth!" Benjy hit Ronam's head with enough force to cause his eyes to tear.

"Somebody please help me," Ronam said. He strained at the handcuffs locking his wrists behind the chair.

"Benjy," Ziller said. "After all the money's in, you and I will carry it down to the bus. Right?" Then to Devereau. "Larry, I think Benjy wants to talk to you."

Barbara turned to Devereau. "Larry, you've got to do something. Larry, please."

The tone of Ziller's voice and then Barbara's reached Devereau, and he looked up. "What do you want, Benjy? Let's hear

328

it right quick. I'm trying to figure out a couple of things so we can get started."

"Just let me out of this chair," Ronam said.

"You don't get out of that chair," Benjy said, "unless I say so."

"Hold it," Ziller said. "Benjy, let's you and me talk about—"

"Don't waste your breath on him," Stroud said. "He's got no goddamn business being in here. He's too stupid." Stroud stood up. "Benjy, let's get your ass outta here and bring in one of the other. . . ."

Benjy scrambled to his feet, keeping the muzzle of his rifle to Ronam's head. Suddenly the gravity of the situation was obvious to everyone.

Ziller stood up slowly and held out his hand. "Benjy, you don't have to listen to what anyone here says. Understand what I'm saying? All you have to remember is that everything will be all right as long as no shots are fired."

Stroud said in a restrained but commanding tone, "Benjy, you put that gun down. You hear me? Put that son-of-a-bitch down."

"Benjy, that's an order," Devereau said, getting to his feet.

Benjy pressed the muzzle of the gun firmly against the back of Ronam's head and held it there.

"Benjy, remember what I told you," Ziller said as calmly as possible. "Everything'll be all right as long as no shots are fired. Okay?" He sat back down. "Larry, I think you and Stroud oughta have a seat. Hear what I'm saying?"

"You heard what Dee just told ya'," Stroud said, a little more hotly. "Put that goddamn rifle down. That's an order."

"I don't take orders," Benjy said slowly. "I take enough orders in the army."

"You little spic," Stroud said. "I'm gonna have to take that gun away from you." He started forward.

Benjy pulled the trigger.

A section of Ronam's forehead disappeared, and a whitish substance sprayed across the room. Ronam's head jerked forward and then flopped back. His eyes remained open. His head finally slumped against his chest. He was held upright only by the handcuffs behind the chair.

The four men remained frozen. The crack of the shot seemed to be circling around the room, gradually fading like a distant sound. Benjy made several uncertain gigglelike noises.

Barbara was unable to take her eyes from the cavity in Ronam's head. She looked down finally at a spot on her knee, a fleck of the white. She reached out as if to brush it away but was unable to make herself touch it. She waved her hand just over it several times. Her face began to grow pale. She looked away and brought her hands up to her mouth. Then she shook her head and fell over onto the couch, unconscious.

"No!" Stroud yelled finally. "You stupid . . ." But before he could get his rifle aimed, Benjy fired again. Stroud went down. Benjy fired a second time at him as he was falling.

Devereau dropped to his knees behind the desk and fumbled for his army automatic. But his holster was empty. He had never bothered to replace the gun he gave to Luis the night before.

Ziller dropped to the floor next to the desk. Benjy watched curiously as Ziller groped inside his fly with his hand, and when he saw what appeared to be the glint of metal, he fired. Ziller spun around, clutching at himself. He fell back and lay still. Benjy fired one more shot through the desk at Devereau.

Devereau slid along the floor behind the desk toward Ziller's body. The shot through the desk had missed him. He plunged his hand into Ziller's fly and struggled with the elastic holster. Benjy still hadn't seen him. Devereau raised up behind the desk and leveled the tiny weapon across the desktop. Benjy was backing toward the door, his gaze still rubbering about vacantly.

Devereau fired. Benjy yelled something incomprehensible

and grabbed at his neck. Holding the rifle in his other hand, he got off one wild shot at Devereau and then dashed out of the room. Devereau fired twice more and then ran to the door. Benjy had already cleared a corner in the corridor.

Devereau turned back toward the office. He surveyed the room, and his body sagged. He pulled himself upright and walked cautiously into the corridor, holding the small automatic in front of him. He stopped, hesitated for a moment, and then retreated into the office.

Benjy continued toward the elevator foyer. The blood from the wound in his neck was beginning to soak into his fatigues. He saw Rick Dominguez and Mattie Foster running toward him, carrying their rifles, and he planted his feet and fired at them, watching them drop.

He hurried on by them into the foyer. He paused, looked at both open stairwell doors, and started down the rear stairs.

When Daniels first heard the shots, he divided the squad into two groups and sent one into each stairwell. The cops moved upward very slowly, pausing after each step to listen. When the cops in the rear stairwell heard rushing footsteps, they flattened themselves against the walls and held their weapons ready.

The three troops on twenty-one had been waiting indecisively for the half-minute since the shooting began. Then they heard someone coming down the back stairs. They went to the doorway and watched Benjy approach. They shouted at him, but he ignored them and continued down, past their landing. They heard the pop of an M-14 round, followed by the echoing thunder of two rounds from a shotgun, and a few seconds later the shouts of several cops. They turned back toward the foyer to face six cops with shotguns and submachine pistols. "Freeze!" said one of the cops.

A minute later, Daniels led seven of his men into the foyer of the penthouse. The door to the office area was open, and they saw the two troops lying unconscious. Both were still alive. With the four downstairs, these two made six. Only two should still be ahead. They moved in slowly, working their way toward the big corner office. All of the floor's employees were staying back out of sight. The floor was quiet as they advanced cautiously.

"Come on in, guys," yelled a voice ahead of them. "I'm not going to shoot. . . . And neither are you."

The cops turned a corner in the corridor, and the open door leading into the big office came into view. They approached warily. Then Daniels took a small periscope from his pocket and peeped around the door frame into the room. He finally located one of the troops sitting on the couch, facing him. The troop was holding the body of a semiconscious young women upright on his lap, his left arm across her chest. The troop used his right hand to hold a twenty-five automatic to her temple. "Come on in, guys," he repeated.

"I'm comfortable right here," Daniels answered.

"It's perfectly safe. Just walk right in."

Daniels stuck his head briefly around the edge of the door. Another troop lay motionless on the floor. That accounted for all eight. He turned to his men. "Cover me. I'm going face-to-face." Holding his service revolver ready, he took a couple of steps into the room.

The rest of the cops peered around the edge of the door with carbines and shotguns ready.

"Just don't try to get too close," the troop said. He pressed the small gun menacingly against the girl's head.

Daniels quickly surveyed the room. He flinched at the sight of Ronam. Then he looked at the dead troop on the floor. He finally spotted Ziller lying behind the desk. He looked back at the man on the couch and noticed the captain's bars. Larry Devereau, the chief perpetrator.

"Sorry about your cop friend," Devereau said.

"Let me take a look at him," Daniels said.

"Forget it. I want you to stay right where I can keep an eye

on all of you at one time. I've got to think about how to proceed."

"What do you have in mind?" Daniels asked.

"To take the money that's in so far and leave. I'm planning
to use her as my ticket out of here."

Daniels was silent.

"I had nothing to do with any of this gunplay," Devereau
said. "It resulted when an injured mind collapsed under severe pressure. Benjy Sanchez. He never recovered from the
things that happened to him in Vietnam. That's where you
can place the blame. Senseless waste, all of this. I did everything I could to prevent this type of thing happening."

Daniels and the other cops remained silent.

"He had been a good soldier over there," Devereau continued. He obviously liked talking to Daniels, another officer.
"Well trained, good record, he'd held up well for me. Perfectly subordinate. Did exactly as he was told. . . . Until a few
minutes ago."

Barbara Meyner began to regain consciousness. She
opened her eyes and looked around her, then realizing where
she was, began to struggle.

"Take it easy," Devereau said roughly, tightening his grip.

She looked at Ronam and screamed hysterically, two,
three, four times. She turned her head away finally, and
sniffled, struggling to calm herself.

"Move him so he's facing in another direction," Devereau
shouted at the cops.

Daniels nodded at one of his men who lifted the chair, pi-
voting it on one of its legs. He touched his toe to an imprint in
the carpet left by a chair leg.

Ziller groaned.

"Captain," said the cop by the chair. "It's Lieutenant Ziller."

Ziller rolled over onto his back and touched his left forearm. After examining the blood on his fingers, he wiped them

on his pants. He pushed himself up on his elbows and frowned in pain.

"Harry?" said Daniels. "You okay?"

Ziller saw Daniels and the other cops, and his face brightened. "Just like in my dreams," he said. "The ESD, coming to save my ass. Help me up. Looks like I got a little nip in my arm, and it smarts."

"Stay where you are," Devereau snapped as a cop started toward him.

Ziller looked around, startled. He could not see Devereau because the desk stood between them. He reached for the corner of the desk and struggled into the large executive swivel chair.

"Looks like your vest stopped the M-14," Devereau said.

"Guess they really work," Ziller said. "The shot must have slid off the vest and nicked my arm. Then I hit my head when I went down. The base o' this chair." He sat back and pulled out a handkerchief, pressing it against the wound. He glanced down, and noticing his fly was open, zipped it up.

"I'm glad you weren't messed up," Devereau said. "I want to use you in getting out of here."

Ziller looked at Daniels. "What about the rest of them?"

"Three apprehended. The rest dead or wounded."

"The little one that made this mess?"

"Blown away. Two rounds of double-O-buck at close range."

"Any of our guys?"

Daniels shook his head. "You."

Ziller looked back at Devereau. "Just me and you now, Larry."

"You and Barbara are all I need. I'm following my final contingency plan."

Barbara twisted against his arm.

"Don't screw around," Devereau said. "I'm leaving with that money. And I'm taking you along. Do you understand? But if I'm forced, I'll pull this trigger."

"Then what will you have?" she asked.

"What will *you* have?" he said.

Ziller said, "Barbara, do what he says." Then: "Larry, your best bet is still to give up. You've got no previous record. And I'm your witness to what happened in this room."

"Ziller, you've been spouting that crap for twenty-four hours, and I'm sick of hearing it."

"You'll have problems making it alone," Ziller said. "Keep in mind what I've been telling you."

Devereau adjusted his grip on the small weapon. "As long as I've got this and one hostage with a head to hold it against, I'm viable."

"Then what's your plan?"

"First, you will have these men carry the money to the foyer. Then you will have the area cleared of cops and a car brought to the door. The three of us will go down together. You will load the car, and drive it to the airport. And see that the plane is arranged. And remember, all this time I'll have this gun to her head."

"Where will you fly to?"

"I'll tell the pilot."

"How do you feel about his plan, Barbara?"

She hesitated. Then her expression changed. "It sounds like it's going to work beautifully."

Daniels and the other cops looked at her in astonishment.

"Why are you all looking so surprised?" she asked.

"He's been saying that he'd shoot you," Ziller said.

"Do you really believe he would?" she asked.

"Would you, Larry?"

"Don't test me, Ziller, I will if I have to."

"How does that make you feel, Barbara?"

"I'll take the chance."

"Larry, if you shoot her, your plan automatically fails."

"But *you* can't allow that to happen, Ziller. Because then you'd lose, too. And besides, at that point I'd have to shoot you, as well."

Ziller studied the girl, trying to make some sense of what she'd said. He got a brief glimpse of Ronam, who was facing him. It was a sight he'd never forget. He glanced at Stroud on the floor and then at Daniels and his guys, who were struck dumb by Barbara's last statements. He looked back at Devereau. "Okay, Larry. Looks like you're still holding the cards. What's next?"

"We're moving out."

"Right now?"

"Let's get on with it."

Ziller instructed Daniels to take his men and clear the building of all cops and all remaining employees. The cases of money were to be left by the elevators, according to Devereau's demands. A caravan consisting of an unmarked car between a pair of white-tops was to be left in front of the door with the motor of the middle car left running. Daniels was to call Ziller on the police radio when everything was set.

Daniels balked. "You sure this is the way you want it?"

"It's okay, J.B." Ziller answered.

"Anything else I can do to help?" Daniels asked, looking directly at Ziller.

"It's okay, J.B.," Ziller repeated with a trace of impatience. He glanced at Devereau. "You think of anything else?"

"Let's just get moving," Devereau said.

Daniels motioned to his men to take the briefcases from the large crate behind the desk. Ziller watched the men walk out of the room with the five briefcases. Five? There should be six! He looked at Devereau. "One case is missing," he said, after the cops were out of the room.

Devereau smiled. "Relax a few minutes."

The three of them sat quietly and listened to the varied sounds of relief and shock coming from the floor's employees as they were led out by Daniels' men. After the floor was quiet again, Ziller asked, "Where's the other case?

"Look under the desk. All the way against the back," Devereau said. "Just a little precaution. I never carry all my money in one pocket. One of the things I learned from being mugged once in this stinking city of yours."

Ziller reached far into the kneehole of the desk and brought out the case.

"Ever see a half-million dollars before?" Devereau asked.

"Not before yesterday," Ziller answered as he looked at the money.

"I've thought over our discussion on the twentieth floor, and that's my offer."

"What?" Barbara looked astonished.

"Now. What will you do for it?" Devereau asked.

"Get you out of here and safely on your way."

"Do you really think I should trust a cop?"

"What do you stand to lose? A half-million out of three?"

"And if I decide to take you along as an extra hostage?"

"Then you've got one more person to keep an eye on. And I already told you, I don't think you'll make it. You're one guy and there's more than twenty-five thousand cops on the force. And like I've been telling you, we know a few tricks, too."

"Such as?"

"If I tell ya, I've got nothin' to sell."

"I can force you to tell me with this gun to Barbara's head."

"How are you ever gonna know if I'm tellin' you everything? Or if I'm even tellin' the truth?"

"If you pull a fast one, you and Barbara both end up dead."

"Then what'll you have?"

Devereau paused. "And if I go along with your proposition?"

"I'll try and get you safely to the plane. But we gotta set it up so it looks absolutely clean."

"Do you guarantee my safety?"

"There are no guarantees. You know that. But look at the percentages. I can't understand why you're givin' me an argument."

"Are you going to trust him?" Barbara asked.

"It's not a question of trust," Devereau answered. "I don't really have to trust him. I've got the gun. If he crosses me, I'll shoot him. But he makes a lot of sense. And it appears he's like the rest of us. He appreciates money."

"A bigger question, Barbara," Ziller said, "do *you* trust Larry?"

She looked steadfastly at Ziller. "Sure."

"Maybe you know him better than he knows himself."

"Don't be a fool, Harry. It'll be her first, and then you."

"Then where'll you be?"

"One thing is certain. You'll never know."

"Then why don't we get ready to leave? We'll be hearing from Daniels soon."

Devereau asked, "Got any ideas on how we set up this payoff for you?"

"We hide this case in here somewhere," Ziller said. "Someplace that's out of sight but accessible. So I can double back and pick it up later." Ziller lifted out a packet of bills and riffled them. "A hundred hundreds," he said, looking at them. "That's ten thousand dollars!" He took out another packet. "Think I'll take these two now." He stuffed them into his pockets. "They don't show."

"You can hide the rest in an air duct on a vacant floor. I'll give you my master key. Nobody'll question *you*."

"Harry," squawked a voice from the police radio on the desk. "Daniels here. You okay?"

Ziller picked up the radio unit. "No problems. Everything set down there?"

"All set. Building's cleared. Money by the elevators. Cars waiting. Coming out soon?"

"Right away."

"That's good. You can pull the string on the caravan when you get down."

Pull the string? "Wanna gimme that again, J.B.?" Ziller asked.

"You can decide on the string on the way down, Harry.

338

Okay?" Daniels' emphasis was on "string," and his tone suggested Ziller should ask no more questions.

The phone on the desk began to ring.

"Got it," Ziller said to Daniels. "On our way. Ten-four." He put down the radio and started to reach for the phone.

"What was he talking about?" Devereau asked.

"Procedural stuff. Let me handle it."

"I'm paying you a half-million dollars for your expertise. At those prices, I expect to be told everything."

"He was just talking' about, uh, how many radio cars we use for escort. Two or more. We can decide on the way. Two escort cars is about right."

The telephone continued ringing.

"Okay." said Devereau. "Now, close the case and let's go." He pushed Barbara ahead of him, keeping the gun to her temple.

Ziller reached for the phone.

"Forget the goddamn phone," Devereau said.

Ziller picked up the receiver. "Yeah?"

"Winnie?" An older woman's voice, a weak connection.

"Who?"

"Mr. Root. Mr. Winfield Root? Do I have the right number? This is Mrs. Root calling from Bermuda. I just heard . . ."

"He's okay, Mrs. Root. He's already left the building. This is Lieutenant Ziller of the police department."

"Then he's safe?"

"Yes, ma'am." He looked at Barbara.

"Oh, thank God. Nowadays, it seems almost anything can happen. One of my friends was just telling me—"

"Your husband's safe, Mrs. Root. I have to hang up now." He put down the phone and stood up. "When we get downstairs," he said to Devereau, "keep Barbara close in front of you at all times. I mean *close*. Don't give anybody a target. Stay inside with her until I get the car loaded.

"And Barbara, when you walk out of the building, make it

look good," Ziller continued. "Act scared. Struggle a little, but stay very close to Larry. I'll go out first and see if everything's okay. Watch for me to nod my head. If I don't nod, refuse to come out.

"When you get in the car, duck down outta sight and stay close together. Once I get in, Larry, stay close between me and Barbara. Okay. Ready to move?"

Devereau smiled. "I'm beginning to like you, Harry."

"Just don't get careless," Ziller said.

They walked out of the office and toward the elevators. Barbara noted blood on the carpeting in several places, without reaction. After Ronam and Stroud, bloodstains were nothing.

They reached the foyer and found the five cases standing neatly in front of one of the elevators. Ziller walked over to it and pressed the button.

"Wait a minute," Devereau said. "Let's use one of the other elevators."

"What difference does it make?" Ziller asked.

"Probably none," Devereau answered. "But we're not taking that one."

Ziller pressed the button on the next one, and the car returned from the lobby. When the door opened, Ziller loaded the cases inside, keeping his apart from the others. "What floor did you say was vacant?" Ziller asked.

"Sixteen."

Ziller pressed the button, and the elevator started downward. Then he saw the string. The small locked door below the buttons on the elevator control panel had been jimmied open and taped closed with transparent tape. A piece of string was tied through perforations in the little door. He looked at Devereau, who stood facing the front of the elevator, holding Barbara. Ziller's knees suddenly felt rubbery.

The car reached the sixteenth floor and the door slid open. Ziller picked up the single briefcase and said to Devereau, "You know where this duct is located?"

"It's just inside there, to the right."

They walked out of the elevator and cautiously looked around. "Stand over there," Devereau said to Ziller, nodding at the entry from the foyer into the office area. Then he carefully transferred the tiny automatic to his left hand and fished in his pocket with his right, finally producing a small key chain with one key. He tossed it to Ziller. "Use it now and return it. I'll give it back to you when we get to the airport."

Ziller unlocked the door and walked through, followed by Devereau and Barbara. He returned the key, and Devereau dropped it back into his pocket.

"Over here to the right," Devereau said.

They approached the small utility-storage room containing the heating duct and immediately noticed twenty to thirty bulletholes through the metal door to the unit. "Jesus," Ziller said. "What were they shooting at this for? We can't leave the money here. Ballistics'll be coming back to take a look."

"The eleventh floor is vacant, too," Devereau said. "Let's go there."

As they returned to the elevator, Ziller stepped in first and put down the briefcase. He stood in front of the controls so Devereau couldn't see the small piece of string. He hoped Devereau wouldn't notice that he was trembling.

After Devereau and Barbara entered the car and turned to face the front, he pushed the button for the eleventh floor. Then he quickly pulled the string. The tiny access door to the elevator's control wiring swung open to reveal a service revolver. He glanced at Devereau and then reached in for the weapon. With a single motion he brought the gun out and put it up to Devereau's throat. "Larry, it's over. Drop the gun."

Devereau looked at him, stunned. "What the hell are you doing?" He had never seen where Ziller found the gun.

Ziller pulled the revolver's hammer back. "I said it's over! Now drop it!"

"No, Harry."

Ziller moved the weapon a few inches from Devereau's head and fired at the ceiling. The bullet made a neat hole, and the noise was deafening as it reverberated in the confined space. He quickly put the pistol back to Devereau's throat. "Now, drop the gun, Larry! It's over!"

"I'm going to kill this girl!" Devereau shouted.

Barbara's face suddenly turned white.

Ziller rammed the muzzle roughly below Devereau's ear and pulled back the hammer again. "Whether you shoot first or not, if you don't drop it, I'm killing you."

"Harry, what about the money?"

"One more second, Larry, and that's it!"

Devereau let Barbara go and leaned back against the wall. His right hand, which held the small automatic, hung at his side. He looked at the thirty-eight aimed point-blank at the center of his chest and relaxed his fingers. The small pistol fell to the floor.

The elevator had reached the eleventh floor, and the door stood open. Just as it began to close, Barbara dashed out.

Devereau reached for her, but she eluded him just as the door closed. "We'd better get her," he said to Ziller.

"She'll be fine," Ziller answered. He pressed the button for the lobby. "Kick that gun over to this side of the car."

"You're an asshole, Harry. Don't you know that? You're destroying a masterpiece."

"What can I tell you?"

"What's wrong with having a half-million dollars? For that matter, we can even negotiate a better deal. It's not too late, Harry. We can always go back to the eleventh floor. Think about it."

"Forget it, Larry. It's over."

The elevator reached the ground floor, and the door opened.

"Stupid fucking cop," Devereau muttered as he walked through the empty lobby to the door.

"When you walk out," Ziller said, "move slowly and hold your hands up so nobody shoots. Okay?"

"Tell me something, Ziller. How's Quirke?"

"He was DOA."

"You son-of-a-bitch! Why'd you keep telling me he was alive?"

"I didn't want you feelin' desperate. Like you mentioned earlier, who says we gotta play by the Marquis of Queensberry rules?"

When they reached the street, cops moved in from every side. Devereau was read his rights and led away.

Ziller asked Daniels, "Hey, sweetheart, how'd you know which car we were gonna take?"

Daniels grinned broadly, "We didn't. We put a gun in all of them. Where's the girl?"

"She got off the elevator on the eleventh floor. I think she needs some time to sort things out. Tell the guys to be extra nice when she comes down. . . . I just remembered one more thing I have to do." Ziller went back into the lobby of the building and picked up one of the radio units off the pile on the floor. "Boston."

"Boston," answered a cop in room 11-S in the Waldorf.

"Joe Palko! This is Lieutenant Ziller. Joe, it's all over. It's okay to come out. Joe Palko! Do you hear me?" He turned to Daniels who had followed him in. "Poor son-of-a-bitch! I hope he's got his radio turned on."

31

In the Sheep Meadow section of Central Park, the large helicopter thundered into life, and after the engines had run for a minute or two, the craft jumped into the air like a mammoth grasshopper, delighting the spectators who had been standing around waiting for its takeoff. It cleared the treetops and headed for the hangar at Floyd Bennett Field.

On East Forty-ninth the ERV tank rumbled into ear-splitting operation, bringing raucous cheers from the gallery around it. After the clumsy monster was back on the trailer, the truck left on its return to Floyd Bennett.

On the upper floors of the building forensic and photo-unit detectives moved around shooting pictures and gathering other bits of evidence, blood samples and the like. Detectives from the ballistics squad examined bulletholes and looked for imbedded slugs and empty cartridges. Members of the observation teams came down from their roosts, their weapons unloaded. They mingled in the street and compared notes with the ESD cops who were sweaty and uncomfortable in their sixty-pound ceramic vests.

Several cops rerolled the huge concertina coil of barbed wire. Sanitation Department workers picked up the remains of the crushed sofa for the Meeker Avenue warehouse in Brooklyn, where it would be stored as evidence. The bomb squad's disposal truck with its steel-mesh igloo was present, and squad members gathered up grenades. Each perpetrator had carried one live grenade.

The area around 330 Park was alive with media men, shooting pictures and TV footage, questioning any cop who appeared to have been involved in the action. A couple of TV stations were sending back a live signal, interrupting their regular programming to update the story. Extra cops, detailed in from outlying commands, struggled to keep the scene from being overrun by the excited crowds. Windows in the Waldorf and other buildings were filled with people watching the action in the street below.

Harry Ziller finally emerged from the building, carrying a briefcase. As soon as he was recognized by some of the press, the word spread, and they all converged on him, TV cameras and strobe units flashing. He was rescued by a sergeant from the Office of Public Information, who promised a press conference within the hour at the Seventeenth Precinct. Ziller would be present after going to the hospital to be treated. Ziller climbed into a radio car, and it pulled away.

A pair of morgue wagon attendants appeared at the door, carrying a corpse in a canvas body bag. They loaded it and returned to the building for another. Eight bodies in all. Not an average everyday haul to be expected from a single crime scene. And these were added to three others that already occupied rolling shelves. Two victims, nine perpetrators. And no cops.

Up and down Park Avenue police barriers were removed and stacked on the edges of the sidewalks. Traffic resumed, and as the lanes began to flow again, congestion in adjacent areas eased.

Harry Ziller entered the Seventeenth Precinct. The wound in his forearm was covered with a small bandage. But it was a reminder of what might have happened. He carried the vest. He'd decided never to wear that one again. He'd have it mounted instead on a big plaque of walnut and then hang it in his cubbyhole office. Or maybe his TV room, along with his various awards and other memorabilia. The crease from the rifle slug was dramatically apparent. He planned to ask Ballistics if they found that particular slug. He might just glue it into the crease after it was no longer needed for evidence.

Ziller was quickly hustled upstairs, where a group that included Weissberger, Daniels, O'Reilly, and others waited for him. The police commissioner greeted him and shook his hand. Elsewhere on the second floor, Barbara Meyner and the other final hostages were still being debriefed. Devereau and three troops were locked in the precinct's cells.

After Ziller arrived, procedural details for the press conference were reviewed briefly with the deputy commissioner for public information. Then the group walked down and filed into the muster room which had been set up with all media people facing the table where six principals would sit to answer questions. Several TV crews focused cameras on the table, and nearly a dozen microphones had been set in place.

Ziller and the commissioner took the two middle chairs. The chief of detectives, O'Reilly, Daniels, and Weissberger took the other seats. The line of men behind the table included Redmond, Bayne, Farrent, Milford from Forensic, Murphy, Killiper from the bomb squad, Feegel from Ballistics, and several others.

The commissioner held up his hand. "May I have your attention?" After clearing his throat, he read the narrative that had been prepared for him. "At ten-twenty-seven A. M. yesterday a call was received by my office which advised that the building at 330 Park Avenue was under a state of siege and all occupants were being held prisoner. A radio car was dispatched to the scene to check out this call and the car was fired on by a rifle. . . .

The commissioner continued his monologue about the army of alleged perpetrators. Nine had been killed and five had been wounded. One was still being sought, and perhaps as much as two million dollars in currency was still unaccounted for. Six hundred hostages had been safely rescued, and the potential for death held to the lowest possible minimum. Regrettably, two were killed, and one was president of the Root Corporation. Minor injuries were sustained by two police officers in the line of duty. One was Lieutenant Ziller.

The commissioner finished and looked up. Further questions could be directed at any of the officers present. The attention immediately shifted to Harry Ziller.

"Lieutenant Ziller . . ."

Ziller surveyed the group. He'd gotten to know a few from past hostage cases and other occasions. Most of their faces reflected genuine interest and empathy. A few seemed indifferent or even cynical. He pointed at one of the reporters with a hand up.

"Lieutenant, how did it feel to be taken prisoner?"

He answered question after question, favoring the men he knew. He nodded at Richter of ABC-TV.

"Lieutenant, how did this man manage to organize and train so large an army without the police department's knowledge?"

"They did nothing to attract our attention. They had no real ax to grind and no psychological need to attract attention to themselves. They were just after money, so they were smart enough to keep a low profile." Ziller nodded at one he didn't particularly like. No point in delaying. The longer he avoided them, the hotter these guys invariably got. "Yes?"

"Lieutenant, I understand that prior to this case you'd never lost a hostage, and your record was, so to speak, perfect. In view of the two that were lost, would you still consider this one successfully handled?"

The question was inevitable. "We managed to rescue some six hundred hostages from a small army of highly trained, heavily armed perpetrators who were unknown quantities. And who were under extreme pressure the whole time. Out of that number, two were lost. And one of these got himself shot by pulling a gun on the perpetrators. . . . . We did our best. . . . It's not a perfect world."

The questioner seemed cowed by his answer. Ziller nodded at another.

"Lieutenant, I understand there was an inside contact for the group. A girl who worked in the building. Could you comment on this?"

"It's still an ongoing investigation. We don't know who was or wasn't involved at this time."

"Lieutenant, what will they be charged with?" Levine, from the *Times.*

Ziller turned to Bayne. "Mike, why don't you take this one?"

Bayne said, in an unemotional tone, "The alleged perpetrators will be booked on some or all of the following charges: murder, attempted murder, assault with dangerous weapons, unlawful imprisonment, obstructing government administration, extortion, robbery, unlawful possession of dangerous weapons, illegal explosives, and possibly others."

"Obstructing government administration?"

"There's a mail drop in the building," Bayne said without a change of expression.

"Lieutenant . . ."

The questions continued, going into more and more detail about the twenty-four hours of the siege. At one point a detective came into the room, walked up behind Ziller and the commissioner, and whispered at some length to the two of them. Ziller's expression changed, clearly reflecting shock and confusion.

"We have just learned," the commissioner said, "that one of the bodies believed to have been an alleged perpetrator has been positively identified as the chief building engineer of 330 Park."

"He'd been shot twenty-nine times," Ziller added. "And he was found with one and a half million dollars of the ransom money."

Ziller sat at the desk in his office downtown. For a while he'd thought the press conference would never end. He had called Ruthie from the hospital. All that remained was to fill out the paperwork reporting his injury. As soon as he could get that out of the way, he wanted to slip down to the pub with Murphy for a couple of scotches and then go home to bed.

Murphy was still with the detective who'd caught the case, a member of Homicide, Manhattan South. They were working on the Unusual Occurrence Report and case folder, which would probably be a "two-volume, six-pound" case before it was over. A monster.

Ziller let his phone ring a couple of times before answering.

"Harry, it's Heinrich, P.C.'s office."

"What's up?"

"The commissioner got a call from the Waldorf, telling him about the tab for those two meals yesterday."

"So?"

"He wants you to collect the funds from the tenants in 330 Park."

"Why me?"

"You're the one everybody knows. Who'd refuse you?"

"Jesus Christ!"

"It's got to come from somewhere, pal. It ain't coming out

of the Revolving Fund. But take it easy. You don't have to work on it till tomorrow. Nobody's there today."

"Thanks." Ziller touched his thigh and remembered for the first time that he still had ten thousand dollars in each pocket.

All police barriers had been carted away, and traffic moved routinely up and down Park Avenue in the afternoon sun. The special police vehicles, including the headquarters van, had been removed from the area. The bus had been returned to the rental agent, who'd scratched his head as he looked at the olive-drab paint job.

Inside the lobby of 330 Park busboys from the Waldorf-Astoria organized the hotel's carts and dishes for transporting back to the hotel. A pair of bored uniformed cops stood around, maintaining surveillance.

At the front of the lobby, Diego Villeja of the night cleanup crew stood by the floor-to-ceiling plate glass and scraped at the white paint on the inner surface. He was making headway, but there was a lot to remove. He was pleased that Mr. Larsen had called him in early. Having missed work the night before because of all the excitement, he needed the overtime. He wondered about the door to the room above the top floor where the big elevator motors were located. If it was still unlocked, maybe later on he'd go look for Teresa upstairs and take her up there again. Like he did the night before all the excitement.

The rest of the building was quiet and empty, except for the other members of the cleanup crew, who moved about with their mops, vacuums, and sprays. On some floors they worked around the carpet-cleaning specialists who'd been brought in to remove bloodstains. They'd probably have to work all night to satisfy Mr. Larson. He said he wanted the place to look like nothing had happened. The next day was to be "business as usual" at 330 Park.